The Last Year

Book Three of the Torus Saga

Michael Berg

ISBN: 978-0-6486874-2-9

Characters and events in this book are fictitious. Any similarity to real persons, living or dead is coincidental and not intended by the author.

Cover design by: Channelee

First printing (paperback): Amazon Publishing 2019

First published as an Amazon Kindle ebook Copyright © 2018

For all permissions contact: torussaga@gmail.com

Michael Berg is a professional writer residing in Australia. He dedicates this work The Torus Saga, to those with an open mind connected to the heart who seek the many mysteries and progressions of life.

Also in the Torus Saga by Michael Berg:

Book One: First Light

Book Two: Volition

THE LAST YEAR

Chapter 1

C rystal contains many facets for light refraction determined by elemental progression. A human being is also like this. Life contains facets of energy and awareness, with each serving to further the progression of experience and actualisation of authentic self. Asper Carter and her good friend Lorraine Stevens – both in their mid to late thirties, were two such people who enjoyed experiencing the many facets of life they always sought and embraced at the dawning of each new day.

On this the first day of the year twenty ninety four, both Asper and Lorraine stood admiring the golden dawn to the east, despite the cold conditions of winter laying down crunchy frost on the grass below their feet. The house where they were living eighty-eight miles north of San Francisco, was a quaint cottage one could say, surrounded by flowerbeds, and an old garden arch over the front path with a rambling grape vine. On this morning, soft misty wintery tendrils flowed here and there about the valley around the house, where at times it would shroud the sun to become filled with a golden glow.

Asper was happy, so too was Lorraine. They were both happier than they had been for a long time. Life at the house was simplistic and rewarding, unhindered by impact of the city being re-built to the south. Being surrounded by the progressive forces of nature where the elements of the weather down to the intricacies of life amongst the plants in the garden, they felt a sense of belonging and comfort.

What else could they want? Asper and Lorraine were not of the type to want, and therefore to suffer from need arising from want or desire never really occurred to them. They did sometimes feel loss, as neither had seen their lovers in years, but neither ever chose to dwell on such things, so in effect they were two of most free people just about anywhere.

Six years before this time, during the year twenty eighty eight, they had first visited the house where they now lived. It belonged to Carmel Madeline then, and still did, but Asper and Lorraine had not seen Carmel since those times. They had met in San Francisco and journeyed north for a while so their partners could do some work with their friend and Carmel's partner Tim. When they had been successful in removing the devices and microchips the authorities had implanted into their bodies, they stayed a while longer at the house. The three men Tim, John, and Tobias were also there working on a new idea for ways to counteract the incursion of technology into people's bodies, until their work had drawn the men away.

Asper and Lorraine had known each other for a few years by this time, but they had never actually relaxed at home in a country cottage before and so fortune had drawn them back to Carmel's cottage years later. It did not take them long to find the house, and they were considerably fortunate, given the restrictions in place for travel, along with the lack of resources almost everyone had to endure in life during these times, and the fact the house had survived intact aside from some damage.

In contrast to what people from decades before may have thought about the world, this day was not of some technologically marvellous age despite some very advanced technology being present on Earth. It was an age where life coasted along more or less in ways so very similar to one hundred years before, but with some startling differences.

First of these was the lack of most things. Despite their drive to re-establish their power over society after defeating the Agent who was now imprisoned in a facility deep beneath New York City, and despite their new flux mechanical inventions trying to break light speed, the authorities still lacked sufficient power to institute their machine planet society. It was not directly their own fault...this undoing of ideals, but it was mostly their fault, for their biggest failure was to have assumed. If one assumes without really checking and re-checking the information, one can tend to become a victim to the assumption, and so this was what happened to the authorities.

They had assumed flux mechanics for technology beyond light speed was within their grasp. They had assumed they could re-take the Earth for humanity to evolve into their trans-human monsters, and they had assumed...simply too much.

There was only one person known who could provide the solution to flux mechanics, yet they had failed even after incarcerating this person. John Matheson had put a spanner in the works of their machines, and so after a few years of using pseudo flux mechanics technology, the authority run systems began to break down and render many of their new machines useless.

Lorraine knew John well enough through their intimate relationship, and so therefore she knew he must have still been alive sometime after they had last seen each other. This feeling provided her and Asper with some hope of reuniting with their lost loved ones. As Lorraine was with John, Asper was in love with Tobias who was a good friend of John's.

One thing did trouble the two women at times, and it was almost impossible to escape thinking of wherever anyone was on the face of the Earth. A growing unstable vortex anomaly was clearly visible in the sky. It appeared as a black star where at night it gave a peculiar purple glow easily visible from earth. Its' nature and comprehension was of vision and of the sub-conscious. Somehow the authorities had opened a physical portal into space, time, and mind.

Through time, the head scientist Eric Gunter had probed John's mind for stable flux mechanics information. John had always remained unwillingly as he resisted the incursions into his mind from the technology Eric had implanted. As

Eric forced information out of him using nanotechnology mechanics, John had implanted a bug himself inside one faulty algorithm, and so their efforts to create a stable vortex for manifesting their power based technological advances, had failed in most part.

The authorities had been able to construct many machines of both efficiency and menace, but most of these machines had failed to deliver as expected during the past three years. Whilst they once again were the dominant and controlling force of people everywhere, they were not much more advanced than they were when they had first brought in the restrictions and identification microchips almost six years prior to this very day.

One victory many people of Earth did hail them for was their capture of the Agent and the near eradication of his macabre viruses afflicting the lives of so many people. People rejoiced at the news of his incarceration along with the retrieval of the stolen spaceship, and this was an advantage for the authorities in more ways than one. Now they were once again seen as providers for the many who were now in desperate need of better living and opportunity. Whilst the authorities intended to enforce strict compliance, they could relax this a little at first as a means to coax populations into accepting them once again as leaders.

Cities were being re-built and food had become available, though not plentiful. Horrifying effects of the viruses sent out to millions indiscriminately and affecting the technology implants in people's bodies, were finally waning as those stricken with the unsightly vortexes dissolving their sense of self, had finally succumb to these affects and left this life on Earth.

After so many years where survival was the best many could do, the authority offers of a life beyond mere survival, was enough temptation for people to allow their laws of compliance to guide life without question. Then as it is with those whose choose power and dominance, there would be new measures, new machines, and new menace, as the authorities sought to develop their laws so they would never come under threat again – either from a maniac, or from an individual citizen.

As such were the times, they reflected those of the past, and such were the times, they barely looked ahead similarly as they did in the past, and…such were the times where moments seemed to repeat from the past. As Lorraine and Asper stood watching the last tendrils of mist drifting away revealing the sun in entirety on this morning in the year twenty ninety four, Tim Collins appeared at the front gate. It had been over five years now since he had done precisely the same thing when he first met Carmel, who had greeted him with open arms as Lorraine and Asper did now. Travel was restricted and most vehicular traffic was subjected to strict curfew, so Tim had to walk the old dusty roads to Carmel's house, and when he arrived after many miles on foot, he was tired and wanted a drink.

They ushered him in, both very pleased to finally see someone they knew well after so many years of isolation from their friends. It was just past seven and time for breakfast, so they made a special feast to start the day – a day when their lives would forever take on change in a way neither of them, or Tim, could have imagined in recent times.

After eating some breads and fruit and over a fresh pot of coffee, they all relaxed to discuss the recent past in anticipation of what may be ahead. The coffee aroma was the instigator of their conversation, as they excitedly talked about their friends and of events since their last encounter.

"Last time I saw Carmel, was just after John and Tobias had come visiting here to catch up with me and discuss some new flux mechanical algorithms John had discovered about five years back."

"You too know something of flux, don't you?" Lorraine asked.

"Yes I do Lorraine. John and I worked closely on the technology when we all came here...after San Francisco."

"And you went with John to test the mechanics back in Vancouver."

"Sort of...um, it was our intention. I had some associates up there who could have helped us test it with a few machines and computer installations they had in secret. But with all those minions of the Agent, and the people afflicted with viruses, we ran into trouble near Seattle. I went on to Vancouver afterwards, but John and Tobias never showed up."

"So you couldn't return here?"

"No. It was too dangerous. Those horrible viruses were rampant...but I didn't have any of the technology implants, so I was alright. Most the entire scene from Seattle down the west coast had become ugly."

"More coffee?"

"Yeah thanks Asper. Um...yeah, so afterwards I retreated into hiding myself at a farm outside of Vancouver. Pretty well stayed there since. Only now with things a lot calmer have I thought it safe enough to travel."

"How did you avoid the restrictions? The authorities have officers everywhere along the main routes."

"I took the much lesser routes you could say...on foot. It took me two months, and here I am."

"Didn't any danger come to the farm? Almost the entire western sector was in some type of mess."

"No, not really. There were a few of those virus people looking for food and places to stay, but we just made them go away."

"Made?" Asper interjected. "You seem a bit uncomfortable Tim."

"Um, yeah, well we had to get rid of them. It was not pretty, but there was nothing else we could do. So...we made them go away. Sorry."

8

"Don't be sorry Tim. I'm sure you did what you could. I think I would have done similar had Asper and I, or just myself, been in the western sector."

"What brought you back here to the west? Surely the eastern sector was still fairly comfortable compared to the destruction the authorities and the Agent did out here?"

"Yes and no. As soon as they were able to use their knowledge of flux mechanics, they brought on a whole new set of rules. They tried force but failed in the end. It took over a year before the gaps started to appear in their technology, and when some of those new trans-human types started going berserk, Asper and I decided it was time to get out. Sort of like going to the new frontier as it was being re-built."

"Yeah, I didn't want to stick around there any longer. Anyway, the authorities set about re-building a lot of things in the east with an ever greater approach to efficiency. Lorraine and I could see it was becoming unpleasant."

"I agree Asper. From what I have heard, the times years ago when they first brought in the identification microchip, are nothing compared to now."

"Pretty well. They have those scouting robots – they are brutal."

"Menacing," Lorraine added.

"To this day, it is hard to believe when you see people suddenly disappear. At least with the first robots they deployed back in eighty-eight, you could see them for a few seconds. The new ones operate invisibly, and people just disappear into thin air."

"Being held inside them I guess," Tim said looking distant for a moment as he recalled his own encounter with the robots.

"I guess so Tim. They also have constant reminders of the security required for an efficient re-building of society, and the drive for everyone to work for the good. Good of what I ask."

"It wouldn't surprise me if they have something new in store to unleash soon. Now with the Agent gone, what is going to stop them?"

"Almost nothing, except human spirit I suppose. It seems however much they try, something comes along from somewhere in the human psyche to get in their way."

"It is why they wanted John," Lorraine added thinking of her love. "The flux mechanics would enable their machines to anticipate almost any move a human could make. And if it is installed as both the primary fuel drive and the computational drive, then it is almost insurmountable."

"So how did you two end up in the eastern sector after eighty-eight?"

"Well, our story is a bit like yours Tim. When John and Tobias failed to return, we decided to leave this place and go to the east. The Agent made things pretty bad here as you know, but the slightly weird thing was how Carmel was not worried about him at all. After being his former supervisor, you would think she would have wanted to get as far away as possible."

"There is something about her though Lorraine. We both sensed it the first time in the warehouse back in San Francisco. Some type of aura or something. She is unique."

"Yeah I agree there. And we made it through to the east at Omaha just before they erected the fence, but only just."

"What do you think John might have done to undermine the success of flux mechanics for the authorities?" Asper asked wanting to avoid the creeping in feelings of concern over Tobias. She secretly hope he was still with John somewhere and would eventually...naturally find his way to her.

"I am sure John gave them a single faulty algorithm. From what I know based on the work we did together, there was never an issue of instability with the mechanics. I can only assume he gave them a snippet of disinformation causing these issues to occur over time. It is my bet he was clever enough to come up with a slow release type mechanism so he could fool them into believing they had all they needed when they first experimented with flux."

"I wonder if they have suspected anything of John since," Lorraine was increasingly thinking of him now Tim was present and their conversation took up the past.

"We cannot be sure. If their nanotechnology mechanics were able to obtain the information from John, it could be they have had to accept John was not quite the expert they thought he was."

"But he is."

"Indeed Lorraine. I have never met anyone who comes close to his intellect for this type of thing...yet he is a bit of a rough, bush type."

"It is why I love him."

The three of them fell silent after Lorraine's statement, thinking of John and wondering where he could possibly be. They thought too of Tobias who had been by John's side for a lot of the time since they had met them in San Francisco. Lorraine noticed the look come across Asper's face as she once again thought of the man she loved, and sensing they were all going a little downward in spirit, she changed the subject to inject a little light heartedness.

"How about we use this beautiful winter's day and go into town to see what we can find. After all, the authorities have not yet concentrated their re-building efforts on these smaller places, so we might find something useful in some way. I just thought it would be something to do. Maybe you have an eye for things we have missed Tim."

"Are there many people about the town?"

"Not many. Just a few newcomers. Most are still in the city I believe. Asper and I went there a couple of months back, and with all the new buildings and systems going into place, it appears as though most people are ready to accept what the authorities can provide for them in the concentrated city areas."

"Alright, going into town sounds great, but maybe I will have a bit of a refresh first. I am a bit tired from walking so far."

"Sure. There is hot water. Lorraine and I re-built the furnace in the basement here. It is old style and runs off fire rather than electricity, but it works well."

"You two are industrious."

"We have to be. There isn't much else to get by with."

"No electricity at all then?"

"Not yet. Nobody has come to tell us anything about it, and there have been no authority officials here to make any claims or decisions. We are still on our own."

"I suppose it is good in a way."

"In many ways. The less attention the authorities give this place, the better."

As they walked into town half an hour later, the Moon was visible in the soft blue sky, with the vortex also visible in the daylight just to the side. It was an unnerving sight to most, and those whom it did not affect were probably too busy with their heads down thinking only of their self-gratification or immediate reality. Any person who thought even in the slightest sense about what the vortex could mean, were prone to feeling uneasy.

"Do you have any idea why we can see it during the day Tim?"

"Not entirely sure Asper, but I would hazard a guess. It probably projects black light."

"Black light?"

"Yeah…it is long wave ultraviolet light. My guess is illumination of invisible plasma in space. Within the state of flux, tachyons fluctuate around light speed and just above light speed. They interact with information at the frontier state as the bridge between the two for the transition where information is laid upon the tachyon pathways for passage then above light speed. I think this visibility is the result...from something John did otherwise it would mostly be invisible."

"The authorities have similar drive mechanisms for their machines don't they?"

"Yeah, the fuel cells they developed almost twenty years ago draw energy from excited plasma. There is a lot of potential there during the transitional phasing. If you know about the studies they did into vortices in space, they looked into the frontier I just mentioned as the accelerant energy source."

"So does matter actually become antimatter inside the vortex?"

"No. It is accelerated beyond light speed using the energies generated within the flux lens, and remains as matter. And the black light…anyone's guess where it originates and how it seems to touch the sub-conscious level. Perhaps this is the bit from John warning us of the potential energies."

"It could be a vibration pattern," Lorraine suggested. "If you see the black light as a resonance bordering on what we perceive as reality, it might emanate from just beyond our perception."

"I'm not sure the authorities even know where it comes from. It might even be omicron particles theorised in science fiction, where they are a by-product of antimatter generation without mass. Or it might even turn out to be true as the state between matter and antimatter."

"It certainly looks strange to see a purple black star in the blue sky."

As they reached the edge of town, a few people could be seen wandering about, and by the looks on their faces, they appeared to be of similar mind, enjoying the crisp morning air. Tim was hesitant to go and speak with them, but Asper and Lorraine were eager to converse with the strangers, and so they encouraged him to join them as they changed direction to meet up with the others.

"Hello there," one of the strangers called out to them as they approached.

"Hi. A beautiful morning isn't it?" Lorraine replied.

"Sure is. Have you seen many others about this town? We have just arrived this morning and are looking for somewhere to stay for a while."

"Hello," Asper and Tim added when they had reached the group of three adults and one child.

"Hi."

"Um, we've not seen many others, have we Asper."

"No. It is mostly deserted here. Lorraine and I have seen a few people now and then over the past six months or so, but they keep to themselves it seems."

"Oh, I see. My name is Derek, this is Esther, Murray, and Celia, my daughter."

"Nice to meet you. I'm Lorraine."

"Asper."

"Hi, I'm Tim. So what brings you here?"

"We are looking to find a new place to live. San Francisco is not to our liking. We tried there first, but with all the re-building and the authorities everywhere, we just thought it was too much, so we decided to look for a town like this."

"Well, there is plenty of room here. Lorraine and I have looked at a few houses in town, and some look habitable, if you are prepared to fix them up a bit."

"Oh, we can fix houses. Um, have you seen any trouble? Any virus people or the authorities?"

"Neither. But you can bet the authorities will eventually come."

"Yeah, we thought it would be the case for just about anywhere we go, but we are willing to take a chance. The city is not nice at all."

"We were last there a couple of months back. We went to look for supplies…you know, anything we thought might help us here, but there was nothing."

"It is in a state of confinement, more or less. People we spoke to said it is getting worse all the time. It seems the authorities are very eager to re-establish themselves now the Agent is gone."

"Well, welcome to the town. We live a mile out on the west side. Call by any time."

"Yeah thanks. What are you doing in town today?"

"A bit like you. We're looking around for anything of use. It is pretty well a free for all at the moment, but it won't remain so when people discover this place."

"I see. I hope we are not some of those people…to you."

"Oh no. We like you don't we Asper…and Tim."

"Sure. It is nice to see people like you. The city is so full of the types too eager to take up with the authorities where they left off years back. It is refreshing to see you here."

"I just arrived this morning myself. The more decent people like you…and Asper and Lorraine, the better," Tim added also feeling he could sense these people as trustworthy.

"Make yourselves at home. I suggest you take a look on the eastern side. The houses there seem in better condition."

"Okay, thanks. We'll be seeing you I guess."

"You can count on it. Bye."

As she watched the group walk away, Asper was mystified as she felt a connection with the girl Celia she could not define.

Lorraine noticed her puzzled look, "What is it Asper?"

"I can't say other than I feel a connection or something. We are going to see them again. I am sure of it."

Tim had walked to an old stone building across the street and called out to them, "Have you two been in here yet?" He was pointing at a doorway towards the rear of one of the old stone town buildings a minute later.

"No, I haven't been in there. How about you Lorraine?"

"No, me neither. I have seen the door come to think of it. I just thought it was locked – there is no door handle. So I must have moved on thinking it probably goes to nowhere worth looking."

"Well, how about we try it. There could be something worth looking at behind."

"I wonder if it leads to a room we could access from the front of the building?"

"It might Asper. Why don't you and Lorraine go and have a look via the front, whilst I put my shoulder to this."

When Lorraine and Asper returned five minutes later, they found Tim leaning against the door, rubbing his shoulder. "Looks a bit tougher than you thought Tim?"

"Um, yeah. Did you find anything from the inside?"

"Nothing we could determine as being behind the door, could we Asper?"

"No. Not a thing. The building is mostly empty inside with just a few pieces of junked furniture. It has seen much better days."

"How about we look for something to prise it open with."

They looked around the rear alley without finding anything substantial enough to work on the door with, so they extended their search back out into the street and beyond for a block until Asper found an old jemmy bar. When they returned to try the bar and see if the door would come open, they were unsuccessful as it was secured tight and would require more than what they had.

Tim was captivated with what may lie behind the door, and stood there trying to work out what they would use and where they could possibly find something to break it open. Then it occurred to him. The door locking mechanism could be a time fusion lock – one requiring an alignment of timing within the lock. By placing a scanning device held against it sending a correlating time, he might be able to open it for them.

"I think we will have to come back for this one. I have a few tools I could use to help with this task."

"Alright then. Where else should we go?"

"Just lead the way Lorraine. Let's look around for anything we might use.

When they arrived at the same museum where Carmel had found the small steam engine she had lovingly restored, the building was in a much worse state than when she had last visited over five years earlier. Clearly some of the virus afflicted people had gathered there at one time, judging by the pile of bones on the main exhibition room floor. The people were now long gone, reduced to bare bones only where some just ended as if they had been precisely cut. They were not cuts though – the clean edges were the fringes of virus affected parts of their former bodies where the vortices to oblivion had opened up within them.

"Hey, come in here," Asper called out from an adjoining room. The other two joined her in a flash, glad to leave the human debris behind.

"I found this," she said to them as they entered the room. She was holding up what appeared to be the very type of scanner Tim had considered would be required to open the door at the old stone building.

"A very unlikely place to find one of these," Tim said as he looked it over. "It needs a charge, but otherwise it looks like it would work. Strange it was here.

Perhaps the holder of this scanner key was keeping it in safe storage. Where did you find it?"

"Underneath the floor. I was standing here and I heard a hollow sound when I tapped my foot a couple of times. So I just wriggled this little piece of board, and there it was in the hollow there underneath."

"Well good find Asper. I'll need to re-charge it back at the house before I can try it. I have a few input algorithms I can use to crack the timing code. Then we can see what is behind the door."

They continued on through the town for the next hour, looking in places where Asper and Lorraine thought they might have passed by on earlier occasions, but they found nothing more of interest. When their stomachs starting indicating it was nearing lunch time, they decided they to go back to the house and then return later if Tim had been successful with the scanner key.

"So you are sure there are no officers from the authorities on patrol out here?" Tim asked as they walked the mile back to the house.

"We haven't seen any as yet, have we Lorraine."

"None."

"We don't want them to suddenly come upon us with this key, or doing anything they might consider as suspicious. They are a lot worse now than back in eighty-eight. It is straight in for their nanotechnology mechanics or cease to exist if you are arrested and deemed inefficient."

"Why do they pursue those ways? They just don't understand the failures they keep having. Every time they try something, it seems to come up against obstacles," Asper said looking a little dazed as her eyes glazed over for a moment. She was thinking again of Tobias and how uncertain of his fate she was.

"They do it as a search for perfect efficiency. One thing turns to the next, and then so on as they try to overcome the obstacles, not realising they are out of the flow of true reality."

"Let's hope so Lorraine, because if they are able to fix the fault in the flux mechanics, there will be a very long time where they hold power."

"All the disruption with their efficiency, their fear mongering, and their you can depend on us propaganda… yet so many people just lap it up."

"It has been happening for years and when it was not all comfortable, or they had to endure a bit of hardship..."Asper trailed off, again thinking of Tobias.

Lorraine noticed her discomfort, so she took over, "People became attached to external reliance on technology and being provided for by the authorities and now they scamper back like lost lambs to the teat."

Lunch was the same food as breakfast. They talked about what else could be done to secure more food as time went by. Tim told them of the foodstuffs in the cities mainly being those protein and mineral compounds fashioned into barely edible blocks, and this did not thrill Asper and Lorraine who had become accustomed to eating normal organic food they grew – though it could be difficult to obtain anything near a decent supply at times.

"Well, I'm going to see what I can do with this scanner key," Tim said when they were sitting around the table quietly after finishing eating.

"Okay Tim, Asper and I will be here if you need us."

"Well, I hope I can have it done fairly quickly. Maybe we could go back to town this afternoon."

It was around four in the afternoon with light beginning to fade, when Tim had told them the scanner key was working, and suggested they could go back to the door.

"It might take a few attempts to align the time in the lock with the one I enter into this key, but I am confident I could get it today."

"We have plenty of time Tim. It's not like there is something we have to be back at the house for."

"What about curfew?"

"Being careful is called for even though we have not seen any officers on patrol around here. It seems a bit odd, considering we are less than one hundred miles from San Francisco."

"I don't like it. They will eventually come here and when they do, it will be with force. You can bet they have something secret. I suggest we maintain the curfew here. You never know if they might suddenly appear. Lorraine and Asper agreed this was a good decision."

On the fifth attempt at cracking the time correlation lock, Tim was successful. They heard a slight click come from the internal workings of the lock, but nothing else to indicate it was open. With a firm push, Tim opened the heavy door to reveal a small dark room with the only light inside being a mix of the light hitting part of the floor through the open doorway, and a few blinking lights on some equipment they could barely see amongst the shadows.

"Just a moment," he said, fumbling for a small flash light he had brought with him. When he switched it on and then shone it around the small room, all three of them were astounded to see an array of the latest authority owned technology sitting there in standby mode. Tim had brought his bag of tools with him, and the moment he saw the power cells connected to the equipment, he suggested they steal as much of what they could see as possible.

"Look, I am not the thieving type, but in this case, I'll make an exception. This is the latest gear, and these power cells will work for years without a recharge."

"Whatever they are. I'll help you. What about you Asper?"

"Sure. If the authorities use this equipment, it is probable they will use it against us, so it is better if we have it."

"We'll have to hide it though…when we get back to the house."

"No problem. Carmel took care of such things years ago with a nice little hidey-hole. There is even enough room to work in there."

"Perfect."

Tim's tool bag was clearly not large enough to stash all the equipment they intended to steal.

"I know! I'll be back in a minute or two." Asper ran off, leaving the other two to wonder what it was she was on about. When she returned after a few minutes wheeling a rusty old hard cart, they laughed for a second at how ungainly she looked when she nearly crashed. The moment she arrived, they set about loading it with all they could remove from the room.

Tim suggested they leave right away when they were finished and go straight back to Carmel's house so he could analyse the technology and determine its precise operation. The cart was hard work over the mile or so despite the three of them each contributing to getting it moving. They all felt a degree of urgency and being so exposed, this began to create feelings of anxiety – adding further weight and awkwardness.

By the time they arrived home, Tim could smell fresh coffee not really there. Both Apser and Lorraine had the same feeling smell sensation and without a word set about making themselves something to eat as Tim hauled the load the remainder of the way around the house so he could unload without being seen.

"Coffee is on Tim," Lorraine called out.

"Thanks Lorraine, this stuff looks good now I can relax a little and see it properly."

"Ha, such things are key Tim," Asper said laughing a little and feeling a general sense of mischief at the time.

Chapter 2

Eric Gunter was alerted to an irregular status report coming from the systems monitoring the spatial anomaly beyond the Moon. He was used to seeing such statistical readouts as the anomaly had progressively destabilised over the past two years, but this time it was different. The normal consistent rate of growth in the anomaly's size and energy output had suddenly increased to a higher rate. Whilst the new rate remained consistent after the initial surge, the increase was well beyond what he considered could happen based on his calculations and experiences – all managed finely by the microscopic mechanical implants in his brain.

Immediately, he set about entering sequential algorithms into the quantum computer in an effort to understand the origin of the changes. Time and time again Eric entered each sequence, and on each occasion he was unsuccessful in determining the cause of the changes to the anomaly. The only facet of the readouts to attract any attention aside from the usual mathematical analysis was the detection of a harmonic component within the results. Whilst this was not a musical score of any type, it was definitely a regular harmonic pulse rhythm at a low frequency inaudible to human senses.

Eric fine-tuned the readouts to determine the precise frequency, and found it was eight hertz. The moment he discovered this, Eric became aware there was a second regular note in the readings. What puzzled him was how it took discerning the frequency of the low note before evidence of the higher note at five hundred and twenty eight hertz could be detected. This was unusual to normal science as the higher frequency was well within the range of human auditory sense, and so it appeared as though detection of the lower frequency was the key to becoming aware of the other higher frequency. He continued to analyse these results and discovered both of the harmonic frequencies were being amplified through the anomaly as if it was a loud speaker.

This intrigued Eric as he had never encountered anything similar during his career as a developmental scientist. What was left of his organic self was sufficient to bypass his internal nanotechnology mechanics at this time, permitting him to experience this brief notion of intrigue. Over the past two years, the tiny robotic brain manipulators were prone to slight failures prompting Eric and those others who also had the implants, to consider further developmental research was required. Yet simultaneously at times like these, they performed exquisitely in analysing the natural feelings and intentions Eric experienced.

They were mechanics of learning, and so the more Eric gave them, the more of him they would take away in a gradual procession of a human mind turning mechanical. In simplicity, this was not evolution of the elements. Rather, it was more an evolution of ego. Eric worked for an organisation determined to have ultimate control over the entirety of humanity with control to be held in the hands of just a few who held a love for such power.

He had re-scanned the mind of his prize inmate John Matheson for any further information on flux mechanics in case there had been an oversight during the initial mind interrogation procedures. Eric had repeated this process hundreds of times now as the mechanics of his mind devised ways to look for answers as part of their ongoing capacity to learn and propose new ideas, but John had held firm, and had successfully denied the stable flux algorithm to Eric of the authorities.

Any improvements to the nanotechnology mechanics were not going to come from the flux technology, and so Eric was at a stalemate in development of the tiny machines and their operational dynamics. This meant he was also stagnated in the development of the technologies he had envisioned when he apprehended John. Viewed ominously by those in high office, his superiors were not pleased with any degree of inefficient uncertainty.

"Gunter! Report to me at once. I have some details I need you to work on," his superior suddenly barked over the broadcomm. Eric had been successful in developing a new type of broadcomm communications system based on pseudo flux technology where he worked to achieve teleporting data, but as yet, he was unable to take the system to the heights at which he wanted to see it operate.

"Coming sir."

"Look at these diagrams Gunter. Tell me what you see?" his superior demanded the moment Eric arrived.

"Um, sir?"

"What is it? Just tell me what you think you can see in this material."

"Um, a geometric design or pattern sir. What is it?"

"You tell me."

"I haven't seen this information previously sir."

"I myself only received this data about fifteen minutes ago."

"Why was I not sent this when it came in sir?"

"You need not ask such questions Gunter. I just want your opinion on what this is."

"Well, as I said sir, it appears to be some geometric designs, but...considering the fact we use a lot of geometry in our systems and algorithm designs, well, these are not of the type we normally use. They appear to be multi-dimensional sir."

"Multi-dimensional? Explain."

"Um, yes, well multi-dimensional designs are what we would expect from stable flux mechanics. It is where the boundaries beyond light speed, culminate in layers and pathways according to the intended destinations for matter where particles are sent in distribution. If say, we were to recover the spaceship we sent through the spatial anomaly, then we would have established an intentional multi-dimensional field where we could see any geometric design. This establishes links to any place where it not only arrives, but is also operational at the moment it reaches the destination. The research into laying down tachyon paths of intention gleaned from our study of geometries and quantum physics has revealed this capacity. It would involve establishing the geometries in multi-dimensional transition states after the laying down of tachyon pathways to accept matter for transition beyond light speed sir."

"So you are telling me this information we see, is only achievable through stable flux mechanics?"

"I can only assume so sir. We have only established this information as theorised data to date. Our unstable systems have not been able to produce these readings."

"But it sounds to be of this dimension Gunter. Matter beyond light speed does not enter another dimension. And what is its use? Is it information we can rely on?"

"Um, you are correct sir, but there is a filament dimension of stasis where for a tiny fraction of time, matter passes the threshold and at this instant, it is between sub light and beyond light speed sir. This is perhaps what you could call a multi-dimension. But...in order to apply the true elemental frequencies for sub light matter to transfer to beyond light, we need to establish these geometries as the initiating uptake point for the tachyon pathways sir. Do note sir, these speeds are only just a fraction beyond light speed."

"I see. Where do you think this is coming from? Can we use it?"

"The anomaly sir, and yes, I will attend to studying the dynamics in order to reach an algorithmic expression of the data."

"Okay but where...beyond the anomaly?"

"It is anyone's guess sir. I have some additional data. There are harmonic frequencies coming from the anomaly only just apparent."

"Then there must be a link between these two."

"Most likely. May I suggest investigation of this immediately? There is not much further work to be done on the deployment of our new robotics. I only need to finalise one last algorithm."

"And then they can be sent into the field?"

"Yes sir. They will be fully armed and ready. We can deploy across any area we choose."

"Without the knowledge of any other nations on this planet?"

"Yes sir. Our systems are substantially more advanced than any other nation."

"But they still need human operators?"

"Yes, but only for monitoring and command issues, otherwise they are autonomous."

"Okay Gunter, proceed with the last algorithm and then get to work on this anomaly. I'll send this data to you. Um, I suppose there are no signs yet of any readings coming from the spaceship as yet."

"None sir."

"And what about these residual vortex problems we have left over from the amplifications by the Agent?"

"We are still working on those. Some of my teams have been able to stabilise their growth rate, but it seems to be only a temporary solution. We need to work much more on this issue."

"Keep me informed. Okay you can go."

"Thank you sir."

Eric made haste returning to his workstation holographic array as soon as possible so he could finalise the algorithm and then get to work on the anomaly data.

When he had finalised the algorithm enabling the latest robotic war machines to become active, Eric sent a command to stand by and await further orders to the officer in charge of robotic deployment. Within hours, the new machines would be sent to all nations on Earth without the knowledge of anyone except for a few people in the underground facility deep beneath New York City.

Ironically, high above Eric at ground level was the building formerly known as the United Nations where almost all nations on Earth had gathered potentially in peace. Soon far below the building, Eric Gunter and his superiors would engage in a new type of war to end the liberties of human beings through a massive overwhelming show of force, snuffing out choice using machines of a new age.

With the introduction of nanotechnology ribbons used in machines, robotics, manufacturing, and for implants in human beings, the authorities possessed the potential for a limitless control mechanism. Coupled with advanced protein string systems, these systems had power supply edging toward infinity with the only obstacle being the faulty algorithm keeping them just out of flux transition to faster than light capacity.

Whilst some of the technology was now decades old, there were no developmental breakthroughs in application of systems until Eric had discovered a self replicating algorithm. This enabled the substance to perform at the levels now demanded by the near entirely autonomous systems in place. Despite his high degree of intellect, he had not been able to extract the stabilising flux algorithm from John Matheson. Eric knew John was cleverly holding back and manipulating the course of Eric's work, but Eric had no other choice than to pursue what was the most efficient method to extract the vital information required to realise the objectives of his science and the authorities overseeing him.

The prospect of John being able to overcome the demands of the nanotechnology mechanics in his brain had simply not occurred to Eric, so sure he was of their capabilities. The implants searched only for any known contingencies – theorising and analysing, but not truly learning, despite their almost trans-human sentient capacity.

Eric had retained John as a captive of the authorities these past few years since his apprehension from the fishing vessel off the coast of Chile. At first there were great lengths of time where he was entirely alone in the vast underground prison. Then came regular visits from Eric who gave him the luxury of a small quantum computer as a means to help develop the algorithm required to bring flux into stability.

John had not complied with Eric's hopes. Instead, he was busy developing his own thoughts and technological advances – all under the guise of flux test failure after failure. Eric had no idea John was using this ploy despite knowing he was holding back on the key algorithms. John's aptitude for deceiving Eric meant he would be spared further implants of nanotechnology mechanics.

On so many occasions John would think of his dear friends he had not seen for so long now, and of course, his dear Lorraine. When he recalled their first meeting in San Francisco, their plight to stay ahead of the authorities, and the journey to Peru without her, he felt a longing for her and yet also an assurance. She was tenacious and sure to have survived – if only to see her, to feel her, touch and kiss.

John was surprised with the sudden appearance of Eric outside his holding cell. He disengaged the holographic cell bars and then came in to discuss his latest findings. This was something Eric did at the times when he had reached an impasse with unstable flux mechanics.

"How are you John?"

"As usual."

"I see. What are you working on?"

"As usual…stability issues."

"Any developments?"

"Nothing new as yet."

"Well, I have something new I want your thoughts on."

"The anomaly?"

"Yes…as always. It is the focal point of our research."

"Okay, what do you have?"

"Some new data. The growth rate experienced a surge earlier today, and I have detected some harmonic frequencies emanating from within the vortex. My superior has also provided me with data on what appears as multi-dimensional geometries."

"What do you mean…geometries?"

"Patterns, um…they appear as layers as if they are pathways or channels."

"And they contain specific alignments?"

"Yes they do. I have considered they might be reflux…as in a mirror signal to the algorithms we established in first opening the vortex."

"Why would they take so long to bounce back to us?" John was confident he knew what was likely to cause this, and now as he had done previously, he was playing a game of innocence with Eric.

"I cannot say. I am not even sure if my hypothesis is correct. I want you to analyse the data and determine their precise origin. They appear closely aligned with our original signals, yet there is this multi-dimensional aspect I cannot get my head around."

"Are those mechanics failing you even further? How dare they." John thought for a second on how Eric had said he could not get his head around, considering there was a fine line of definition between Eric and the nano mechanics.

"Don't be sarcastic John. I want these results."

"Why come to me? What more could I give you?"

"Your intellect John. I am only asking you to apply your mind to this conundrum."

"What if I come up with nothing?"

"Then at least I would have investigated the possibility of you seeing something I cannot, and thus, I could eliminate the possibility."

"I see. When do you want this by?"

"There is always a degree of urgency John. In this instance, I want thorough analysis from you and so there is not so much urgency attached to this research. I will also keep working on this data, but…I also have other duties."

"I can only guess…with a degree of certainty."

"It is inevitable John. The Earth is on the brink of change…finally. After all the setbacks the authorities have experienced in recent years, they are now finally in the position to assert the new rule of efficiency and consumption based order."

"Through those machines you built?"

"Mostly, but eventually people will see the opportunities awaiting them through our new technology. How they can live longer, how they will never want for anything, and how they will be cater to for all their needs."

"There it is…their needs."

"Don't start again John. You know as well as I do, there is no fantasy world ready for uptake…waiting to be realised. What happens on Earth is entirely the creation of those who deem whatever is necessary for the good of the people. Anything outside this is too inefficient. After all, how can we take care of the Earth through constant inefficiencies?"

"It would manage."

"Perhaps, and as poorly as it has done in the past. No John, we...everyone needs these measures and as soon as we have stable flux mechanics, there will be no turning back."

"So you think."

"So I know. Anyway, get to work on this data. I'll come back the day after tomorrow to see if you have made any progress."

"Why not just monitor me?"

"Your system is in isolation. I'll be back in two days."

John was not bothered with Eric telling him his system was in isolation – he had expected this from the beginning. What Eric did not appear to consider, was how John was able to manipulate technology to his advantage in almost any instance.

Eric did not know John well enough. His implants made assumptions, they built on Eric's own personal experiences, and added scenarios of response and prediction based on what Eric's superiors saw as superior offensive technology. Their offensive was to seek, to target, to learn, and to use artificial intelligence algorithms for what they saw as an enhance trans-human being. Part technology, part organic – it would be a fusion beyond the mere DNA implants used to maintain telomeres and therefore retain higher cell reproduction integrity for longer. Life spans of one hundred and twenty years were common if one had avoided intrusion by the Agent.

This reliance, this dependence, and the sheer audacity to willingly forget the intricate human systems born authentically and organically, was the ignorance apparent yet those who sought to rid humanity of such inefficiencies, entirely missed the point...according to John.

He began to work with the computer immediately taking a course where only he would know the destination and despite being isolated from systems and as a person, it was his tenacity now inspiring his imagination.

Chapter 3

Tim was delighted with the technology he had set up in the secret room at Carmel's house. The more connections he made, and the further he engaged the systems, the more he realised how much of an asset their stolen booty would be in coming times. He had initialised the holographic array and brought the small quantum computer into operational status. Fortunately, the entire system they found included its own power cells, and the readout showed him there was enough power to run the computer for more than one thousand days before a re-charge was required. Tim deliberately kept only one part of the system out of operation - the link to authority central systems.

Failure to keep this computer out of systems registration would invite enquiries from the authorities as soon as they detected a system in operational status when it was meant to be on standby. He hoped they had not detected it going off standby during the time they had taken to bring it from the small room to Carmel's house, but it was a risk he calculated as worth taking.

"We are lucky to have come across this system," he told Asper and Lorraine over breakfast. They had left him to his own devices during the night after they had returned with the computer system.

"Do you think there will be danger when the authorities find out it is missing? Surely they will not take it too lightly," Asper said sipping her coffee.

"I would think so. They will go looking for this equipment, but they will not find it here. I think we are really going to need it so I will set up an energy field to throw off any scanners. This gear we have is their latest. I am fairly confident I can beat them at their own game."

"Any idea why they installed it here…in this town?"

"Your guess is as good as mine, but I would suffice to say, they intend to upscale their impact in places like these…as we correctly assumed. From what I can tell, this little system has a very large capacity. Much more than anything I have seen in recent years, and experience tells us they are almost always planning something."

"In their never ending pursuit of dominance," Lorraine said looking bored at having to conceptualise the mundane power struggle of the authorities.

"This time I think the stakes are much higher Lorraine. With the Agent as captive and no more new viruses around, there is virtually nothing in their way."

"Except the anomaly." Asper said this sentence in a deeper than usual voice as if it was coming through her from somewhere else. Both Tim and Lorraine turned and just stared at her for a few moments as she remained still with a solemn look on her face.

"Are you alright Asper?"

"Huh?" Asper came to from her trance-like state. "Um, yeah, I'm okay. Weird though."

"What about the anomaly?"

"Um, not sure Tim. I don't know where it came from. It felt like a moment of precognition."

"Oh great. Are you a psychic now?" Lorraine laughed.

"I don't know. It was weird as I said. I don't have a clue where it came from. Perhaps I am a psychic. Watch out or I'll read your thoughts you two. No funny business."

"Okay Miss Psychic, the anomaly?"

"Cannot say Tim, other than the authorities will be very distracted by what happens with it I guess."

"Well, you have given me an idea. I am going to set up this computer so I can scan the anomaly. Not thorough tests, it is too far away - just some observational scans and some tests to see if I can detect anything coming from its vicinity. There could be some residual waves of some type reaching the Earth."

Whilst Tim was working with the quantum computer after they had finished breakfast, Asper and Lorraine were out the front of the house enjoying the sunshine on a fine winter morning. As they talked a little about what Asper had experienced, Esther and Celia appeared around the bend in the road a few hundred yards from the house. Asper noticed them first, and gave them a wave indicating for them to come to the house.

"Hi Esther, and Celia."

"Hi…Asper?"

"Yeah, Asper…and Lorraine."

"Hi Asper and Lorraine."

"Hi Esther and Celia."

"Hello."

"We thought we would come for a walk and say hello as the men are doing a few building repairs. We're glad we found you, aren't we Celia."

"Yes, we are very glad to find you." Celia and Esther immediately felt welcome. "I don't like the hole in the sky. There is going to be trouble with it."

"Really Celia. Asper was saying the same thing over breakfast. Have you eaten?"

"Yes thank you."

"We left the men to it after we had breakfast."

"Who told you there would be trouble with the hole in the sky Celia?"

"They did Asper."

"Who are they?"

"The people who know what it is doing."

"Who are these people?"

"I don't know their names or anything silly. I just listen."

"Where are they?"

"I don't know, but they are close enough for me to hear them."

"Maybe they were the ones talking to me."

"I don't know. I just wanted to come to your house this morning. I thought it would be a pretty house and it is. Esther, can I play in their garden please? It is a nice garden."

"I'm sure Asper and Lorraine won't mind dear, but be careful."

"I'll be okay Esther."

Asper and Lorraine took Esther inside to sit and have a chat as Celia was left to play outside. The simple notion of a child set free to play in the garden amongst the wintry frost under bare trees where at times she would run through the archway with the rambling grape vine, was not lost on the three women as they watched her through the main lounge room window. As they sat in silence for a time, they each went back to their own childhood years recalling similar experiences where innocence in all its beauty was such a gift to people.

"It has been a long time since I thought of such things," Lorraine said. "Such simplistic beauty has been so lost and forgotten by many."

"Yes it has. It is good to see her play after the recent horrors she has been through."

"Her mother?"

"Yes. She was a victim of the onslaught by the authorities in recent times. A pure woman herself who happened to be in the wrong place at the wrong time."

"I suppose Celia was confused."

"She was…and still is a little. She would often ask me why, when her mother had never done anything wrong, did not have any viruses from the Agent, and was always a giving person."

"Where was she living?"

"We were all living near Redding north of here. I was working as an executive assistant until the system began to break down. Redding was free from the Agent's flights of destruction, and there were very few virus affected people about. Sort of an oasis really. We managed well after the authorities even came and destroyed most of the west coast a few years back. Now they have made it difficult as they round everyone up and force them into compliance with their new technologies and efficiencies. It's why we left to find a smaller town, or a farm, and this town felt good when we arrived and so here we are."

"So what is it with this anomaly thing? I had a weird moment about it earlier today as well."

"I cannot say really. A sudden realisation or something dawned upon her. She had never really spoken about it until just a day or two ago. Then suddenly, she was coming out with messages about it becoming very scary…to use her words.

But she also says there are people who know about it and they will tell others what to do."

They watched as Celia quietly stalked a raven sitting on the front fence, and then laughed as she ran to it at the last moment, sending it into the air squawking.

"She's beautiful...a free spirit."

"She is great. Her father Derek loves her dearly. Naturally he was shaken up by the loss of his wife Joanna, Celia's mother. They had been through a lot together. It is good now he has found a house to work on and keep his mind occupied."

"Hello Esther. I thought I could hear a child laughing. How are you?"

"Well thanks Tim. Yes, Celia is outside running free."

"Good on her."

"She had a moment like I did Tim...about the anomaly."

"Really. Some sort of message?"

"Esther said Celia knows it is going to be a problem and there are people who will know what to do."

"Interesting. I suppose a lot of people are wondering if it is going to be some type of disaster. Um...I've finished setting up in there." Tim cast a sideways glance at Esther, unsure if he should make it known to her precisely what he had set up.

Celia came running inside, looked at Time for a few seconds and then spoke, "Your computer will help." Then she turned to Esther, "Can I have a drink please?"

"Sure honey...um, is it okay?"

"No problem," Lorraine replied as she went to the kitchen. "Coffee anyone?"

"You have coffee?"

"Yes, not much though Esther. We were able to get some the last time we were in San Francisco. If you know the right people, they can put you in touch."

"I suppose people still grow crops to earn a living somewhere."

"There is a black market the authorities do not know about. It is not big, but it is growing."

When Lorraine returned with four cups of coffee after having fixed a drink for Celia, they all sat at the dining room table together.

"What do you know about my computer Celia?"

"I just know you have one. I can see in your eyes you are the type to have such things."

"Oh, I see."

"Yes and your computer will be a big help to us when the authorities come."

"Do you know when it will be?"

"Of course not silly. How can a little girl like me know such things? I just figured they would come…like you all did. And, the computer will be good for us."

"Do you know anything about the anomaly?"

"The hole is going to get scary. Lots of people will be scared and run around like they are mad. They told me this. And they also said there is someone who will know what to do when the time comes."

"Did they tell you what it was?"

"No. They just said to be watching out for the time and to be awake."

"Awake?"

"Yes, awake. Otherwise they said, people could miss it and then they will be asleep for a very long time."

Esther saw this last sentence as meaning death, so she changed the subject thinking death might stir emotions for Celia. "So Tim, how long are you staying here? You said you had just arrived."

"Um, I guess as long as these two lovely women will permit me to stay. I don't have anywhere else to go really."

"Should we?" Lorraine looked questioningly at Asper.

"Um…let me see. Give me a minute. Okay, you can stay." Asper replied feigning deep thought about weighing up the issue.

"Thanks. Well there you have it Esther. I'll be staying indefinitely."

"Perhaps you could get to know Derek and Murray. They are both decent men and I am sure you could find a few things to discuss."

"I'm sure we could."

"Yes, they know a little about technology like you do, if what Celia says is correct."

"It is Esther. I know," Celia interjected. " You know I speak about true things."

"Yes, she is right Esther. I do know a little about technology you could say. In fact, I know quite a bit. You are perceptive aren't you Celia."

"It seems as though it has just started happening with her, but you are smart aren't you Celia?"

"If you say so Esther. Remember, we need to be awake. Can I go back outside now? I want to watch the last of the frost melt. I love how it goes from crystals to water drops."

"Sure honey. Go right ahead."

"Well, now I am finished here, I think I will return to my little project and see what else I can make it do. If you will excuse me please?"

"Sure Tim."

"Nice to see you again Tim. Call over at any time. I'm sure Derek and Murray would love to chat."

"Thanks Esther. You can count on it."

Back inside the hidey-hole secret room, Tim went about finalising the calibrations for the quantum computer to analyse any signals coming to Earth from the anomaly. He had completed the masking field to prevent detection of the device from any officer of the authorities who might scan the dwelling. He was able to reverse the type of installed algorithms he retrieved from the quantum unit, effectively cancelling out the signal. Now with most settings established, he was confident in completing the calibrations within the hour.

The quantum computer impressed Tim with its capacity to process data almost entirely simultaneously in pseudo flux. From one small unit connected to the holographic projector and the power cells, he was able to do much more than he had ever done on previous devices up until this time. With the added components they had acquired, Tim was now moments away from a fully operational quantum device capable of scanning, deciphering, and communicating. He was now at a distinct advantage over previous times where he had managed to put a few devices together and hack central systems. Now he felt confident of at least working in parallel with the latest algorithms from the authorities as he saw the prospect of access to nanotechnology manufacturing.

He had never been in contact with any such system previously, and now he potentially had the ability to manipulate atoms into whatever he told the nano robotics he wanted. All he would need to do would be to set the co-ordinates of the nano containment field, and then any atoms within the field could be re-shaped into any atomic form.

Without warning, Celia suddenly opened the door to the secret room. "If I can find this, they will find it. You need to do a better job at hiding this Tim."

"How did you find this room Celia?"

"Easy. I just listened. I can hear what you are doing and so will they. Bye."

"Bye Celia." Tim turned back to his work at the computer, but could not help being distracted by thoughts of Celia, and about what she had just said to him. Despite her being a young girl he estimated to be around eleven years of age, Tim took her words as wise, particularly in regards to her being able to hear him in the secret room. After half a minute, he left the room to find some materials for soundproofing, and others to help conceal the doorway into the small hiding place. When he went out into the lounge room on his way outside to the rear shed in the backyard of the small house, Celia and Esther were about to leave.

"Remember what I said. Keep the place secret...and your computer."

"What have you been doing Celia?"

"Just looking around Esther. I have been careful."

"I see. I hope you were not an intrusion."

"No Esther, but he had better be careful...and all of us will need to remember to be awake."

"There you go again with being awake. What do you really mean Celia dear?"

"Just how it sounds. Be awake. So many people have been asleep since before I was born, but they had better wake up, otherwise they will never wake up and it would be a shame."

"A shame?"

"Yes. Then they will be just like they were when I was a baby. They will be like babies. You know what I mean Esther. I think we should leave now. Father and Murray will be wondering where we have been. I don't want father to worry. He has had enough worry lately."

"Okay Celia, let's go then. Thanks Asper and Lorraine…and you too Tim. Make sure you all come over to visit. We are on the east side. You were right as the houses over there were in much better repair than on the west side. It is called Johnston Street."

"Okay Esther, we'll come around. How about tomorrow afternoon? Maybe Tim and the men could have a chat and we can help you about the house."

"It sounds great, doesn't it Celia?"

"Yes it does, but you are going to need to bring something with you when you come. Don't ask me what it is. You will have to work it out. But we will need it…all of us."

Tim found enough materials in the shed to conceal the doorway by making an external panel the same as the surrounding wall. There was nothing around sufficient to sound proof the room, so he decided to search for materials elsewhere as a priority.

"I think I'll take a walk into town and see if I can find anything. Anyone want to come with me?"

"Um, Asper and I were going to collect some firewood…for you to chop later on."

"It's fine. I'll do it when I get back. I'll see you in about an hour or so."

Tim walked the mile into town under a sky beginning to turn grey with inclement weather coming. A sudden gust of chilly air suggested there could be snow in the weather – something he thought would not occur too often at this altitude. Tim estimated the town was at around two thousand feet, so any snow meant the weather system would likely be significant.

At the centre of town he scouted around until he found some internal insulation panels from behind the wall in one of the newer buildings. As he worked them from their mountings, Tim came across a sound he had not heard on any previous occasion during his entire life.

The sound seemed to be coming from within the walls of the building. There was nothing to indicate the sound source, nor was there any power to the building from which the device generating the sound could be powered. When he removed the last and largest insulation panel, he discovered a small hatch embedded into the wall, and it was from behind this door, where Tim could finally discern the source of the sound.

Excitement began to well up inside him at the prospect of discovering something new. It sounded like a mix between a mournful cat and low base drum coming in a regular pulse and rhythm but at very low volume. As he prised open the door, the sound became louder, though only slightly.

There inside the alcove, he found what he instantly thought was a small vortex amplifier. As soon as he saw the small device six inches wide with two horned torus and a ring torus in the centre, he knew what it was for. What confused him was the fact it had been located in a completely separate building from the quantum computer he had found a day earlier.

It was clear to Tim why the hardware installation had taken place and how this small amplifier was designed to be connected to the computer system he had removed, but the separation of the two mystified him. All he could conclude was there would be further installations to follow at both locations. The amplifier was working as evidenced by the sound it made, and the faint glow within all three torus, so he left it running as he stowed it inside the bag he had taken with him.

Tim knew the authorities would definitely come looking for the amplifier when it was discovered missing, so on his way back to the house, he retrieved some additional materials to help conceal the secret room even further. By the time he arrived, he had enough materials for soundproofing and to build an entire false wall over the panelled section containing the doorway to the hidden room.

"Come and have a look at this. I found a vortex amplifier in town."

"What? An amplifier. I thought the Agent was the only one to possess one of those."

"Not so Lorraine. Apparently the authorities have been busy making them. I can only imagine there will be one of these in most small towns and cities."

"Did I hear correctly? A vortex amp…"

"You did Asper. Tim found one when he went into town. I wonder what they are going to be used for."

"We can only imagine it will be needed for a new crackdown and control the authorities will soon bring about. Perhaps they have learned enough from John to make these things work, but then it could be just as dangerous as the Agent, given their flux mechanics are unstable."

"Maybe it is why these systems are not yet on-line and the authorities have not yet overwhelmed these types of places. Perhaps they are waiting until they have stability and then everything will be switched on."

"A good guess Lorraine. Look at the ringed torus. I would guess it is a nano carbon composite with silica elements, but only traces."

"Take it out and see what happens Tim," Asper said with a keenness she could not place in origin.

"Okay, but first I will need to connect it to the quantum computer and create a field to then be able to remove it properly."

Tim made the necessary calculations and then entered the required algorithms. Five minutes later, he was able to remove the ring torus from its situation between the two horns. The moment he did this, the torus took to showing a slight pink hue similar to the Torus of Eternity Asper and Lorraine had seen years before.

"You know what it means don't you Asper?"

"Sure. There is something activating this torus not derived from a power source or cell. And...the authorities are edging closer to enabling these devices to accelerate atoms for flux. Chan would not like this."

"Nor would Jenna. I think you should keep it out of the amplifier Tim."

"But the authorities could have thousands of these. What difference would it make?"

"A world of difference Tim. Don't ask me how I know, but it will."

"Okay Asper."

A light snow was falling as they walked towards the town on their way to visit the others the next day. The house in Johnston Street and Carmel's house were still the only two occupied residences in the town, so there were no encounters with other people on the way. Under the grey skies amidst the gentle flakes, the town had taken on a ghostly feeling, devoid of colour and stark in contrast where the snow had begun to settle on the derelict buildings. When they reached the house, a faint warm glow was a welcome sight after the two-mile walk. As soon as Celia answered the door and had ushered them inside to the kitchen, she turned to Tim with a questioning look on her face.

"Did you bring the torus Tim?"

"Um...ah, yes I did in fact."

"Can I see it please?"

"Um, sure. Here it is." Tim handed it to Celia and the moment she cast her eyes on it, the pink hue within increased.

"Can I keep it here with me? You can come over to use it for the amplifier thing it was in. I know you will need to."

"How do you know this Celia?"

"They told me I would be able to have a torus at this town."

Everyone looked at her after this statement, confounded by what she was telling them and how she knew of things only Tim could known.

Chapter 4

"So tell me of your results John. My superior has demanded I make significant progress with this issue efficiently. Results with tangible outcomes are the only way to proceed."

"I am sure he means you well and he has your best interests in mind."

"Now John, you know it is simply not the case. He…and I, have neither of those issues on our minds. We strive for efficiency only. So tell me, what do you have?"

"I have some readings concerning the geometric layers being sent through the anomaly. There is a correlation between those and the harmonics."

"Um, yes John. I know this already. Unless you have something further to tell me, then there is no purpose behind our meeting and no cause for you to pursue this any further. Perhaps it is best for you to continue analysis of the flux mechanics. After all, the stability issue is our primary concern."

"I am sure it is."

"So?"

"All I can tell you is the correlation at this stage. It will take some further calculations."

"Have you applied flux differentials in order to establish the dynamics of both harmonic frequencies?"

"Yes. I can see why you needed to detect the lower eight hertz frequency before you could detect the higher frequency. The lower frequency is a carrier wave. How this is done, I am not sure at this stage, as harmonics are normally just…harmonics. The idea of one sound wave carrying another is an issue for further investigation using flux. I can only suggest the higher wave is dimensionally phased slightly different to the lower wave. The lower frequency operates as a tuning key element for transition to the high frequency."

"And the patterns?"

"Similar characteristics, except there is no carrier wave. I am going to apply the harmonics to the geometries using flux as my next experiment."

"So you have determined the required algorithms in order to conduct this experiment?"

"Yes, it is mostly what I have been working on since you last visited."

"Then I too will work on this so our studies are in alignment. This is sufficient progress for report to my superior. As long as we have a direction, then we can continue to look for your assistance John."

"Whatever you say Eric. I will do what I can, but you are holding me against my will. I can never be entirely compliant with your needs."

"Now you know our position as well as I do John. We are unable to release you until we have this problem solved. You know our vulnerabilities arising from unstable flux John. I can imagine you could take this technology and use it against us."

"You have all I know."

"Indeed you say, but a mind as intelligent as yours could serve us well once we have established stability...and also, such a mind could be capable of keeping secrets. Imagine the technology you could be a part of. You could make history John."

"How absurd. You know..."

"I know there is yet more to know John. You will give us the way."

"I would think the authorities are seeking to eradicate history anyway. Such desires are an ego trait...to make history. It seeks notoriety."

"Not all is to be lost John, otherwise how do you think people will make decisions for the good of the population?"

"They don't."

"So you see it to be, but believe me, there is a lot more to come. We have installations at the ready for engagement as soon as stability is achieved John."

"What installations?"

"Just be aware there are machines ready to institute the new wave of mechanics we will soon deploy. Even I consider we are mere moments away from stability John."

"How do you know? And what will you do when you have it?"

"Oh I do know John. My own thoughts are still evolving despite the faults with my nano mechanics. You may be surprised to hear I could soon know almost as much about flux mechanics as you do John. As for what we are going to do, I think there is enough time to allow you to wait and see. All I can say is there will be far fewer people required to for the efficient goals of the machine John."

"So you are simply going to kill off people not seen as required for your machine?"

"In a way John, but they will still have purpose, so they will not all actually be killed...rather, um, utilised."

"Great, more of your human values coming through."

"Our humanity is prevalent John. It is just a different vision of this we have in opposition to your aspirations, but in the long run, you too will come to realise the value of our methods and our objectives."

"Again...objectives. You are not dealing with a manufacturing process here, these are people."

"Correct on both accounts, except...we are looking at the manufacturing of people John. And then, we are going to send them to wherever we need to send them. We need to manage society thoroughly John."

"What do you mean by sending them?"

"There are many things to discover and yet many things have been discovered since you have been with us John. When you have helped us, or even if you cannot, within a relatively short period, humanity will express itself in ways and in places people could have barely even dreamed of…ever."

"Ha…expression. You have been quashing it since eighty-eight!"

"Oh no we haven't John. We have been quashing it for much longer than the past recent years. Think with your great mind and you will realise such things have been happening since long before you were born John. It is just we have allowed people to believe they are free…"

"Free! It has never really been the case throughout all history."

"See, you are already realising the truth John. You are right. People have never really been free. The authorities and the corporations have just made it seem like it is."

"You lot own the corporations."

"It has not always been the way John. When the authorities saw the dependence the people had developed on large multi-national corporations by the middle of the twenty-first century, they began a gradual takeover, but the people were never allowed to see this. Remember one thing John. The corporations have mostly been responsible for the products, but the authorities have always made the laws. Since those times, collusion between government and corporations has begun and a managed society has emerged. It is this simple thing most people have overlooked as they have had their head down for so very long now."

"But you haven't fooled everyone. There were people back in eighty-eight who were against the identification microchip and they resisted. There will always be someone…"

"No there will not be John. Our directive is to finally eradicate all levels of dissent through the use of stable flux mechanics John. Such issues will simply not occur to people come future times."

"You already have robots…why not use them and let people be themselves?"

"Then there would be no use for the authorities John and then the population will lose direction and aspiration of a better world will be lost."

"You are seeking to eradicate aspiration."

"Not entirely John. Status will play a part as people are driven to depend again on technology to better their lives. It will be a staged release John…it always has been. We need them to generate the capital and continue a world of economic dominance. Otherwise there will be nothing to hold the populations to account for."

"So this is your purpose…or should I say, the purpose in life you want people to have. To work for status and to consume and therefore create capital for new development, whilst they are being controlled by the elite few."

"Your words sound accurate John."

"It only takes a mildly warm brain to see this has been happening a long time anyway. I don't need any credit."

"And you shall not receive any John...unless you align with our purpose sufficiently to gain yourself superior status, and then you shall receive all the credit you deserve."

"But it is outside..."

"Our directives. Remember John, not all is to be lost. There will be the onus upon status for all. Eventually this will lead us into a new sphere of human evolution where the inefficiencies of the ages past will not even be a memory. We will wipe all those instances from both memory and the records John. And...there will always be the elite John...as we leave the confines of Earth behind."

"Where..."

"I cannot say as yet because you have not stabilised flux mechanics for us John. So please hurry up and make a breakthrough, otherwise I will have to do it, and at present I have a number of projects to complete."

"What for?"

"Machines John. Machines."

Eric left John to do his work, telling him he would return again in two more days to discuss any progress on the issues at hand. John was not a smug person, but at this time, he felt a slight sense of this despite being incarcerated deep inside the facility below New York City. He had managed to keep the one algorithm to stabilise flux mechanics away from Eric's knowledge for three years, and he had almost entirely determined the coding used within the nano mechanics working against him inside his brain.

There was one other thing John had reason to hold a sense of smugness for, and it was his knowledge of the anomaly he had not given to Eric Gunter. In the time since he had been ordered to work on the sudden surge in size of the anomaly, and the strange energies being beamed from within its swirling vortex, he had discovered there were areas to study in multi-dimensional physics of which Eric or his superiors were barely aware.

By providing the one faulty algorithm within the enveloping multi-dimensional field required to lay all tachyon receptive pathways upon, basic elements of flux mechanics were held back by John. Without precise allocation of receptors at the verge of the antimatter and matter threshold, successful stable flux phasing of atomic and quantum atomic fields, could not occur.

He was now delving into this one algorithm as he studied the recent changes in the spatial anomaly. John was convinced he was on the right path as the results showed the origins of the geometries and the correlating harmonic frequencies as being deliberately beamed in a regular pattern through the vortex for reception on this side. Eluding him at this time was the precise location from where the energies were coming from, and the reason why they were coming through. One thing he began to consider was the idea of the spacecraft sent into the anomaly three years prior beaming these transmissions from a point where it was being held in stasis.

In his own sense of wonder, John felt compelled to pursue this without the knowledge of Eric and his superiors as he considered the many questions he could ask the pilot of the craft. What it was like wherever the anomaly led to, and what dimensional shifts had the pilot experienced, were the two foremost questions in mind.

His next move would be to clarify wherever possible, the precise configurations within the geometries, and then to run some theoretical testing to ascertain their purpose. With this information, John felt then he would be able to work more in depth with the correlating harmonics and then build an overall picture as to the reason and origin of the beamed energies. In a way, he was seeing the anomaly as both a sound speaker with the harmonics, and a pathway for the sending of data forming the geometric pattern layers.

He worked as late as his alertness would permit – well beyond the hour of midnight, into the early hours not long before sunrise. John had not seen the sun or a sunrise since he had been captured with Tobias after journeying west from Concepcion in Chile to board a fishing vessel on the coast for eventual passage back to Mollendo in Peru. They had ventured far on the return seaward leg when Eric had tracked them down and taken them both into custody.

Eric had provided John with artificial lighting to replace the essential elements a human being required to obtain from sunlight, but it was nothing like the real feeling one has standing in the open air, feeling the warmth caressing skin. As a consequence, work of this type had become difficult at times for John as he struggled with health issues arising from his incarceration. Such was his strength and determination however, he held the vision of eventual escape from this prison, and so all the work he did also encompassed researching ways to use this knowledge and some technology to make good his escape. Often too in his thoughts was the fate of his friend Tobias and how he was faring.

Chapter 5

Tim was looking at a small device Murray had possessed for some years. "Do you know what this is?"

"No Tim. It was something I found during the dark days under the Agent. It was in a small warehouse and I thought it might be of use some day."

"Well, you were right. It will be of use. It is microchip injection device. I can make it work after a few adjustments and by replacing a couple of the capacitors. They look burnt out to me. I wonder why it was left behind? Maybe because of these burn outs."

"What can we use it for?"

"If I make a few adjustments, we can reverse the injection module and use it to extract microchips."

"Surely there are not many people left with those inserts."

"Probably not. The Agent took care of a lot of them. Nevertheless, it could be handy sometime in the future."

"Do you think they will try a new round of injections then?"

"Maybe, but I am more inclined to think they will be using far more advanced technology these days."

"I'll bet they have something pretty bad in store for all of us."

"Not for me. I'll never have any of their rubbish inside. I extracted the first round of chips. This device can help ensure we won't have to keep anything they try to force on us."

"So what is it you do Tim? You seem fairly technologically skilled to me."

"You could say so. I just dabble in various things. Wherever I can get by, I do so. Working for the authorities or any of their corporations has never been my thing. I prefer to work alone...or with a friend or two should they come along. How about you?"

"Foodstuffs research and development. It has been a while though since I have worked in a front line developmental facility. Not since eighty-eight actually. As soon as the restrictions on fresh food came into force, the authorities shut down any new development of foodstuffs. They said the population was to rely on what had already been developed as it met the minimum nutrient requirements for survival and efficient work ability. Apparently the nano technology was to take care of the rest."

"Except it didn't."

"No. What do you think of the Agent's viruses and those holes he opened up? I have heard some say they will become dangerous if the authorities cannot close them."

"They have managed to eradicate many of the small ones I believe. It is the joined holes they are having problems with. I have heard they have rounded up all those affected and have them contained within one or two centres where they can work on them. It is my guess they are more likely just to dispose of the people as most of them are well beyond any help now. As far as the vortexes go, I think they will be using flux mechanics to manage those."

"But the anomaly is unstable isn't it?"

"It sure is. So there is still a long way to go before there is any certainty."

"What do you think about Celia?"

"Yeah, what do you think Tim?" Derek added. He had arrived on the scene undetected by either Tim or Murray.

"Um, I'm not sure Derek…and Murray. It is a bit weird how she knows these things. Some precognition maybe. Asper had a similar experience the same day as Celia and Esther showed up at our place."

"Yeah, I am grappling with it both as her father, and as a psycho cybernetic specialist. All the work I did in the past did not come close to anything like Celia is demonstrating. We just looked into constructing autonomous cybernetic responses…through algorithms. We did not even imagine exploring the aspects of precognition or anticipation either."

"It shows how far the authorities still have to go for nano mechanical trans-human values to parallel those of real sentience."

"If they obtain stable flux though…they will come a lot closer."

"So you work deep inside authority central then?"

"Yeah, for a time. I was in the eastern sector up until the Agent took to flying over and launching viruses in his laser fire. My situation was at the fringes working on ancillary response mechanisms. As soon as the Agent took to the east, we were shut down and left without any work, or anywhere to live. The authorities just shut us out completely…not to mention thousands of unfortunate others as well. When all hell broke loose with the war-like onslaught and the resulting disarray, Celia's mother and I took her away from Baltimore and headed west to see if we could find a new style of living. With the Agent being apprehended, we figured it would be safe…but then Joanna was killed during one of those clean up initiatives."

"I'm sorry to hear."

"Thanks Tim. She was a great lady. Full of spirit and such a giving person. Celia looks just like her."

"She is a fine child Derek."

"Yeah, I think so. What are you two discussing anyway?"

"I just showed Tim the device I have been carrying for years. He told me it was an injection unit he can modify to be an extraction unit after he fixes a few parts."

"Oh good. I always thought it was something along those lines. The only injection units I saw previously were the bigger type, connected to the chairs they used back in eighty-eight."

"They were ugly things those."

"You're telling me. When I watched people use them, it bloody well nearly made me sick. One administration officer I was working with was all for them for a time, but when I told him of the long-term affects coming he gave them up. His dad helped him to do it. We were in Boston at the time on a special project. I didn't see him again, but I heard his dad was on the run somewhere. Apparently he had some knowledge on how flux mechanics works, according to his son, the officer…Chris, I think his name was. It surprised me how an administrative officer would know of such things at first. Anyway, he did all he could to get his dad to stay, but in the end, he had to give him up. It was a shame. The authorities have ruined a lot of good relationships over the years."

"Interesting you mention him because I am almost certain I know the person you are speaking of. There are not many people at all who have substantial knowledge of flux. The one person who is an expert is a friend of mine, but I have not seen him in a long time."

"The authorities probably have him."

"Indeed, they likely do have him as captive and probably used his knowledge to make the anomaly."

"Couldn't they make it without flux mechanics?"

"No. It takes the specific phasing properties within flux to create a stable vortex unlike those the Agent created."

"But it is unstable isn't it?"

"Yeah. I um…am watching it myself."

"Watching it?"

"Yeah, I came across a bit of technology not long ago and have it set up to monitor the anomaly."

"Yeah Tim is a bit of a technology expert Derek."

"Hey, they are your words Murray…but I'll go with them for now."

"You know, I have a little whiskey I found. Perhaps we could all do with a drink," Murray suggested. He was becoming tired of the technology talk.

"Sounds great Murray. Ask the ladies if they would like a drink. All this technology talk gets a bit much after a while."

"I would have to agree there Derek. It's good to step away now and then."

"Whiskey Asper…Lorraine? How about you Esther?"

"Sure! Where did you get whiskey? I haven't had a drink in a longer time than I can remember."

"We found a stash a couple of months back. I'll get a few glasses."

"I'll help Esther."

"Thanks Lorraine."

"Where's Celia?"

"She is in her room Derek. She said she just wanted to play with the torus Tim gave her."

"Oh okay. Sure she is alright?"

"Don't worry. Have a drink. Let's all have a drink…or two."

For a while, all the adults could relax over a drink and allow themselves to loosen up from the on-going tension often rearing its head each day. After a time when the snowfall became heavier, it prompted them into action.

"I'll better get firewood. Snow is the heavier," Murray slurred.

"I'll help you Murray. You sound a little drunk," Esther replied smiling.

"It's only been tree drinks Esther. Maybe because it has been a while."

"You stay here Esther. Tim and I will help Murray."

"Yeah fine. Where is the wood pile?" Tim asked.

"Out the side of the rear shed. Let's go."

The three men donned their heavy coats and stepped outside into the steadily falling snow. As they reached the rear shed and stacked a few logs into their arms, a low droning sound could be heard from some distance away.

"What the hell is it?" Murray asked as the three of them stood motionless.

"I don't know. But whatever it is, it cannot be good. Let's take this back inside quickly."

"Esther, close those curtains will you. I'll keep the fire low," Derek said as he dumped his armful of logs beside the fire."

"What is it?"

"There is something outside. Not real close, but close enough."

"Where?"

"In the sky, which means it can only be the authorities. We best keep quiet."

"Here look. I can just see it off in the distance. It looks like it is hovering a short distance away near the centre of town."

"Any idea what it is Tim?" Derek asked.

"Cannot see it clearly, but from I can see, it looks like a type of flying craft I have never seen before. Sort of spaceship like but then again not."

"What do you mean?"

"Well…here take a look yourself. There is a bit of a break in the weather. You can see is a bit clearer now."

"Oh…no good. I have seen schematics for those craft when I was still in cybernetics. They were looking to build flying craft piloted by robotics. It looks like they have succeeded."

"Are they armed?"

"I would expect so."

"What do you think they are here for?" Esther looked concerned as she pondered a fast escape and more time on the road.

"To take this town Esther. I found a little device they will likely go looking for after they land. Lucky it is well concealed and not at this house. If they come here and start asking questions, then we will have to say we all live here. Um, just arrived. Okay?"

Everyone agreed it was a good plan, and the three women went about making it appear as if they all lived in the house by scattering a few things about. In the meantime, they conducted themselves as if they were doing normal things anyone would be doing in such a situation inside a house without power whilst snow was falling outside. Tim remained looking out through the window trying as best he could to see where the craft had landed and if anyone decided to visit the house. After watching for almost half an hour, he advised there were officers in their street who looked to be checking all the houses for any signs of life.

"They'll be here in a few minutes. I suggest we just keep doing what we are doing. Don't be nervous or they will think we have something to hide."

The three officers did not knock on the door to the house. Instead they just opened the door and made their way inside.

"Everyone in this house come to this room now."

Celia had appeared just before the officers had arrived, so there was no need to go and fetch her from the room where she had been playing. She had hidden the torus as her feelings told her to do what she could to protect it at all times.

"What are you all doing here?"

"Just trying to survive officer."

"Names?"

"I am Derek, this is Esther, Celia, Murray, Lorraine, Tim, and Asper."

"Right. Who else is here with you?"

"Just us officer. We all live here together. We only arrived here from San Francisco a few days ago and found this house to stay before the weather set in."

"We'll take a look. You two go and search the house."

The other two officers proceeded to go through the entire house, looking in each room, opening cupboards, and upturning beds. They returned a few minutes later as it was only a small house."

"Nothing to report sir."

"Why did you come here? The city is a much easier place for you to survive."

"Um, we like the country officer. No other reason."

"Did you know this town is marked for direct authority control?"

"Um, no officer. We do not even know what such control means."

"Well, it means there will be an appointed officer in charge of this town to oversee its re-shaping into a rural efficiency centre. It is to become a hub for authority control in this region."

"I see."

"Do you all see? This is very relevant for your choice to live in this town."

All the others except for Celia nodded to indicate they understood.

"Have you seen other people in this town?"

"No officer. Just us so far."

"I don't believe you. Others must be here. Do any of you know where they are?"

"No officer. As I said, we have only been here a few days. Maybe they are in another part of town."

"For your sakes, let's hope you are right. There is something missing and if we find those responsible for its theft, they will be imprisoned. The authorities cannot tolerate the inefficiencies of people going about stealing property clearly not theirs."

"Um, we will keep an eye out sir."

"You do keep an eye out. You two go and check all around this house, including the shed out there."

The two officers once again went on a search, but returned a few minutes later to report nothing.

"Right. For your advice I will tell you this. In five days this town will become integrated into the regional authority network as new systems are brought online. For you this means there will be officers all over this town here to ensure all goes according to authority planning without any inefficiency. You will be permitted to remain here as long as you meet all obligations for compliance to the laws as they will be set out. Do you understand?"

Again, everyone except Celia nodded to indicate their understanding.

"One last thing. Do you have any technology?"

"No officer. None of us have anything. Besides there is no power to run any technology sir."

"There will be. As soon as we have installed a replacement node in the town centre, electricity will be beamed into this town. An officer will call by this house in five days to provide you with further advice. Until then, I suggest you do what you can to prepare for the new laws. There will be no tolerance of anything outside of strict compliance."

"What do you think he meant by electricity will be beamed into this town?" Murray asked a few minutes after the trio of officers had departed.

"I suppose they have some type of new technology to transmit electricity rather than carry it through lines. I have heard of it being converted into microwaves to transmit and then convert it back to electricity, but they would have to install technology at each and every residence, building, machine, and so on, so it is still a bit of a guess."

"They will get the tiny robots to do it," Celia told them. "They might even be here now, waiting to be activated so they can start building. Then they will be able to control people."

"Of course! Nano bots to replicate. You are a wonder Celia."

"So they will just build things basically out of nothing?"

"Almost Esther. They program them to convert any matter at the atomic level from within specified co-ordinates."

"A long way then from the old three dimensional printing?"

"Oh yes. The nano bots can operate out of sight without the need of a machine to conduct the process of manufacturing like the printing used a few decades back."

"Then we had better watch out. Maybe they can also manufacture surveillance devices without our knowing."

"They will be almost too small to see as well. We need to keep our conversations to code or avoid anything deemed as suspicious for most of the time. Anyway, it becomes tiring discussing the authorities for too long."

"But we do need to try and stay a step ahead of them Tim. After all, I think we are all gathered here because we share common motivations and intentions."

"You have me for such things…and Asper. We know about the anomaly don't we Asper?"

"Um, yes Celia."

The low barely audible hum sound of the flying craft indicated the officers were departing the town. Everyone in the room except for Celia relaxed a little knowing their presence was leaving. Celia had simply remained out of contact with such feelings of anxiety – somehow resolute she was going to be all right without the burden of analysis the adults carried. When the craft was gone, a faint smell of electricity burning was in the air for a time.

"I think I'll get to work repairing the device you have Murray, now they have gone. I am more certain now we are going to use it sometime in the future."

"Sure Tim. Maybe Derek can help."

"Um, yeah, I suppose. My expertise is more with the cybernetic algorithms though. But perhaps I can help with some of the re-configuration work."

"The more heads working on it the better."

"Okay, I'll stoke the fire though. Now they know we are in town, it won't be an issue if we have a roaring fire."

"What if they visit Carmel's house and see it has been lived in?" Lorraine asked as her anxiety suddenly rose when realising they were likely to visit.

"We can only take it as we will see it Lorraine. At least the room is hidden."

Chapter 6

Eric was in charge of the Monolithic Directive. This project of immense proportion was the next imposition the authorities were to force upon the population. It was to be characterised by its massive size and effect, and by its intentional rigidity to deliver total uniformity and compliance. In contrast to its internal operations conducted by billions of microscopic robots, the machine itself was enormous – stretching some five hundred feet along each side.

The heart of the machine contained a replication star measuring two hundred feet in diameter - held in an anti-gravity stasis field. The star was nothing short of spectacular as it glowed a low electric blue in standby mode. Eric still had work to do on the final calculations to enable internal fusion processes to commence, and so had not yet proceeded to activation of the star in full. For now, it glimmered barely visible to the naked eye.

The project was unknown to all except those directly responsible for its approval, and those employed for its development. When Eric had finalised all calculations necessary to activate the star, it would generate sufficient energy to supply the authorities with the power for all machines, and would serve as an atomic generator for creation of base elements required by nano mechanics in the manufacture of whatever Eric programmed them to create. Drawing on other dimensional manifestation through a torus vortex, the star would potentially power the authorities to eternity.

The stability of flux mechanics was a key issue impairing success for the star at present. Whilst it could be mostly operational without flux, the benefits of the mechanics in stability would enable the authorities to amplify energy beyond dimensions to create as many stars as they deemed necessary for their expansion motives.

Eric and his team were servants to their superiors, and their superiors were increasingly looking to extend their reach far beyond Earth with the Monolithic Directive as their vehicle. As their first imperative, Eric was to rectify the instability of the spatial anomaly, so they could send the manufactured star into the vortex.

"Well John. What information do you have for me today?"

"What, not even a hello from you Eric?"

"I think you have come to expect me whenever I see fit. Such cordiality is beyond us now."

"Another one of your efficiencies then. Um, not much information for you today Eric. All I have is a little more on the construct of the multi-dimensional geometries. From what I can see, they are deliberately being sent through the vortex. As for their purpose, I am still uncertain. However…"

"Yes?"

"My data shows they are not likely to be originating from the spacecraft sent into the anomaly."

"So you think they are extra-terrestrial?"

"Perhaps as a possibility only Eric. You know as well as I do of the mathematical probability for other intelligent life in the galaxy."

"What have you done to follow up on this particular point?"

"What can be done? You might send a transmission through the vortex in an attempt to contact whoever might be sending these transmissions to us. But...personally, I would hold off on such things at this time. If you will permit me to investigate further, I could run some tests to see if they are not transmissions at all. I am speculating...only speculating at this stage, on the idea of these geometries being phase wake."

"Phase wake?'

"Yes phase wake. Think if you will how an ocean vessel creates waves as it travels. These waves are formed by the vessel's course through water in response to the angulations of the physical vessel in opposition to the wave forms it courses through. When these waves flow on to a point where they may encounter a stationary object, they reverberate and thus create additional waves at angulations to the original waves."

"I see, and..."

"Then these geometries could be similar but different where they are results from the algorithmic reverberations perhaps created by the spaceship riding the tachyon pathways."

"What about the time since John?"

"Time is immaterial for flux mechanics...particularly when conducted through spatial anomalies. These could be such wave forms bouncing back and within the vortex."

"What of the issue of them only now becoming apparent?"

"Interesting you ask. As far as I can tell, it is likely a result of the immeasurable variations created through its instability. It could be only now they have made their way back to us. Who knows the extent of the anomaly's reach?"

"I have made some progress John...into the effects generated by the Agent's viruses. I do know there are some limitations incurred due to their instability."

"True. I have seen similar, but we are still yet to actually define these limitations. There still remains the uncertainty of how far they reach in either continuum. For all we know, they could be reaching places we are yet to even consider – be they great in distance and in time."

"Then you will need to proceed further with this line of research and expeditiously. I am being pressured to engage our latest developments very soon John, and..."

"But you cannot deploy whatever it is until you have stability. It could open up a plethora of instances the authorities would see as very inefficient."

"I know this John, which is why we must hurry in a way. You know what my superiors become when impatience is a factor."

"I would have thought like you, they would have the same nano mechanics preventing them from such inefficient behavioural traits."

"They don't."

"So it is you with your mechanical eyes and your nano mechanical systems coercing your organics as their guinea pig?"

"I am not a guinea pig John. I am the way forward. As soon as we have success, so too will it be the way for all."

"I don't know if I agree with you there Eric."

"It is irrelevant John. My superiors only want what is best for all...and for themselves. When we reach stability, they will not hesitate to take on the trans-human values I myself espouse to."

"I see. And what if we are unable to reach stability?"

"Then they will proceed with the best they have at the time, regardless."

"Precisely what the Agent did without regard for anything or anyone."

"Except as I have said previously, the authorities have a definitive objective in mind, whereas the Agent did not."

"Where is he, the Agent?"

"He is located nine floors below you John where he has been these past years."

"What will you do with him?"

"We are already doing things with him. His mania is very much the focus of some studies for our cybernetic division. We wish to fully understand such character traits in order to ensure they do not feature in human evolution as we move ahead. However...we are doing some research into his heightened adrenaline states for use in future applications."

"So you are developing algorithms to apply?"

"Yes."

"Do you think they will work Eric?"

"Of course. Our next level of nano mechanics will successfully eradicate all such inefficiencies within the human mind, whilst perhaps being able to draw upon increased efficiencies based on the adrenaline state."

"But it will be a mechanical mind."

"In part. There will still be elemental human characteristics John."

"Minimal."

"Yet present. Keep working John. I need this information as soon as possible. In fact, consider this...everyone needs this information as soon as possible."

"Two days then?"

"I would think it would be appropriate."

"What do you really have in store Eric? I can sense there is something else. There is a large part of me given still to such things."

"Whatever else I am working on John is not really of consequence to you at this point in time. Suffice to say, there is something looming as there always has been."

"I realise this Eric. It has been the way of the authorities for some time. People come to expect it. You cannot say something looming is anything except what is simply to be the way for you Eric. I think people have the idea by now."

"Not all John. Some may have a notion of what is transgressing, but there is very little knowledge about what is really happening."

"You state the obvious. Again, you speak of what has been the normal way, for so many years now."

"Indeed, yet so many have not so much as questioned the way on which they have been led. This indicates efficiency John. After all, this is simply what is meant to be. There is no other alternative. What transgresses as an intimate moment for anyone is merely another moment ill spent. Substance of what is called intimate or empathic is merely a sense distracted from the overall purpose John. What else could people want other than to feel their lives are complete? They can still have the pleasures, those moments of inclination based on actualisation in the moment. It is just they will combine with all other moments in a lineal strive towards efficiency. There is no other feasible way in which to reorganise the frailties of human experiences, other than to refine them through nano mechanics John."

"What? You cannot be serious."

"Oh very serious. You wait until you see the results on a wider scale. There will be an ordered and efficiently functioning society. One moment people can feel ecstasy, and then the next they can be removed from contemplation by the mind...unthinking and to be actualised John."

"Cybernetics. You are planning to use this intrusion into self, to construct a trans-being. The idea of trans-human is superseded by your motives."

"Not my motives John. I am merely in service to the manifestation of this ideal from the authorities."

"Mind as data. Data as mind. You are turning minds into computers – managed by the data you see as most suitable."

"In a way yes. Understand within this crucible there will be those elemental facets of self-servicing to the enhancements. Misery will be gone. Sorrow and loneliness will be forgotten."

"And with flux...in stability?"

"Then I have it all ready to go John. Machines await your deliverance. They also await mine. They will be unstoppable. This is no mere crackdown on liberties you may have seen in the past. This is going to be a swift and comprehensive change…for the good, forever. It will be an enthralling time to be human alive on this planet. We will take it so much further as well."

"I can only imagine. These concepts you speak of are the progression ahead for humanity anyway as they learn more mindful approaches to living. They are not in the sole domain of what you can do with flux mechanics."

"Yes, but those ways are inefficient John. Ultimately we must reside with this notion for the sake of ourselves, and for the planet."

"I get you Eric. I can also see you Eric. But I ask. Can you really see me Eric?"

"These mechanical eyes are fully functional John. I can see you clearly."

John noticed how Eric had said these instead of my. Their conversations had begun to take a slant as Eric became more and more aligned with the directives of his superiors. He could see Eric losing his sense as a human being, now being smothered gradually by the infusion of robotics into his mind, and throughout his body – including his heart.

Turning back to his work, John became even more vigilant in keeping his other results secret from Eric. His lie about the signal not being from the space craft appeared to go undetected by both Eric and the nano implants in his brain. Whilst the nano mechanics in his own mind, constantly plagued him with notions, and directions into his synapses, and with influence over his overall mood, he was able to enter places of concept at an increasingly successful rate. The mechanics were failing inside him, as they were also failing inside Eric.

John had watched as Eric had gradually become less and less aligned with the elemental intentions arising from the central heart vortex in his body. He could see the loss of relation to core values aspiring to uplift progressive life senses. Eric was misaligned, yet becoming very much aligned with the directions as set out by his superiors along with his own work to shape his future.

Chapter 7

"Twelve sides, see?"

"Yes I do Celia. It is a lovely shape."

"It is called a dodecahedron. See the pentagons? Each of them has five sides, and the dodecahedron has twelve sides."

"It is a beautiful thing Celia. Where did you get it?"

"I found it when we were out in the town before the snow came. It's mine now, but...really it belongs to nobody. And, it goes so well with the torus you gave me Tim."

"What do you mean Celia?"

"Well the torus is a powerful object. It is why they put it in the computer you found. They can accelerate atoms."

"Really!"

"Yes, and now I have this dodecahedron, there can be much more power for the torus Tim."

"I see."

"Yes. Perhaps you can study this some more and then we can talk about it again. I am not a scientist, but I do know there is much to learn from these things. So I recommend you study them. Use the computer you have. I know you stole it, but it is alright, because your ideas are good...the authorities are bad."

"Thanks Celia. Maybe I will study these shapes," Tim replied a little confounded at what Celia appeared to know.

"You could do no harm studying them. It might help you with what you will need to do."

"Okay...and what am I going to need to do Celia?"

"Help others fix the anomaly. Gee...I thought you would have figured it out by now."

"Um...who are the others Celia?"

"I don't really know. All I know is you will trust them to help fix it. They will come, but don't wait for them. You need to get working now. It is why you have the computer isn't it?"

"I guess so. I just thought it would be an advantage for us...somehow. I have looked at the anomaly with it."

"Well, now you know it is. I'm going to play now. The sun is out and the snow looks very pretty and so white."

"Do you think Esther will mind, or your father?"

"They won't mind. They can see me. I'll just be out the front of the house. One last thing. When you study these shapes, think about the light helping us to see the anomaly in the daytime. I don't know what it is called, but they told me this is important."

"Who are they Celia?"

"I don't know Tim…just voices I hear. Okay, bye, I'm going to play now."

"Celia was telling me some interesting things just now Derek. Do you know about these voices she is hearing?" Tim said as the two men stood watching Celia play in the snow out the front of the house.

"Yeah, she has been telling me about them since before we came to this town. She even said we were meant to come to this town as they had told her we would meet people here who could help us."

"Perhaps Asper, Lorraine, and I are those people."

"More than likely. She has been a little mysterious of late. I thought it was due to her mother's passing, but it seems like something else."

"She asked me for the torus from the vortex amplifier I found."

"Really. When I was in cybernetics, they were looking at building such amplifiers. I guess the authorities are looking for it."

"Yeah, I stole it from their little hidey hole. Anyway…Celia has suggested there is a correlation between the torus I gave her and the dodecahedron she found."

"She found? She didn't tell me. What is it?"

"Just a crystal about two inches in diameter. She said she found it in the town here, before the snow came."

"I wonder where it came from. It is not like such things would just be left lying around. Did she say precisely where she found it?"

"No she didn't. I didn't ask either."

"Maybe we should ask her. My work involved using geometry in building cybernetic pathways for neural transmission. We looked at torus and dodecahedron for their specific geometric properties."

"She did suggest I study both as it would help us with the anomaly."

Celia was still running around outside when they went to ask her about the crystal, "So where did you find this Celia?"

"At Tim's, Asper's, and Lorraine's house when I was playing in the garden."

"Why didn't you tell us then?"

"They told me to keep it secret until it was the right time to tell you, which is today."

"Who are they?"

"The voices from the hole…um, the anomaly."

"Voices from the anomaly?"

"I think so. I don't know where else they would come from."

"Do they say bad things Celia?"

"Never. They are good people. They want to help us. But they say we must help ourselves for them to be able to help us."

"I see. What else have they told you?"

"Nothing much other than to get working on the anomaly, and to remember the geometry."

"Remember the geometry?"

"Yes. They tell me and they asked me to mind my words and only speak to the people I can trust. They also said there are others they are talking to and we are not the only ones."

"Others too. Okay Celia. You can go and play some more, but don't get cold. If you do, please come inside straight away."

"Yes father."

"I suppose we should listen to her and put our heads together on this. It will at least give us something to occupy our minds other than just trying to survive here at the moment. I wonder though if it is all just childhood fantasy after her mother died."

"I too though similarly but her words seem to have something, and doing something will prepare us for the coming of the authorities Derek."

"Indeed. It mystifies me though. These voices. She does not seem alarmed. Esther told me she has had nothing from Celia I should worry about."

"Maybe it is just something we go along with. It is weird…and Asper had a moment yesterday about the anomaly. Best we keep an eye on them both and just see what they have to tell us…or listen. I'll talk to Asper about it and see if she can shed any light on where these voices or notions might be coming from. Her experience was more of a feeling or precognition, rather than a voice."

"Celia did say there were others, so I guess we are amongst a group somehow being communicated with…but from where? It sounds impossible."

"Anyone's guess. It could even be a deception being broadcast by the authorities. We need to be wary of any such incursion."

"Good point Tim. The work I did in cybernetics looked long and hard at mind manipulation including subliminal suggestion. It was all for the push towards more and more efficiency and less and less opposition. There was a point where even the officials and employees of the authorities were being subjected to subliminal sounds to enhance their efficiency output."

"Maybe you could come over to where I have the installation and we can work on some test scenarios to see what we can find out about the torus and dodecahedron connection."

"We can go now if you like. The weather is not so bad, so the walk should be easy enough."

"Right then. But I think it is best just the two of us go in case there is any surveillance now in town. I suggest we take alternate routes and then meet up outside the house behind the rear shed. I'll come in from the front, and you can meet me from the rear. I'll have a look around before we go in. No doubt the authorities would have visited."

"I'll keep my eyes out as I go. We should stay well clear of the town centre and where it was you came across the computer."

"Good idea. Keep to the smaller lanes and stay close to walls and fences. Make it look as if we are out looking for fuel. Actually, grab a little on your way and then also when we leave, we can take more on the return trip."

Tim could not see any signs of there being any new surveillance hardware, but it was no consolation considering the size of the technology required to capture images of movement about the town. As he walked in the vicinity of where he had stolen the quantum computer from, he could see the traces left behind by the authority officers – where they had landed, and their footsteps in the snow. He did not glance directly at where he had found the hardware, but kept to looking in places where he might find wood or any other fuel to keep warm and to cook with. By the time he reached Carmel's house, Derek was scrounging around the rear side of the shed, and so they greeted each other in surprise under the guise of being out looking for fuel.

"I have these few pieces of wood, but I think there could be something at this house. It looks like it has been occupied more recently than most of the others."

"Yeah, I agree Derek. Being here on the edge of town may have contributed to it being a preferred choice by whoever lived here. Let's check inside this shed, and then go into the house."

After checking around for the authorities and seeing the front door open as they had left it, both men hoped the officers had seen the house and decided those who were living there were either gone or out somewhere.

Two minutes later they were both situated in the secret room where Tim had set up the quantum node array.

"See the processor unit is only tiny, but with all these peripherals…well, you can understand now why we needed the cart Asper found to bring it all here."

"Is this the energy transmitter?" Derek asked as he touched the main device.

"I guess so. I was hoping you might confirm."

"I didn't see any of this equipment during my cybernetics work. But, looking at this small rectangular antenna, it is most likely the electricity receiver or relay."

"You are probably right. I was not sure at all what it was for, but now with the advice of electricity being beamed into this town, I think it is a safe bet it has something major to do with microwave beams of electricity. We can work without the torus Celia is minding. This thing will do calculations fine as it is the booster within the vortex amplifier more or less. I have run a few monitoring tests through it for the anomaly."

"Any results yet?"

"Just a few energy level fluctuations and some scratchy audio."

"Audio?"

"It sounds like a regular pulse rhythm, but I need to refine the scanning parameters to hone in on it and obtain a clear result."

"Why don't we start there then? You have some preliminary results for us to work on. We shouldn't stay here too long though."

"You have a point there."

"What about the amplifier Tim? Perhaps if we connect it…or activate it, then it might provide some results a lot faster. Also, what about the sensitivity? Surely it would increase by a huge amount."

"Well Celia still has the torus and to engage the amplifier without it may prove unwise. I suggest we continue with this and then we can make some projections to focus on when we return with the torus and power up the amplifier."

"Alright. Good idea. I was a bit eager there for a moment. Maybe it was my cybernetics work. Back in the lab, we were constantly pushed for progress. It was seen as inefficient to move on development too slowly."

"I can only imagine."

The holographic projection array flickered into life illuminating the small room brilliantly as Tim entered the start up sequences for the quantum computer.

"Is it shielded Tim?"

"You bet. I built an algorithm to shield the array in less than a millionth of a second after it initialises."

Tim entered formulae to calculate the radius of the inscribed sphere and then determine the tangent to each face of a dodecahedron. At first he worked with two dimensional symmetry projections of the object to establish the orthogonal calculations giving rise to the contextual real vector spaces, before he moved onto a three dimensional perspective. As they studied the object and the equations showing at its side, one focal point emerged. The dihedral or torsion angle between the two planes during an edge on view showed vividly within the golden ratio. Both men knew the relevance of this aspect through their work and studies, and by knowing the essences of many facets of artistic expression and life force energies residing in focus at this golden section.

Within a few seconds more, a three dimensional dodecahedron floated in the air in front of the two men. They took no further time to study the object, other than to consider what they had just realised.

"How does Celia have any clue on the meaning of this?"

"I don't know. I have had nothing to indicate she is a genius. I know she is smart, but this is material you would not normally expect to come out of a child eleven years of age."

"Now…see this, I've just had a thought. The dodecahedron is made up of pentagons, and pentagons have diagonals in the golden ratio to its sides."

"I'm beginning to see a consistency here Tim. We looked at these angulations and ratios during the cybernetics development. One officer was sent on a study to Germany back in eighty-eight, and her report was ground breaking in the development of algorithms based on this for use in cybernetic autonomous processing."

"You know who it was?"

"Um, no why?

"Carmel Madeline is her name. She and I were lovers for a few years. We met at this house…this is her house!"

"You're kidding me. This is getting to be a bit unreal. All this co-incidence."

"Some of my friends would say it is much more than the mere pass over co-incidence has often been regarded as."

"Celia also said to study the torus in relation to the dodecahedron."

"I think we can already see the relationship. The torus is an atomic accelerator. And this golden ratio or section – it is where the essence of focus and creation resides. We established the dihedral angle during the construction of the dodecahedron, and this is a characteristic of DNA as well. It is all coming together if I consider what I know about the Torus of Eternity. The others told me it was being awakened or activated through the recollection of human values aligning with elemental intentions... over those intentions born out of negative ego traits of conditioning and the persona of self."

"I know of some of this Tim. We looked at this in preparation for torus based technologies ourselves, until it was lost."

"So you would have an idea on how this all links together then. I wonder why Celia is being told we should look into this to help fix the anomaly."

"Perhaps an understanding of these angulations is required to bring it into alignment and stabilise the vortex. Maybe she just has such an open mind this comes to her easily and not analysed like an adult mind."

"I have a feeling we will find out more in the coming times Derek. But the question is, how do we align these geometric properties to find some solution to the vortex? Without John here to help us, we are still at a point where application of this knowledge is restricted by our own capacity to work with flux mechanics. The phasing I do know of, but the application into the dimensional planes is his speciality."

"We can only continue with what we can do. Celia did say someone will come. Going by her intuitions of late, perhaps the one she refers to is your friend."

"Now you have me thinking..."

Chapter 8

John was wondering why Eric had not come to see him during the two days since their last meeting as had been scheduled. Such inefficiency would certainly be in contrast to the outcomes sought by both Eric and his superiors. After all, John's knowledge and research of flux mechanics was important to their forthcoming visions of successful integration of the next stage of nanotech mechanics. He knew Eric had a lot of work to do, with most of it being of sufficient complexity demanding significant attention, but he also knew most of it was awaiting a successful balancing of flux energies in order to enable these other developments to come into fruition.

He knew how to do this. He had always known. Despite the ever-present intrusion of the mechanics into his own mind, he was still keeping his thoughts away from disclosing the true algorithms required to repair the faults Eric was seeing in his daily statistical readouts. Now as he continued to research the spatial anomaly using the quantum computer Eric had provided, John had a new battle in his mind. Retention of the information obtained through discoveries he was making each day, was now a new frontier he encountered as the tiny machines attempted to shape him into revealing all he knew.

John was clever enough and Eric knew this. Each new discovery he made was primarily in his own mind and based on scenarios he entered as sequences into the quantum machine. Whilst the readouts projected an array of three-dimensional probabilities and even possibilities, John always remained one step ahead by ensuring the computer was only responsible for his results in part. Eric could easily come and seize the data he was working with, and if he did so, this would result in nothing more than what John told him at each meeting.

Yet Eric could not seize John's mind, for the nanotech mechanics were failing and as each day passed, John could sense their diminishing capacity and their diminishing efficiency. His knowledge of flux mechanics would be the only way the machines could become fully capable of their integration with the normal organic synapses of the brain, and whilst ever John held this information back, the robots would always come to a finite point unable to accommodate fluctuations in emotive based thinking.

He was certain the finite constraints of the nanotech mechanics would ensure their eventual failure, and all he needed to do was to find the point where he could begin to reprogram their software based intent to finally escape their clutches. John never tired of this battle, for to succumb to exhaustion would open the channels to the areas of his mind they had not penetrated, and so he took to each moment and each second of the experiences with vigilance and determination. Soon would come a day where he would see the path he sought clearly, and on such a day his escape would commence.

At first it was going to be a realignment of the nanotechnology mechanics and not a total escape removing his physical self from deep within the prison facility beneath New York City. After changing his mind, John would find the way to match his mind and also free his body from the cell he had been forced to endure these near three years..

Eric's holographic image suddenly displayed in front of John, taking him from his thoughts.

"John. I am unable to attend your cell today as I have a directive meeting with my superiors. I trust you have some further news for me."

"Hmm, trust. I do wonder about such things Eric. Anyway, I have nothing much to add regarding the multi-dimensional geometries. All I can say is I have fine-tuned the spectrum analysis algorithm and this has resulted in my determining these geometries are nothing to be concerned over. I am unable to pinpoint their precise origin, but...you can be assured they pose no threat to your work."

"Okay John, I understand this. But...I really need more solid information. I am certain these geometric projections are something to be seriously considered for us to enable stability here. We need precision, nothing else. I am being asked to push ahead with my other major project..."

"The directive meeting?"

"You will arrive at the place my superiors deem necessary for your sufficient understanding of the project as you assist in the stability of the vortex John, but you are not there yet."

John knew what the geometric projections were – they were being transmitted through the vortex as information from an unknown source showing how to bring the anomaly into stability. Their origin eluded him even with his focus being on the space craft, but his assumptions as to the significance unfolding, led him to regard this as one of the most exciting and thought provoking moments of human history.

At times his mind did wander within its nanotech enforced constraints as he now considered the signals could possibly be coming from another sentient race of beings. John was well versed enough in the basic statistical probabilities of this being possible, and so now to be at the frontier of this discovery, he found this research alluring to his ever inquisitive nature.

"Well Eric. I can only do what I can. Allow me more time to stay with this angle of research and I will bring you results." John was already planning a set of false results he was going to supply to Eric.

"Not too long John. My meeting is about to start so I must go. But...I want you to give me a summary report and then some backup data within the next few days. Otherwise, my superiors are going to proceed with this project despite..."

"Despite the instability. You know what it could do. The Agent has shown you this already…everywhere."

"He has John and as I said, we are still trying to overcome his mistakes. If you give us the information we require, then we might be able to plug all of those holes in an instant. Until our next meeting then."

John seriously considered giving Eric the information he required to fix the unstable vortexes opened up by the Agent. Whilst the numbers of people suffering from the viruses he had sent out over the years past were now quite low, there still remained enough uncertainty and suffering to trouble John's conscience. It was a double bind for him for to give this information would inevitably lead to Eric finding true stability.

In the moments after Eric had disengaged his holographic image, John sat there considering this. And then in the moments following, he began to carefully construct an algorithm to do what he could to fix some of the problems caused by the Agent, without providing the true dynamics of flux.

Up until this time, he had been constrained, but now with his latest discoveries concerning the multi-dimensional geometric projections, John suddenly came to realise where he could do something to help overcome the horrors of the Agent's viruses.

For the rest of the day, John concentrated on building an algorithm based on the geometries he had detected. By working with the results Eric was already aware of, John was sure there would be no suspicion of the information coming from any other source. When at last he was satisfied with the work, he ran a test scenario through the quantum computer. As the results showed in the holographic display, he could see how the stabilisation would come into effect, and also how the calculations could also be used to circumvent the affects of nano mechanics.

Eric would not see this in the results however, as it was only evident to John through his knowledge of flux and as such was not actually displayed in full before him. Hidden within the data, was an algorithm to commence a gradual break down of the efficiency of the mechanics as they manipulate the chemical reactions occurring within the axon located at the end of each neuron in the brain. At this place were the synapses or electrical impulses where a thought was thought, a memory recalled, or a decision was made.

Essential to the successful allocation of energies in manifest of a flux mechanics field, is the establishment of the threshold between matter and anti-matter in a hyper state. Within this elemental contingency resides the opening through which transgression of matter and intention flows infinitely in toroidal progressive magnitude allowing transfer onto tachyon pathways beyond light speed. At the diamond shaped intersection just above the middle of the toroidal field there resides the potential to align and determine other dimensional influences.

Yet, as this is perspective derived from the third dimensionality of human cognitive relativity, then a paradox occurs as the resulting emergence of matter into flux is not bound by the laws of ascension in an upward vertical sense. The alignment of elemental human intention with the elemental pathways constructed are the foundation possibility giving rise to projection of self into concept of accessing potential dimensions at this point. Without this projection then the separation of the equation and the self manifests an unstable holistic situation.

John knew precisely how to calculate the parameters for the acceptance of material into dimensional subspace based on the precise allocation of the focal dispensation for matter. He knew to allow constraints of relative light bearing photonic connection residing within the golden ratio relative to this third dimension. He often wondered if this was true and in fact, humans may be in the fourth dimension. John never saw time as the fourth – time to him was a frequency of data rate like a clock speed of a computer processor.

Calculation of parameters and seeing the constraints ensures anti-particle entanglement carries the properties of both dimensions whilst opening access to other dimensions. There the algorithm could carry an intended or programmed circumstance to manifest matter inside a phasing flux lens.

His genius was reverent in itself as he successfully enabled this capacity with a constructed mask taken from flux calculations to keep it hidden from view or detection within the quantum device Eric had given him. He knew if they were able to decipher this information and proceed to be fully flux enabled, their machines and their nano mechanics would know no bounds. Advances of this nature would only be used for negative purposes he was sure, and this would enable the authorities to go places and affect change beyond where they could presently conceptualise.

His next step was to run the solution through a virtual unstable vortex containing the same properties as those generated by the Agent's vortex amplifier. After first constructing the scenario, he ran the algorithm through it over and over again to test both its success rate, and to ensure the information mask did its job. Both worked splendidly as did his own deliberate misconceptions of the data in steering away the mechanics in his mind and keep them from being able to relay any record of the experiment back to central systems. He had become skilled at this self deception over time since his first ever capture as John knew the data retrieval of the mechanics in his mind, was capable only of accepting the information provided and not actually searching beyond despite their inclinations trying to force his thoughts.

Now after this test, he had something he could give to Eric for his superiors to look upon favourably. John decided to take the initiative and relay the information through prior to Eric visiting him. He thought this would cause sufficient distraction as they were able then to focus on using this information for a time, somewhat easing the pressure on him to provide more results.

Whilst they looked elsewhere, John could work on his ideas and calculations for establishing a stronghold over the nanotech mechanics, and ultimately aid in his escape. He compiled the report along with an instruction set for Eric to implement the sequential algorithms he had built, and sent it off.

He did not wait for any response from Eric. Instead, he focused on working further with the dynamic ratios within the calculations to see if any further improvements could be made. Secretly, he ran through a few tests on the quantum computer, and for once he actually felt glad.

Such feelings had mostly eluded him over the past two years as he had been subjected to endless days and months inside the cell. Now he felt a genuine sense of being glad and feeling happy Eric had unknowingly given him the means to overcome his incarceration, and eventually, overcoming the motives behind the developments Eric was constructing.

The one thing troubling his mind was the directive Eric had briefly mentioned. There was never an instance where John took Eric's words lightly as he knew the real people behind the developments were the superiors within the authorities and they held a stern uncompromising view on the way forward for human evolution. This directive could only be a large project of significant proportion, and with the hints Eric had given about their intent to use it in association with the spatial anomaly, John knew problems were coming.

John saw what potential issues could arise should the authorities try anything like what he suspected the directive was to be. Since the anomaly's creation, John had felt a sense of guilt for the loss of the trans-human military officer who had piloted the spacecraft inside. He was never given any information such a test flight would occur when he first was probed for the flux mechanics information, and so he also felt a degree of disassociation from the guilt whilst still bearing responsibility. It had been a journey into a new frontier never taken by a human before and John knew the risk could be oblivion. He felt sad for the unknown officer – regardless of not knowing his face, his life was at the mercy of John's work and John had never held such responsibility, nor had he ever wanted to or contemplated.

Chapter 9

Celia was dreaming. She was sound asleep on the eve of when the authorities were to return and then remain as a permanent presence. In her mind's vision, she was running through a field of wild flowers – it was mid spring and blossoms carpeted the valley. As she ran endlessly without any specific destination, bees rose in swarms as her legs brushed them aside. Birds flew in flocks overhead where now and then, a few would dive down to retrieve worms as they wriggled out of the fertile soils amongst the flower stems.

A gentle stream meandered through the valley centre, and Celia ran in a zigzag pattern for a while, jumping across it at intervals. When it grew too wide to take in a single striding jump, she carefully jumped from stone to stone.

Its' clear waters bubbled and gurgled as they pushed around the stones, and fell over the tiny falls of low rock walls trying to halt the flow now and then. For a moment she paused, leaning over to scoop some water with her hand to take a drink. How lovely it was – so clear and sweet as it caressed her throat. Then she was off again, buoyed on by the taste of both the sweet water and air around her.

Nothing here was tainted. It was as pure as her intentions. She did not even spare the time to think about where she was, or what she was doing, as everything just occurred and just happened as it should do for an unhindered free spirit.

As the sun peeked from behind the little fluffy clouds making their way from west to east, its' rays warmed her skin, sending her off in a different direction as she chased the edge of the shadow from the cloud overhead. Celia giggled, laughed, and then fleetingly took on a slightly serious look as she momentarily pondered the entire scene, but it was not a serious discerning view – it was a look cast to nowhere, looking at everywhere to feel the connection of all surrounding her and inside of her. When a bee stopped and landed on her shoulder, she did not panic at the prospect of its sting. Instead, she admired its beauty and its presence, before running off again without direction, sending the bee into the sky.

There was no hole in this sky, no spatial anomaly for her to think about, and the voices were not present. She could feel freedom amongst the tall grasses and sea of flowers as if nothing else ever mattered, and nothing else was ever going to matter. She was there and now and in this sense she was a true child. A child who was unaltered by the misgivings of what so many had created before her time. A child who was purely at one with the observations and insights around her, and a child who was leading others she could not even see, back into their memories and forward into themselves.

As the Earth was an entity of biology and systematic organic infinite ecological progression, so too Celia was indeed feeling similar as she bounded unbound through the fields. Where patterns and designs are inherent in nature, so too is the random expression of these geometries, and Celia was this expression like many others – the others she was rekindling memory for to invigorate true apparitions of their intentions.

Celia was running without exhaustion, on both her own energy, and on the energy of the Earth as part of the universe. She required no sustenance for this other than to feel as she did, and to be as she was in essence and intention, as pure. Like the clear waters beneath her as she jumped, then inside her as she drank, her spirit was the resonant connection.

When she jumped the stream again to look westward where the gentle winds were coming from, Asper appeared as if she had been there all along, so comforting the look on her face was to Celia. Although she was not her mother, she was her mother in apparition as was the Earth in essence, and so Asper's appearance was in confirmation of the motherly figure. Celia immediately grabbed both of her hands and they danced around in circles, sending spirals of pollen skyward, and bees to match. After a few seconds, the gentle winds caught the pollen and cast it upon the waves flowing away to the east across the valley, so they turned and gave chase. So too did the bees, and for a time they continued on as a precession of life force being energy meandering back and forth like the stream.

The sun shone on, the water flowed flawlessly, and the fields of flowers gave to the bees where they gathered pollen to take back to their hexagonal homes for making honey, and it was all a system yet not, for it was ubiquitous in design and was neither lineal or finite – it was toroidal and infinite with progression like their running hand in hand to nowhere, yet everywhere.

Asper had not spoken and neither had Celia for words were not required in this expression. Words could not suffice in these instances as they were beyond the restrictions of language. They only laughed, and through their laughter they spoke so much more than they could have ever conveyed through normal language.

On and on they ran and on and on they laughed, then upwards…spiralling and taking to the heavens, which were also present upon the Earth. Skyward they ascended to see the valley far below yet they were still amongst the blossoming flowers and the bees moving in the air. Then in a gasping breath of exultation, they both realised they were all apparently below and within. This sent forth signals out across the vastness of inner space deep within their DNA and yet further still to no place but to all places as if they could reconcile all…of which they were, to become, and had ever been.

Images flashed hurriedly before them, yet their visions remained steady with each image confirming a presence despite its fleeting course. Geometries, simple life connections, and the flowers so full of colour, were all there to render an artistic golden moment lasting forever, and would do so never to be clouded and never to be forgotten, for once rekindled such a flame is eternal.

This made them both laugh and giggle with excitement and a warmth in their hearts not dependent upon the sun caressing the valley below from above them – it came from within, and it came from nowhere specific. It just was and just is and from this they felt freedom.

When at last Celia did awaken from her dream, there were two officers of the authorities at the front door to the house. As she approached the open door where she could see them talking to her father, Celia simply stared for a time without any sense of foreboding, and without any sense of fear. One of the officers noticed her look and returned her gaze for a moment. In this instant, Celia knew he had begun to awaken. A moment later when his eyes looked away, he left the scene for his fellow officer to finish giving the advice to Celia's father. He walked back to his transport where he sat in silence for a few moments thinking yet not…until his fellow officer returned and they departed.

"Father?"

"Yes Celia?"

"What were those men speaking about?"

"Oh just some information about the electricity soon to be available in this town. Why?"

"Just curious father. One of them did seem to be stronger than the other."

"What do you mean by stronger Celia? Are you speaking about the man who stayed whilst the other one walked away? He was behaving very much like an official."

"No father. I mean the one who did walk away. He was the stronger one."

"How so Celia?"

"Because he had the strength to walk away. He was listening father."

"Listening?"

"Yes. To his inner self. I could tell. He had the strength to act on his inner voices."

"What voices are they Celia?"

"The ones inside telling him about who he really is."

"What were they saying to him and how do you know this Celia?"

"They were telling him to listen to them and I know because they are inside me…and all of us. It takes strength to listen to them father."

"You are full of surprises lately Celia."

"We all are father. It is just so many do not remember. I am just a child, but so too are you and all the others here…and there."

Celia had been keeping the torus Tim had given her in her pocket day and night. In the other pocket, she kept the dodecahedron she had found at Carmel's house. She thought this was the best way to mind them as one complimented the other and by keeping them at either side in a balance of their energies. It was not as if she consciously went about thinking of this in even the slightest of scientific terms – it was more to her. It was a feeling, and a knowing. Despite her youthful age, she was a soul beyond the mere lineal measure of time, which to her was a count of how many times she had travelled spaceship Earth on its course around the sun shining brightly on this winter morning.

The snow around the house was brilliant white with a purity matching her own, and the sight of it invigorated her. It gave her energetic buoyancy aside from the usual characteristics of childhood, and despite the recent trauma with the loss of her mother, Derek could sense her release and her unabated fervour emanating to all those around her. Whenever he felt this from his daughter, Derek went along with what she gave to him, and so his own feelings of despair and loss were quickly receding to be replaced with the grace of what his recently passed wife had given to him through Celia.

"Father, there is one more thing I want to say before I go and have breakfast."

"What is it Celia?"

"You have chosen well to bring us to this house father."

"Why is it so?"

"Because it has the elemental flow of energy, and it is why we are making these connections father. Since we left our other place, we have travelled and sought a place to become happy, and this is the place father."

"I see."

"Yes you do father, though you may not realise this. Asper knows what I am speaking of. We have similar intuitions. Can we go and see her again soon please father? There are a lot of things I want to talk to her about."

"I am sure it can be arranged Celia."

"Good. And you and Tim can discuss the entropy for alignment of the spatial anomaly. You know what it means don't you?"

"Um, yes I do. I am surprised you have a grasp on such things Celia."

"Don't be surprised father. Well…maybe you can, but just for a little bit. You and Tim will need to do a lot of work father. There will be others to help you, and they will come from different places to this town. But they are not here yet and you will need to work with Tim to prepare for their arrival. I can't wait to meet them."

"Who are they Celia?"

"Friends father."

"Okay. Maybe you should go and have some breakfast now Celia. We are going to be sent some electricity today, so things will get better here for us and we will…"

"It is not happening the way you think father. The electricity will help, but it will also bring others who are not as kind as our friends. It is why you need to work much more with Tim so we can be prepared."

After breakfast, Celia returned to the front of the house where her father was out clearing some of the snow on the front pathway leading to the gate. She decided she would spend the entire morning helping him, and so she offered whatever she could to clear the snow and make the front of the house tidy. Derek watched as she went about diligently tidying up and piling snow well away from the pathway. With each load, Celia added to the form she was shaping with the snow, and by the end of the morning she had created a near perfect dodecahedron.

"It is lovely Celia."

"Thanks father. I wanted to make this for you as a reminder how important it is for you to keep studying this shape and its relationship to the torus. There is a lot to be learned father."

"Yes I know. Tim and I spent a lot of time on his computer…"

"Quiet father. Don't say it too loud. The authorities might hear you. They are in the town already and they will be listening."

"You are right Celia. I will be more careful." Derek was thankful for the reminder from his daughter. He decided to immediately speak of this to the others as it would become an increasingly covert operation especially now with Tim. If the authorities detected their possession of the missing quantum device and knew of the type of work they were doing, they would not hesitate to incarcerate them all without remorse and without any hint of empathy to their survival.

"You know what?"

"What Celia?"

"There is a part inside all of us very important to remember."

"And what is it Celia?"

"It is a very small thing…inside our brains, but it connects us much more to our heart than we realise."

"Our pineal gland?"

"Yes. I was talking about it to them…well, they told me."

"The voices?"

"Who else father? Of course it was them. They don't have conversations or really speak though. It is like they put the ideas into my mind father."

"Well I studied the pineal gland when I worked in cybernetics."

"Then you will know about what it can do then. It helps us wake up father to see life more spontaneously."

"So you think I should study this as well?"

"You already have. If we don't use it, then it can fade away or become dormant. We should use if more often. Mine is working now. It works every day. Adults sometimes lose this sense father. They become concerned and worried about things in the world and they forget why they have this little thing."

"Okay Celia, I will promise to remember mine then."

"It makes me much happier to know you might be a little like me. After all, wisdom is not about what you have necessarily learned because some of it can trouble you. Wisdom is being open to remembering and to knowing you have a lot to learn. It is why I said the man who left this morning when he was listening to himself, is strong. People who do not listen but simply obey and do not think for themselves, are the weak ones father. It is easy for a person to be like others and accept what they are given or what they depend on to think they are happy. But, if a person goes away from this and listens, then they show strength and they will remember the little thing inside their brain connecting them to everything. It will give them the visions to see ahead and to see themselves, instead of just looking down the narrow tunnel they spend a lot of time doing in life."

"Really Celia?"

"You know father, otherwise we would not be here talking about it together."

"I suppose so. Well, now we have finished here, I guess it is time I did some of the work with Tim."

Celia then whispered to her father, "You do not need the torus yet, so I will keep it in my pocket. It is a lovely pink colour, but I won't show you out here. They might be watching."

"Okay. I'll talk about it to Tim. Maybe he knows why it is pink."

"He might. Can you ask Asper to come over soon when you are there please father?"

"Sure. I'll see if she can come over today. I'm sure she would love to see you again Celia."

"I know dad. It is why I asked…well, in part. She is very nice, and so too is Lorraine and Esther does like spending time with them. Also, I think mother would have liked them a lot too."

"I am sure she would have dear."

Derek left Celia to play with the snow and make his way through town to Carmel's house on the west side. As he passed through the centre, he saw there were four officials there who appeared to be setting up a base of some type in the building where Tim had stolen the quantum computer. When the officers saw him, they motioned for him to change direction and come over to them.

"Where are you going?" the same official who had remained at the front door earlier, demanded from him.

"Just over to another house where I know some people."

Lucky for them all, the two officers who had visited four days earlier were now gone from the area, and so Derek did not have to explain anything about them now residing in two different locations.

"Who else do you know of in this town?"

"Just the others I am going to see."

"How many people live there?"

"Three adults in a house a mile out on the west side."

"What are they doing?"

"Same as us. Just surviving."

"Why didn't you tell me this at the start?"

"You didn't ask. I thought you would have surveyed the entire town anyway and discovered them yourself as part of your efficient…"

"Don't get wise with me."

"I'm not officer. I just thought…"

"Well don't think. Soon enough we will have measures in place to ensure such a thing. What are you going there for?"

"Just to see how they are getting on after the snow and if they need any help repairing their house. Most places here are in a state of disrepair and I just thought I could lend a hand."

"Make sure it is all you are going to do. We'll be watching."

Derek could see a shimmering off to the side of the building the officers were setting up their base inside, and for a moment was baffled by the sight. The lead officer noticed him staring for a few brief moments and told Derek to keep moving. As he walked away, Derek went through what he had seen in his mind, at first still puzzled, but by the time he had rounded the corner and was out of sight of the four officers, he knew he had been looking at a well concealed flying craft rendered almost invisible. He knew of some developmental substances the authorities had been working on for refracting light, but this was the first instance he had witnessed the technology in actual use.

"They are here in town, and they have one of their new type of flying craft," Derek said when he arrived at Carmel's' house.

"Yeah, I was out before dawn scouting around. I saw it land. Well…sort of saw it land. It sure looked weird seeing thruster wash coming from almost nothing aside from the faint shimmering I could see."

"So they have not perfected it yet then. From what I could tell, they have a few adjustments to make in order to render complete invisibility."

"The refraction of the upper wavelengths still requires a bit of work."

"Most likely. Once they establish flux angulations in those, only the thrusters wash will remain."

"They have the sound wave frequencies bouncing off using white noise cancellation to make it silent…hey, it reminds me of something I noticed last night about the anomaly. Don't worry, I have set up a masking field to prevent them detecting the computer. But, there are two harmonic frequencies coming from it, and it took the detection of the lower frequency first, to then be able to hear the higher frequency."

"Interesting. Show me your readouts."

"Okay, let's go inside."

"Hi Derek," Asper said as the two men entered the house.

"Hello Asper. Celia was asking about you this morning. She really wants to see you again."

"I had a feeling she might. I had a strange dream last night with her in it. Maybe Lorraine and I could go over shortly."

"Good idea. Esther will be glad to see you as well. But, don't go through the town centre. The authorities are up to something there."

Celia and Esther answered the door together to greet Asper and Lorraine. Murray was out the back of the house repairing some of the guttering loosened due to the weight of the snow over the past few days. He gave them both a wave to say hello when they arrived in the kitchen to sit and talk with Ester and Celia.

"I'm so glad you came Asper...and you Lorraine. Esther and I love having you here. It can get a little lonely at times without any visitors."

"We are glad to be here, aren't we Lorraine?"

"Sure we are. How have you been?"

"Oh good thanks. Esther is well too aren't you Esther?"

"Yes I am thanks Celia. I have a little tea, would you like some?"

"So long as you don't dwindle your supply giving it to us."

"No problem Lorraine. What else is it good for other than to share with friends?"

"So...Celia, how have you been lately?"

"Very well thanks Asper. I had a wonderful dream last night. You were in it with me."

"Really! What was it about?"

"About us and about how we hear things. We were running through a field of flowers and then we went up into the sky and could look down on the valley below. It felt wonderful and it was like we knew what to do about things. We could see what made life so simple and so beautiful and we both felt like we would never ever have anything to worry about."

"It sounds wonderful Celia. How amazing it sounds. I had a dream too, and it was very similar to yours..."

"I knew it. I was talking to father about the voices talking to me and I felt then you would know the same things. Now I know I am right. What was your dream about? Were you running through the flowers too?"

"Yes I was Celia. We both were. And there were feelings about the warmth in our hearts and to remember about who we really are."

"It is what I was saying to father. I told him about the little thing inside our brains connecting us to our hearts. This is important for us to remember ourselves and it takes strength to do this."

"The pineal gland?"

"Yes. And did you see the bees and the swirling pollen we made when we were running through the flowers?"

"I did Celia. They showed me the biorhythms in nature and they work in harmony to create life."

"Because they pollinate the flowers to make the seeds and they also build houses in pretty shapes."

"Hexagons."

"Yes, hexagons to store their honey. Did you see the spiral patterns we made as we ran and the pollen taking to the air around us?"

"Yes I did. Then we lifted up into the sky and were laughing."

"See how excited you get with these simple things. It is what so many adults forget when they use too much of their brains. They become all worried and think only and forget the link with their heart and with their spirit. After all Asper, it takes spirit to laugh doesn't it?"

"Indeed it does Celia."

"It is why we have spirit, to connect us with ourselves and all what makes us alive, and then we laugh because this excites us."

"People forget how to laugh."

"Yes, the authorities do not like people really being happy at all. They want them to use technology to be happy, but they are mostly only fooling themselves aren't they?"

"Yes they are. Many things in the world are supposed to make them happy but they only do it for a little while before they want something new again. Real happiness comes from within."

"You two are certainly on a tangent there." Esther commented.

"I was thinking the same Esther. They have a connection," Lorraine added.

"It is okay though Lorraine…and Esther. It excites us."

"Sure it is okay honey. Lorraine and I like it don't we Lorraine?"

"Yes we do. Don't stop talking because of us."

"Oh we have so much to say and there will be more when we hear it too, won't there Asper?"

"Um…yeah, I guess so Celia."

"But now we have to concentrate on what we have just been dreaming about. We need to call the others to join us here. If we concentrate, they will hear us and then they will come."

"The people behind the voices?" Esther asked looking puzzled.

"No Esther. They are not really voices – more like ideas. The people who will come will help with the anomaly and they also know what the torus really means to us and to everyone. They are funny too. One of them speaks a little strange but we will get used to it. But I mostly want to meet the lady."

"How do you know this Celia?"

"It is easy Esther. There are others who can hear the voices and they will come to this town as well because we attract them. Maybe they will go to your house Asper, where I found this."

Celia took out the small dodecahedron and showed it to the women.

"Where did you find it Celia?"

"At your house. Carmel's house. It was buried in the garden but a little piece of it was sticking out, so I dug it out and kept it. I hope you don't mind."

"Not at all. Take a look Lorraine."

"I wonder why it was there and where it came from."

"One of those little mysteries of the times I would say. A bit like this dream we shared."

"There is a reason, but we just don't know it yet. It works with the torus somehow. Don't ask me how or why – father and Tim are looking at finding the reason."

"It's beautiful. I wonder what type of material it is."

"Search me Lorraine. Murray might have a clue. I'll call him in." Esther went to the window and asked Murray in for a coffee.

"What do you have there Celia?"

"A dodecahedron I found. Esther said you might know what type of material it is made from. Do you?"

"It looks a bit like a crystal and gold mixture."

"See it is a beautiful thing then. Gold is always beautiful."

"Take care of it won't you. It is very valuable."

"I know Murray, but not how you might think. You could never get money for such a thing. It has valuable powers though. Tim and father are researching those powers. I do like how it is gold, like the honey and the bees and the pollen Asper and I saw in our dreams."

At Carmel's house, Tim and Derek were looking at the golden ratio angles within a dodecahedron and how they might relate to the torus. It was a puzzle to them both as the answers were not easily forthcoming, aside from beginning to establish a type of relationship with the dihedral angle in the golden ratio and the atomic acceleration properties of the torus.

Derek remembered investigations for the possibility of multi-dimensional facets to human DNA where meridians based on ancient studies included additional strands of DNA beyond the accepted double strand model. When he applied a few theoretical sequences to the shapes floating in three-dimensional holographic projection in front of the two men, a series of results erupted from within. In an instant, they could both see the application of the twelve-sided shape as a reflection of the relational twelve helix DNA based on the twelve meridian count.

His next thought was where on Earth, or beyond, was Celia receiving the information leading them to pursue this path of investigation. It was best kept to himself as a thought to save distracting Tim now. In deciding this he then experienced a sudden insight about the torus shape and despite the simplicity of his words, they did not belie his thoughts.

"Well at least we can be sure of the relationship now when you consider how the torus relates to the human energy field."

"The human is part of the entire system reflecting the geometries of the torus. It is a fundamental to building what we determine as physical reality. Ha…I remember Chan Lee having mentioned spirit sets the path for light to follow. Perhaps he meant the intention of consciousness sets the intention and material matter is then a derivative of consciousness.

Derek then realised how this intuition was now gaining momentum as Tim's response built upon the thoughts he was having. It invigorated him further as he set about contributing to Tim's work wherever he could.

Chapter 10

Eric was pleased with the results for repairing the unstable vortexes as he scanned data on his holographic array. For a moment, a slight sense of elation resonated within him, before his nano mechanics again directed his mind to further analysis. He could see how the information from John worked on stabilising the vortices where in some instances they began to wink out of existence. This test bed scenario for later application to the actual physical instances was enough for Eric to see success when he deployed the data. He then allowed himself to consider he might be breaking through deeper into John Matheson's mind.

Eric's work on the monolithic directive was now almost complete, and with this additional information, he would commence testing data for inserting the manufactured star into the spatial anomaly. One final result was pending prior to him being able to report this breakthrough to his superiors – the stability and finite nature of the results themselves.

As he ran a periodic test sequencing the passage of precisely one year of time, the array projected the results as expected. Eric managed a faint smile as he realised the significant turning point for his developmental research. In another moment of rarity, he felt a remote sense of being glad as John had finally provided tangible information for him to recommend proceeding with the objectives for the monolithic directive. This potential breakthrough also held the prospect of assured status for Eric – something both his mind...his ego, and the mechanics within his mind, took shape as data for officials secretly monitoring Eric.

The next stage for the manufacture of atomic material for use by nano robotics to manipulate atoms into whatever substances Eric programmed them to create was close. This was the main purpose of the directive – the creation of seemingly endless raw atomic material drawn inter-dimensionally for the authorities to manifest in technology presently awaiting realisation.

In contrast to the motives behind Eric's sense of feeling glad, John was experiencing a similar feeling in association with the progress he had made toward deactivating his internal nano mechanics. A few more calculations was all he needed before he could render them inoperative in a much shorter time than he had initially projected. In parallel, he was hacking into the central systems to find an escape path both through data, and through the physical labyrinth of the deep underground facility. In a moment of personal triumph celebrated silently, he stumbled across an algorithm he could use for communicating to the external world beyond the confines of the facility outside the usual channels used by the authorities.

From deep within his memory, he recalled the signature his friend The Fixture had used to bypass the systems authentications for the identification microchip the authorities had deployed six years prior. In another win over the internal robotic ingress into his psyche, he was able to bypass the effect of the mechanics and realise the data he required for his latest test whilst the robotics were busy working endlessly probing his thoughts as they did.

Within half an hour, John had refined the data sufficiently to transmit communications across the entire globe without the authorities knowing he was doing so. The only issue facing him as he engaged the system for the first time was if his friend still had a device of any type capable of receiving his transmission. John felt confident The Fixture would have retained something of use, as the authorities and the Agent limited the availability of new technology stringently in the recent past.

Across the gulf of distance from the east coast to the west, Tim's old communications device suddenly illuminated to indicate an in-coming transmission. So seldom had this occurred in recent times, at first he ignored it, thinking it was likely to just be an internal error as there was nobody who was capable of sending a communications request – except for John. When this dawned on him, Tim immediately stopped what he was doing and powered up the receiver to filter the transmission sufficiently for audible recognition. After a few adjustments of the settings, he could discern a regular pattern of pulses. The pattern was old, but he knew its origin. He and John had established this method of communication some time before, and now as Tim recognised it for the first time in years, his heart seemed to skip a beat.

Instantly he went about returning the transmission with the acknowledgement he knew only John would recognise. Derek watched on with interest not knowing precisely what was going on, but intrigued at why Tim seemed to be so excited suddenly.

Tim noticed Derek's interest out of the corner of his eye when he had established the response transmission and had a moment to look away from the device as the message used the same carrier pathway John had established in reverse, carrying it back across to the east coast.

"It's John. It can only be him. I'm sending a response to acknowledge his signal."

"How long since you had contact?"

"Not for about three years. This device is set on a frequency the authorities used back during the times of the identification microchip, so they will not be looking for transmissions in this range. I guess he has been able to access something to configure and send this message."

"So he's using an old frequency then. Quite a good idea. During my last times in cybernetics, the authorities were so sure they had closed off all channels for the old settings, they simply gave up on them."

"Sounds a bit like in times long past when some nations gave up on Morse code and stopped looking for it. Then there were the dissident groups in the thirties using it and bypassing all the authority filters then…around sixty years ago."

"Yeah, I saw it as a bit of a laugh in my opinion. Well before my time, but I recall reading about how it made a lot of leaders look stupid back then."

"It seems as though they did not learn from those mistakes."

"Yeah, it appears so, as goes for many of the population. What is he saying?"

"It is just a call out for acknowledgement. Once he confirms my response, he will send some more code through. I can work it out fairly easily. It will be co-ordinates and other similar stuff."

"What about conversing?"

"Yeah, after we check the coding only us two know…unless the authorities have probed his mind for it."

"I cannot see a reason why they would. They have him as a prisoner, so you would expect they are focusing on the flux developments using cybernetic algorithms in their devices to detect only flux information he might think about. Gee, he must be of strong mind being able to circumvent the nano tech."

"He is reliable Derek. Anyway, we will soon see. I expect he will send some more code through shortly."

A minute later, Tim received co-ordinates information from John to show he was being held deep beneath New York City.

"I know of the place. It was being built when I was in cybernetics. I suspect it is all up and running now."

The last piece of the message was a code to indicate John was working on studying the logistical functioning inside the building, and then it ended.

"It means he is looking for a means to escape. You know a little of the place. What do you think his chances are?"

"Going on what you have told me about him, I guess he has a reasonable chance of success. The place he is in has a number of viable escape routes if he has the ability to make it past the security screens."

"Screens?"

"Yeah, they are DNA scanners basically. When he was taken there, they would have scanned his DNA signature."

"Then how will he get past?"

"He will need to mask his signature with someone else's…a guard or an officer. The screens are always on and so long as you have authority, you can always pass through. No authority and the screen will stun you. At least it is how I understand it from the pieces of information I know."

"I can imagine John will devise a way to scan someone else's DNA then. He has been able to escape from some pretty tough places before."

An hour later, the entire group was discussing the communication from John in code after agreeing to act on Celia's advice in keeping it secret. Lorraine was especially happy at the news, and felt a taste of contentment she had not experienced since she was last by his side.

"John. What are you up to?"

"I'm just running through some scenarios to further test the data I sent to you Eric."

"I have achieved significant progress through the data you provided earlier. In fact, I have actually taken some of the unstable vortexes out of existence."

"How did you obtain access to…?"

"We used some afflicted people subjects for the tests John. And because of you they have been healed to almost normal health."

"What lingering effects are there Eric?"

"Oh just a few physical problems where subjects have issues with missing tissue. We are trying some injected nano technology to manage these conditions."

"And you expect them to then be okay?"

"Yes, without a doubt. Our new technology will effectively mend these problems and whilst they may have some degree of disability, the subjects will be able to live healthy lives."

"Well then, a positive result for you Eric."

"And for you John. I will be able to use the data you sent me in application for other uses. I am proceeding with the directive based on your provisions."

"What else do you want me to do Eric? I have the data on the anomaly, but it is at a sticking point with nothing new really showing up."

"Your computer will be linked to the main systems John. I want you to run through these tests I have been devising in real time with me. The directive is going to require your application of knowledge…"

"Then will you tell me what it is?"

"Not so John, as it is highly classified. But…I will permit you to have input into the readings I gather, hence your connection."

"How can I work on something I know nothing about?"

"Oh but you do. All you need to know is already apparent through your work with flux mechanics. I need you to provide me instantaneous feedback as I run the tests. Simply put, there is nobody else who can come close to carrying out the work I require. I will say this – the directive is for the manufacture of new atomic alchemy technology John. It is a resource base from which nano mechanics will thrive and construct our new phase of operations."

"What precisely will I be required to do?"

"Just run the tests as I said, and help me with some algorithms whenever the need arises. Otherwise, this reporting back and forth scenario will take too long and cause too much delay."

"Today then?"

"Yes John." Eric disengaged the holographic cell bars and entered John's cell to make the necessary adjustments enabling his quantum computer to have access to the wider network.

"Stay vigilant John," he said as he left the cell and re-engaged the bars. "This requires the utmost of attention from both of us. And consider this. If you are successful, you may be granted access outside of this cell in the near future, but only with the strictest of conditions."

"And they are?"

"Compliance John. Compliance. You will only be permitted to work on this with full compliance to my conditions. Otherwise, it will be back to this cell for good...until I perhaps find some other use for you."

"You don't sound very forthcoming there Eric."

"I do not need to be. When the time comes, you will see our way is the only way forward. The machines we are about to unleash will make anything you have experienced in the past, pale in comparison."

John knew he must work much harder to escape the clutches of the authorities and take what he knew with him. Within minutes of Eric's departure, he recommenced his work to nullify the affect of his own internal nano mechanics. He was at the brink of a major personal break through, and so he stayed awake the entire night to focus on achieving the release from the mechanics he sought.

When morning arrived, only evident to him by the time indicator on his holographic array, John had successfully rendered the mechanics inoperative by re-programming them to operate only in a status sufficient to communicate nominal function to Eric's monitoring systems. With this link they would appear to be operating as normal but would actually be without the intrusions into his mind.

Now with his computer connected to the main systems, he went to work on building a DNA profile for himself - stolen from the data banks containing information about the hundreds of officers inside the facility. Eric was confident of having covered all viable access paths to prevent John obtaining this data, but his confidence was ill placed, as John was by far the more intelligent of the two, and so he had been able to bypass the filters and hack into the central systems for the information. When at last his body told him to sleep, John had built the required profile. Building a field resonance device to store the profile and then disengage the holographic cell bars to escape, were now his remaining tasks to gain freedom.

When Eric asked for the required sequence to commence testing the following day, John did as he was told, but simultaneously he reformatted the hardware components of the quantum computer. It was a perfect cover for his motives as Eric concentrated on the output data and missed the unrecorded but visible reformatting being carried out during the directive testing. After numerous tests, all of which were successful for Eric's needs, John was advised the session was over for the day, and he should return to working on determining stability for flux mechanics – a seemingly endless and futile task to him as he had always known what was required to align flux for stable use.

By the end of the day when his body prompted him to rest, John had carefully constructed a quantum computer with a profile storage device and also configured an emitter to place a field around his body for transmitting the DNA profile taken from a prison officer's record.

John stood at the cell bars on the third day. Eric had mistakenly linked John's computer overlooking John's ability to hack systems. The time was precisely three in the morning – a time when he knew many officers would be lulled into a lax state given the hour. Whilst the authorities espoused to efficiency and many of their officers were fitted with nanotechnology mechanics, they had not yet been able to overcome the simple condition of the human body being susceptible to periods of inattentiveness.

Incorporated into the profile device, John had included an input peripheral via a small holographic projection sequence pad. He entered the required code to disengage the cell bars using information he had hacked during the previous days' testing. In such contrast to his long incarceration within the confines of one room, he simply walked out of the facility taking the service stairways connecting each floor all of the way to ground level. When he arrived at the perimeter, he coaxed his way past the guards on duty by telling them he was carrying out systematic maintenance checks. All at the facility were clothed in the latest Geiga wear – a mandatory requirement for the monitoring systems in place. John was fortunate he was no exception and so he was clothed identically to all officers and all other inmates at the facility. In their vision of efficiency and decision to use the latest suits for all, the authorities had made this mistake. As confident as they were relying on their DNA identity profile scanners, they had overlooked John's ability to bypass their systems. Whilst all of the other inmates, of whom there were almost two hundred, were unable to do as he had done, John was an exception. Only one other inmate could come close to repeating John's capacity to affect the authorities, and he soon would also make his presence felt as his maniacal disturbances provoked his actions.

His first idea was to simply run, and he did. John ran until he could run no longer, and when he was too exhausted to continue, he hid amongst the darkest streets he could find in the old section of New York City.

Simultaneously Eric was forced to run the entire length of the corridor from his residence to his work station as alarms rang throughout the deep underground matrix of the facility. Eric knew what had happened and he knew it was his responsibility. He despatched teams of officers to search for John as he ran, to arrive then at his workstation as his superior officers were demanding explanations – their demanding presence being full three-dimensional life size holograms.

Immediately Eric went into reporting mode as his mechanics took over influencing his every move.

"I have despatched recovery teams to apprehend Matheson sir. His capacity for brilliance is again reminding us of a need to be…"

"I certainly don't want to hear about needs Gunter. This oversight is now a precarious position for us. You realise there is more at stake here than you can imagine."

Eric could imagine the extent his own work could go but there were two factors out of his control. His superiors were always prone to sudden changes with the drive to deliver results for new projects almost immediately. They were unkind to delay and so as Eric counteracted their propensities, he was also aware of the frontier the authorities were approaching and with such uncertainty there came developments as yet unseen and unforseen.

Chapter 11

"This torus is just a copy of the real thing, but copies can also be good for a purpose."

"And for what purpose Celia?"

"For acceleration Tim. The torus is an atomic accelerator."

"I had a feeling..."

"A feeling. I think you know it is the way, rather than just being a feeling."

"Feelings can lead to truths Celia."

"Yes they can, but for science you need your mind too."

"I might need to use the torus again in the computer when I do some more studies of the anomaly."

"Okay Tim. You can have it whenever you need to. I just want to mind the torus when you don't need to use it. After all, it does feel good...and kind of warm."

"Did the voices ask you to mind it Celia?"

"They did say something, but it was more my own idea Tim. They like it when I am minding it though. They tell me it is right for this to be happening."

"Have they told you anything new since we last spoke about them?"

"Oh yes, they speak to me every day Tim. Not with talking words though as I said. They told me something is going to happen soon and our DNA will be changed. Tim, what is DNA?"

"It is something inside making us who we are."

"Well, they say it will shift and change so it can become more aligned."

"Hmm, interesting." He also thought of what he knew about the implants affecting DNA. "Anything more about the anomaly?"

"Yes. I just told you silly. The DNA is part of it."

"Really. I think I will have to spend some time finding out what it means."

"Do so Tim. It is best when you do find something, to then come and get the torus. They told me when you are aware of what it is you need to find out, the torus would help. They don't say your name. It is like they are saying this for all people but I see why we are here and so I think of you Tim."

"But there are some things your father and I are not quite sure about Celia. We have done a lot of work to find out what we do know, but something is missing and the best person for help is a long way away from here..."

"But he did contact you didn't he?"

"Um, yes. How did you know?"

"They said he would. They know he is important to help as well. He will come Tim, you can be sure. It is his way to be here and be a part of something he has always been a part of."

"Oh well, I guess you are right. I wonder how long it will take."

"Not as long as you think. Don't see it as time. See it as how aware you become."

"Well, those voices do seem to be wise Celia."

"Maybe. I don't get those thoughts about them…just a feeling. Maybe feeling is wise. Maybe a lot of people could feel things more than they do."

"Indeed, for many are lost to their external experiences."

"Look inside to see very far they say. Open your mind and the answers will come."

"Oh okay. Have you spoken to Asper today?"

"Of course I have. She is just in the kitchen with Esther. We are all going to have a nice lunch together and Asper is helping to prepare lunch with Lorraine. I'll come and get you when it is ready."

"Okay, see you then."

Derek and Murray were making repairs at the rear of the house when Tim arrived to offer help. He had turned up after Asper and Lorraine had left him at Carmel's house to finish off some calculations he was making before coming over.

"It looks like you have a bit of snow and ice damage."

"Yeah Tim. How are you? The gutter has come away from the roof edging here. Murray and I nearly have it all done though."

"I'm well thanks, and you Murray?"

"Good thanks Tim. Any progress with those shapes as yet?"

"Yes, a fair bit in fact. But you know how it is lately. You get somewhere then Celia throws a spanner in the works to make you think of things from a different angle."

"I know what you mean. Her innocence gets you thinking. Any more contact from John?"

"None yet Derek. I suspect he is up to making good his escape. He'll probably try again as soon as he can. Celia said the voices told her he would come to us. It seems a bit unreal. But…maybe it is like what Chan said in respect to the co-incidence thing. Anyway, it will be tough for John."

"It is a long journey all the way from New York to here, particularly in these times."

"I'll say. If I know John though, he'll find a way."

After lunch, the entire group discussed the coming of the authorities to the town bringing implications for them in the near and distant future. Tim mentioned the contact he had received from John and how if he made his way all the way west from the east, they could both benefit from his presence, yet also come to the attention of the authorities. Lorraine was still feeling particularly pleased with the news of John, and Asper felt good too, though a little despondent at having been reminded of Tobias.

Celia noticed the look on Asper's face as they talked, so she silently took hold of her hand in an effort of reassurance. Asper and her shared a connection, and so Celia's effort did have some effect on Asper's state of mind and heart.

"He will help you Tim," Lorraine said. "I know it might be dangerous because the authorities will be after him, but he is smart enough to overcome the power of the authorities."

"Places a lot of weight on his shoulders Lorraine."

"He is used to it is a certain way. You could imagine it is his path ahead. He told me once about why he left employment with the authorities when he did. He said he could see what was coming and he was intent on doing something about it, but he was not entirely sure on precisely what it was back then. I suppose all these years later, he has a much clearer idea."

"Do you think he will try and find Chris?"

"You can bet on it. When I first met Chris in London, John was so saddened by what he had become, and then a few years later, he was able to convince Chris to have the nano implants removed. Thankfully he listened to his father and likely saved himself from the tyranny of the Agent."

"Chris was in Boston. I met him there when I was on a special cybernetics project," Derek added.

"Then I would imagine it will be the first place John will head towards. He has a talent for turning out information when he has almost nothing to go with."

Lorraine suddenly thought of Asper and her loss of Tobias all those years ago when she had lost contact with John. "He'll come though. There was something in him similar to John. They might have captured him, but you can be sure he will eventually come around. When he woke up to what was really happening, he started something inside they could not totally suppress despite their efforts."

"Yeah, I have a feeling he is still alive, but it has been so long now, I just wonder about what has happened during all these years."

"It will be okay Asper. You wait and see. Think about our dreams. In your heart, the connection has never been broken and it will always be there for him as well," Celia said softly.

"Such wisdom Celia. You amaze me more and more every day dear," Esther said looking surprised again at how bold and assured Celia was.

"It's because I can feel what my heart tells me Esther. I listen as well."

"Well you just keep listening and feeling, and tell us whenever you think you have something to say. Wouldn't you agree Derek?"

"I certainly do. She makes me very proud Esther."

"Our love is enough to speak dad."

Everyone broke into laughter at how Celia could suddenly direct the conversation and seem to present all the adults with these moments of wisdom. It was not a mocking laugh. It was more in the sense of acceptance, and from the joy she emanated as she gave to the group.

After a minute, Celia brought out the torus she had in her pocket bringing their laughter to a stop as they all gazed at the object with a distinctive and alluring electric pink hue. It was not a time where the joy of the previous moment was lost, rather a confirmation of the feelings they all felt. Celia looked at each person sitting around the table one by one, meeting their gaze directly through eye-to-eye contact. She had a different look on her face – a serious yet loving look, and for each moment in turn, the adults felt a connection and a knowing sense of purpose together. When she had finished, she joked at them with a feigned air of authority, telling them to be easy and soon the real torus would come to them.

"What is this real torus Celia?" Murray asked.

"The one the others have Murray. The one Carmel and the others have been keeping safe. They will bring it here because Carmel's house is here and she wants to return, even though she has loved where she has been since she was last here."

"She is a remarkable woman."

"You must miss her Tim."

"Yes I do. I hope you are right Celia. I would dearly love to see her again."

"Don't hope Tim, just believe and feel. She will come. Wait and see."

Asper could see the radiance about Celia. The others could feel it, but Asper could see the energy she was giving, though not so specifically as a sight in normal vision – it was almost as if she was in a dream state when she looked.

"Do you like my aura Asper? I can tell you are looking at it."

"Um…yes Celia. It is a beautiful glow."

"What do you mean dear?"

"My aura Esther. Surely you know what an aura is."

"Yes I do, but I cannot see your aura."

"Well you could. But don't look harder for it because then it will never show. Asper knows."

Everyone turned to look at Asper in expectation of an explanation, but all she did was to continue looking at Celia. The others could see Asper was not focusing intently - appearing to be staring through Celia if anything. Without any response forthcoming, they each in turn, looked back at Celia trying to gaze upon her as Asper did. Celia knew what was happening and she just let it be so by just sitting there and enabling them each to have their own experience.

"So what is it you see then?"

"I find it hard to see, but you do seem to have a shimmer."

"There. Soon you will see more father."

"The nature of progression like our dream Celia."

"Yes Asper. I think it is like our dream in a way. I'll put the torus away now. Somebody is telling me it would be the right thing to do."

Within minutes, two officers of the authorities appeared, demanding to be let inside. Murray left the group to answer them, whilst the others did what they could to conjure an appearance as if they were innocent of anything approaching meaningful thought.

"You are all advised electricity is now available in allocated amounts. This device connects to the main junction box for this house in order to receive transmitted energy for dispersal throughout the premises."

"What do you mean by allocated amounts?"

"Precisely as stated. Energy is no longer a constant for normal citizens. Instead, each residence is to be allocated a specific amount of energy per week. Use it all up, and you will then be without power until your next allocation. The authorities will also be monitoring all energy use."

"Why?"

"You do not need to know why specifically, other than to realise you are all to be closely watched. In fact, every citizen is to be closely watched. Do you understand this…properly?"

"Yes," everyone except for Celia said in unison.

"Any attempts to access more energy than allocated will result in your arrest. Understood?"

Everyone nodded in acknowledgement again, except for Celia who appeared to be closely studying the faces of the two men. When the officer who had remained silent noticed her stare, he became uneasy, "What are you staring at little girl?"

"Your energy."

"What are you talking about?"

"The energy you have normally unseen."

"So you can see it now?"

"Yes, I can always…"

"Now Celia, please don't interrupt these officers. They have a job to do."

"Okay father."

The first officer again confirmed all present understood the implications of the energy provisions, and after receiving the answers sought, he indicated to the other officer it was time to leave. The other officer had mostly looked at Celia this entire time, and for an instant was unresponsive to the directive from his superior. When at last he did respond, he was left somewhat aghast as somewhere deep inside him doubts about his life were emerging.

"Be careful what you say to the authorities, won't you Celia."

"Yes father. I'm sorry."

"Don't be sorry. Just be smart my sweet. If they suspect anything, they will be brutal to us."

"But we are not doing anything wrong really."

"Yes we know, but in their eyes, we would be seen as dissidents and they would put us in prison."

"And the torus father?"

"Yes, they would say we stole it and then they would ask why. If they begin to know what we are doing with it, then we would be in a lot of trouble."

"I understand father. They don't understand...but some of them do. I saw the man's aura. It is in conflict father and has holes. I think people like this are unsure about what they are doing because the holes show what they are doing is bad for them."

"What if someone is doing bad things but they don't have any holes?"

"Then it is simple silly. They are learning what it is to be like what they are experiencing in their life...without the conflict. But they too will begin to ask why one day. Almost all people do father, it is a universal question."

"A universal question hey Celia. Where do you get this idea?"

"From within. It is my heart and my quest."

"Your quest. Do you mean it is what you want to do with your life? Just follow your heart. What about what you want to be?"

"Oh it will come when I listen to my heart. When I see people with the aura holes, I can see they are not really listening to their heart. They think what they are doing is what is best for them."

"But they can often be correct..."

"Because they listen to their heart father. Even if they are those bad people of the authorities, they are still listening to their heart. It is just they do not understand any further. When they get older they might, and so they begin to ask questions about what they are doing. If I listen to my heart, then all the rest will fall into place."

"So the torus helps you do this listening?"

"In a way, but it is only showing this. It does not make me listen."

"Celia...and I have a knowing feeling about all this you know Derek. We have shared dreams and emotions and they are the evidence of the connection she is talking about."

"You know there were a few similar moments with her mother before she passed Asper."

"I can imagine so. The energy in her is very pure and there is always the mother and daughter connection."

"Yes father. Mother and I did have a few of these moments. It is why I am now so happy to be here and to have met Asper. Remember how I thought it was best we come to this town without really knowing why? Well, I think we are all beginning to know why now."

"Yes Celia, I think we are beginning to see this wonderful relationship you are sharing."

"And listen because the universe speaks through all of us."

Chapter 12

The dark streets in the old section of New York City had remained mostly unchanged for many decades. Amongst the litter discarded by humans, and of humans, John was hiding in a small disused warehouse smelling of vermin and dampness. It was accessible by a small almost indistinguishable door – an ideal indiscreet location for him to gather thoughts and plan what to do next. Above him he could see through a section of broken roof to a sky of dull light, haze, and a near full moon. For a moment he remembered life back in Alaska – the freedom beside the river in the moment knowing place in mind and spirit, the spontaneous wildreness, and his inherent place as part of it all. He could see a few stars now, but otherwise he felt the sky looked dirty. There was nothing really aside from a sense of staleness in the air with no movement – not even the slightest breeze. He loved the winds and the sharp coolness of Alaska. He had always felt more alive, felt clear, and life always held a sense of invigoration.

Now, the haze reached into the streets here and there to form soft amber hues coming from sparse yet regular street lights, with the odd soft blue spot indicating a technology installation. He dreamed of being back beside the river. For a moment then he thought of Tobias. It was his arrival those years ago when John had to leave his serenity behind. Since...it had been a life on the run, in prison, and in the company of others he held dear. It was then his determination decided it was best to remain in hiding for the time being so he could devise a sure method to avoid re-capture by the authorities when he escaped the city.

Rats infested the floors, were inside the walls, and could be heard scuffling throughout as each night he worked over ideas on how he would first travel to Boston to find his son Chris. The rats failed to bother John, instead he saw them as a shield in a sense aiding in keeping anyone away from such an undesirable place. His thoughts were focused on how he would coax him to come along and how they would require some type of plan to then head west all the way to Carmel's house north of San Francisco.

Travel would be difficult without any means to bypass the now mandatory security checks for all citizens whenever they boarded public transport. Private ownership was still restricted as so many were forced to limit their travels to wherever the public transport systems were in place. The authorities were not of the mind to encourage any distant travel, restricting many to efficient work related journeys.

Food was an issue. Availability of foodstuffs was restricted with payment by cashless means in New York, using one's personal DNA profile to purchase any kind of item. John only had the limited technology he had taken with him from the underground facility to work with as he spent nearly all his waking hours building a new DNA profile mask for himself. In the meantime, his survival depended upon scraps he found during the few hours each day when he wandered the old streets in search of food.

"What do you want?"

"Just looking for something to eat. Is it a problem?" John replied.

"It is if I want what you have. What have you found?"

"Just a few scraps. I don't want any trouble with you, but I am very hungry, so don't try to take them off me."

"A wise guy hey. Maybe I do want your few scraps. You are not the only one who is hungry around here."

"I bet, but you won't get this food. I'll stop you."

"Oh you will stop me will you? I think I see it differently. Why don't you just hand it over and save yourself a few significant injuries. I have a weapon."

"Where?"

"Concealed. You don't think I would walk around with it out in the open do you?"

"What is it?"

"Why should I tell you?"

"I can make weapons."

"So?"

"So if you show me, perhaps I can help you."

"What the hell are you talking about? How can you help me? You look half starved and weak as piss."

"Don't underestimate me."

"Maybe I will show you the moment before I shoot you. How would you like..?"

"It depends. If I can avoid your weapon, then it will not matter, and then before you know it, you will be looking down its' barrel."

"It doesn't have one. First mistake to you."

"So it is a discharge weapon then. I think you just made a mistake."

"So what of it? I still have the weapon."

"But now I know its type, I can defend myself against you."

"Not bloody likely. Even if it is a discharge weapon, it will still take you down in an instant."

"Not bloody likely yourself. Don't try it. You will regret it."

"Screw you. I am bloody hungry enough to take whatever you have and stun you at least on the spot. In fact, I think it is just what I will do."

"I warned you."

"Screw your warning. How are you going to move fast enough to avoid the electrical bolt?"

"I don't need to move an inch."

"Ha, all fool you then." The stranger quickly drew the weapon, levelled it at John, and then fired, but during the course of this, John pressed a button on the small device in his pocket. When the stranger fired, the weapon simply discharged a small bolt too weak to even cover the distance between himself and John. As surprise took hold of the stranger, John made his move, and after a few quick movements, he had taken the weapon, and was now levelling it back at him.

"See, I told you."

"How in hell did you..?"

"I said I could help you, but you declined. Now see who is in the shit."

"Hey look, don't fire on me. I'm sorry. It is just around here, things are often desperate..."

"I can reason there. But still, you intended to stun me. It is hardly a nice thing to do and now you ask me to take it easy. Lucky for you, I could not care to kill anyone, but don't take me for granted, I might change my mind."

"Okay...and thanks. I am sorry."

"Well maybe we could work together. Are you a fugitive?"

"Um, yeah of sorts. I don't want the latest shit coming from the authorities with this DNA thing. It pisses me to have them take over my body and my life. Screw them I say. They don't like it though. Just three days ago they tried to force me to take the DNA scan, but I wouldn't do it, so I ran. I guess they will be after me in some way now."

"You're in luck then. I think similarly. They have had me imprisoned for the past few years."

"Shit man, whatever for?"

"See there?" John pointed to the anomaly visible in the evening sky. "They had me tell them how to make it. Now there is all hell breaking loose if I don't stop them for good soon."

"How do you mean?"

"I gave them some faulty information and so the hole is unstable. If they don't fix it soon, it is going to make a mess."

"Why did you leave?"

"Because they had me against my will, and I have information sufficient to make the authorities more powerful than ever. I don't want them to obtain the knowledge I have. It would only be a matter of time before they did. I have fooled them for the past few years, but once they start their next stage of technology deployment, there would be almost no stopping them. So I had to escape, otherwise we would all be stuffed."

"Gee man, you must be pretty smart then."

"There are plenty of smart people about, doing stupid things...for years. I know about some decent tech, but I keep it mostly to myself."

"You're not the guy the authorities talk about are you? I overheard a few people who said they were after one person who could give them flux...um, flux..."

"Mechanics. It is faster than light technology. And yes, I am the guy. But don't think of turning me over to them, or I will use this weapon. They won't give you a reward anyway...more like some of their nano technology and then send you on your way."

"Oh don't worry mate. I don't give a shit about rewards and all the material rubbish. I work from the heart. Count me as on your side."

"Where do you live?"

"One block from here in an old warehouse."

"It seems we have similar tastes then. I am one block in the other direction, in an old warehouse."

"What is it like? I've been here for months and have managed to put a few things together. Some of them I don't even know what they are for."

"My place is a shit hole. Full of rats and dirt..."

"Then come to mine. I have plenty of room. Maybe we can work together. Perhaps you could tell me what some of the stuff I have could be used for."

"Sounds reasonable, but can I trust you?"

"Look man, I am as much against those bastards as I think you are. I am not going to spill the beans. Anyway, my name is Gareth. Pleased to meet you."

"Yeah likewise Gareth. I'm John. Maybe we can get along a bit better in the future than we did at the start."

"You bet John. I am sorry, but you know how it is."

"Yeah I can understand, but don't be so aggressive. It will be your undoing, and maybe ours. Stay calm and alert...fortune will come your way."

"I think it already has. This way mate. As I said, only one block from here and then we'll be at my place. It's pretty discreet and there are not many others around."

"I noticed. These streets look almost deserted."

"It is the authorities. They are rounding up a lot of people."

After a fast walk to maintain cover, Gareth led John in through a small partially hidden doorway into the warehouse where he lived. Almost immediately, John exclaimed with delight when he saw the various pieces of technology Gareth had managed to find over the past few months.

"This is quite a treasure trove you have here mate. You say you don't know what any of it is for?"

"Only a few of the pieces. Their use is fairly obvious, but all this other stuff sure beats me for what it is meant to do. I'm originally a musician back in the days before eighty-eight, so the only tech I know about is related to composing tunes...melodies, you know."

"Well you sure have some good pieces here. Eighty-eight was a big year for just about everyone I think. What about food? You did say you were short earlier."

"I was lying of sorts. It has been hard around here, so I was going to take what you had to add to my own booty. Here, take a look. I have a few days worth of food and these bottles of whiskey I came across inside the basement of an old hotel a few blocks from here. They were a lucky find."

"Well, let's crack one open and celebrate. Afterwards, I'll get to work with some of this gear you have. Perhaps you could help me?"

"Anything you want to help mate. I'll grab a bottle. It is pretty good stuff too, and worthy for the occasion."

During the course of finishing half the bottle of whiskey, John analysed the technology Gareth possessed, and was thrilled to see most of it was still in operational condition. When he was satisfied all had been examined sufficiently, John selected a few pieces to begin working on immediately.

"See this? It is an elemental processor."

"What is an elemental processor?"

"It is used to analyse the status of subtle elemental forces affecting the integrity of data transmission when filtered through a pseudo flux generator. Connect it to the output terminal of any quantum computer, and it will balance any variables affecting the data integrity."

"Which means?"

"It means if I can make it work, I can modify the output variables to shape true flux mechanics."

"Don't you already have gear to do such tasks?"

"I did. For years I had my own gear, but when I was captured, they took it all from me. I only have the modified device I was able to build when I was incarcerated."

"The one you used to squash the output of the discharge bolt I tried on you?"

"Precisely. It is also capable of masking some data and creating false profiles for other uses, but I have been struggling to come up with something solid. Now with this, I can resume full flux mechanical output."

"But after a few modifications. How long will it take you?"

"A day or two if I stay on it. Then I can build a small DNA profiler for us both…and we can start buying food instead of scavenging."

"Won't the authority systems register some type of false file?"

"Good question. They would if I overlooked a key component within the data. I have a trick I can use to create a real time file, so when it is first used, the authority systems will create a file as if it is a real DNA profile…of a real person. The only problem is as if someone took the time to scan the profiles and seek a history. It would take a hell of a lot of work considering the hundreds of millions of profiles in existence."

"So almost infallible?"

"Almost. Sometimes you have to take a chance. Anyway, if we did use the false profiles and then they were discovered at a later date, we would be well on our way somewhere else. And to counteract, I will build an algorithm so it creates new profiles regularly."

On this first night during their drinking session, both men had decided they would leave New York City together and make their way to Boston where John thought his son Chris was living. Then over the next two days, John concentrated on working with the technology, whilst Gareth tended to gather food and any other supplies they had agreed would help their cause. In contrast to how they met, both men now considered the other as a friend. Over the course of time since their meeting, they had easily grown accustomed to the other's company, and they agreed on many philosophical discussions.

On the third day, John was satisfied with the work he had completed, and decided it was time they test the new devices he had built to provide them with false DNA profiles.

"We will need to stock up a bit if we are going to travel to Boston. Normally, the authorities restrict the amount of food purchased in one transaction."

"Prevents people from being comfortable, and keeps them on edge I suppose."

"Maybe we can do a few days purchasing and then go."

"Sounds okay to me Gareth. I want to test some more of this gear I have been working on anyway. We will need as much as we can muster to keep on top of things once we leave. How are the travel restrictions?"

"Work and authority related mostly. Nobody is permitted to travel for the sake of anything else, unless they have a very strong reason."

"Well, it will have to be in small stints then."

When it came time to leave Gareth's warehouse, the two men had been able to successfully purchase a decent supply of food to take on the journey to Boston. John had also built a small flux mechanics generator for use with the quantum computer he and Gareth had stolen from the authorities the night before when they broke into a regional power distribution node. Along with a few pieces of technology he had salvaged from Gareth's collection, John now had the capacity to build flux mechanics and most other small devices he considered they might require.

"I'll hack into the authority database and map their transport facilities from here to Boston. As soon as I have the data, we should prepare to leave."

"I do know the public routes are fairly good out of the city to the north as far as Bridgeport. With the Agent now out of the way, the authorities have opened up these channels again so they can get people back to work."

"It's basically all city up to there anyway."

"Yeah, but until recently, anywhere out of the New York city limits was shut down more or less. People were being confined to their immediate areas. We can ride in sections up to Bridgeport, and then we are going to have to try our luck until we reach Providence."

"Why Providence? I would have thought the lines would be drawn in pretty close to Boston."

"The authorities have a new type of facility up there. Some sort of new residential block, I believe. With all the re-arranging after the Agent, they decided to develop Providence to accommodate the influx of people who had ventured all the way to the east."

"Keep them under their watchful eye I imagine."

"You could say so."

John spent the next few hours hacking into the authority database, looking into all possible transit corridors.

"So how are you progressing John?"

"I pretty well have all the information we need. The authorities have some checkpoints in place. From what I can see, people require special permission to pass through. They have some type of new systems in governing these permissions, which I have not been able to access."

"Where will we go then?"

"I have it figured. We will have to take an inland route and then approach Providence from the west."

At the end of their first day after departing New York, the two men had made it to Stamford north of the city, where John had decided it would be best they then go inland from there to avoid Bridgeport entirely to keep their distance from the authorities.

"I will be able to hack into the authority systems to locate my son Chris once I have finished one last algorithm to bypass their encryption."

"When you have found him, how likely do you think he is to just up and leave Boston?"

"I don't really have an answer. When I last saw him, he was pretty solid on being anti nanotech. I had managed to persuade him to have the implants removed before the Agent did his worst...thankfully. But he was still fairly keen on pursuing some type of status, and we both know, only the authorities are able to provide there. I think if I can convince him of how we can build a life free from their direct influence, he will join us."

"But how will you do it John? There are no guarantees at all, and I imagine it is going to be hectic in the west now the authorities are stepping up their re-building."

"Life is hectic in some way all the time now anyway Gareth. I am going to contact Tim again, but this time I will send a message and see if I can obtain some information from him…and his thoughts on my ideas. With the flux capability I have again, there is definitely a new incentive for positively making some big changes."

"Will the authorities be able to intercept your transmission? It sounds risky."

"Not if I can help it. Flux will give us an edge."

John and Gareth stayed in a deserted farmhouse over night before the last leg of their journey towards Providence. Travel had been slow, as they had to be very cautious to avoid any officers of the authorities. During the course of the evening whilst Gareth spent most of the time standing guard on look out for anyone who might present as trouble for them, John worked on developing a communication channel to Tim. He adapted the signal for transference to the old communications device he used to contact Tim prior to escaping the prison, and was in part hoping the message would reach him. Within the data, he requested Tim reply with any information about the state of affairs for him, and of how much influence the authorities now had.

Minutes later, John was surprised to see Tim's response originating from a quantum computing source, and then he saw the content of the message. Tim had a quantum computer. Lorraine was with him in California, along with Asper and some other people John had never met, and they were staying at Carmel's house where the authorities were present, but yet to be over bearing. After reading the contents of the message, and then re-reading to ensure he had it all right, John felt the happiest he had felt in years.

When Gareth came in from one of his regular scouting rounds, he immediately sensed John's uplifted mood, which added to his own.

"I can tell you have had some good news."

"Indeed. Much better than I expected. My friends in the west are all doing well and there is good reason for us to go there as soon as we can."

"After we find your son."

"Yes. I reckon we could go on to Boston directly from here. It will take us at least two days."

For two days they travelled under guard to keep away from any authority observations. It was arduous going taking a toll on their psyche despite their recent good news. When they arrived at the outskirts of Boston, they decided to stick to the old section of the city to find a place where they could stay hidden whilst John hacked the authority systems to locate his son. After a few hours work, he had determined Chris' residential address.

"We'll go first thing in the morning and see if we can catch him before he goes to work."

"Then what? Even if we do find and persuade him, then we will have to find transit west."

"I've been thinking. There are limited HyperJet flights to major destinations all over the United States. We just need to get on board one to San Francisco. I have travelled a lot of miles on foot and horseback in recent years, so a quick flight appeals to me a great deal."

"System hack? We'll need a lot more credit than you were able to allocate to our false DNA profiles we used to buy food."

"No problem Gareth. The actual amount does not matter a bit. Ten credits or ten thousand. Once I am into those systems, I can allocate as much as we need. There will be a data trail and so we actually have to limit it to essential credit only."

"What about Chris? What if he needs to purchase a flight and he is not permitted? I know you can bypass the systems to authorise our false profiles, but he is an entirely different case."

"Same story as us. We're going to have to first persuade him to come, and then to use a false profile for the trip. He is going to have to commit, as they will see he is not working and is no longer located at his residential address. Once he comes with us, it is all or nothing for him. He won't be able to turn back."

"Do you think he will?"

"I am pretty confident. He has changed since the early nano tech days. You know I told you he turned me in when I saw him in London back in eighty-eight. Well, he was different the last time I saw him. I just hope he will turn his back on it all and hopefully see it along our lines. When he knows the potential of what flux mechanics can do and what the authorities are likely to do with it should they ever gain stability, I am banking on his heart opening up to some truths."

"There is much to be said for the heart mate. I hope he comes around for you...for us, and others."

Chapter 13

Since John had escaped and so far evaded recapture by the authorities, Eric Gunter had concentrated his efforts on priming the Monolithic Directive for its first test run. The artificial star was in standby mode, positioned as it had been in the vast underground facility since its construction. At its core, a toroidal fusion module was generating only enough power to retain integrity of the stars' basic formation as Eric's superiors supervised his every move and every outcome.

There was no immediate punishment in store for Eric. His superiors deemed it too important for him to keep focus on the Directive and the implications of stabilisation of the spatial anomaly. John's escape would not pass without repercussions Eric knew would come, and strangely to him, a degree of gratitude arose for a moment before he could feel his mechanical self directing his thoughts.

Standing at a vast holographic array, Eric was busy beyond what could be considered natural as his implants drove him harder and faster to enter algorithmic sequences in preparation for the first stage of testing. Without any hint he was nearing the end of this initiation stage, Eric suddenly ceased entering sequences and with a deliberate stand out motion, pierced the engage systems holographic control with his forefinger. Almost instantly a low resonance hum sounded throughout the enormous room housing the star. Within a fraction of a second after engaging the device, a large as yet unseen spacecraft housed immediately above the room, also came to life.

The spaceship designed for transferring the monolith to the spatial anomaly had been concealed within the structure of the building until this time. Utilising the latest invisibility technology, the craft had remained unseen to anyone not authorised to know of its existence. Measuring four hundred feet long and one hundred wide, it was the most immense spacecraft ever built on Earth or on any other known planet to this time. On its underside was a phasing anti gravity cage designed to lift and hold the Monolithic Directive without the use of any physical grappling device. With operations to bring the monolith into semi-operational status, the spaceship was engaged in case removal of the two hundred foot wide artificial star and immediate evacuation into space was required.

Eric engaged the star's internal atomic generator to begin the first instance of atomic manufacture in a relatively stable state. It looked incredible as it began to emit a low blue radiance for the first time where even at this low semi-operational level, it dazzled all who viewed.

As the first results appeared on his holographic array, Eric could see the generation of atoms was proceeding as planned. Billions of potential building blocks of matter coursed along intense gravitational forces generated within the valleys between plasma outbursts from the star. This second result pleased him, as he was now certain the star could be used to manufacture large amounts of energy in addition to the atomic material. Within the next few seconds, the test results showed the star to be ready for an increase in output level, prompting Eric to increase atomic output from the stars' core.

The centre of the monolith comprised of a part physical core interfaced with a holographic generator to process flux mechanics data provided by John. Unbeknown to Eric, were the algorithmic misalignment subtleties John had disguised as stable equations enabling the star to operate at full capacity and then in time change the monolith.

Eric engaged a full power test. The star increased to a brightness requiring all personnel present to wear filtering goggles against the immense radiation of blue light, except those who like Eric, had entirely mechanical eyes capable of filtering out the blinding glare. As the glare continued to intensify, Eric studied the holographic readouts measuring the torus based fusion within the star.

Three-dimensional imagery showed nuclei of atoms fusing together from sub-atomic states and further beyond the brink of quantum particles towards the very energy giving rise to matter. As they were released beyond the photosphere in wave after wave, the atomic prominence collector gathered them for storage inside a constrained tachyon field.

For the last stage of testing, Eric applied the atomic acceleration algorithm John had devised, casting the atoms into a toroidal pattern of flow. This was a crucial stage to gauge success, as this point was the nexus between normal matter and faster than light transference. When Eric observed the establishment of the tachyon pathways and the subsequent unhindered uptake of atomic matter being accelerated beyond light speed, he was satisfied both in a professional sense, and in a more remote personal sense.

The objective had achieved what his superiors would see as the foundation of flux mechanical development – a potential endless energy. Eric then shut down the test, returning the monolith to standby status as the space craft above simultaneously shut down. Testing was now complete and the next task for Eric would be to deploy the star for insertion into the spatial anomaly.

"Gunter?"

"Yes sir?"

"We have observed the testing results as positive. You may proceed with construction."

"Acknowledged sir. Anything else?"

"Yes. Once you have completed production of the monolithic robotics, you are to report to me for readiness and deployment of all monolithic technologies to the anomaly."

"Understood sir."

Eric now had a two week period to finalise the construction of monolithic derived robotics for accompanying the star into the spatial anomaly. In parallel development to the star itself, this new type of robotics operated using torus atomic generators for the production of material output based on the nanotechnology atomic manipulation. No longer would machines be designed and built for a specific purpose. They were to be replaced by energetic machine entities simply existing as generators of atomic mass ready to accommodate any purpose Eric and others instructed them to perform. Through replication of nanotechnology robotics available for atomic transference as required, they were to be the first machines approaching infinite capacity.

Interrogation machines, medical surgeons, weapons enabled devices - all were within grasp amongst the many other purposes the authorities would deem necessary for managing society.

Flux mechanics was about to take on an entire new meaning where the forces of geometry giving rise to existence, were within reach of those in control. Eric had worked hard on these machines – much harder than he had worked on John to extract the necessary information.

Eric's work would reduce people to become only what they could serve as part of an efficient work process for the authorities. No guise of opportunity would be necessary as people would be shaped to believe the choice provided was the best option where all life's best pleasures, most needs, and almost all dreams could be realised. Eric and his superiors were well aware humans are prone to forgetfulness and are quite adaptable when circumstances demand, so many would accept the way of being as normal as the generations passed and those who Eric and his superiors deemed a threat now and into the future, could be efficiently eradicated thus rendering effective opposition as obsolete.

Chapter 14

Life in the small town north of San Francisco had changed somewhat since the authorities had returned and made their presence felt. Ten more houses were now occupied and electricity whilst available was being rationed to homes as a measure to keep people in a state of need at the line bordering hardship. This did not cause too much issue for at least two of the houses in the town – both with occupants resilient to these motives by the authorities.

Those few who were in control had no mind to suddenly release the stranglehold over the populous, nor did they want to attract many new comers from the cities to a life in smaller country areas. Their onus was very much on control but they also realised to have an effective operational community with security in place, there needed to be centres of smaller populations who would go on to provide for those who lived in the new cities they were building.

Gone were the central collections of interlinked high-rise, now replaced with massive blocks of towers built to accommodate most of the populations within the cities. Status was no longer a focus for many to gain residence on floors high above the decaying streets below for life was to be lived by almost all at the dizzying heights where buildings reached to the sky approaching two hundred floors. No care had been taken to restore the character of city streets. Instead, life was to be lived almost entirely within the towers where the streets below would become the service corridors for those above. Cities rapidly began to lose their historical values – even the famous wooden houses in San Francisco, would soon come under threat.

Tim was busy working on data for study of geometry Celia had mentioned relating to the spatial anomaly when the message arrived from John. He immediately knew it was him as no other person could possibly be in contact, though the thought of it being the authorities attempting to solicit illegal behaviour from citizens, did cross his mind. Tim considered it very likely they would attempt to coerce people into such behaviour as a measure of investigating citizens opposing their motives.

"What are you doing Tim?"

"More of the study you recommended I take on Celia."

"I have heard you talking to father. It is best you continue to look at this information. Your friend will come here soon to work on this with you. He feels responsible for the anomaly and he wants to fix all the wrong things."

"What do you think those things are Celia?"

"Oh Tim, I know they are bad, and so does he. It is why he will get here as soon as he can."

"It is funny how you have turned up to speak to me the moment I receive a message from John."

"I'm just making sure you keep thinking about this. Nothing else."

"Well you can be sure Celia. I think you are right about John coming here as soon as he can, but I am mystified as to how you know this."

"It is simple Tim. Remember the dream Asper and I shared? Think about it and how we aligned together as two different people and you will begin to understand the answer to your question."

Celia then left Tim to himself, choosing to go outside and play in the light dusting of snow. She ran freely about the yard stopping now and then to look closely at something before setting off again throwing handfuls of snow into the air and watching their crystal veil in the sparkling winter sunlight. Now and then, Esther, Lorraine, and Asper would see her stop and just stand motionless as if she was in a trance. Her gaze would fix on something and she would just stare at it for a few moments, before suddenly erupting again into frivolous play, bounding about and laughing. Her innocence and purity held the three women as each of them recalled their own memories of play, and thought of the burden free heart and mind of childhood. When it appeared as though she had exhausted herself for a time, Celia turned and ran into the kitchen startling them out of their day dreaming.

"Esther. How long until lunch? I am starving."

"A little while Celia dear. It is only around eleven."

"Can I have something until then please?"

"Sure. What would you like?"

"I think one of those pieces of fruit we have would be nice. I know there are not many, but I do feel like having a piece."

"Okay. Why else would we have them? Apple or orange?"

"Orange please."

"You know what?" Celia said as she ate the orange with the three women looking on. "Orange is a colour in the light spectrum. I have seen it in rainbows and I have been reading about it in those books in the lounge room."

"Yes it is in the spectrum. It is a beautiful colour."

"Well Esther, orange is also the colour of the Sacral chakra. Asper knows it too, don't you Asper."

"Um, yes. It is the colour of the Sacral chakra. It is for meditating on the creative forces into all aspects of one's being. High soul procreation and devotion...according to those texts. Why have you been reading this Celia?"

"Oh, I was interested. I don't know why. It is true though isn't it Asper? We do need to bring more creativity into our lives. Human beings I mean. I am talking about the meaning. "

"Yes, I suppose it is true. For a long time, people have been going about routine and working, then the suffering when the Agent was here. It sure did a lot to stop creativity."

"People have been very dependent and have been seeing status as the most important thing for a long time as well Celia," Lorraine added.

"I guess you are right Lorraine. I don't know much about those things. I like to think about the beautiful things we see around us, and my dreams, and also what the voices say to me. Do you like these things too Asper?"

"Sure dear. They take all the worries away…"

"But why do adults worry so much? They make things to worry about. Life is free isn't it? It seems silly to give your life to things to worry about."

"Yes it does. Adults can be quite silly at times."

"But not you, or Esther, or any of us. We will see won't we? The dream we shared is telling us Asper."

As Celia was finishing the orange, Murray and Derek burst in through the front door after returning from a scouting mission around town. She did not look up at them as they began to explain the situation about to occur, as she knew what they were going to say. Celia knew the men coming to the house would not hold much respect for anyone they ordered about, and their actions would attempt to bring on a state of dependency and force withdrawal of people's natural inclinations to be creative.

"They are aggressive and fearful from being people who are insecure instead of just being awake," she murmured to herself as Derek told the others to prepare for the visit from the authorities.

Tim heard the words from the adjacent room, so he quickly set about shutting off the quantum computer and closing the secret alcove just in time to conceal its existence. When the two men arrived at the front door, he had joined the others in the lounge room of Carmel's house.

"You lot do spend considerable time together don't you? Every time the authorities come visiting, their drive for efficiency is boosted with only having to visit one house instead of two, except if we were to visit the wrong house first, which we have not done as yet. Hmm, remarkable."

"I guess we are just becoming good friends. It is pretty hard to find people who…"

"I wonder how good and what type. There is absolutely no allowance of dissent or any pathetic notion of resistance to the coming measures."

Celia could sense the anger within the officer who stood at the door with his partner. For a few seconds it gave her a feeling of angst and of sliding downwards into despair, but she was able to grab hold of something strong inside of her and stop herself from submitting to the negativity she could sense radiating from the officer.

"We would never consider dissent or any other measure as appropriate," Tim replied. "We were hoping things would go well for the authorities and for the restoration of some services. How else will we survive?"

"Yes. Indeed. Keep your thoughts on such things for they are the only truths to seek. Without the authorities, the population is useless…helpless and pathetic, unable to cope with the world, and unable to cope with themselves. Look at them. Always dependent on something and someone to make their existences seem worthwhile. How else will they realise any happiness? The services provided by the authorities who have affiliated so well with the few large corporations left in existence, will provide all the people need."

Celia knew the simple answer to this question and it began as a feeling welling up inside her, but she dared not say a thing in order to avoid any type of trouble. She let it go. To her, even thinking about why the officer was thinking this way, simply dissolved from her mind. As it dissipated, she let out a gasp loud enough to attract his attention.

He studied her for a moment, looking her up and down, and in some distant sense momentarily felt a slight threat coming from her. Within in a moment, his nanotechnology mechanical implants dismissed the idea of a girl posing any type of threat to him. 'Anyway, I have a weapon,' he thought stupidly. The mechanics were not entirely overwhelming him as his were customised for his work operations, and so he and others like him, retained a significant degree of their own thoughts.

Looking away, he shook the last few distractions Celia had posed to his mind, and ordered the adults prepare for the authorities to come visiting quite regularly in the coming weeks.

"All houses will be fitted out by the authorities in order for them to be considered efficiently habitable. There will be absolutely no allowance made for anyone to exceed their quota of both energy and foodstuff supplies." He motioned to the other officer who had remained at the fringe of the group, near the front door. Immediately, he opened a small compartment on his sleeve and gave the object to his superior.

The object was a cube precisely one inch square, and for a moment the superior held it carefully between his forefinger and thumb, so all could see.

"All this house requires to commence its integration into the new authority network is in this cube. All of your communication needs and data transfers for processing will be managed by this device. Think yourselves privileged in fact, as you are amongst the first to be given these quantum computers. And… twenty-four hour holographic broadcasts will soon recommence to service all your entertainment needs. The resolution from these will put you in any scene. Try the holographic virtual reality mode too – no eye wear required."

He then turned and walked over to a wooden panel above the doorway separating the lounge area and dining, removed the panel and set the cube into a housing obviously designed for this purpose. It was placed there either before they had lived at Carmel's house, or sometime after. The second option was the most likely scenario and this troubled all of them greatly when they considered the authorities having been in the house without their knowledge.

The officer could sense something as they all felt this and turned and looked Tim directly in the eye, "This trouble you hey? Well all I will say is yes it will if you cause trouble. Otherwise, be a good citizen and there will be nothing to worry about. We'll be watching you…especially. I am no scientific expert or doctor or whatever, but I know enough to be aware of when it might be a good idea to be a little suspicious. A group like you. All of you seem too pretty to me. I'll be watching. We'll drop by your other house and pop the cube in there too. No need to come, we'll see ourselves in."

"What do you think he meant by 'pretty' father?" Celia asked when the two officers had left.

"I think he means we look like people who are not fooled by what he tells us all the time sweetheart. Why don't you go and fetch yourself a drink from the kitchen. I think it is time for us adults to have a talk."

"I know what you are going to talk about, but don't take too long doing it father. It could make you feel more negativity. Those men like people to feel bad things. I'm going to play anyway. The sun is out now and then, and with the snow falling, it looks lovely."

"What was with him? Half of what he said sounded like orders, and the rest was like a sales pitch," Asper said looking baffled and distant at the same time.

"They want you Asper. You will soon see their way is the only way. They not only want you to do it, but also believe it."

"Oh shut up Lorraine silly. We would never fall for the sales line."

The others laughed thinking as if they would ever simply believe what they were told, and in doing so, broke the seriousness of the time up until now. Celia then passed by the large window facing the yard where they could see her running here and there with her face upturned to the falling snow. Lorraine gave Asper a mischievous look, and they both turned to see Esther who clearly knew what they were thinking.

With a quick jab to Derek's ribs, Esther took charge, "No time for talk now. Everyone outside."

In a flash, all the adults utterly let go of their concerns from the meeting just prior with the authorities, and ran to join Celia playing in the snow.

The very moment they were outside, each of them caught the essence of why she had decided to do as she continued to run about catching snowflakes with her open mouth. It was a beautiful sight with the clear winter sun streaming from between the snow-laden clouds sending large flakes cast in sun rays falling gently to the ground. Magic had descended upon the town and the valley in those moments despite the incursion and threats. A simple elemental progression in nature was all it took to strike wonder in those who could feel it, easily overwhelming any notion of negativity. The cold did not bother them. In fact, the sunlight gave to their sense of warmth inside even though its' rays delivered mostly light.

The two officers did one last survey of the house where Celia, her father, Esther, and Murray lived. They were both frustrated from not having come up with any results from a detailed search, especially the disgruntled superior of the two who was convinced this group was up to something. He was glad they all spent time together so often, allowing him to have entered Carmel's house, install the cube receptacle, and conduct a thorough search. The fact he found nothing, only served to frustrate him then, but it did not deter him from continuing to watch the group. He knew of the missing quantum computer installed to operate as the central hub for this town mysteriously going missing during the time where only two houses were occupied. He hoped to watch them in secret where if he caught them in the act of something, he could claim credit towards his status for arresting them. Status to officer, officials, and the population was no longer a purely material pursuit. It had become focused on earning status credits in the system through actions of efficiency, citizen duty, and alignment of the mind to the directives as set out by the authorities as they sought to psychologically and socially profile people.

"Well, just leave the other device and we'll get going," he said to the other officer.

"I wonder why the cube just doesn't do voice surveillance and why we need this extra device?"

"Someone would find out. A computer hacker would find it and as soon as the public knew, they would object and lead to inefficiencies. The thing you installed is being deployed wherever there is enough suspicion. My orders are to keep it strict to the conditions. The authorities don't want anyone to find them."

"Then they will have to keep building new codes or something. If people were suspicious about the cube, then they will be looking for other things as well."

"Yeah, but it is mostly only hackers and their friends. Most people don't have the first idea of how the tech stuff works. They just come on board as soon as they are told how good it is for them."

"I guess pretty soon all people will be totally dependent on technology. You know…twenty four seven."

"You can be sure it is their goal. It scares me a bit. I want status, but I worry a bit about becoming someone like a machine."

"Fully trans-human?"

"Yeah, if such a thing exists. Sure a longer life is good. Don't get me wrong, but…so much of you becoming machine. It worries me."

"Yeah, me too. I really only joined the services to ensure I had a half decent life. I'm not entirely into gaining status, but I do believe in the cause for how this planet should operate. If you look at it with common sense, you can see the benefits."

"Mostly governmental, logistical, efficiency…all about organisations and operations. I don't mind it. I believe in striving for a common goal…"

"Yeah, but is it the right one?"

"Don't let anyone else hear you say anything. And don't ever say it to me again. Just keep your head down and do your job. Whilst times sure are better now the Agent is safely locked away, they sure are going to get bad in a lot of other ways, so keep quiet."

"Father." Celia had suddenly stopped playing and was standing looking at him with a serious, but not concerned look on her face.

"What is it dear?"

"Those officers are suspicious father."

"Yes I know dear. Don't worry about yourself…"

"I'm not father. I know they are up to something. Men like them usually are."

"Well…yes, an accurate observation Celia."

"We need to be careful. Those cubes are suspicious. I don't like them."

"Yes, all of us adults feel the same Celia."

"Then we must avoid them…and we must look out for other things. They will be watching us father…and listening."

"Indeed, I think they will."

"Actions speak louder than words, but sometimes words speak very loud when there is little action."

"I guess you are right. I really didn't think too much about it yet."

"I know. And I am so glad you all came out to play. How could you miss moments like this couped up inside being all serious?"

"You are right there Celia. I am also glad we came outside to play with you. The snow is so beautiful in the sunlight."

"It sure is dad. Here."

She threw a small snowball at Derek, hitting him square on the chin. As he blew the remnants of snow from his face, he set out chasing her around the yard where they each scooped up snow to throw at each other. The others could not help but to join them, as they were drawn in by Celia and Derek's loud bouts of laughter. For a time the yard was a melee of snowballs being thrown at all angles and of chases resulting in snow being pushed down the inside of collars, and then when finally they all felt exhausted, snow gently gathered as it fell on their upturned faces and bodies whilst they lay on their backs together in the centre of the yard.

At the end of the day, they sat around eating dinner discussing nothing of the events or issues relating to the authorities after deciding they should only discuss such maters outside. Despite the urge in all of the adults to live together in the one house, they had decided against it immediately upon suggestion for the authorities would see it as confirmation of their suspicions. Even though they had not gone through anything too distressing, somehow they all felt a stronger sense of determined togetherness now.

Murray led the group out to the front gate after dinner. "We'll take the main streets home and present exactly how they would want us."

"Don't overdo it though Murray. None of the acting stuff you like. I've seen it..."

"What? You don't like my sudden expressions of prose, given from my heart, emotively conveying the tragedy and ecstasy of Shakespeare or..."

"Oh, don't get me wrong. Let it be known I, Tim Collins do hereby appreciate the arts, but...and I emphasise this, there cometh a moment where time seems to slip away and the verges become blurred. Focus is taken to the enactment, be it pleasure, business, or pain, and thereupon the stage of life is set the scene, ambivalent in nature, yet from the depths of knowing, cast in fate. It is then, when this evocation forthwith compels one to study the finest expressions of the psyche through the embodiment of performance, one, and may I say, others, surely must observe what falls in a cascade not unlike beads of sweat upon the brow of the discerning and troubled. This finality is yet drawn against outcomes if aligned in context for the ongoing infinite progress, resulting in evidence of where the truth does lay. And...this truth is one to observe not only, but to also respond over react. Failing this measure is the circumstances...of an actor descending beyond the worn stage boards into the dark abyss below and sent back to the yearning status of an amateur."

"So you are saying my acting is not so good?"

"It is indeed good. So good, it may be seen as too good, too normal, and therefore a little suspicious. Be yourself and keep watching and listening."

"Um...Tim?"

"Yes Asper?"

"You okay?"

"Sure. Why?"

"Um, just never seen you...all those words..."

"Ah, there are surprises in life yet I say, and you...along with I too, just had one, though let it be known, through these times of years of recent, I have found a lot of time for reading. And when I think of John, I relay the very depths of the human spirit where those who seek shall find as their reckoning the ability to see beyond and begin to take those steps not as mastery, but of allowance for the perpetual nature of existence will see collective effort based on this realisation."

"Do you speak of undertones my good man where this is matter of fact?"

"Indeed Murray good sir. News of passage coming to me...us in reflection of our wonder amongst the falling snow in the sun."

"So we'll see you in two days time. Agreed we need to keep contact," Esther said looking uncomfortable at the prospect of the walk across town. She wanted to be underway so she could be free of uncertainty sooner. "Are you okay Celia?"

"Yes Esther. I know what to do. And don't look so worried please. We will be alright if you just allow yourself to feel it will be alight. Otherwise being worried or concerned too much, will just keep you in the same place of worrying and it gets too heavy wouldn't you agree?"

"I would agree dear. Shall we go?"

"Sure," Celia replied heading immediately towards the front gate. She stopped at the gate and grabbed Asper by the hand, "Keep dreaming Asper. We might meet again."

"I can't wait. Bye Celia."

"Bye."

Chapter 15

Elated as he was at seeing his son Chris again, John knew it was going to take some effort to bring him anywhere near close to considering what he would tell him. Every sentence he spoke, though genuine in affection for his father, or truthful about a particular fact, was underpinned by the language of the authorities. John could feel it emanating from him as if his son had practiced it so often for so long it had become part of his nature and projection of himself. This brought a depth of dismay for John when he considered how deeply the authorities had penetrated Chris' soul, despite the long since removal of the trans-human implants. He dared not allow himself to show any of this to Chris, instead remaining steady and firm.

John decided he would speak about it later with Gareth and plan a strategy to gradually win Chris over. Still, one aspect of this idea really troubled him, and it was how long Chris would take to be convinced.

Deep inside he knew there was some great upheaval coming and as a father, he felt compelled to do what he could to protect his son. At times his life was an endless challenge with the years of incarceration, beating Eric Gunter and being able to escape, the escape itself and travelling to Boston, and now to convince Chris to leave his life of status entirely behind.

For a brief moment he considered the gravity of recent times, as if he was about to succumb and languish somewhere low in spirit. But...it was only a fleeting moment, as he cast it off laughing when he thought of the regular challenges he had come up against since leaving the services before escaping from Alaska with Tobias six years ago.

Memory of his close friend added to his determination for success this moment, take Chris, and head west with a faint hope of some day being able to find Tobias and help him as well. A second later he thought of the times just a few years before when he was in Peru with Carmel, Chan, and the others. He had often thought of them during his time in prison, longing for the simplicity of the steam powered farm in the valley surrounded by towering Andean peaks. John liked the outdoors, so the years locked floors below ground level had tested his courage and determination to their fullest. He knew those at the farm would have thought of him...and Tobias, and of how they would have expected them both to return a number of weeks after taking the HyperJet from Arequipa in Peru to prevent them being traced.

John knew they had implanted him soon after capture almost three years ago. In the time since, he often wondered if there was anything left of the real Tobias or whether he was now more machine than man.

"Hell bad....höllen bad, time I made a..."

"What did you say dad? Hell bad?"

"Yeah. I was just thinking of a few of the experiences I have had in recent years and thought, yeah they were hell bad at times, but I always made it through."

"I can never forgive myself when you came to see me from Germany. It was…"

"Don't worry about it Chris. You couldn't help it. Anyway, we talked about this when you had your implants removed, and … we are here now."

"What are you…you and Gareth going to do dad? Surely the authorities will be after you. Don't worry as I won't repeat what happened before."

"I know Chris. Um…I am not really sure besides going west as soon as possible. I know people there and they can help us…"

"Help you? What way? You will need help just to get there first."

"Well there are two of us. The more the merrier so they say. At least we should be able to settle a while and stay in hiding."

"They won't give up looking for you. Flux mechanics is their goal. Everyone who works in the services knows this now. Whilst many cannot see the value or agree with the authority motives, they are happy just to do their work and gradually gain higher status. There are a few though who are beginning to question their motives."

"Are you one of those people Chris?"

"Not really. Sure, I have thought about what they are trying to do since I had the implants removed. I was so blind and willing just to take everything on face value previously. It is hard to believe what I actually used to subscribe to having them. I guess you were pretty freaked out seeing me in London."

"Um, yes I was. It hurt me a lot. So?"

"I'm okay with working and keeping a degree of safety dad. You helped me see their greater goals and how you can still be functional without being ultimately committed and dependent, but I am not sure if I would want to take it any further. Life could get difficult. You just said so."

"Yeah it can."

"Well, I'm not sure I would want to be actively against the authorities or whatever you consider your position to be dad. I'm glad you showed me the truth and I think I can safely say I can live well enough knowing this without giving up the things I have worked for. It also helps me foster my own interests with a steady income…"

"Yeah, but soon income will be data only in a real sense. Credits attached to your DNA profile. They'll force it onto everyone."

"I know what they are planning, but just look at it as the evolution of how payment is made. DNA, chip, hardware device. They are all attached to the person."

"I see your point. Gareth and I would be looking to stay in Boston for a short while…away from your place."

"Yeah, this meeting is risky, but something inside me just wanted you to come here at least once. I've been here for a while. It gets lonely at times. Life can be such a solitary affair attached to work, status, and routines. I wonder if I'll always be this way."

"See, you do question the legitimacy of…"

"Wait on dad. I see where you are heading, and maybe you have a point. But, I think it is best you left now. You and Gareth have been here an hour. I think we cannot risk any more time. Meet me tomorrow at these location details."

"You're cutting it a bit short…"

"No dad. It is best you go now. Lucky I live in this old place. These buildings have a few hidden surprises for access to and from without being seen, but I don't want to risk it any further. If you were caught again, and so soon, it would be…"

"Yeah, hell bad. Okay, we'll meet you then…and there. Come on Gareth. It has been great to see you son. And thanks for these supplies."

"No problems dad. I love you dad. See you tomorrow. Bye Gareth."

"See you mate."

John and Gareth left Chris' building to find somewhere to stay for the night. For a while their conversation was muted until Gareth raised a point tentatively, not sure how John would be feeling in respect to Chris.

"I heard you and Chris talking when I was in the next room earlier. He sounds like he is a fair way off giving all this up."

"Yeah. Still…I think there is some promise, and at least even if he doesn't come, I know he is okay and we have been able to see each other."

"Do you think he is genuine? Not another set up?"

"I'm sure we can trust him, but regardless, we need to stay alert for anything."

"Agreed."

"I want to take a look at the tech gear we have with us when we settle for the night. I have had a few ideas on something else I could build, but I think we will need to source one other item if my memory serves me correctly."

"What item John?

"The best holographic lens we can find. I have seen a few of the toroidal lens type I want, so it could be difficult."

"Why the reason for the torus type in particular?"

"I can program one to amplify flux mechanics…the torus thing. Not as good as a real torus like the one I have seen, but sufficient for what I anticipate could lay ahead of us in the west."

"What about sourcing one when we get there?"

"It may have to be our last resort if we have to. I'm thinking there would be a greater chance here in the east, considering the west is only now being reoccupied by the authorities to any real extent, and the technology will not be so widespread."

"Yeah you have a point. Any suggestions on where we might look?"

"The largest authority occupied building in the city."

"So you mean one of those very high risk type missions?"

"Unfortunately, yes. They are brand new technology. I came across some data on them and how they will be deployed almost everywhere eventually. My guess and I think I am fairly close to the mark, is to project holograms all over the place. Furthermore, and now this is the disturbing part, I am sure the authorities will deploy a holographic force of some type using these lenses."

"What? To move around?"

"Think of a holographic security force. They will manifest almost anything using these systems."

"But what would a projection be able to do?"

"Emit a radiant field transmitted as data on the photons…light. They are at a stage where they can almost begin to look at serious testing for transmitting nanotechnology robotics using projections. They take the light component of matter and splice it in a nucleonic sense…"

"You're losing me there."

"Um yeah. Let's just say they can use these fields to affect people. How they act. How they think...even to use light weapons like lasers. I'm not one hundred percent, but from my time inside and the work I did, I can easily see this as being at the cusp of deployment."

"So they won't need nanotech implants to manipulate people?"

"Probably not."

"And you are going to use one of these lenses to try and stop this happening?"

"It would be part of the picture. I'm…we're going to have to stay well ahead by doing what we can to anticipate their next moves. The lens will enable some affective data transmissions to help us."

"So when do you propose we go and find this building?"

"Right now. Then, if we find the right place, we can come back at a planned time to get the lens."

"A building can be a very big place."

"You're telling me after spending so long underground. There will likely be installs already if the building is significant enough. The data I saw indicated these projection nodes have been deployed to all authority central run buildings. We just need to find the discreet little housing. I know what they look like."

"Security is going to be high."

"The reason why we need a little time to plan. I'm going to run a scan when we find one, and I'll do this so I can work on an algorithm to make it appear as though the node is in normal situation when we take it."

After a short walk and search, John indicated he had found a torus device, "See the small circular recess five feet up?"

"Um, yeah, but it looks just as if it is part of the building material."

"They make them appear invisible by blending in. The lens can shift light around and so reflect whatever material it is mounted in. And at one inch wide, they are basically out of sight anyway."

"The scan?"

"It is running as we stand here. I don't need to hold the device or point it at the lens. I just calibrate it to look for or work on what I want."

"If you look closely at it, you can see the ring."

"The torus. Yes. It needs to be unattached to its housing though."

"How does it happen?"

"They suspend the torus using sonic waves we cannot hear. Let's move so we don't attract attention looking at it."

"What?"

"Yeah, sound waves. The torus is ultra light and barely solid - almost in a state of flux.

"So they just calibrate the sound waves to affect the frequency resonance of the torus?"

"Yes. You're catching on."

"How will you bypass the readings and remove the lens?"

"Use the scan. It has detected all relevant frequency data and I have over sampled to ensure there is no encrypted security back up."

"What time do you think would be good to return and take this thing?"

"We should wait until people are indoors to lessen the chances of us being seen, so just before nine tonight would be good."

"Alright. How long will it take you to remove the lens?"

"About a minute for removal and replacement with a dummy device."

"But you don't have anything to fit in the alcove for the lens."

"I'll make something and embed a transmitter so it appears as though the lens is still in place."

Over the next few hours, John went about building a device and installing algorithms based on the scan of the lens, whilst Gareth mostly kept watch at the door to the abandoned warehouse they had found. When he was satisfied with his results, Gareth was impressed with his skills.

"We'll go now. I know it is a little early, but I reckon on getting this out of the way as soon as possible."

"Are our false DNA profiles still updating?"

"Yeah, they would never see us for who we really are. If anyone chances on examining the security data for the time we are there, they will see nothing as the algorithm will mask our presence the entire time."

"Good. I don't fancy being caught and locked up as you were."

"Believe me Gareth, it is not even the last thing on my mind. There is no way I ever want to go near the place again and you can be sure I will be doing my best to ensure this is the case for me…and anyone I know."

When they approached the scene where they were to take the torus, both men cased the area first in a casual way. Satisfied the opportunity was upon them, John instigated the action.

"Just stand beside me talking to me as if we have stopped to discuss something important. It will only take a minute."

"Sure. How is it coming?"

"On track. It'll be free in about forty seconds. I just have to ensure the dummy device is connected to their security at the instant I remove the lens. You can thank flux technology for helping us there."

"Can it still spark an alert?"

"If anyone sees data for this device, I am hoping they will interpret it as a temporary system anomaly, and simply pass it by."

"Or?"

"If they investigate, they will see the device experienced a fluctuation for a tiny fraction of a second. By the time they properly investigate, I am hoping we will be a long way from here."

"They'll come looking?"

"Sure. But just focus ahead and on staying one step in front of them and we should be all right. Just a few more seconds now."

"Um John. There are two officers heading our way."

"Stay calm and keep talking, five more seconds…"

"You two! What are you doing?"

"Just talking officer."

"About what?"

"Work sir. My colleague and I stopped to discuss a problem we have at work and how to overcome it in the most efficient way."

"We have a scan readout indicating elevated data signals here."

"I don't know what it could be officer. We have only stopped to talk for a minute."

"I don't like the look in your eyes…both of you. Something tells me I should run a check on your DNA and see if my suspicions are correct."

"By all means officer. You will find we are employees of the authorities and our credentials are in good order."

As the officer conducted the scan, his companion stood watching Gareth and John, checking for any sign of body language indicating guilt.

"Your profiles check out, but they tell me you both work for a division not requiring you to be out at this time of night. So I ask again, what are you doing here?"

"Just talking officer. We decided to take a walk and try to get a fresh perspective on our work issue."

"You don't need to walk around to develop ideas. You are best using your energy on the thoughts and not actions. What is your level of implants?"

"The DNA scan should indicate sir."

"Um…yes. It says here you both have minimal identification and telomeres implants. Perhaps you should consider upgrading to the new mind implants. Then you will not need these inefficient night time walks to work out solutions for your work related problems."

"It is a consideration officer. We have discussed this as well, but have been so busy it has seen us overlook the upgrades."

"Well, there will be a large scale deployment of the new implants very soon, and then uptake will eventually become mandatory."

"So you are saying we cannot choose to refuse the implants."

"Precisely. It is for the better anyway. You will find yourselves less affected by emotions, and able to focus on efficient life style choices and work commitments."

"Well it sounds great," John replied careful to mask his sarcasm.

"It will be. I can schedule an implant session for you now if you like."

"It's okay. I'm sure our divisional employer will provide us with an employee scheme."

"Indeed they will. You are free to go, but go home."

"Yes officer. Let's go mate. I think I have the details we need…"

"Details?"

"Um, yes officer. I mean the solution to our problem. It seems as though this walk despite being inefficient, has assisted in working out our dilemma."

"Good. Then be on your way."

"Of course sir. Immediately."

John indicated to Gareth and the two men left the scene. After walking the two miles back to the warehouse, they both felt elated at the success of their mission, and they were finally able to relax a little.

"How about a drink of whiskey?" Gareth asked when they arrived.

"Sure. How about a few drinks of whiskey?"

"Now you're talking. All this serious side to life is taking its toll on my fun genes."

"Yeah, it can take over entirely and you lose yourself at times."

"At least it is not as permanent as losing yourself through technology implants."

"Totally agree there. You get the whiskey and I'll re-calibrate the torus so the authorities cannot detect its presence, and then hide it."

"What happens when they go to switch the lens on?" Gareth asked as he poured two large glasses.

"There is the weak point in our plan. As soon as they go to use it, they will find a non-responsive dummy in its place…"

"So they will immediately investigate."

"You can bet on it. My worry is they are going to figure out who took it fairly quickly, so it will give a lead on where to find me."

"So you are the only one who…?"

"Yeah. The only one who could remove the lens…aside from an officer trained to do the task."

"When will they try to activate the lens? It could happen tomorrow and then the authorities will be looking everywhere. They will be looking even harder for you."

"Which means I have to try my best to convince Chris to come along with us tomorrow, otherwise we will have to leave Boston and Chris behind. We cannot take any more chances. Time is very much of the essence here."

"Here mate."

"Thanks. I certainly feel like I need this. The past week or so has been far too intense."

"Sure has mate. Drink up."

The two men finished the entire bottle of whiskey over the course of about two hours, until they both fell asleep from tiredness and drunkenness.

When the sun cast a weak wintry light in through the old dirty glass window panes above them the following morning, they awoke to a vast cold empty space and feeling quite small for a moment.

"I'll check out around the exterior while you prepare the gear."

"Okay. We'll meet Chris at the arranged time, and then we leave Boston for good."

When they arrived at the co-ordinates Chris had supplied John with the day before, his son was already waiting for them. John wasted no time in proposing what he and Gareth were doing and how Chris could be included.

"Dad, I know you mean well, but I cannot just give all this up so easy."

"Why not son? You know their motives are to basically enslave the human race…even further."

"Yes, but through being employed in my position at the authorities, I can avoid it to an extent. There are more liberties available to official employees than to the general public you know."

115

"Yeah I know, but how good are these liberties? Back west, we could live free from the author…"

"But they will go there in droves dad. Since the Agent has gone, they have been eager to re-unite everywhere under their one umbrella of control. The town near San Francisco is sure to have officers all over it any time soon."

"They are already there. But I have friends there who are striving to live out of authority control as much as possible. Look…we have technology and you know I am a master at flux mechanics. We are going to be the best chance anyone has at getting past the new levels of slavery…"

"Listen to your dad Chris. He has really impressed me with his expertise and his commitment towards you. Look at how he has risked so much just to see you."

"Thanks Gareth. I know dad is smart, and dad, I really want you back in my life, but it would mean the authorities regard me as a fugitive. I don't know if I want to live on the run."

"Well think about this son. You can continue to work out your life serving the needs of the authorities for your so-called status and security, or you can take a chance and add a bit of spice to life. I know it is a dangerous proposition, but generally people have become too afraid to step out and take such chances so they have become stale and routine. Is this what you want? A stale life repeating the same work every single day until you have enough status to leave the services."

"There is always a degree of repetition with anything dad."

"Yeah, but so much? Look at it this way. How does living in a house out of the city, breathing real air, and activating your senses and instincts, compare to the same old thing every day going to and from work and consuming technology in your spare time to make it seem worthwhile?"

"It sounds good dad, but I worry about the future and how such insecurity might impact my status."

"What is a status anyway? Does it make you better than the next person? Does it bring you spontaneous happiness in response to sensations, emotions, or feelings you get?"

"I see what you say, but without it there would be so much uncertainty."

"Where is the problem? Certainty can be an illusion. The authorities could re-structure at any time and you could find yourself out of work. At least with uncertainty there is mystery and you put yourself to the test."

"I know dad, but I just don't know either. Some days I feel like my life is being wasted. The work I do is not for the good of people. I am just processing authority data really. All they want is to rule an efficient machine planet."

"Which is why I am asking you to come. Do you want to be a cog in the machine, or to strive for self-actualisation?"

"What if we all end up in jail? How good would it be then? At least by staying out of trouble, I can be a little free."

"Yeah, I suppose. You know the day in London when I cried?"

"Yes."

"I was crying not only for you, but what life is becoming. I thought I had lost you to the nanotech forever. Soon enough, people will lose themselves to the technology and become mere shells of humanity, operated in part by machine to serve a machine."

"How would I leave dad? The authorities will be watching me."

"Simple Chris. We all leave now. The three of us together just get up and get going now."

"Gee dad. I knew you would ask me again, but I did not prepare for something so immediate."

"I know it is a difficult thing for you. Consider how much new experience means to you."

"I am dad. I want to come, but…"

"But what? The issue of security?"

"I guess."

"Then let it go. Both Gareth and I don't have any security, yet we live well considering. I haven't had anything secure for years, but I survive and I experience life. Gee, Lorraine is there at the house. I have to go. Come with us…please."

"Here Chris, drink this. It might help you decide." Gareth passed a small cup of whiskey to Chris, who after an initial hesitation, then downed the drink as if it was a shot. When John saw him do this, he was able to conjure a little confidence Chris maybe was coming around, considering he had declined to drink any alcohol in recent times.

Chris sat there thinking to himself for the next five minutes as they all remained silent. John knew he had to consider his options without any further influence from the two men. It was a difficult time for all three of them. Chris would have to launch himself into the unknown, John was eager to free his son of the bind his employer had over him, and Gareth knew they would have to leave as soon as possible to avoid any chance of apprehension.

After beginning to speak a few times, then holding back, Chris finally spoke, instantly sending relief deep into John's heart. "I'll come dad. I am pretty scared but I'll give it a chance."

"Good for you Chris. I knew there was some of me inside there."

"Yeah. If only mother could see us. She would be happy."

"Yes she would. I miss her too. So then it is settled, and in order to confirm our decision, I suggest we go about starting to leave now."

"What about my things?"

"I suggest you go home and gather a few items. It is your day off today, though I don't know how you work thirteen days per fortnight. Anyway…grab some gear and food if you can and meet us back here."

"Okay. I'll see you in one hour."

"Good. See you then."

The next hour was one of the longest hours of John's life as he struggled with the idea of Chris not returning because he changed his mind, or perhaps the authorities had detained him. It was unfounded though, when Chris returned fifty-five minutes later carrying a small bag of clothes, food, and some technology.

"There are a lot of similarities between us dad. Look here."

Chris showed John his bag of hardware. Inside he found two devices Chris had built for detecting nanotechnology and for sending messages outside of the authority run data network.

"I'm impressed. Both of these will come in use. This communications device is what I was thinking of building myself. I just have not been able to find the necessary parts and now here they are. I think you are right. There are similarities between us."

"Two technical experts are better than one from my perspective."

"We'll try and live up to your expectations then Gareth. Are we good to go?"

"Yes dad."

"Yeah. I'm good John. Let's do it."

Chapter 16

Again Eric was taunted by his remaining natural thought patterns providing him a feeling of being slightly pleased with his efforts. Whilst he considered his work was progressing well, his internal mechanical implants were the actual source of this direction. Progressively over time, the implants learned the ways his remaining natural mind worked, and so they gradually began to replace him.

Realisation of this for Eric was being lost with each moment. At first he could make a distinction between his own thoughts and those directed by the mechanics, but now even deciding to make the distinction was slipping away from him.

The source for his sense of being pleased with himself, stood as an army before him in the large underground warehouse. Two thousand four hundred robots were on standby - motionless in readiness to be engaged. They had all been tested and were now ready for deployment as part of the monolithic directive project. The monolith itself was ready, as was its carrier ship, along with the hundreds of personnel who had been assigned to implement the devices the authorities would use to affect their most ambitious plan since the defeat of the Agent.

Within the next fleeting moments, Eric's mechanics directed his thoughts back to his duties. "All robotics are now ready," he said quietly into his broadcomm device on his lapel.

"Report at once in person. I require comprehensive details for presentation to senior officers."

"Acknowledged sir. I will be there in ten minutes."

"Don't delay Eric. My superiors have stressed this deployment must take place as soon as possible."

"There will be no delay sir."

Eight minutes later, Eric stood opposite his superior waiting patiently as his work was assessed.

"You have done well Eric. I can confidently make a recommendation for full deployment of the directive at any time. You are ready at any time aren't you?"

"Yes sir. I can go now if you like."

"Not so fast Eric. First we need approval and then you will have the go ahead."

"Understood sir."

"I will advise you the moment I have received a response. You are best to go and get some rest now, as I am sure this objective will involve long hours and a great deal of work."

"Yes sir."

As Eric walked the corridor towards the location of his living quarters, he thought he could sense a slight feeling of pride. It seemed to well up in him suddenly before just as suddenly, the mechanics washed it away as they told him he simply needed to sleep. Upon reaching his quarters, he immediately went to bed where he slept the following five hours to then be awoken by a request from his superior.

"Eric?"

"Yes sir."

"You have the go ahead. You may commence deployment immediately."

"Understood sir. The carrier craft is on standby. I will order the robotics to be loaded on board prior to lifting the monolith."

"Deployment of the robots is to commence once you have reached the designated altitude. They will fly won't they?"

"Beautifully…um, yes sir." Again, Eric had been taunted with expression based on emotion, but was immediately corrected by the mechanics to direct his attention only to his work. The use of descriptive language was no longer an efficient consideration for any employee who had been given the implants, and soon enough, traces of emotive input would almost be eliminated.

The implants could never entirely work without stable flux, so in each instance where Eric passed through moments of emotion as residual elements of his former self, the mechanics were actually showing their gradual decline in effectiveness. Those responsible for his implants worked even longer hours than Eric as they knew this was occurring. Many hours were spent striving to align the algorithms for the devices, but as yet, success eluded them.

"I will attend immediately if I may have your leave sir."

"Certainly Eric. Go now, but keep me informed during every stage of the deployment. I am also required to make constant reports to my superiors."

Within three hours, the craft was stationed at an altitude of thirteen thousand meters, with the blue radiant two hundred foot star suspended below its fuselage. It would not commence full radiance until just prior to deployment into the anomaly. As each of the near two thousand robots was ejected via portholes, they cast a faint blue glow on their way to their designated coordinates. The star itself though not fully ignited was blinding to anyone up close who was not equipped with either mechanical eyes, or anti glare goggles.

People below could see this operation taking place, but they were not astounded and they barely gave it any thought. To many, they saw it as the latest move by the authorities to ensure their security, so they actually welcomed the sight without any real knowledge about why or how. It appeared as though the authorities could deploy virus free hardware finally now the Agent had been overcome and they welcomed the possibilities ahead. Those who did not bother to even make these considerations, were simply attracted to the sight taking place for a moment or two, before turning away to direct their thoughts back to work or to where they were going. Only a very few in contrast to a vast majority considered the real implications for what might be occurring.

Once all robotics were despatched from the spacecraft, it immediately ascended beyond the atmosphere on a heading to the anomaly beyond the orbit of the moon. Eric stood on the bridge beside the operational flight crew with the captain, monitoring the glow coming from underneath the ship. Unveiled for the first time to most aboard and to the people who caught a glimpse of the craft prior to insertion into space, the latest authority spacecraft appeared almost holographic in places as near flux mechanical construct took it to the verge of light speed. This velocity was not in its' lineal progress – rather, the very atomic resonance properties generating a solid manifestation of spacecraft. With an atomic resonance preparing it for transition to tachyon pathways crossing the speed barrier where its' own light properties immersed within a flux state, from what appeared to be from deeper within the craft's constructed surface, emerged colours of the blackest blue accompanied with a bright electric blue identical to the star beneath.

Within four hours, the spacecraft had reached its destination. The captain then ordered an all stop so Eric could begin insertion of the star.

Once it had been disconnected from the holding energy of its' carrier craft, the star now brilliantly glowing blue and set against the purple black hues of the anomaly, was given a gentle magnetic push. On course directly towards the middle where the tunnel of magnetic plasma already showed an excited state from the star's proximity, it would only be seconds now until Eric would see his work culminate in a technological age humanity could barely have imagined less than a century before.

At the point of the anomaly's threshold, the star illuminated to full operational status casting electric blue rays all those on the scene and those who witnessed this ignition from other places in space and on the Earth, admired with a sense of awe. For those like Eric whose thoughts were directed only towards efficient work, they simply monitored statistics on holographic banks, barely casting their eyes towards the sight.

All of his calculations indicated the monolith would commence atomic generation once inside the anomaly. If the information John Matheson had provided proved to be correct, then the star would commence stable transmission of this energy back through the anomaly for uptake by the waiting robotics now in standby position. Eric knew other nations of Earth would be watching this event unfold and he knew there was nothing anyone could do to stop him. Nobody aside from the very few had access to the technology. It had not been shared and so was the sole dominion of Eric and his superiors.

"Captain. Stand by for transmission reception."

"Okay Eric, we are clear to go."

"Three, two, one."

The star disappeared entirely from view with one last flash of intense light. Within a second later, data began streaming in, visible on the vast holographic array Eric was using.

"Report Eric."

"Yes sir. The monolith is transmitting. Operations are nominal."

"The robotics?"

"Engaging now sir."

Eric sent the commands to initialise all robots waiting on standby.

"Results are as expected sir. We can begin torus initialisation."

"Then do it."

"Yes sir."

Eric entered the command for transmission of data from the robotics to every torus situated with quantum computers located in towns and cities. It occurred as the toroidal drive for the artificial star began transmitting inter-dimensional dihedral force at the golden section angle of torsion against the physical plane when measured laterally.

"And...?"

"Successful sir. All torus are now operating."

"Excellent. Your work is exemplary Eric. Instruct the captain to return to Earth immediately."

"Yes sir."

Chapter 17

Celia was very upset. She had been dreaming with Asper there beside her in the visions, but now she was fully awake and she felt frightened. Her dream was quickly receding in her mind as the impact of what upset her began to overwhelm her normally calm state. She jumped out of bed and ran to her father's room pleading for him to awaken and listen to what she had to say.

"What is it dear?"

"I am scared father. Very scared. They have done it."

"What have they done dear? And who?"

"The authorities. They have sent something into the anomaly. It is very bad father."

"Calm down dear. What do you mean they have sent something into the anomaly?"

"Ask Tim. His friend John will know. We need to contact him so he can come here quickly."

"I'm not sure we can help him get here any sooner than he can Celia. I think we can go over to Tim's house."

"Now?"

"It is very early in the morning. I am not sure they will be awake."

"It doesn't matter father. They will want to know about this. I think Asper already does."

"What do you mean?"

"We were sharing a dream again when I suddenly woke up scared. Ask her. She will know."

"Alright. I'll wake the others and we will all go over together."

"Thank you father. I will be waiting by the front gate."

Celia kept urging the adults with her to go faster as they walked to Carmel's house. By the time Esther, Derek, and Murray arrived, Celia was already inside the front gate beneath the rambling grape vine and calling out to Asper.

"Come inside," Lorraine called to them from the front door. "There is some coffee on. We need to talk."

"The anomaly isn't it?" Tim asked as he made a loud clamour bashing kitchen utensils and pots in an effort to mask their conversation from any potential eavesdropping.

"Yes Tim."

"I thought so. Asper woke me after her dream. She is just in the bathroom freshening up. She will be out in a moment."

Immediately upon seeing Asper emerge from the bathroom, Celia ran to her and grabbed her hand gripping it tightly.

"It's alright Celia. We are all safe together. You suddenly left the dream we were sharing."

Tim then interrupted Asper with a suggestion they all go outside to continue the conversation.

"The anomaly. The anomaly. Asper, they have sent something inside. The voices came to me the moment they did it. They sounded worried. Tim?"

"Yes."

"Can you call him? He needs to get here. He is the only one who can really help. Can he come faster?"

"I'm not sure Celia. He sent me a message to say he had left with his son and a man named Gareth. Travel will be dangerous for him and the others. I can contact him again and see what his plans are, but it is up to him when he gets here."

"He needs to come quickly Tim. The anomaly is going to get bad. The voices told me it will become very dangerous unless something is done."

"Come with me Celia. Let's go walk around the garden. You do like the garden. We'll leave this to the other adults to work out."

"Okay Asper. Yes I do like the garden. It is pretty."

Asper gave the others a quick glance as she lead Celia away. Her eyes settled on Tim for a moment as she indicated towards the hidden room reinforcing the urgency Celia felt. She had felt something surge inside just before the share dream had ended. Now with what Celia had just told them, she knew there was something serious happening.

"Tim must be careful. The authorities are going to be checking everything much more now. They have started something horrible."

"He will be careful dear. We all will."

"And Carmel..."

"What about Carmel?"

"She must come too. I know I haven't met her yet, but I know she is needed."

"We don't know where she is dear."

"I know. But she will feel this calling too. She must come so we can all join together. If we don't do this together, they might get away with it."

"I just hope she does come for all our sake."

"And Tim's. When they meet again, they will both shine much more than when they are apart."

"Shine?"

"Yes. Like a bright star. They are so beautiful together and they will help a lot."

A moment later, Esther came running outside looking for them. When she found them, she called them back inside saying breakfast was ready.

"First we need to have breakfast, and second, keep talk low."

"It is pink," Celia said as she crunched some toast. "I checked outside."

"Show me the torus Celia," Tim asked ten minutes later as they casually strolled about the frosty yard. Everyone could see the faint pink hue as Celia held the torus in the palm of her open hand.

"Okay. You can put it back into your pocket now Celia. I think we have all seen the lovely colour."

"The colour is lovely Tim, but it is a bad sign. The voices told me to warn you and anyone else about it being activated. It is a false torus Tim. Do you know what it means?"

"Yes I do Celia. It was made by the authorities and appears to now be connected to their network somehow."

"Yes, but it is false because it is not a true representation of the real torus. The one your friends have."

"The authorities have a lot of these I suspect Celia. They use them to power the tiny computers they have put in place to control energy and other things..."

"The way people communicate. They will use them to make big changes Tim. The voices said if they succeed with using these torus, then there will be very hard times ahead for people."

"There have been plenty of hard times since..."

"Much worse than what they did just before I was born Tim. And there might not be any way to stop them."

"I think John will try."

"And you must help him, along with all the adults." Celia looked into the eyes of all present in turn as if she was talking to them without words. Asper picked up on this the most as if Celia was able to communicate strong feelings this way. "And...Carmel needs to come back to her house. I wish she was here too, and the man you told me about. Ch, ch..."

"Chan Lee. Yes he was very wise and helpful. He will know what to do."

"We need him to be here. There is going to be a lot of energy and he knows how to control it."

"Okay Celia. I think we have talked about this enough now. Why don't you go with Esther and take Asper and Lorraine for a walk into town, while Tim and Murray and I talk about what we need to do."

"Alright father. Good idea. Come on Esther." Celia had taken both Asper and Lorraine by the hand, leading them out to the front gate.

"See you soon then."

"Yes father. We will not be long."

As they walked through the streets in the middle of town, the three women and Celia noticed the increase in activity with people about. Aside from there being more officers of the authorities around, a number of new families appeared to be settling into houses they were being directed to by the officers. When one of the officers noticed the small wandering group, he came over to speak directly to them. As soon as he was close enough, they recognised him as the quieter of the two officers who had visited them a few days before.

"How are you today?"

"Um, well thanks," Lorraine replied. The other two women nodded in agreement, but Celia was just staring at the man.

"As you can see, things in this town are changing now. The authorities are moving in right across the west. We have finally closed the case on the Agent."

"No you haven't," Celia said keeping the same straight face.

"What do you mean little girl? The Agent is in prison and now the authorities are taking back all of the places he ruled over for too long."

"Yes, but he is not finished. I know enough about him to think he will try bad things again."

"But he is in prison, far below the ground and out of the way where the authorities can control him and study him."

"Only for now. He is too bad to give up easily."

"We will see. Anyway, I just came over to tell you to stay away from trouble. The authorities are watching you and any others they think will be a threat. Just stay safe. I like you. I am not like my superiors..."

"I know. I can feel it. We will be okay. Thanks for the information." Celia had taken over the conversation, leaving the adults a little lost for words.

"Just remember what I told you," the officer said as he walked away shaking his head. Celia had caused him to feel and think for a moment as she had done previously in a challenge to his normal composure, but all the efforts he made to shake free of this did nothing with her presence staying with him for the rest of the day and beyond. She had an affect he was unable to describe, and whilst it was unsettling, he also found it comforting in a way.

"Let's keep walking. I want to get away from this part of town," Celia said in such a way the adults just followed her without question.

"What is the matter Celia?"

"Oh nothing much Esther. I guess it is the scary things I have been feeling. And the officer. He is waking up and it makes me think about how many others might be waking up."

"Waking up?"

"Yes. Ask Asper. She knows what I am talking about. I think Lorraine might know too."

Esther looked at the other two women searching for answers. From the look on Asper's face, she began to realise what Celia was talking about.

"See. They know about it. It doesn't matter anyway. You are already waking up Esther. It is part of the reason we are here in this town."

"I think I know...or feel what you are talking about dear. Where shall we go? You seemed eager to get away from here."

"Yes I do. Let's go for a walk around the edge of town. We can see how many people are moving here then."

Asper and Lorraine agreed a walk on the edge of town would be good and take them away from the watchful eyes of the authorities.

"Do you remember our dream together this morning Asper?"

"Yes I do Celia. It was a lovely dream."

"Hmm, yes it was. We were dreaming about beautiful people without hate or greed or anger."

"Yes I remember. The fields of flowers were lovely too."

"It was like the dream we first shared. I think we have something we both like to create the same thing in our minds."

"A lot of people would like what we see in our dreams."

"Yes they would, but this is different."

"In what way Celia?"

"It is because we are waking up and we are beginning to remember ourselves properly."

"Funny how our dreams show we are waking up."

"Often it can be this way Asper. Our dreams are just the first thing. All the rest will follow soon."

"All the rest. What do you mean?"

"The voices will come for you too and for others. Then we will all begin to listen to them when we are awake."

"Really awake or..."

"Yes. During the day and at any time."

"Why would the voices do this Celia? And do you know where they come from?"

"They just will, and the voices are from places I do not know other than they are inside us and all around us."

"Well we will wait and see then."

"Yes we will. When they come properly, it will be a very good thing. They will help us too, but we also need Carmel."

"We don't know where she is dear," Esther added.

"It does not matter Esther. She knows where we are. Um, well not really, but we are at her house and she will return here because it is in her heart."

"I see."

Chapter 18

"Gunter! What is going wrong? Such inefficiencies cannot be tolerated."

"I do not know sir. All data appears to be nominal. The monolith is on the planned trajectory. I cannot explain it."

"Is there any news on Matheson? Perhaps he could help you. This is an unremarkable failure Gunter. Even my superiors can see there is something wrong."

"No news on Matheson yet sir. We have officers scouring all conceivable ways he could escape, and we have operatives in places he could likely frequent."

"It is not good enough. The readouts show instability at a minimum within the anomaly, but it is growing. What else can you suggest?"

"I will go through all of the data until I have an answer sir. As long as it takes..."

"Yes you will Gunter. I want answers already. This incompetence is unforgivable. You said Matheson had nailed all there was to know about flux mechanics."

"Yes I did sir. Matheson is the most prolific in this area of research. Very few others come close."

"How close, and who?"

"Some of our scientists could assist with this problem, but they are far behind Matheson in knowledge of flux."

"Who else?"

"The only other person I know who might be able to help with vortex amplification is...is..."

"Spit it out Gunter!"

"Um, the Agent sir. He acquired a good deal of knowledge on flux over the years..."

"He is a very high security risk. How could we use him?"

"Admittedly he is a high risk, but I could take measures to ensure risk mitigation sir."

"Well take them. I have had enough of failures already and I want this technology working. But do not allow the Agent any leeway. I want as many personnel as possible monitoring him every time he takes a breath. Do you understand me Gunter?"

"Yes sir."

"In the mean time, see to it all flux robotics are working according to phase one of planning. Bring the entire network into control mode."

"Control mode is on standby sir. I can confirm all localised operations for all robotic sites are ready with systems initialised at level one."

"Then take them off readiness and deploy the first phase...and get the Agent onto this...now. Otherwise you might find yourself staring at level one status Gunter."

"Yes sir. I will attend immediately." Eric could feel a faint sense of what it would mean to descend to lower status, but it was a mere faint sense as his internal mechanics focused him on the tasks ahead. As quickly as his personal feelings arose they were suppressed, with only a slight sense of fear remaining.

The scientists continuously working on updating internal mechanics for all those with implants had been instructed to include a degree of fear. This last vestige of humanity was one of the darkest, and those who were of darkness in high office had decided it would be an efficient method to prompt compliance for all those who managed to reckon with any sense of their remaining self.

Eric knew he must go to the Agent now and attempt to extract anything he could provide about vortex amplification. Whilst his assistants had provided valuable insight and support during the development of the monolithic directive, they could only do so much in theoretical test scenarios.

Eric interrupted his actions for a moment, instructing covert operations to broaden their search for John. Knowledge he possessed would be the only solution – anything from the Agent would be a short term measure.

Now without Matheson at hand, the Agent was the only person possessing knowledge of vortex amplification surpassing some of Eric's own. In preparation for engagement with the most notorious criminal the authorities and most of the world had known in the past century, Eric collated data for the Agent's assessment and recommendation. He was not nervous in any way as his internal mechanics simply would not allow such inefficiency. Rather, Eric was poised to make demands from the Agent without any sense of submission.

The Agent relied on others to submit to his presence such was his megalomania, and Eric was in no way prepared to do such a thing. All of his work was about to rest on the shoulders of the most despised person known to be alive, and whilst Eric had no real sense of dislike for this fact, he knew his status was under threat. For Eric to lose status, it would mean relegation to a far more inferior level as a scientist bored with the mundane repetitiveness of processing work other scientists of status had completed. This itself was again a failure of his nanotech self as he momentarily thought of status in an egotistical sense. A battle was beginning within – one Eric could not ignore much longer. Dare he reveal to those monitoring his mind of his personal feelings and status as such could become irrelevant. Now almost in second nature, Eric was beginning to be aware of his mechanical self aside from his true identity or reckoning and so was in turn manipulating this emerging duality.

The Agent was located in the deepest cell within the complex, twenty stories beneath New York City. Eric walked the long passageways deep underground struggling at times with himself and the mechanics in his mind.

When he finally arrived at the outer door leading to the hallway for passage to the Agent's cell, he had reached a state of urgency within based on the scale of conflict in his work and also of inside his workings. His mannerisms and patience reflected this state of being as he demanded the guards give him access to the Agent. The moment the Agent saw Eric, he knew Eric was in a less than optimal state, and therefore open to manipulation.

"What do you want? I don't get visitors. Have the authorities decided to relax and allow me something resembling human contact?" The Agent was looking directly into Eric's eyes seeing immediately they were non-human.

"I am not here on a visit. And no, the authorities have not decided to allow contact for you. I need your advice about some technical issues."

"I know, otherwise you would not be here. Let me guess. Is it vortex amplification?"

"Yes. We have a slight issue with stabil..."

"Stability is not a slight issue."

"Well yes."

"Ha ha. The anomaly. You are responsible for it. I know. The only other person you could talk to is Matheson. I could kill him after what he did to me."

"You would have to find him first."

"Ah, so he escaped you then. You could not have built the anomaly without him and now it is not working...but he has escaped and you have nobody else to turn to but me."

"You could say so."

"I just have you idiot. Don't screw with me though. I am prepared to die and get this over and done with at any time. You bastards have been keeping..."

"Oh save us the rhetoric George."

The Agent hated anyone using his real name, and he already hated Eric, so this just made him more determined to manipulate him at the first opportunity. "What makes you think I will help you?"

"Nothing makes me think this George. I have orders and you are to obey every..."

"Obey! We will see."

"Enough! You are to come with me now so we can analyse this data I have prepared."

Two guards fell in beside the Agent on either side as Eric led them all to his holographic bank for commencement of work on solving the problem.

When they reached Eric's workstation, the Agent immediately began to analyse the situation. His mind was already nearing overdrive looking for any means to gain advantage. Eric knew it would be a difficult assignment to work with the Agent – now confirmed during these first few moments. As he considered the best way to approach extracting information, his nanotech implants began to take over with logical thought patterns to accommodate any problems.

"As you can see with this holographic data, there is a change in the instability within the anomaly since insertion of the monolith."

"The vortex is unstable to begin with. By adding this thing you have built is only going to amplify the instability."

"Yes, I realise. I need you to look at these algorithms and determine a path ahead so we can make gradual adjustments to..."

"Why gradual? I have never liked gradual. It is always too slow. Why not bring it in line immediately?"

"It would cause a rupture in the progressive manifestation of particles approaching light speed, which would send them off course from the projected beyond light pathways of tachyon emissions."

"Ah, on a path to oblivion. Show me the specific data on the monolith's cycle."

"Here."

"And what is this other data you have running simultaneously? Oh I see. You sent a space craft in there previously. Was it my space craft?"

"No. And it was never your space craft."

"Yes it was...for quite a few years."

"We analysed the modifications you made to it as well as the amplifier you built. It is what brought you here. You certainly learned a lot during those years."

"Not enough so it would seem, otherwise I would not be here now."

"You might think so. Anyway, what is your approach?"

"I will need time to analyse data in respect to the constant required to hold the vortex or anomaly as you call it."

"And then?"

"How can I tell you? You already ask stupid questions. I am surprised you are in charge of this project. And your eyes. Where can I get those?"

"One thing at a time George."

The second he heard his name used again, the Agent spoke sounding infuriated, "Don't use my name!"

"Why George?" Eric's mind mechanics were guiding him through this conversation with his choice of language coming from live updates well behind the scene. "Now I have your attention fully, I want you to work on the algorithm."

"Well it is why I was brought here in the first place."

"Yes it is, so get to work."

"Indeed I will." The Agent was feeling a bit smitten given his covert nature and the plans he was already conjuring for escape from the clutches of the authorities.

"We'll be watching you." Eric knew the extent to which the Agent was a threat and what it would mean for him if the Agent was to undermine his efforts in any way.

'And I will be watching you,' he said to himself.

Eric left the Agent under guard to initialise phase one as ordered by his superior officer. Within an hour, all systems were operational and for the first time in years, reliable transport became available to the population for domestic and international travel. Life for many would now return to a semblance of normality with society being restored to the new type of order the authorities were building. After years of suffering and deprivation, people could now begin to feel confident the authorities were there to provide for them again with a new type of deprivation and suffering unbeknown to the their otherwise pre-occupied minds.

Chapter 19

Celia was playing casually with the dodecahedron and the torus as she thought about the dream her and Asper had shared the night before. Everyone was gathered at Carmel's house discussing what life may be like now the authorities had restored power.

"They will bring us holographic broadcast vision today," Celia said without looking at anyone else in the room. She remained focused on the two objects in both of her hands and it took two attempts from Tim asking her how she knew this before he was able to draw her attention away from them.

"Celia, how do you...?"

"Sorry Tim. They will bring one today for this house and for all of the other houses. Ask Asper. We shared a dream last night and we both saw them go through town handing things out."

Tim looked to Asper whose expression confirmed what Celia had said. "They will Tim. Trust her."

"Then we should prepare. It was no doubt inevitably anyway. Installation of holographic vision will incur some type of system to monitor all those who tune in."

"They won't tune in Tim. The vision will be on all day and night. People will begin to live by holographic vision like they used to."

"You seem to be a step ahead of everything Celia."

"Um, well if it means I know things before they happen, you might say so. But it is the voices and the dreams really telling me and Asper. And it is sensible."

"Tell us more about the dream dear."

"Asper can tell you. I am going to play." Celia suddenly left the adults to discuss this news by running throughout the garden to stop and gently touch icicles hanging from tree branches.

"We dreamed the same thing again. I think Celia feels why this is happening more than thinking about why it is happening. I am trying to come to terms with it myself, but in my typical adult ways, I am analysing too much I think. She just feels it and being a child, she is not trained in such analytical ways."

"A good thing for her I suppose."

"Anyway. A lot of the stuff in the dreams is about healing the Earth and ourselves. The images present as ways to let go of our ego telling us to analyse, and to just open up to the patterns of life and nature surrounding us."

"Why do you think she was so intent just now playing with the two objects Asper?" Derek asked.

"I can only guess, but to me and I suppose more so to her, they represent life force and energies of creation. We did talk about them once, and from what I gather, she likes them as they keep her in touch with these, these..."

"Of course! Sorry to interrupt Asper," Lorraine said looking for forgiveness. "The torus is like the one Chan and the others sought. It is called the Torus of Eternity and represents life being eternal in elemental progression."

"Yes the torus does represent this aspect."

"I wonder where they are."

"Don't wonder Lorraine. They will come here." Celia had returned quietly unbeknown to the adults. "But I told you. The men are here now with a holographic viewer. I saw them coming down the road."

"Okay dear. We should leave now," Esther interjected.

"I agree. Come on Murray."

"Yeah...coming."

"We'll see you later today then as planned...for dinner?"

"Sure."

Celia was right. The authorities wasted no time installing the holographic vision devices in all houses considered liveable – those with occupants and those yet to be filled.

At the end of the day, they all gathered for dinner together as planned. Celia was delighted to see Tim, Asper, and Lorraine appear just beyond the front gate. She welcomed them in staying beside Asper the entire time. She could sense her sensitivity from their shared dreams and thoughts and from her distractions with the news of John where this led her to think of Tobias.

"They came to this house not long after we returned this morning," Derek said as he, Murray, and Esther came outside to greet them. "What do you think about these viewers Tim?"

"Far more advanced than the holographic banks of the past. We have good reason to suspect everything more or less. I would think the authorities are bent on intruding into the everyday lives of people much more than they have previously."

"They are," Asper said looking towards Celia.

"Yes. They want control and the anomaly is part of it too."

"I can only guess at this stage, it has something to do with them using the anomaly for some power source. John would not have given them true flux mechanics, and...he would have made sure they did not know it at the time."

"It is what the voices say. You must work hard on this Tim. They are worried about what might happen. The anomaly is dangerous to them too."

"If only he was here now. Last time he made contact with me he said they had made it almost all the way to where the perimeter dividing fence was."

"They must have opened access through the fence by now. Those afflicted with viruses the Agent would have been collected. Hmm, it sounds harsh, but what else would they have done?" Murray said looking a little embarrassed at his almost cold words.

"We can only imagine Murray." Esther looked at Celia and then back to the other adults as if to say not to explore too much detail on the subject. Esther and Derek had shielded her from a lot of the details about what had happened around the world since she had been born, figuring it would be in her best interests to remain naive to it all.

"The voices say they can fix those bad things."

"Oh do they dear? Anyway, let us go inside and eat. I'm sure we are all famished by now considering it is well past a normal dinner time."

"Lead the way Esther."

They all kept discussion of any details to a minimum after Tim once again reminded them they had let slip with too much already with the discussion of John, despite being outside the house.

On the other side of the continent, travel had been difficult for the trio since they had left Boston. Whilst they had remained clear of the authorities, they found the going slow and tough. HyperJet travel was too risky and so they had made their way any way they could. Without any transport readily available, they were resigned to seeking out people in the darkest corners of towns and cities in the hope they could find someone with access to finding them a ride.

When the main transport routes did begin to open up again, they were restricted to public transport transit tubes. This meant John had to continually update their false identification DNA profiles in order to avoid leaving any trace of a group travelling so distant. This troubled him as he considered the biometrics units they would be using for facial recognition, so he suggested they should look at disguising themselves. By the time they had reached Omaha in the former state known as Nebraska, they were exhausted.

The authorities now disbanded all sense of individuality and they had started by changing society into one collective territory, thus erasing all previous state borders. John took them to the house Tobias once occupied, only to find it was now occupied by new tenants as part of the drive to re-populate essential areas with authority employees. His disappointment showed clearly to the other two men – the first instance where they grasped a sense of this from him during the entire journey.

Whilst relatively stoic in character, he had counted on staying there for a short time to work on some technology collected along the way from Boston. Now he would be without a workshop to re-invent devices as weapons and communications hardware. He still had the small quantum device used to contact Tim, but he knew as soon as the authorities brought the first phase of flux mechanical robotics on line, they would be able to trace every time he used the small device.

"Dad. What about the farm you once stayed at? Maybe it will be free."

"Good idea son. I had overlooked it entirely. We'll get there before dark if we leave now."

"Well let's go then," Gareth replied. "I'll spearhead this mission if you direct me. You look tired mate. I'll keep a watch out as we go."

The fence was indeed gone. The watch tower was gone, and Tobias was gone. As they left, John thought long about his friend feeling a sense of sadness at times not knowing of Tobias' fate. Upon seeing the house where Tobias used to live where he broke through the fence with Kerry-Ann not so long ago, John felt such a moment of sorrow. "We need to go around the outskirts and head north. It is about twelve miles further."

"Okay mate. I'll lead. You and Chris follow. Keep a look out Chris, your dad needs a rest."

When they arrived at the farm, night had just fallen and luckily it was still unoccupied. They had a small stock of food supplies, so John directed them to the barn he had stayed in previously with Tobias and Kerry-Ann. Immediately after they had a meal and then they all fell into a deep sleep.

As they slept, officers of the authorities were en-route towards the recently dismantled fence gate. They had established John's previous access through the fence during his escape from the western sector, and considered it a likely place he might try again.

Next morning dawned very cold and icy. Snow lay about here and there, but the cold temperature defied the lack of a deep snowy appearance to the landscape. John estimated it must have been at least ten below freezing as the three men shivered over a cold meal of biscuit and dried fruits.

"We need to stay here at least a day or two so I can build a device to get us around the new mechanics the authorities have deployed."

"A rest will do us good. We have barely stopped since we left."

"Yeah...but, they will look everwhere for us, including here. We need to be vigilant."

"What then dad? We will have to find some transport. This route is the only main one for miles around. I guess it is why you brought us here."

"It is...and I was hoping to stay at Tobias' house as you know. The only other option is to head north and take the public transit tube from there."

"What about the disguise you mentioned?"

"I have been thinking about it Gareth. What do you suggest though? These beards help but to avoid facial recognition entirely means we need to re-shape our faces...bone structure."

"Yeah it is a hard one to counteract. Chris and I will think on it while you work on your device thing."

"Okay. Maybe we could find some type or temporary thing to just get us past checkpoints for the transit."

"I was thinking the same. First thing is we could look for some clay. I noticed the soil here is pretty hard packed, so maybe there is some we could use."

"Sounds very temporary to me."

"We need to try it John."

After searching nearly all day, Gareth and Chris had found some clay and had also searched the abandoned farm house where they located some applicator implements they imagined a woman who had lived there in the past would have used.

"How is the hardware coming along dad?"

"Good Chris. I'll be finished today in fact. What about our disguises?"

"Gareth and I have found a few things to help us. I think we should be able to affect sufficient face changes to make it through the check points."

"Good. I have a feeling we need to leave here as soon as possible which means tonight."

"Well, we also found something to help us there. Chris and I came across some old rusty bicycles in another shed..."

"Oh, I remember those. I saw them when I was here last. Are they good to ride?"

"Yeah. Four of them are good, if not a little rickety. But I reckon we could ride them for a while before they fall apart. There was even an old pump for the tires."

"Well done. So it is a night bike ride then. Let me finish up here and then we should eat."

"Agreed. Chris and I will prepare this disguise stuff so we can apply it as soon as we are ready to go..."

"We won't need it tonight Gareth. It is going to be a few nights of riding until we get to the transit tube. Get it ready for then."

The bikes were indeed a shaky ride all the way until on the third night of riding by moonlight, they saw the transit tube in the distance - its' lights a beacon in the otherwise grey landscape.

"Right. We stay here until mid morning and then we walk to the tube. I hope there is an entry point here in this town, otherwise we will have to ride until we find one."

When the time to enter the transit tube approached, the three men went about disguising themselves.

"Hey watch it son."

"Sorry dad. I'm not used to this kind of thing."

"I'm sure none of us are. It was a good idea to send Gareth ahead to see if there is an entry point here. How you holding up mate?"

"Not bad. I sure wonder how women could ever stand to have muck all over their face back in the past."

"Yeah. Since the advent of nanotech, they probably agree with you now they no longer wear makeup. I don't know how they did it either."

"Okay dad. I've finished now. We are all set to go."

Three bearded men with their faces altered and half covered in scarves to keep out the bone chilling cold, approached the transit. As they made their way to the DNA scanner, they all kept their minds focused on remaining calm. The scanners were equipped with sensors to alert the authorities if anyone presented as nervous or anxious to detect anyone who could be acting suspiciously. John had given Chris and Gareth a quick lesson on focusing their minds – something he had learned in the days of incarceration by the authorities.

"You three there. Remove those scarves!"

"Yes sir," Chris replied as they all did as they were being told. Fortunately the officer did not look any closer at the three men, confident the facial and DNA scanners would do their work. Within a minute, all three were comfortably seated inside the public transport carriage for the long trip west along with other people were also taking the same trip as part of authority efforts to re-populate the west.

"Not so bad," was all John said careful to not say anything possibly deemed suspicious. Chris and Gareth merely nodded in agreement and the instant the doors to the carriage were closed, the transport quickly accelerated away.

At the last moment prior to approaching the transit, John was able to upload images of their recast faces as part of their DNA profile file. He was happy with himself seeing his work fool the authority systems as a plan well devised and executed. He had also added credits to their false identities using the new devices, sufficient for them to purchase travel all the way to Seattle.

"Citizens. Welcome to the new west. This journey will take all who have been allocated new residences to their designated connection point for re-settlement. Paying passengers are advised to register themselves once they reach their intended destinations. All citizens must comply with orders for using this transport."

"I see they have not decided on being polite or..."

"Don't talk about it Gareth. We'll just sit here and have the odd conversation as if to appear natural."

"Understood. Let's hope it is a bit warmer where we are going, and out of this thing. It stinks. What is the smell?"

"Electrical burning. Maybe because it is new."

Since the destruction of Reno with a delimited nuclear event almost six years prior, all travel to the west was restricted to passage via Denver and Salt Lake City before it turned northward to Seattle. The only other route was southerly from Denver then through the former state of New Mexico, and on to Los Angeles. They had decided the northerly route was more to their liking, avoiding the masses of people and the authorities centred on the Los Angeles region.

When the transport stopped for a short while at Boise in the former state of Idaho, John felt a degree of sorrow for his lost friend Tobias again.

"What is it dad?" Chris asked seeing the downward expression come across his father.

"It's Tobias. We met up in Boise back in eighty eight on our way to San Francisco. I suppose it is those memories and..."

"I understand. Maybe he is still alive or he could be looking for us."

"I only wish it were true son. I am sure he was taken by the authorities to be implanted with technology just after we were captured in South America."

"I'm sorry dad."

"Thanks. Anyway, we must look on the brighter side. If we ever do find him again, perhaps we'll have the means to liberate him from the technology."

"We must look on the brighter side. After all, you have convinced Chris to come with us. There is a start."

"You're right Gareth."

An announcement advising the transport would be departing within the minute ended their conversation, once again reminding them to keep quiet as they boarded the carriage for the last leg of the journey.

Just over two hours later, they could see the outskirts of Seattle. The city came more and more into view as they neared, yet it held a silent gloom as opposed to its once sparkling grandeur. Most of the central towers had damage and all still were coated in matte black at the Agent's doing. He chose this sombre shade to reflect his own self, and to deprive the people of any light in reflection.

When the three men disembarked, they immediately went to register their intention to travel south.

"And what is your reason for deciding to travel to San Francisco?" an officer asked them as they stood at the registration desk.

"I used to live there some years ago and we all thought it would be a good place to re-settle and offer our services to work re-building the city," John replied.

"What services are they? You do realise all employment is subject to authority approval."

"Yes sir. I can offer my skills with engineering," John replied.

"And you two?"

"I am also skilled with data engineering and I thought the authorities could use any personnel they could get to assist in re-building," Chris replied.

"And you?"

"I am a chef, but I also have other skills and aptitude I am sure the authorities could make good use of."

"Well. We are not really going to need any chefs at any time. You do know all foods will be provided on a ration basis by the authorities don't you?"

"Yes."

"Well then, what are your other 'aptitude' skills?"

"I am a hard worker and I have ability to quickly assimilate information and then get to work."

"Hmm. I like your choice of word there, assimilate. Okay, you can proceed, but be sure to register with the authorities as soon as you arrive so you can be allocated residential premises."

"Certainly sir. Will they be using the high rise like it was used in the past?"

"Only some sections. The Agent destroyed a lot of the good work the authorities had completed to look after people. You will most likely be allocated residence in one of the outer buildings."

"Great. The sooner we can settle, the sooner we can get to work. It is great how the authorities are now working so well to restore the damage done by the Agent."

"Indeed it is. You may proceed."

All three men had managed this contact well, ensuring they kept their heads a little bowed and at angle.

"Oh, you can remove those scarves now. It is nowhere near as cold down south."

"Thank you sir."

John led them to the connecting transit, eager to board quickly and be away from any prying eyes of the authorities.

"We were lucky the officer did not have mechanical eyes. They have in-built scanners. Otherwise we could have been in a difficult situation."

"But soon all of their officers will be equipped. We were told this at work just two weeks ago."

"Then lucky you came with us son."

"It was part of my decision dad. Sure, I was hesitant for many reasons and also in a bit of conflict wanting to be with you, but the thought of more implants was the catalyst for my decision really."

"And a good one. How could your dad have looked into your eyes if they were those stupid machines?"

"I'm sure it would not have been good at all. Quite heart breaking Gareth. Well, here we are. Let's get aboard. They have repaired these transit tubes well. I think the trip will be about as long as from Boise to Seattle. All of this will become a bit harder for us again when we leave San Francisco. I can imagine the only settlers outside the city are being allocated by the authorities, so we are going to have to avoid the next round of scrutiny and interrogation."

As the transport approached San Francisco, they could all see the damage the Agent had brought upon the once beautiful bay city. Buildings lay in ruins everywhere, with just a few still standing unaffected by his rampages. When they drew closer, they could see why the high rise would only have limited occupancy for some time, as three of the eight towers lay in ruins, and the remaining five were being re-built. Only a few sections of the many floors in each appeared to be unaffected. There were no longer any usable elevated passageways between them, and the city sky was devoid of the Jetcab traffic so often a feature of the past as it buzzed people here and there.

"Once we are directed to the registration desk, we follow orders like all these other people. Then after registration we are likely to be directed to a transport for a trip to an allocated residence. Once we reach there, we are going to have to find a way to avoid the compulsory order for new settlers to remain in residence until we are called to then be assigned work duties."

"But won't it raise suspicion dad?"

"I have thought of it as we travelled from Seattle. We are going to have to find somewhere to hide during the time so I can create data records for us. If all goes well, the automated system will not even call us up as it will register us as having been allocated employment."

"Always a step ahead John."

"Yeah, it pays to think well in advance Gareth. But I also need you to take on finding us some method of transport north out of the city whilst I work on those dummy data records."

"Yeah sure. What about us having to stay at this home they allocate?"

"I am going to enter some data to provide you access outside at this time. This work will take me a few hours, so I will do you first so you can get under way. Once you find something or not, come back after a few hours and we will take it from there."

"Okay. Well here is the registration desk. How is my mask doing?"

"All good as far as I can tell. And ours?"

"You could never tell those slight alterations to you cheek bones were even there."

As soon as they presented to the desk, the officer was able to access data on each of them, and so this process took only a few minutes before they were sent on their way to a residence at the western side of the city block near the old Golden Gate Park. When they reached this destination, they stood staring for a few moments at the now wrecked famous red bridge further to the west.

"It will have to be re-built entirely by the looks of it."

"Yeah, I reckon so Chris. John, what will we do for food? Being a food person myself, it tends to often be a thought for me."

"The authorities will have provided some food stuffs inside, but don't count on them being any of the chef's delights you have been used to Gareth."

"Not unless you think protein supplements are corde en bleu," Chris added with a little laughter seeing the discord come across Gareth's face. "Don't worry Gareth."

By evening, Gareth had returned with news he had located a vehicle at least twenty years old in a warehouse about a mile from where they were.

"I checked it over and it appears to be operational, even the fuel cell."

"Good. I'll need to check the cell. If it hasn't been used in a long time, it is going to need some refurbishment before a re-charge."

"How will you charge it John?"

"With this." John showed them a small anode cell he had brought with them from Boston.

"Always a step ahead."

"You can be sure I will be...need to be. We'll go after the curfew the authorities have in place. Say around ten."

As a hush closed over the city, the three men made their way to the warehouse where John quickly set to work restoring charge to the fuel cell whilst Chris and Gareth stood watch. Within half an hour he was able to start the vehicle. As soon as he had it running, he ran to the others to tell them the good news.

"I have it working. Good news is we can move."

"And the bad news dad?"

"Actually driving this thing out of the city without being caught. This will be a make or break for us. If the authorities see us then they will not overlook..."

"Dad. Why don't you build a data algorithm to fool them?"

"Of course. Gee, I must be getting vague in my old age. I had completely overlooked the idea."

"Hey, you're not old dad. You've just been very busy. How long do you think it will take to build the algorithm?"

"About an hour. I have to key into the systems using this quantum device and retrieve the necessary schematics from analysing the build of the vehicle and then insert the data."

"Then get to it man. Chris and I will keep watch again."

An hour later as they sped at top speed over the Bay Bridge, an officer of the authorities watched their transit on her holographic array. The vehicles credentials checked out in the system, but she wondered why such an old vehicle would be making the journey at this time. She entered the vehicle identification codes to initiate a full check, and luckily for the three passengers, John had foreseen this event, and so he had created an entire dummy data file as if the journey had been officially logged and approved. When she was satisfied the use of this old technology was just an efficient measure, she gave it no more attention and returned to normal duties.

Two hours before dawn, John, Chris, and Gareth were standing beside the road after having just hidden the vehicle in thick undergrowth amongst one of the last remaining sequoia forests five miles from the town north of San Francisco.

"I have killed all operations for this vehicle at this time," he told them as they began the walk the last leg of the journey. "As far as anyone could tell, this vehicle simply broke down and could no longer proceed. I left a log entry for the supposed officers who were driving it, saying they were returning to San Francisco via the transit tube. Luckily it was such old technology. It was a good find Gareth. If it had been any one of the new vehicles they have developed using the flux information I gave them, it would be immediately tracked by the system, but due to its' age, there is not the same capacity for data reconciliation."

"Do you think our progress has been too easy dad?"

"Such thoughts did enter my mind. I cannot be sure, but we are just going to have to go with it so far, but...remain vigilant. We don't want to put the others at risk."

"But surely we are already. And what will happen if the authorities do find this vehicle and then see the two supposed officers did not return by the transit?"

"The vehicle was a necessary risk, so we will have to wait and see. And yes, we may have put the others at risk but the authorities probably do not have any knowledge of my history in this town.

"They'll do a lot to get you back from what you have told us," Gareth added mirroring Chris' concerns.

"You're right. Their inroads into inexhaustible energy using flux mechanics would be showing instability and since I am the only real expert in this area, they would be frantic by now."

"Could they get the information from anyone else?"

"Their scientists don't have near enough knowledge about flux to fix the problem. The only other person who might come close due to his exploits trying out vortex amplification is..."

"The Agent?"

"Yes. But...even he could not fully rectify the problem."

"It would be very risky if they use him though, wouldn't it?"

"So long as he remains in custody. Otherwise, if he escapes then the whole world will be involved."

"Why?"

"He no doubt would have spent many days and weeks...even months conjuring up some type of means to escape them and return to his megalomaniac ways. He is smart enough to know what to look for and advance his knowledge of flux, so if he goes free, he'll no doubt put it to use. And you never know if he would have made some secretive store or the like for him to return to. His operations covered a lot of places. I don't think the authorities are likely to have covered them all as yet."

As the sun breached the horizon lighting up the frosty ground about the town, Celia awoke with a cry of joy. She ran to her father's room, waking him up with her exclamations. "Father, father, he is..." She stopped herself short remembering it was likely their house was being bugged. Instead, she went over to his bed as he rubbed his eyes and whispered into his ear. "John is here. I know he is."

"Okay dear. Go and wake the others. Maybe we can all go to Carmel's house for breakfast."

Half an hour later, they were discussing what Celia had said to her father. Lorraine was visibly moved and appeared to be distracted, far away in thought. Asper shared her feelings and thoughts, and for a while held on to the idea Tobias might be with John.

When John, Chris, and Gareth did appear from around the back of the house shortly after, her hopes were dashed. Lorraine felt a sense of both joy and dismay at seeing John and at seeing her friend this way, and so drew her into the hug she gave John and Chris. After introductions had then been made, they all went back inside to eat.

Holographic vision was playing as they sat enjoying the meal. Propaganda bulletins about the authorities restoring order and encouraging compliance for all people, were showing.

"Don't believe a word of..."

"Quiet Chris," Celia said to him.

He looked at her with a slightly puzzled look on his face, but after looking around at the other adults, he quickly realised it was best to keep quiet near technology.

They all turned back to the broadcast again for a moment then as the news service began advising travel was now available to international destinations.

Chapter 20

Carmel felt restless. Life in Peru at the farm near Arequipa had been trouble free since capture of the Agent who had terrorised them when seeking return of the Torus of Eternity. On this day, she was perusing the marketplace in the city with Raynie, Jenna, and Lyle, looking for some electrical parts they could use. In contrast to her usual attentiveness, she was distracted from their shopping as they walked the city streets.

"This could be an end to our relying on steam power," Lyle commented when the group had stopped at a street corner whilst an announcement about services being restored by the authorities was playing.

"I kind of like the steam though," Raynie added - her sentimentality for old things was as strong as ever. "It does have a romantic element." She looked towards Carmel seeking her agreement. Carmel's small steam engine had been her only treasured possession since she had restored it, but Carmel appeared to be far away in thought and did not return her look. "What is it Carmel?"

"I'm not sure Raynie. Something is bothering me...an unsettled feeling. I feel both good and bad, as if there is a significant positive event on our horizon, yet with it will also come a lot of danger."

Her words stopped Jenna and Lyle who were talking quietly to each other. The mention of danger drew their attention. Whilst life had been fairly sedate living on the farm in the valley, they were aware danger could present at any time, particularly as Chan possessed the actual pink diamond Torus of Eternity.

"Is it to do with the torus?"

"Well sort of Lyle. Not directly though. All I can say is I have a distinct urge to return to my house in California."

"Or what used to be according to the announcement with North America now a collective territory without any borders any longer."

"I am concerned about it too Lyle. It can only mean the authorities are clamping down on individual distinction from the very top level. Taking away any sense of individuality from the collective whole is their objective...it always has."

"A paradox in a way. Where humanity could do with some collective thinking and feeling for its' own good, the authorities are trying to implement such a thing but for their own motives and not for the population as a whole, though many think they are."

"Everything has been going so well for us here," Raynie added. "We have not had to run from the authorities or anyone else for such a long time now. I was...I'm sure we all were, very tired of constantly trying to stay ahead of being tracked down. Jake and I love it at the farm. It has given us time to really fall in love."

"I know Raynie. I can see all what you say, and feel it too. I cannot explain other than I know I am needed back at my house. I have been having some strange dreams lately. All of them have featured a young girl, and I have woken up each time thinking of her and strangely of Asper too. I don't know why."

"Do you think Asper could be at your house?"

"I cannot say. Perhaps discussing this with Chan might help me gain a clearer picture. His meditations could reveal something to help me reason with why this is happening."

"Now travel is restored, I suppose going back to your house may be a little easier, though we could expect the authorities to be vigilant on checking the credentials of all potential travellers."

"Well, let's get what we came to the city for and return and see what Chan thinks," Lyle suggested.

With evening casting the high snow capped peaks aglow with hues of orange, red, and gold, they had taken to sitting together for dinner outside on the veranda of the house.

"It is inevitable this time would come," Chan said. "Such as it is in the elemental progression of our intuitions, our quest for enlightenment can intersect with what we consider as the normal and constant way ahead, by what can I say...um, present being perpendicular to where we think we are going. When we understand this we are able to accommodate and relate to the intentional path for our exploration of life and actualising true potential, meaning we can also accommodate this angular issue."

"I am thinking this may lead to feelings enabling healing within ourselves and of others," Carmel said looking intent on determining why she felt as she did.

"Yes, this is right Carmel. Whilst it may be apparent our ways are leading us to where we naturally align, these instances show us wisdom is within when we can accommodate change, and thus realise our paths are forever meandering like the flow of water returning to its source. True vision comes from this ability to observe and act upon feelings rather than to think mostly with our minds and make decisions on how secure we may think we are."

"And the torus. Does it reflect this for us?"

"See for yourself." Chan showed it to the group revealing an increased vibrancy of a rich and deeper pink fragmented with what appeared to be flashing instances of gold. "It has clearly gained in colour from the paleness it has held for some years now. Your feelings for returning are in parallel with its awakening. It is not to say it is the instrument for this ascension, for it is merely reflective of the nature of all within, indicative of the nostalgic return to authentic self."

"Will it be more dangerous for us if we return?" Raynie asked. She was still captivated with the idea of remaining at the steam driven farm with its' historic sense and removal far from the authorities.

"It is a question to only be answered when embracing the feelings one may be having now. Life is full of challenges and dangers as we have experienced. Consider...we have overcome these times."

"Because of our intentions?"

"Yes Raynie. Elemental in progression, like the meandering flow, they cannot be stopped. One may lose their life or experience hardships testing the motivation to continue, but there remains always an element of the source, driven to remain on course towards what some have described as nirvana, though it is not some kind of mythical heaven."

"So I guess we are to face these types of events again then?"

"Your guess is not so much a stab in the dark as some would say. Rather it is your inner intuitions coming from your heart and realising themselves at the forefront of your mind enabling you to respond."

"Rather than reacting to the situation?"

"Yes. Response is important over reaction in these instances for us to see the real choice rather than the reactive choice."

"They will have systems in place where payment for travel back to the United States is required. How are we going to overcome such an obstacle? We don't have John here to fashion any devices or build algorithms for us to evade the strict requirements they will have in place. And what if we are still on the authorities' wanted list?"

Jenna was feeling positive for accompanying Carmel back to her house, but presently held a logical frame of mind as she analysed the proposition of returning north. Life at the farm for her and Lyle had allowed them to develop their relationship in relative peace, but something in her own enquiring mind wanted to return home. She felt her previous scientific work had never been completed and she would have to do more to feel this pathway Chan had just been describing.

"No doubt we are still on some list Jenna, for we hold the eternal torus and they will ultimately want it to fulfil their own desires."

"I think so Chan, but what if we were able to do something before they...?'"

"Only our willingness to embrace uncertainty will tell."

"I am most willing to embrace this uncertainty Chan. I feel compelled," Carmel said looking as if she was now resolute on returning.

"Then you must go with this Carmel."

"Who else will come with me? I can go alone. I have no fear."

"We can talk. I can see what it means for you by the look in your eyes and the emotion behind your words," Lyle added looking at Jenna. He knew she would be resolute once she had made up her mind, meaning the decision if he would leave was already made.

"Don't include us Lyle honey. Steve and I are very happy here and neither us would like to go back." Kerry-Ann felt secure and much in love. Steve and her had discussed the idea briefly when the others first returned from the city and had mentioned what Carmel was feeling.

After searching their inner most desires including where they felt they belonged, both Kerry-Ann and Steve had decided to stay at the farm. Kerry-Ann was pregnant with their child to be born in only a few months, so the idea of a dangerous life back in the United States could not compare with the serenity in the valley. Alongside her, Steve devoted considerable energy and attention to working and maintaining the steam driven machinery at the farm, spending many days with Diego methodically learning how to repair and service the mill and also the steam driven harvester they had built together.

For Juan, Diego, Manuel, Ricardo, and Lolita, as owners of the farm, the question of going anywhere did not mean anything. They had never even visited in years previous, and now devoted their lives to making the farm work where they had chosen to spend the rest of their lives.

After lengthy discussion on how the group could secure passage back to the United States, Lyle and Jake decided to travel into Arequipa the following day to determine if flying was possible. When the next morning dawned crisp and clear, they took to the road out of the valley early and headed towards the city. For over an hour they meandered through steep mountainsides as they followed the hurried river washing over large round stones where the water created a low roar echoing off the rocky cliffs all around them. When they started to leave the valleys behind, mist gathered in patches reaching out from the hollows to cross the road now and then suddenly thrusting them into an eerie nothingness for a time where Frieda was slowed to a walk. For a few moments both men realized the task ahead of them as they considered what was at stake. Then coincidently they seemed to both come around feeling determined to beat the odds, only then to be matched without hesitation by Frieda as she broke into a trot eager the leave the mists behind. As they approached the fringe of Arequipa, they saw many more people than they had anticipated heading in the same direction.

"Why are you going to the city?" Jake asked a small group of travellers.

"The authorities have some important announcements and we do not want to miss the news," was a reply.

"What announcements?"

"We do not know, but a friend called by last night saying there was notices broadcast all over Arequipa for people to gather in the city centre the following day. You must have come from the rural district to the north, which is probably why you have not heard."

"You are right. We live on a farm..."

"Then you must come with us to find out what is happening, and then return home to tell your families. Our friend told us this information is very important."

"Can we travel with you these last few miles then?"

"You are most welcome to come with us."

Upon reaching the fringe of Arequipa, they were surprised at seeing many more people than anticipated. By the time they had reached the city, Lyle estimated at least two hundred thousand people had gathered there to form a crowd which crammed the square at the city centre and spilled outward along the main arterial roads leading away. In the middle of the square, a stage had been built where large numbers of armed officers could be seen in preparation for what could only be a more senior figure yet to arrive. Both Jake and Lyle looked at each other as soon as they saw the contingent of officers, knowing it could not be a good thing for so many heavily armed personnel to be about.

"Citizens of this city. We are here to give you good news. With the defeat of our enemy the Agent, the authorities are now proceeding with reassignment of settlements, cities, and citizens into the new order of society. Fear no longer as the authorities are now in an unchallenged position to provide all of your life comforts and requirements. Once again, life can return to normal for all here who gather to welcome our institution properly back into this city. As you may know, travel is now available to all people who require passage for employment and other approved movement. You may now proceed to other parts of this nation, and for those in strict compliance with regulations, you will be permitted international travel."

"The authorities have established a central office for enquiry and administration of this location, so please feel free and allow us to inform you of anything you are unsure of. And in order to please you and make your life easier, the authorities have built a vast new data network and array of machines to compliment your life. You can now be certain of your security and capacity to achieve status. What was of the past stays in the past. There will be no nanotechnology identification implants. A simple scanner can do all the work required to make your life as simple and efficient as possible."

"Over the next few weeks, the authorities will commence installation of the machines designed for you, designed to efficiently process your needs, and designed to ensure security.

So welcome to the new order of life and welcome to the next age of human evolution."

The announcement continued outlining the conditions for work and family life as the two men walked away feeling alarmed. Lies were already being extolled upon the population as the announcement made news of information not actually true. Local authorities for Peru and most other nations were now falling into line with the events taking place in North America, with each dependent on the scraps of information they were permitted to access in order to develop sufficient technology to manage their local populations. The very issue of strict compliance was not welcoming to them at all, and this also showed on some of the faces in the crowd around them.

Arequipa had been at the frontier of authority control with minimal influence in recent years, but now with what seemed to be an increased presence in the city at the foothills of the Andes Mountains, people were visibly uncomfortable with what may be in store for them in coming times. As the crowd dispersed, some others appeared to welcome the promise for an easier life where concerns would be looked after by the authorities.

"We should return back to the farm and pass on this news. I want to talk to Jenna and see what ideas she might have in response to this turn of events."

"Agreed Lyle. It looks like we are going to be maintaining a covert profile again."

A soft glow from within the barn where they lived greeted them and calmed their intense feelings a little. Jenna was inside working and had already begun to consider profile data when the two men returned to discuss the issue. As clouds gathered bringing stormy weather amongst the steep Andean peaks atop the valley behind them, so too they all now gathered as a group knowing they were to be the provocateurs of the storm they felt they must face ahead. Jenna felt compelled inside to align with her work as an elemental intention – it was who she had remembered herself as with the help of Chan and the others since they had met in San Francisco.

She greeted Lyle with a hugging kiss, exuberant and keen to share good news. "This is great Lyle dear. See this reading?"

"Um, yeah...appears to be operational code for establishing the parameters for protein string activation. I remember seeing this in the cupboard we were using on the Moon together."

"Yeah...the cupboard. It was a challenge at first being stuck in a room no bigger than a cupboard near the lunar south pole...alone and distant. Anyway, watch this."

The small holographic array showed what Lyle had correctly stated. Even through such a small hologram, Lyle could recognise the stage Jenna was showing being immediately prior to the activation of the strings where they began to take on a light carpet appearance. Jenna then entered a command via the light panel to convert the data to activation status.

"I think we could use this as a carrier source to obtain information on how the authorities systems operate, though from a limited angle. This could be a long shot as I am going on the presumption they would be using the strings I developed...and likely have upgraded them. Fundamentally the technology should be the similar as the foundation for building the strings is almost guaranteed to be the same."

"So where is the real connection?" Jake asked.

"It is here. Strings have a unique algorithm set according purely to their atomic and sub-atomic properties. It is as if they are elemental alignments you need to establish in balance so they actualise their distinctive...um, atomic intention."

"Elemental alignments...being in the flow, meant to be. I get it."

"Oh cool. Check these elemental arrays out – you will see the carrier wave after I do this." Jenna said as she entered a further sequence, resulting in one wave being singled out from the entire group consisting of billions of pathways.

"What capacity does it have to access their systems?" Lyle asked.

"Lyle dear, you know it has a massive capacity for data. I imagine the authorities will have a central hub as a place to manage everything efficiently, and this will connect to all nodes, devices, places...despite their machines having a degree of autonomy. Even with there being a lot or most data being processed away from central, there is still the requirement to oversee the management of it all. Therein lies our link."

In present times reflective of the past, Lyle, Jenna, Jake, Raynie, and Chan along with Carmel, set about planning life under the authorities. They were to return to North America as a group on a heading to the small town north of San Francisco. As to the conditions at their destination, they were unaware, yet they knew all the tenacity and courage they could draw upon would be needed.

Life at the steam driven farm had been one of reprieve, alignment and healing, and of simple living. Soon all those times would be behind them – they were anxious in a way as it is for human endeavours into the unknown, but they were resolute. A stirring had come to them and from within them, bringing forth feelings compelling them to respond.

Late into the night and beyond into the first light of the coming day they worked on how to secure travel and maintain cover. When the roosters began their first calls in the pre-dawn misty grey of the morning, a plan had been devised and Jenna had constructed the data they would require to help them on their way.

"It is prudent for us to take yet a few more days here at this farm and round off our time here in view of our next progression," Chan suggested over breakfast. "Ensuring an aligned approach to the journey ahead beginning from this within ourselves, will give us the many strengths required over coming times. This is all energy as we know – it is our requirement to tune this energy for its' potential to be realised especially in these times as it becomes obvious what we have worked for is about to be realised."

"We have become used to this from you Chan."

"Yes, but consider also. It is imperative for you to not become used to anything, for there is always change and progression and so you always require vigilance in feeling what is best. Complacency comes from experiences of comfort and as we have drawn many comforts during our time here, we have indeed become a little complacent."

"What do you mean Chan? We have been mindful," Raynie said almost sounding defiant.

"Yes for it is appropriate where mindfulness reveals our complacency and our thinking of where we are in a moment rather than actually being in the moment. Time can be frustrating and deceptive. It is now our complacency is to be shown and for us to be delivered away from its' grasp."

Chapter 21

Sound wave vibration systems came on line to engage the next level of robotic systems integration. Within each menacing robot there existed the processes for meta-material manufacture using the shaping affect properties of sound waves for propulsion and internal mechanical functions to define flux parameters for normal operations. A mere swipe of his hand was all it took for Eric to engage phase one of autonomy for the array of these ominous beasts.

They were of this beastly ilk, yet somewhat dissimilar to the beast represented by the Agent's vortex amplifier. Though dissimilar in appearance to the complex holographic manifest of two horns with a centre ring built to wreak so much havoc, the purpose of these beasts was not dissimilar. As the Agent did undo the integrity and sense of purpose for many during his years of debauched maniacal pleasure, these machines were an evolution of this motive, gathered now in sinister force to send the minions of humanity on a similarly parallel path. This path was of order, void of the chaos bestowed near and far by the Agent during his mania.

Now this phase of their autonomy was activated, the monolithic robotics were capable of integrating decisions in real time. Any encounter with any object or living thing could be responded to according to the sound it made and the phonetic values of emotion attached. A robot could detect fear, guilt, contrition and more, and then learn from them for application in determining its next action. Heuristic in nature, these beasts were designed to learn and adapt taking all humanity could present to them.

"I see a perfect integration Eric."

"For this time it would appear so sir."

"For this time. What do you mean Eric? It looks perfect...results are as expected."

"Precisely sir. Those expectations contain the issue of instability. Hence for only this time the results are expected within this context sir."

Eric's superior looked intently at him for a few fleeting seconds, considering if the mechanics in Eric's mind may be doing too well. "I am aware of such things. You have nothing from the Agent as yet I assume."

"Nothing. He is not being very helpful. I would suggest..."

"You are not in a position to make suggestions considering your lack of progress in the one area we all know. You are aware of the directives Eric?"

"Completely sir. I ..."

Eric's superior cut him off knowing well Eric would have knowledge of almost all facets of the directive plan about to be actioned.

After a few moments of silence, the superior spoke calmly, "There must be progress with the Agent. Do what you can Eric...if the mind of yours knows how to play a game or two in order to achieve efficient outcomes."

"Um, yes I do sir."

"Then do it if you need to. We are going to have to launch soon and you know what it means. I need stability, and what about Matheson? No...don't tell me. Double...triple your efforts to find Matheson. Investigate any known contacts he has had. Look back as far as it takes Gunter." As his last words sounded, Eric's supervisor disengaged holographic view – his life size three dimensional image disappearing in an instant.

Eric stood staring at the point where he last observed his supervisor. He was not lost to thought, quite the opposite in fact. With methods to find John Matheson racing through his mind, disturbed now and then when he thought of the Agent, Eric then walked directly to the Agent's cell to ask him what he knew about Matheson.

"You ask me about a person I hate. Matheson was the reason I am here now. Not your pathetic ways of...what is it? Efficiency? You know nothing of efficiency at all, yet you claim in the name of righteousness to protect and look after however many people are left out there. Since I acquired my spaceship, all you could muster was your ridiculous compliance. Nothing compares to my methods. You know it to be true."

"Why so angry G...?" Eric left it knowing he was not likely to appease the Agent any if he used his name. "We can work together on this. You hate him and I need him. Our work here is slow. Surely you can see some reason."

"You have merit, but there is no reason to give you anything. You will do nothing for me in return. I know you cannot afford to have me freely seeking the torus."

"Of course. We can make life for you more interesting though. Maybe you have a fascination with nanotechnology mechanics."

"So you can infect me with a virus?"

"Perhaps not. This is where your help or Matheson's can deliver for us. You can see something can't you. Imagine stable flux mechanics...you could become eternal. Best of all, they tailor to individual DNA signatures, so even if you ever re-acquired your beloved torus, or any other, the days of viruses will be coming to an end."

"You cannot guarantee. I can already see a flaw...beginning with you the fact you don't have stability, so there would likely be contingencies you are yet to consider."

The Agent was correct. Until stability was reached there would be a degree of uncertainty. Eric changed his angle a little, "What about if we do get Matheson though?"

"I'm not convinced. If you have him, then it is back to how it was anyway – I gain nothing. With him free, he will always be there for my taking."

"There is no always."

"You were just talking about eternal. Do you actually have an accurate grasp on what it means?"

"We are going nowhere with this. I want information from you. If it turns out to be of value, then your existence will become similar."

"I don't care...I'd rather die."

"Would you?" Eric then left the Agent immediately without waiting for an answer, nor did he look back after re-engaging the holographic cell bars.

The Agent just sat there staring into space for a few minutes after Eric had left. His severe bouts of maniacal behaviour had subsided in recent times – the dull greyness of the authorities was once his own type of aspiration, and so it had begun to have some type of long term calming effect on how often these sessions would occur. His mind was racing with ideas on how to affect an escape as any instance of a normal sense of calm was as distant as his dreams were disturbed.

Ideas had taken on a new dimension for him this night far below ground. Any leeway he could establish, he would amplify to serve his cause. His spaceship would not be there if he escaped, and those useless minions were probably so marginalised and fractioned, garnishing their support for a new offensive would be difficult. They mattered even less than himself if it was possible, but the Agent knew in order to make something of his mania, he would require some type of collective to unify behind the cause – the same dark cause they had espoused to for centuries.

With this sudden recollection, his confidence grew as he took to devising a plan to give Eric only some of what he wanted.

The first part would be to lure Eric into having a degree of confidence in him and thus lessen the stringent opposition to his very being. Any hint of compassion was a weakness and the Agent knew the upper hand for his motives could be gained in the moment this showed itself.

Eric's mind mechanics were sure to smother this typical human trait lost to so many in recent times, but the Agent knew of the issue of instability for the mechanics as they diminished in functionality. Once he had this advantage, the Agent would then commence his gradual overwhelming of Eric. He had tried this tactic years before on his way to Mars and it had proved successful then. Despite his mania, the Agent knew how to evoke the inner frailties of human beings in support of his successful bouts of manic action.

Without awareness of the self, his automatic mania set to work and action his plan. With his familiar half grin, George engaged the holographic controls of the quantum computer in his cell, making particular effort to expand the display to full size, thus immersing him within its projection field. This was a notion of exhibition by the Agent, in reflection of his inner mania manifesting as confidence and purpose. Ironically, he never had feelings of actual confidence – simply manic driven purpose, and there was no actual purpose to his life other than to fulfil the mania of his self until his expiration.

When his work was complete, he returned to a listless state - his awkward grin gone. The moment he sent the report to Eric, was the moment his fiery tinge of manic lust waned. The grey lights overhead replaced this immersion of his being from within the light of the hologram, now lulling him into a period of waiting.

As soon as he received the Agent's report, Eric set to work analysing the information as he felt a slight tinge of satisfaction. His ploy had worked so he thought, and now the Agent could be moulded for his needs. Eric had considered the idea of mind mechanics for the Agent as a type of experiment for understanding the extremes of megalomania in human behaviour. As an advance project for incorporating these contingencies within the monolithic robotics, Eric was on a direction to control this and shape it into an efficient mode of processing and action. He knew the Agent had a surge of self power during these manic intrusions, and Eric wanted to harness this as a controllable energy to deploy within the robotic beasts he was unleashing.

It was a lateral consideration, rather than a lineal process and wherever process could take quantum leaps in efficiency, Eric saw it as his duty to respond and please his own superior officers. The lure of status advancement was one strong remaining facet of his natural self, particularly as those above him had access to the latest in technology enhanced living. Eric wanted this, for it would enable him to merge his mechanical self with his work, as opposed to having to go to work. As the most mechanically affected individual on Earth, he would become part of the actual machine planet of the monolithic directive.

Eric worked endlessly each day to understand the dynamics of alternative dimensions and then to bring them through the monolith using the torus to accelerate atomic resonance. Stability was still the issue in his attempts to overstep the divide between the essence of human nature and the notion of artificial intelligence. Eric wanted this for his last remaining self as a means to establish his own presence as the model of efficiency for what humanity was to become and this was a form of mania unknown to him yet sanctioned for study by those very superiors he sought to please.

Eric would reach the goal on behalf of his superiors, ushering in a new phase of human occupation conquering both mind and cosmos. Within his determinations mostly mechanical, was the need to take humanity beyond the solar system – outward amongst the deepest stars lining the avenue to galactic exploration through dimensions as knowledge of flux states of matter in torus fields was more understood. Through dimensional shift and particle flux acceleration, Eric wanted to be the pioneer scientist taking humanity where they had never previously ventured.

Beyond time and space on some eternal quest, Eric's and the authority motives were in accordance with facets of seemingly natural human experience. The quest for power and recognition is nothing new, yet within lay dissimilarities of essence where natural authentic foundation of the self was to be challenged by an artificial intelligence meld of humanity into deepest technology dependency.

Chapter 22

With authentic embrace, the entire group who had been living together at the steam driven farm these past years gathered in farewell. Chan, Carmel, Lyle, Jenna, Raynie, and Jake were set to depart. Frieda the white horse was also amongst them receiving special attention from Carmel who loved her as a dearest friend. She had shared in the turmoil of Carmel's journey with John through North America, and then on to Peru with the group - probably the first ever horse to ride in a passenger HyperJet. Her life at the farm had then become what it should be for horses in their element, with many days spent free amongst the valley grasses, only interrupted now and then when Carmel took to her for a ride, or there was a little work to be done. Her name meant peace, and she had found its expression.

Beloved in a way by Carmel, her little steam engine was to accompany them back to California, or what once was California.

The steam engine had been carefully disassembled by Carmel. She knew it intricately after having first restored it to magnificent condition and then maintaining every component over the years since, including when Frieda had drawn the cart so far with it stowed at the back. With a last soft few strokes of Frieda's velvety nose, Carmel let her go for the time being. She did not see this departure as final – such things simply did not occur to her now. Frieda gave her a soft sound in response, accompanied by a slight shuffle. All living things respond to touch, and Carmel's touch was especially responsive for her.

As horses do with humans, Frieda had become used to her being around, being in touch, and they had shared many fine rides journeying to the foothills around the valley at the base of the jagged high peaks immediately behind. The winds had tossed her mane and sent Carmel's long wavy hair to the sky. Carmel felt strong emotion for her lovely companion – they had shared experience in their authentic element together. At the last, Carmel gently kissed Frieda's face as a tear fell from her eye. Frieda gave a soft sound and one last velvety nose nuzzle before Carmel then pulled away.

Juan then drove them out the front gate in the large wagon drawn by two of the original farm horses. Lolita, Ricardo, Diego, Kerry Ann, and Steve waved their goodbyes as a group with their arms around each other's waist. When they had gone, a downcast feeling took over them as they realised their dear friends had actually left.

Kerry Ann noticed the gloominess. "Cheer up honey," she said to Ricardo. "They'll be sure to all come back."

"Yes I know this is not the end. It is...um, just we are not so many here and I will miss their company."

"We all will honey. Won't we Lolly." Kerry Ann had taken to calling Lolita by this nickname over time as their friendship had grown.

"You are right. I will miss them too, but I have a feeling we will all be happy in one place again someday."

"I know we will honey."

The ride into the city was a sombre time with little conversation. Nobody wanted to feel burdened with goodbyes or about what might be coming. When at last they did arrive, Juan bade them farewell and safe travels ahead as he watched them walk into Arequipa airport. He too felt a sense of loss at their departure, and like the others back at the farm, felt as though they would all be together in one place again in the future.

For Chan and the others there was a sense evoking mystery at what might lay ahead, mixed with emotions of departing their dear friends as Juan disappeared from view. They had all worked in mind and soul in preparation for what they would encounter, but now they felt a strong sense of loss as they realised the final moments of their time in Peru.

Jenna had worked wonders with limited technology in constructing false profile personal details and data to enable their travel and then subsequent method of payment when they had reached their destination. Her access into their systems via the protein strings had proven a success, and then she had discovered the authorities were giving new settlers sufficient credit to re-establish their lives. It was by no means a payment one could ascribe to as wealth, rather a provision to facilitate efficient process for new arrivals returning or relocating to areas undergoing rebuilding since the end of the Agent's manic era.

Within two hours after arriving at Arequipa airport, they were aboard a HyperJet climbing towards seventy thousand feet leaving South America behind them on their way to San Francisco. Officials had welcomed their plight of return to make good in North America, especially as they provided just enough details alluding to their technical skills for use in the effort of re-building. The authorities were eager to place as many valuable and efficient people for the sake of their cause as soon as possible, and so they had easily been allocated travel back to the area most devastated by the Agent.

For the first time since escaping the Agent, they flew once again near the cusp of atmosphere and space admiring the view of the Earth spread out far below contrasted against the blackness just above them.

Near the end of the two hour flight, they took in the marvellous view of the Baja Peninsula as the jet made approach towards San Francisco. At velocity nearing four thousand miles per hour, approach to landing was always a carefully mapped course for a HyperJet as it descended through the layers of airspace where much slower manned craft and drones operated. When at last the view of the city appeared, a sense of dismay came over all who were aboard the flight, as all could see the widespread devastation wrought upon a place once considered so beautiful.

Jenna was keenly looking towards the city in the last moments before landing, hoping to see streets of old wooden houses still standing. She would never be able to see her own place, but the appearance of so many houses like hers, gave her a feeling she would be greeted with good news when she finally made it to her own home not far from California Avenue.

After the new JetCab had delivered the group to one of the passenger disembarkation points near the city, they had walked the partly ruined streets towards the south-west. Jenna's hopes sank a little in seeing the house was standing but in a state of disrepair from neglect and damage caused by others over the years since she had last lived there. When they all entered together, they first stood within the musty dust riddled lounge room surveying the conditions. For a few minutes they all felt somewhat in a trance like state as they each came to terms with their memories of the house and the past.

Raynie was the first to break the moment by beginning the process of tidying up the lounge room to clear space for them to gather and take stock of the situation. Jenna and the others set about doing the same immediately after and within a few minutes they had cleared most of the room. During the walk back to her house from the JetCab terminal, they had purchased a few drinks and light foods as provisions. When they were satisfied with the lounge room, they sat at the main table by the large bay windows looking out towards the glittering waters to the west all the way to the still wrecked Golden Gate Bridge.

"Well despite this mess, at least your house is still standing and liveable Jenna."

"I am grateful for us to be here, but Carmel...you will want to return north, so we will need to decide if it is all of us there, or some to stay here. Sorry, I am a bit flustered. Perhaps it is seeing my house this way."

"Perhaps there is also the notion of your past attached to this house as well. We have lived far from here in such circumstances it is like our lives went beyond our past somewhat in leaving it behind. Now we return, and I too recall my first contact with you Jenna and Lyle, in this house. After all since, we are perhaps reminded of times when life was so different from the time prior to the upheaval in recent years. See beyond this for living is now and at this time, where we take the best of essence from the past as all progresses into alignment or place. Magic can happen when all is in place where it should be," Chan said this looking calm and assured. He took on the moment guiding them to retain mindfulness in stressful situations as he had done many times over the years.

Carmel had watched Chan closely as he spoke. She noticed he had taken to showing a heightened sense of enrichment, and she knew then the torus must have activated just a little further.

'How was this a key moment?' she asked herself. She need not have bothered, for as she asked this of herself, she realised through feeling why she wanted to return to her house.

"Your beautiful house Jenna. Should we all clean it some and secure it before we go to my house?"

"I think so Carmel. We may need this house again. It has stood the test of recent times, so let's hope it continues..." Jenna trailed off as she considered what she was saying. The authorities were re-building San Francisco, meaning she had to leave her house behind for it would eventually fall to their re-building efforts. Even before they had spoken, Jenna knew they would have to continue away from the city.

Everyone had felt they did not want to stay in San Francisco as soon as they had arrived. Carmel had instigated this journey in the beginning, and they had all felt their final destination was with her. Chan was of the mind to allow what must be to occur and Raynie had urged Jake to see if they could find some peace with Carmel.

"Let's go tomorrow then," Jenna said looking a little downcast.

Everyone agreed and then for the entire afternoon, they cleaned and fixed as best they could. When the time came where they all agreed it they had done enough, the sun was setting across the distant ocean visible through the remnants of the famous wrecked icon. There was no electricity in the house – their only power source being the small cells Jenna had built before they left the farm. Lyle, Raynie, Jake, and Chan were preparing a meal in the kitchen, where remarkably, they had found some candles Jenna had left there years before.

Everyone made for celebration as they sat down for dinner where at times they all felt a tinge of sadness knowing this meal would likely be their last together for some time after having shared so many memorable occasions in recent years.. They knew what this time meant in view of the house destined to be consumed by the massive re-development the authorities planned for the city. Gone would be so much of its charm, the character, the many vistas of association where couples would kiss, street deals would be done, and rendezvous made. It was to become rather bland in comparison with facades of false representations distant to what San Francisco had once been. Many were likely to not even care, rather thinking of what lay in store for them to consume after so long of nothing new.

Carmel had managed to smuggle some wine all the way from Arequipa. They drank all the wine as they talked of what they were to do once they arrived at Carmel's house, if indeed it was still there. This made them consider other plans where they considered staying at Jenna's house for a few moments, until they again sensed going north was where they were meant to be.

As the near full moon rose over the city, the machines of the authorities relentlessly went about building. There were no visible operators of these machines for most of them were entirely autonomous. They were the first phase of monolithic robotics with a capacity soon to dramatically increase.

After a restless night for all but Chan, they rose in the early hours of the morning to stand at the bay windows looking out to the Golden Gate Bridge. Before their eyes, they watched as the remaining wreckage of the once famous landmark was reduced to an atomic mass. A faint blue haze could be seen about the bridge as the robotics did their work compressing matter, leaving a small object approximately the same size as a chair.

Eric Gunter had been instructed to carry out this task – it was a propaganda initiative to gain favour amongst the populace. As the lead feature of the morning's news story, it would be fed to the public and shown in full three dimensional holographic glory. In place of the bridge, would be a new transit way of grandeur rendering the Golden Gate forever to the past.

Raynie was holding Jake's hand as the entire process unfolded, but neither they or the others been impressed with this exhibition.

"Jenna. Do you have any idea what we just saw?"

"I can only guess with at least a slight degree of accuracy Raynie. They must be using nanotech robotics for material shaping. They have been around for years but I have not seen anything compress material so quickly before."

It was about eight in the morning and although this was a time for many to be about, the city was still fairly quiet. The empty shops lining the streets reflected a low gleam through the coating of dust on their windows. Long abandoned bars and restaurants displayed faded signs from times past – no longer visited by anyone and so derelict to their purpose and empty of character once attached to their appearance. Many of the older character buildings were still standing amongst the rubble, listless, dulled and senseless. They attracted no custom. They offered no respite through fantasy from the realities found on the streets. And they were in their death – slowly decaying before being lost in form and forgotten in memory.

Jenna's success with data had ensured they were able to escape this vision of misery. The misery was not the intense violence of the Agent. It was more the misery of slow decay to then be met with sudden finality. The old world was quickly being disposed of and being replaced with a world in true vision of the authority's motives. It was to be a machine world in all facets of existence and the people were to reflect this in who they were to become.

The JetCab took them to the northern most point to which the service operated. It had flown the only city bound passage along the length of the intact

Bay Bridge onward then further to the new satellite centre being constructed in the area near the facility where Raynie and Jake had been incarcerated years before. After this it would be a case of walking. No other means of travel was available as the only transit tube veered well away from the small town and Carmel's house. They had considered riding it to a point within twenty five miles of the house, but had decided against it when Jenna had been able to access details on what information passengers to rural locations had to provide. This prompted them all to agree registering an intention to live at the town would only expose them to potential danger despite their false profiles. Jenna knew the authorities would be collecting personal information on them almost where ever they went – she had warned them of the potential systems for DNA scanning they would possess.

Fifty miles of walking now lay ahead. They were all strong after having lived and worked together so well at the farm near Arequipa, leaving behind any remnants of the devastation the Agent had brought upon their lives when he had held them captive.

The walk was of no deterrence when they had set off happily in each other's company away from the physical and spiritual confines of the city. It would take two or three days at the most. Their provisions and proper clothing would ensure they were not troubled other than if they encountered anyone who might be aggressive.

Carmel had remained firm on being the one to carry all of the components of her little steam engine after offers to spread the load came from the others. Chan had admired her for this moment as she was determined to be solely responsible for the heavy weight. He had grown very comfortable in observing and feeling from the intentions Carmel displayed since he had first come to know her, and so at this time he was admiring her strength of will for he was sure she would need to draw upon it often in coming times.

A chill was already in the air when they found a deserted farm after walking twenty three miles on a long first day. Sun had warmed them as they strode country roads past derelict buildings and around abandoned vehicles often found in large craters, but as it slipped below the hills to the west, a chill descended prompting them to gather wood and make a fire at the entrance to the old barn. They had lived together for years in a barn at the farm, and so this first night the familiarity of the setting prompted them into discussing times recently passed.

They did not consider concealing their flame as fear simply did not enter into their psyche. Nor should they have as they were the only people for miles around the isolated farm.

When time had passed and the women had taken to sleep leaving Jake, Lyle, and Chan sitting by the flickering flames at the barn's entrance, the three men simply stared out into the darkness beyond the reach of firelight. A gentle breeze then suddenly caressed each of their faces. It was laden with cold air indicating coming snow, and so it stimulated conversation.

"It will not be too much snow," Chan said seeing the look in response to the cold on the other two men's faces.

"Cold though," Lyle said.

"Let us see," Chan took the torus out of his pocket to show them. It had increased yet again in intensity. The pink hue was now showing a radiance somehow tricking the eye. Looking at the torus for more than a glance, prompted one to think they were seeing golden shapes form and change within the radiance.

"See how those shapes form and then progress onto another shape? They are representations of our intentions for we are in most proximity to the torus and such are our strengths in alignment it shows this energy."

"It will be useful Chan when the time comes. We have discussed this at length in recent years, and how it is to act as if it is a confirmation of our own intentions."

"But is it Lyle? Can we be sure what the torus is at all? After these years we see this activation gradually progressing and we have speculated on what the torus may be able to do...if anything. Why it could be a representation only. It could even be a work of art."

"It is both of those and more Chan."

"Yes, but we know nothing of what it is to become. It may be nothing or it may be something. I am reminded of John and his work with flux mechanics. They are either something or nothing or both as they go beyond light speed and such concept is difficult to grasp."

"It will become evident as we progress," Jake added. "Now we only know of its atomic acceleration properties...but this is perhaps all it is meant to be."

"Is it Jake? Maybe you are right, or maybe it is merely a picture of ourselves."

Snow began to fall not long after the three men had retired for the night. It was a gentle caress to the scene – Chan had been right as it was only a slight fall. When they all awoke early the following morning, a dusting lay upon the ground, upon the buildings and fences, on pine trees, and it traced the bare branches of the deciduous trees. The day was not sunny though. It was cold and grey and so the snow would hold and not melt away. This made for a delightful scene, somehow virgin in nature and inspirational to all of them when they set out after a brief breakfast.

As they walked the crunchy country lane away from the farm, Chan spoke further about what they had discussed the night before, "We are to ensure we maintain our view of the torus as open and not defined by anything. Whilst we have talked at length about what it may represent, we must remain vigilant in seeing the torus as merely a geometric reflection of our own selves. As we know, it is said human beings manifest around them those things they feel inside. As warriors of our own lives, this is our focus."

"When we first met you Chan, you told us there was a dangerous power or energy at stake. If the torus is a reflection of our own activation, then how is it a dangerous power?"

"We have spoken of this before Lyle. The energy or power can be dangerous in respect to those who can attune their intentions to the potential torus activation can provide. It is prudent though, for us to focus only in seeing it as this potential for we cannot foretell the future, so we are yet to learn the precise reason for it being here. What has taken place is only a sample of what potential lies within the torus. All the technology, the episode of the Agent – this is a precursor to the potential."

"We do have a strong indication though."

"Indeed. But...this is a journey of wisdom and to recognise we are forever learning is the foundation to our intentions aligning with being open to the path we seek in our hearts during our recollection of our ancient self and the memories of our DNA and genes connected to all there is. Simply allowing this without thinking."

Jenna had been waiting to contribute and spoke the moment she could, "I have a reasonable assumption beckoning. I think the torus will provide us insight into the other dimensions in existence. After all, it is an atomic accelerator, so my scientific thinking is along these lines."

"You may well be correct Jenna. Again though, we are to avoid seeing it as an answer...to all these issues in life. Such things can be misguided for outcomes anyone may seek, always begin within as intentions of the heart. And the danger may well have been indicated to us through the exploits of the Agent with his use of the torus..."

"And the resulting instability?" Jake asked.

"It was indicative of the misaligned intentions of the Agent."

"There must be others like us who are activating their memories forgotten for so long" Raynie added. "Jake and I were talking about this as we lay awake for a while this morning."

"Of course the human heart spirit is awakened in many. It has always been this way as it represents the torus energies of the universe in existence and so is this connection to creation and sustenance, though to sustain is to provide respect to self for opportunity. Indeed, this is an exciting aspect for us and for those others as they too consider who else may be out there. There also is reason to focus on intentions as I have said, for there is the energy we have discussed and this is a matter for people to connect through mindful application of their authentic intentions not controlled by negative ego. Where the authorities and their pseudo corporations have delivered technology so widely for the purpose of people connecting, this has often been in a way channelled through devices and so through habit, many have lost their personal touch, their responses to others in situation, and often their mannerisms."

"Often they hide behind the veil of technology and this can lead to unauthentic presence where idioms of expression emerge from disparity manifesting from a deep sub-conscious yearning for alignment. This causes unknown but felt...experienced angst for those not aligned in elemental flow. People are led through life with offerings to satisfy the mildest desire of balance, equality, and humanitarianism, but this is a mere facade or a facsimile of the potential naturally lying in waiting for them to experience."

"Chasing status opportunities as the only way to live leads to an on-going insatiable hunger."

"This has been true for many decades and centuries Raynie. To awaken from this veil or cloud is to allow one to see clearly without measure. Just to be. Few seem to realise happiness in pure essence as their dependency is a distraction and often they might not see they are dependent. They are not feeling so much of themselves, rather than an idea of themselves. It is mostly just an attitude and an apparent need really only existing because of the attitude or view on life. Many would be reluctant to let go of this as it is their version of security. All life is secure in being elementally progressive, yet people can mostly only see the material provisions as a guide to measure the success and security of their lives and leave these other aspects of self unanswered. This affects thinking and how thoughts are shaped as the frequency of the material mind not just thinking of consuming, but how it views and analyses without realising this is a condition."

By midday they had covered another ten miles when they decided to look around a small deserted town for a while. There were only a dozen houses and what appeared to be two former small businesses. They concluded one must have been a general store after seeing a small number of various advertising materials stuck to the inside of the windows to the main door. No signs indicated this or otherwise, but they had come across similar buildings during their travels in years past when such establishments may still have operated. The other building appeared to be an electronics sale and repair store. The ground at the front of the building had broken hardware scattered here and there with the obvious odd thing out being the recent work to cover over the front door. Immediately they were both alerted and intrigued.

When they checked out the back and came across a large stockpile of more broken hardware, they saw the only door into the building. Jenna and Lyle confirmed it was made of a brand new type of nanotech material. A moment later Chan suddenly felt a pang of urgency and concern. He sent this to them all as a notion or feeling and within seconds the others could sense Chan was uneasy.

"Let's go Jake," Raynie said grabbing his hand and leading him on a swift walk back to the street at the front of the building. Jenna did the same with Chan, leaving Lyle there for a few seconds more as he thought about the material used to make the door. He began to imagine what other technology may lay in store, but then decided against it and ran out to meet the others who were standing on the opposite side of the street waiting for him.

When he arrived to them as they stood in a close huddle, nobody spoke except with their eyes. They guarded their speech as they guarded their feelings, and without word, they walked quietly and quickly out of the small town determined to finish their journey this day or into the night if necessary. Chan knew the authorities were using torus based dimensional technologies when he heard Jenna and Lyle explain the door. He could feel a vibration come from the torus he carried – it was physical vibration. His slight look of consternation kept them quiet for the next hour of walking north from the town. They felt this day had become very significant based on reasoning as much as feeling, and this fine balance required attention.

During their years together, and since Carmel had joined them, they had established this connection where moments of significance were apparent to them all simultaneously. Carmel had remained separate during the entire time they had investigated the building. She had simply not followed their curiosity, instead calmly remaining at distance. She had felt awkward upon arrival and so had removed herself in a way for a short time. As they walked now, she remained silent but in no way sullen. She was invigorated by her senses regardless of what they told her, and despite the feelings warning, she was similar in steadiness to Chan in mind and heart at this time.

Chan had noticed all this from the outset and he continued to notice Carmel as they walked. Her presence at this time was giving or adding progress to his own feelings and yet she was doing nothing outwardly to project towards him. She simply was giving without conscious effort, and somehow the incident at the store had amplified the recognition of this in Chan. For a moment he admired her as she walked on showing no signs of exhaustion despite the weight of the engine and few belongings on her back.

When they stopped to eat a meal as the last light of the day receded behind nearby hills, they had covered a great distance and could recognise the area where they were in respect to its proximity to Carmel's house. The hills formed the same low range as the hills visible from her house and she estimated they only had around twelve miles to go along the valley.

Around three in the morning after deciding to push on and reach their destination, they arrived at the front of Carmel's house to see a glow in one window from what appeared to be candle light. They immediately became wary, except for Carmel and Chan. Upon seeing a smile on both of their faces, Raynie, Jake, Jenna, and Lyle could feel an ease coming from them, allowing them to let go of their wariness.

Carmel walked the pathway to the front door, delighted to see the arch still there with a bare but living grape vine strewn wildly across it creating a tunnel effect. She paused for a moment before going up and lightly knocking on the front door. Nobody answered for a minute, so she knocked again slightly louder. This time she heard footsteps coming towards her. Someone then arrived behind the door but opened it only a little. In a split second Tim and Carmel's eyes met, so he thrust the door wide open and they embraced in a long tight embrace - kissing and laughing, looking deeply into each other's eyes, and feeling the best they had for so many years.

Chapter 23

Monolithic Directive systems were heightened to engage level two status. Deployment of preliminary programmable matter was now taking place after torus operations had been started and sufficiently stabilised. This was not the stability of true flux mechanics, rather just reliability for operations of the technology as planned. True programmable matter would come through flux drawing in resonances from other dimensions during phasing of sub-atomic and photonic oscillations.

Energy systems, monitoring systems, imaging systems, and identification systems were now all on-line. Robotics had been deployed to take care of both policing the state and for overseeing operations in replacement of personnel. They were primed to manage preliminary programmable matter, and now with strong signals coming from within the star positioned out of sight within the anomaly, harnessing and channelling multi-dimensional potential energies could take place. Similar to laying tachyon pathways for uptake beyond light speed, preliminary programmable matter rendered a state ready for full programmable matter.

Eric knew of the amplification properties the anomaly would have from his work, and as he stood immersed in a holographic control array, he remained diligent to ensure this next phase of operations was to be a success. With the connection about to be established in status level two, he would commence the process of building towards funnelling atomic matter manifestation to wherever he or the system decided. It would emerge from the anomaly not as actual matter, but matter within a flux state and so it could be transmitted along the projected pathways programmed within the manufactured star at speeds just beyond light. This carriage proceeded to atomic collectors for dispersal to wherever it was required.

Eric engaged the control for initiating status level two and within seconds the entire system of manufacture, collection, and dispersal began.

Next in line would be status level three where human influence was the objective. Eric knew he would activate a system to forever alter the human evolutionary path physically, emotionally, and mentally. He was not troubled by this apparition, for the image of such events was as clear to him as the immense three dimensional holographic array he now stood within. He could easily project such images within his mind as his internal mechanics sought to influence his thoughts in a sense complimentary to his imagination. In service to striving for more and more efficiency, trans-human hardware was now to be powered by Monolithic systems designed to learn through prompting ideas and extrapolating for efficient developmental purpose. In a sense, an autonomous conscience in construct would begin life within human beings.

For an instant or two, Eric felt a sensation associated with the speed his mind was able to expand a concept. This occurred for just a brief time as his mechanics sought to over ride such inefficiency entirely, but they were unable to complete this direction. With capacity subtly diminishing due to instability, such moments were bound to increase. Eric knew what was happening to him and in some self residual moment his arrogance allowed him to see his personal solution in line with his Monolithic outcomes.

"Matter construct is proceeding as anticipated sir. Systems are at full reception status."

"Good work Eric. Now with this star situated inside the vortex and capable of drawing multi-dimensional energies, we have inexhaustible resources to manufacture and develop fully programmable matter."

"We do indeed sir. Full programming will evolve as star based geometries align at angulations in readiness to access dimensional boundaries."

"Your work developing robotics in this area is exemplary Eric. By using those algorithms the Agent developed, we are able to support this endeavour."

"They were useful. His efforts in destroying the HAARP facility and what he did in reducing many cities and towns to rubble, did give us the angle we required to proceed sir. It is imperative for us to remember the work we have done to expand on the Agent's ideas and manifest these systems now where we can continue refining the data required to ensure progressive efficiency of these construction systems."

"Very good news to me Eric. I can tell you now with phase two operating, those in office far above my status are learning of your efforts. Continue to progress as you have and enrichment of your status will follow. Why, I could even see you in a director's role Eric. Your work managing these deployment teams has ensured me personally of our efforts to render your internal mechanics as a worthy success."

"They do serve me well sir. With phase three, many will learn of their benefits."

"I am sure they will Eric. Now we have engaged this next phase, I want you to continue working towards phase three, but...I want results about Matheson. Your work with the Agent is our only course of action at this time and it is not enough by any measure."

"He is difficult sir. I have set him up to help us, but I must remind you he is a vindictive and maniacal individual sir. He will be trying to turn this arrangement in his favour."

"I am well aware of the Agent's tendencies Eric. I need no reminder of the setbacks he brought personally upon me and upon the motives of the authorities as a whole. We need this information. I don't need you to tell me we need true stability known by Matheson. Don't think I am not aware of the details Eric.

So...work with this maniac and get us Matheson or at least something we can use to tide us over until we have the strength of knowledge Matheson has on this subject."

"Understood sir. I will return to work immediately."

Eric's superior officer disappeared leaving Eric standing amongst the many readouts projected into the air around him. The latest developments in holographic vision with its ability to project light to designated co-ordinates and excite atoms on which to render a projected photon field as an image, pleased Eric as far as his modifications would permit. Now with access to atomic particulate refraction, Eric could see everything in perfect detail and not one command or vision would ever fail.

He activated a test for the programmable matter collectors to check their storage capacity dynamics. All collectors were operating normally storing matter in a data state with readouts conveying statistics. Each collector took on enormous loads of data for conversion into sufficient energy or matter to use on a massive scale. Through directive manufacturing, pure elements could be created without any contamination or large scale processing. Eric had unleashed a version of alchemy seen as pure fiction in the past. Ironically his own personal alchemical experience through nano mechanics, failed to realize the true self in the subjective broader sense.

Eric was satisfied all systems were now ready to commence matter manifestation, so he entered to required secure sequence to begin. Within a second, results appeared in the projection around him. Basic elements of solids, gases, and liquids were being formed and conveyed as atomic constructs within the imagery. A second later, transmission to building robotics began where the matter was received and then programmed into physical objects, or converted to energy.

Used as field operatives, each robot could then direct the intended or programmed matter to location and manifest as an object. Capable of directing this to any place on the Earth at a tiny fraction under the speed of light, a robot could send enforcement to any place where they would manifest on location within seconds.

In a few days, Eric would release the authority for the advertisement of a new line of nanotechnology mechanical devices to fully enrich people's lives...or so they thought. Then, just a few days afterwards, the first secretive incursions of the technology would then start to take up residence in the unknowing population, affecting their bodies, their thoughts, and their emotions. All in office took the same justification – it was efficient with minimal risk and therefore best for the people.

Eric had a system in place for communication with the Agent, and now its' small signal in amongst the hundreds flashing around him, told him the Agent had some information. Immediately he confirmed reception, advising him he had a few things to complete and he would see him shortly. Unknown to Eric was the Agent's ability to hack into the system he shared with Eric, and whilst Eric confirmed his request, the Agent was analysing the data Eric was managing.

The Agent could see the monolithic forces running through the entire process now in operation. He could see how the matter was transmitted as data for convergence into atoms via the robotics, and he could see how this could help his own cause. Within the processes, algorithms emerged as the basis to the elemental forces constituting the programmed matter, so the Agent copied them. The Agent did marvel at how effective this process was in drawing energy from other dimensions into the Earth dimension. In a way it was like alchemy, often seen as a dark art and so it reminded him of more maniacal moments where he himself tried his own blend of matter transformation.

He knew how this worked through his years amplifying vortexes using the torus, but now to see such a massive scale of replication, he began to take on the mystique of possibility. It was not the mystery one with aligned elemental intentions would see. It was more of the type of mystery one could explore when tainted with maniacal tendencies leading to acts of deprivation.

By the time he took the effort to read Eric's confirmation, the Agent had retrieved sufficient data to understand the dynamics required to instigate this act of replication. This was by no means his avenue for escaping the facility where he was being held, but it would surely serve his endeavours once he had escaped.

Matheson had escaped and the Agent knew of how he would do similar. He knew Eric and his officers would have upgraded security in lieu of the blunder allowing John to gain his freedom, but the Agent was pre-emptive in most instances, and so this consideration was merely just something else he would overcome. Despite his mania, his will...his volition of selflessness served him where he would seize upon it to be free.

Within the data, the Agent noticed some key elements he discovered and could help in his escape, and so this came as an added bonus to his system hacking efforts. He could see the algorithm for initiating the transfer process and in the last few seconds before Eric arrived, the Agent found the means to bypass the security systems. Ironically the unstable algorithm he discovered and help in his escape, was supplied by John Matheson. In effect, John was to provide him with the means to escape so the Agent could pursue him as far as the Agent's mania permitted. George felt glee for just a fleeting second as Eric approached.

"So what news do you have for me?"

"Nothing much aside from some analytics I have worked through. These should narrow down the field of probability for finding Matheson. I have looked at his associations over a period of time and have found a recurrence in the data."

"Indicating...?"

"Look around this area north of San Francisco."

"It covers territory all the way to Seattle. Why so far?" Eric suspected the Agent may be trying to steer him on a wild chase in the wrong direction.

"I know your suspicious nature. I too have been an officer with the authorities. Whether you trust me or not is your problem. But...this is here for the taking. You decide what to do."

The Agent was prepared to provide this much detail as it would ensure the authorities would likely be able to put pressure on John if indeed he was to be found in the rough area he had indicated. This would work in his favour he was sure, and so in effect, the authorities could do a lot of the work he required to expose John and thus he would be able to carry out his own plans.

"I'll work on it. Do you have anything else?"

"No."

"Then why call me here? Surely you could have sent these details to me."

"I just wanted to show you I am willing to co-operate and engage my superiors."

"You really let yourself down George. A line as such an idiom coming from you is entirely unconscionable. I know you are looking for ways to get the better of me. Just don't think it will work. Our systems are watching you and they are continuously adapting..."

"I am sure."

Eric looked at the Agent for a moment considering him and his air of confidence as he spoke, then his internal mechanics told him the Agent was likely to be in one of his delusional states. "Oh I see," he said to play along with what he thought was a simple mind game. "Well, continue on with your work then."

"You can be sure I will."

Eric departed the cell without a word of goodbye. The Agent was grateful in his way. He had no liking for idle chatter with Eric, instead preferring to be both direct and evasive. Within a minute, he had returned to analysing the data he had stolen just prior and within his thoughts, a return to his former state of inglorious glory.

His visions were not of a rampaging maniac prone to erratic incursion to make life difficult. Instead, they began to take on entirely new dimensions of grandeur where he would have the secret to monolithic directive manufacturing and the knowledge possessed by John Matheson, and so then, he would finally rein his brand of never ending hell on Earth.

Once he had both, he would surpass any previous power held. Whilst he held no value for the idea of a collective seen as a dark sect, he had once led them for in essence he was the darkest of them all, and his type of darkness was from all as if he was the single manifestation of all seen despicable in nature with George as its' catalyst. The Agent denied the validity of life, of soul, and of love, instead existing for the suppression of light and the disintegration of soul or the human spirit...anything representing the energy of progression.

He laughed as he had done previously when he considered their feeble plight against him. He laughed when he realised how close he was coming to freedom from this hated place, and he laughed when he anticipated how much disassociation from self he would purvey upon he people. His previous efforts were merely a taste of what was now to come, and this inspired him ever more as such a taste was alluring to want – the want of more, yet want of less. His pathway to oblivion was eternal as is all energies of the cosmos and in his misunderstanding, George enacted his true self at this time, this moment, and place within his entire destiny of futile foray.

Chapter 24

If there was ever a reason to hold a party of cerebration of any magnitude in recent years, it was now. After so much time apart, the entire group were all together once again, along with new friends, yet missing one, for whom Asper felt pangs of sorrow in amongst the joys. Tobias was the only person she adored who was missing from the scene. The others could all feel for her during these moments, yet despite their years of experience in life, it was Celia who comforted Asper the most.

"I know you are hurting while everyone else is feeling good."

"The others probably know as well dear. See how they talk to me now and then?"

"Oh I know. I can see it...and feel. But I know really. They can imagine based on their own experiences, but we have a connection Asper, and I know how you feel now. Remember I lost my mother..."

"Alright Celia. Thank you for being there for me. I really do..."

"Don't thank me silly. We both know why. Come on let's go outside into the garden. I am sure the others will follow. They can speak about things then."

"Okay Celia, sounds like a great idea. The sun is out and the mist in the valley is pretty."

"See. Better already." Celia took Asper's hand and led her out to the garden, where they went about soaking up the crisp air and feeling a connection to the elements. She had been right as within a minute, all those present had joined them outside embracing the atmosphere and drawing invigoration from the morning air.

It had been a very late hour when the travelling group had arrived, and not long afterwards they had all retired for the night. Despite their long night, now they were up early at winter's dawn where after resting, they had embraced each other again, eager to discuss details of their recent lives, yet restricted due to the inevitable surveillance from the recently installed computer.

Now outside and somewhat free from prying, they all at first stood together feeling a sense of engagement.

Celia noticed the affects as she saw people appear more at ease and less burdened. Without their realisation at the conscious level, they were all connecting at the sub-conscious elemental level of sentience. It was if something they knew about and had feelings over, suddenly became a surge much stronger than an analytical perception for understanding.

It was energy connecting outside the manifestations of what resulted from conscious decision making. Perhaps it was similar to a trance like state, yet everyone was alert and interacting. Amongst all their conversation and genuine affections for each other, this energy continued to grow, progressing elementally from infinite source in construct of the next experience.

Times were approaching where fundamental questions and answers could prove decisive – John knew of this all along in his quest to take flux mechanics to its maturity and build a platform for it to become elementally progressive. Tuning into the energies and pre-empting the path by which light or matter would follow was more than laying down tachyon pathways to accept transmission a fraction above light speed. This technology would open doorways to other worlds within the minds of people, and within the hearts of pioneers.

Celia laughed out loud when she noticed Carmel and Tim during a passionate kiss in the garden at the back of the house. There was a slight hill at the rear of Carmel's house with long grass by the pond near the back fence. Asper had been keeping it this way and Carmel liked it so much, she had quietly taken Tim away from the others at the front for this kiss. As soon as Celia had erupted into giggles, they both broke away laughing and pretended to chase her. She ran off from them to go and fetch anyone else who might come with her, returning a few moments later with Lorraine, Raynie, and Chan. Immediately she convinced them a game of chase would be best done around the Mulberry tree to the side of the pond near the long grass. They all joined her in a frantic game of laughter and acting with deliberate tricks and a few spills and tumbles, before exhaustion took to all of them for the time sending them falling to the ground despite the grass being wet from melted winter frost.

For the remainder of the day the entire group sat on the grass around the Mulberry tree. Carmel had taken to wanting to prepare lunch by herself as a gesture to welcome all to her house, and in thanks for them all being there and for those who had arrived before her and taken care of the house. They had discussed the fact of it being somewhat remarkable it had survived intact all these years, but there were still other even older buildings around the town, so they surmised this town and perhaps others were of no significance for the Agent to bother with during his reign of terror. When chill took to the air and the last red ochres of sunset were glowing low over the hills to the west, they were all situated inside for dinner and a night of enjoying each other's company. Conversation over sensitive matters was not an option. They were to be free from deliberations indulging in some alcohol Gareth had secretly brought. John immediately set about searching for any other deceptions Gareth may have in store as he muttered a few sarcastic remarks on how the newly presented bottle of scotch could have helped them along the road before they had arrived at the house.

"Well then, what would we have to celebrate with now? Careful planning you see so we get to have occasions like these. What better measure?" Gareth said as he feigned a few punches into John's ribs. John pretended to not see them coming and so fell in a crumpled heap acknowledging the merit of Gareth's point. "I see now," he said in a strained voice.

"Good. Then remember your lessons dear sir, and always consider there is much to learn always if one is to be wise."

"Am I getting this right? Tim has a way of breaking into talk like...and Chan, and... hmm, I'll bet there will be a lot for you yet you have not realised Gareth."

"Why thank you dear lady Carmel. An essence of creativity... of art, is within us food connoisseurs as well you know."

"Indeed I do know. Bless you dear...all of us. Well then, open the bottle you are so proud of."

At nights end, Derek, Murray, and Esther took Celia home after leaving with thanks and an invite for all to visit and stay at their house. As Celia walked through the front door, she waved at the others and then her eyes settled on Asper, telling her it would be nice for her to come and stay at their house. Chan had noticed this connection between these two previously as he did at this moment, and it filled him with a sense of warmth amplified by the torus he carried in his pocket.

Celia also gave him her eyes, but for less time than she had given Asper. Chan knew what she was saying and soon he would learn from her, despite his appearance of apparent wisdom through greater age. The feelings and knowledge being activated were not confined to the bounds of lineal lives of acquired experiences, though they were very much in alignment with experience. It was coming from a different place in all people waiting to be remembered through their elemental spark of all pervasive consciousness.

After they had left, the others lingered around outside talking to stay away from any surveillance.

"It is inevitable for us to face much stronger challenges now we have returned here to Carmel's house," Raynie said pre-empting Chan as he was about to speak.

"Indeed. We are all of such knowledge, for ahead of us there are the challenges for rebuilding our lives here."

They been focusing on human and torus activation for some years now and their intentions were becoming far more influential than they realised at times.

Chan brought them to thinking of the dodecahedron Celia had so proudly shown them in the garden. "When energy is properly focused as we see through many mediums be they human contact, machines, computers, the universe and dimensions at large, exponential growth in progression occurs where measurement begins to take on much less significance. But...it also bears significance for many contexts in order to control the machines, gain the correct results from data input for computers, and for us in maintaining correct focus. The strengths of our elemental intentions can be sub-consciously received as energy without definition by others who may be considered as dominated by the negative ego. In these instances, the negative ego attempts to reconcile what is detected sub-consciously into familiar patterns for it to feel in place within the embodiment of an individual. As we know, this is very much a blockage to synchronised alignment and so in reaction, behaviour, health, and decision making can bring forth the results of this misalignment."

"What about the dodecha...?"

"I am getting to it. Be not impatient and feel as I speak as I know you do. The shape represents the angles where energy points or meridians come together in construct of the overall object. This principle is evident in all forms of energies interacting be they physical, emotional, or beyond, for the sake of constructing the intended outcomes. You can see this in machines, in relationships, and through the acts and motivations of the authorities. In past times as well as present, most of this has been largely ignored by humanity and so often it has then led to disparity and misalignment, disease, or the break down in many parts of society. As we focus now and in reflection we witness this object Celia holds so dearly, we are bringing into our lives what our intentions seek. As exponential energy, there is more beyond what we see or understand in direct consequence, which as you understand, is energy of potential."

"Celia doesn't hold the object as one of affection though. It is as if she is aware of the meaning behind its presence," Lyle said quietly.

"I too sense this Lyle. She is much aligned as it is an emerging and growing common place for people her age, and also could be for those yet to come. Therein is reason for us to be extraordinarily mindful and of genuine heart ahead in life, and I mean from this very moment. We have discussed this at length over time, and whilst some of those times seemed quite arduous requiring the best of our focus, ahead of us lies yet greater tests for this activation process reflected to us through the torus."

"So you are saying we need to make even greater effort?"

"Yes. We are here to enhance alignment whilst never being complacent, a pertinent value for acknowledging the intentional behaviour of children free from bind and thus of authentic presence."

Next morning, Celia and Esther woke everyone at Carmel's house as the sun was beginning to rise. This day dawned grey though, and so there was no visible sunlight, just the light of day gradually emerging through the misty veils throughout the valley. Celia was the first to reach the front of the house calling out to all wake up as she knocked persistently on the door.

"Wake up, wake up. Esther and Celia are here."

Carmel was the first to answer their calling, appearing sleepy and dishevelled when she opened the door. Neither of the two visitors were concerned with her appearance, instead they gave her a fond yet solemn greeting. As she cast her eyes beyond them to the sky outside, Carmel could sense the grey misty light as something reflective of the mood Celia was in particularly. Esther looked less concerned but was visibly feeling similar to the young girl.

"What is it dears?"

"The authorities are here with weapons and they are going through the entire town. Father and Murray told us to come here and tell you whilst they stayed at our house for when the officers came."

"What is their take on this Esther?" Jenna asked when by the time Celia and Esther were in the lounge room as her and all the others had risen rubbing sleep from their faces.

"It looks ominous. They do have laser weapons which means they are not being friendly."

"Perhaps the weapons are for some assurance to force people to comply with their objectives, and not for use other than outright dissent."

"Let us hope it is all and their objectives are not too demanding Jenna."

"They will be demanding Jake. Recall what we discussed late into last night. What I spoke of is so prevalent it has come to us almost at the very first opportunity. The presence of these armed officers is a reaction to uncertainty. For their ideas of control to manifest according to their desires if one can call them such, then they are going to strongly exert themselves. It is their way."

"Then what are we to do?"

"Nothing other than placate their requests in the most sensible way to avoid trouble. We must retain strong focus and not give anything away or be seen as suspicious through our body language coming from fearful thoughts."

Carmel then spoke invoking a sense of calm, "Just treat this all with a casual approach and not allow any situation to distract us away from our true selves. Only when we see uncertainty in a way where it affects our stability inducing fear, do we begin to distance ourselves through separation of heart and mind. A strong heart remains true to its intentions, its alignment, and true authenticity. No circumstance is outside or external and so despite tests of courage, our strength of will, or where we are meant to be in life moments, we will be in the aligned place through elemental contact to who we are, not what we think we should be."

When they were all gathered as a group free from sleepiness, Asper and Celia were drawn together without any conscious mind to do so. Their connection was very evident and growing stronger - now they sat snugly together on the couch with Celia remaining mostly quiet during the discussion. Asper spoke only to confirm agreement with the points of issue Chan, Carmel, and the others were discussing, content mostly to go with the feelings she was sharing with Celia.

"Watch them. They will be suspicious anyway. Now so many of us have gathered, they will look closely. Big groups don't show up much. We didn't see any on the way to this town did we Esther."

"No we didn't dear. What is it John?" Esther noticed he looked distant to the others, and instinctively she then looked at Tim to see both men seemingly sharing similar concerns.

John looked up and spoke though only softly interrupting the entire feeling of the conversation, "We need to move now to ensure we do not have to endure any potential situation. They are going to have technology far surpassing anything we have seen on a wide spread scale and this means we have to take counteractive measures. Perhaps this is where you are very correct in one sense Chan, so we must keep in mind, the fact our technology and our collective group, coupled with their propensity to be suspicious could be awkward. Tim, let's start."

Both men immediately went outside to discuss how to set about taking measures to hide the technology they possessed. Carmel was impressed with Tim's secret room, but John told them they would have to do more to prevent any detection of technology.

"I will build a force field. Yep, you heard it right. It won't repel forces, but it will cast a shell around things effectively scrambling any scanning."

"What about their results data John? A scramble is something."

"I know so I suggest we get to work straight away and determine the resonant operational and crystal status of the quantum computer you have, plus all I have...and the torus. All of it."

"But there is no time."

"We have to do this as soon as possible. As chance may have it, any visit we receive from armed officers may not include a capability for running scans. From what I know of the technology Eric was so pleased with, I anticipate we have a window of only a few days. My own scanning device confirmed he has placed the star inside the anomaly. It is a simple residual frequency scan...harmless and easily overlooked, but the patterns are there and the signature indicates there was a large surge of sub atomic energy when the star went in, followed by subsequent moderated energy flashes likely to do with engaging different phases of the monolith systems."

"What we were dealing with in eighty eight and since, is nothing compared to what you are telling me John. We will have to draw on this Chan knowledge with focus on the torus. I know its flux application...but we are going beyond aren't we? And what about the scramble though?"

"You're right. It will go well beyond my current capacity to generate flux mechanics. And, I am confident the signal will disappear through fine tuning the scramble to mask any output from our gear."

"I won't say I hope it works. I know you'll give it your best shot. Tell me what you need hardware wise and I'll start on it while you get to work scanning."

"Agreed mate. Let's go. I have a few small bits I am sure will be good enough to create the energy field we need."

As both men worked, they held their strongest focus for probably as long as they could remember. For John, his battle with the internal mechanical devices in his mind, had subdued to a manageable state. He could sense their impact less and less as each day had passed and without any proximity to Eric, he was able to free his thinking knowing his knowledge would not be detected.

"How's the mind?"

"Yeah steady mate. I am going to have to get your expertise to remove them though."

"Hey, chip removal is one thing but brain surgery is another case."

"I'm confident you and I can find a way. Here, I have the scramble. We are covered. Let's finish up."

Almost the instant they had finished and emerged through the door to the secret room, two armed officers were pounding on the front door of Carmel's house.

Celia met John and Tim in the hallway on their way to the lounge room, "Now use your brains."

"Um...what, we just did."

"Yeah I know, but do you know?"

"Know?"

"Yes. Really know. You can tell those men what you want to say if you use your brain properly. They will ask you questions, but you can decide the answers. Awakened brains are like this...they talk different. Knowing what will really be happening is beyond those men, so you can um, order them around. It is how their bosses do it."

"I thought we were awake Celia."

"You are...much more than anyone else I know besides this place. Plus you know how to make little machines. You are very awake."

"Thank you Celia."

"No need to thank me John...or Tim. You are both good men and telling you these things is what I have to do."

"Okay, we should hush now. I can hear the officers talking to Jake and Lyle."

"Alright."

At the last moment, John directed Tim and Celia to remain out of sight from the officers in the lounge room. He felt confident the men did not know of their presence as they had not spoken since he had heard the men talking. He hushed the other two indicating they should just stand and listen, but Celia would not do as he asked.

"You didn't use your head," she whispered as she walked past him into the lounge room. John and Tim followed immediately after for all three to have appeared before the officers could say anything.

Carmel, Lorraine, Asper, Raynie, Jenna, Gareth, Chris, and Chan were standing silently to the side as the two officers directed their talk at Jake and Lyle.

"We were advised only two adults lived in this house. Who are all of you? Present yourselves for an identity scan," the senior of the two officers said to John and Tim, eyeing them carefully. He completely ignored Celia passing her off as a simple child.

"No others officer. We came as soon as we heard the talking."

"I see."

Chan coughed twice to mask, "Do you?"

The officer picked up on this immediately, turned to Chan and gave him a dismissive look. "What relevance do you have old man. It will not be long before we see the last of your types...inefficient and contributing nothing to the cause."

Chan felt the irresistibility of the moment, "What cause?"

"For the new phase of how life is to be for all. For the measure of compliance to guarantee a safe and productive life. Not one part of it includes wastage like you old man."

"All you officers seem to say the same thing. Perhaps there could be a way I could contribute to the cause. Surely everyone has something to offer."

"We will see." The senior officer broke off there as he remembered there were still some properties to visit this day, and the shortest amount of time he had to bother with the general population, the better.

"We are here to advise there will be stricter measures than what has been put into place to this day. The authorities seek only to better humanity through productivity in leading efficient lives for the greater cause of progress. During the days ahead, you will see new allocations for improvement in your day to day living, including the new network of technology and entertainment the authorities will provide. In order to maintain access to these new services, and to generally maintain access to the energy grid for domestic purposes, people are required to work according to their capacity in order to strive for the best possible outcome in status. Are you listening?"

Everyone present nodded in the affirmative except for Celia.

The officer continued whilst second in command stood blocking the front doorway as he had the entire time. "Since the days of the Agent, the authorities have deemed it necessary to strengthen all security measures to ensure safety at large. The authorities also advise officers will be stationed at regular positions through all territories to ensure compliance with all regulations. Non compliance and dissent will invoke punishment. Be assured, any dissent will be severely dealt with. Are you listening?"

Celia thought it was funny how the officer asked this question considering he was the one who was not listening to himself. Carmel thought similarly to Celia, except her angle was on the wording of the question asking if people were listening rather than if they understood.

"Finally, all systems for your available use will be productive within the next three days. Be sure to register yourselves for work and allocation of credit as soon as possible. The best jobs will go fast."

The senior officer then gave the impression they were then about to leave, but instead he indicated to the other officer to commence a scan search of the house. John, Tim's and everyone else's heart skipped a beat during the first few seconds as the officer engaged his holographic scanning device. Seconds later it returned a negative on any other DNA profiles being present at this location, thus giving them all respite. Nobody had outwardly showed anxiety at this time - they had all worked well holding onto their strength of intent.

Without further word, both officers departed the house, leaving the entire group standing in silence as each thought of what the officers had told them. Celia could notice how the adults appeared to be unconcerned when they thought about what had been said. This was very good to her as she shuffled about a little on the spot watching them. In all, it was only a matter of about fifteen seconds before she spoke calling out to Asper.

"Come and live with us today please Asper. Please?"

"Sure dear. I think it is a good idea."

Carmel noticed there was a chill in the air, not present before the officers had visited. She went over to the large window looking out on the garden to see it had begun to snow quite heavily. "This is unusual. Take a look at how much snow there is. Tim dear, please fetch some wood."

"Come on guys, let's grab a load each."

All the men went out immediately to fetch wood from the stack at the back of the house, leaving the women and Celia alone inside.

"The way the officer spoke was horrible," Asper said. "Such a lack of something with the way he spoke and the words...an emptiness."

"Just an order for a spiritless system," Carmel responded feeling similar.

"Spiritless...yes," Raynie added. "I am fascinated with spirited character. His manner seemed to lack both."

"I'm glad you feel about like I do. When I said it was an emptiness, it is also about what he said and life in the future."

"I saw this coming when I was a former Superior Officer. I am so glad to be Carmel rather than being so often being addressed in formal tones. This is where they were heading back in eighty eight, and the Agent interfered."

"Their deals with overseas nations began to fall apart too. It seems the nature of the schemes they put into place invokes the historical divisions in the long run. They don't have enough awareness to really cross cultures and embrace different concepts."

"This time might be different though," Jenna added. "With this new level of technology, there are going to be large incentives to do deals ensuring all those involved across different nations can exert a level of control. It will become a militaristic corporation. Energy in, products, weapons, and technology out. All the while these people become removed from authentic presence in life with a packaged lifestyle robbing them of experiences much greater than anything their providers can supply."

"It is a shame as we have discussed this before and now we are likely to be facing an even tougher challenge," Lorraine said looking a little tired with the whole idea. "John and I have talked about this some in context for the technology he works with. Perhaps you could join him and Tim in looking at technology Jenna."

"I think it is a good idea Lorraine. It will be a challenge ahead, but I know enough of John's ability to be confident."

"You adults have a lot of complicated things to undo don't you," Celia stated. The adults all turned to her knowing she was right.

"They have all this silly stuff to make it complicated, and they don't need it. Silly silly."

"I think we all agree with you dear and we all love you."

"I know Esther. I think this is the best place we could have chosen to live."

"Me too dear. Hey, here come the men with some firewood. Let's help make the fire."

"I wish father and Murray were here."

A few seconds later, Murray was knocking at the front door calling out saying it was him and Derek. Celia smiled in an instant and she felt really warm despite the fire not yet being started. Chan looked at Asper, and then focused on Carmel for a few seconds. They could all sense the rise in energy amongst the group the instant the other two men had arrived, but it was Chan, Asper, Carmel, and Celia who felt it most.

Raynie opened the door to them, ushering them inside out of the heavy snow. As she helped them with their coats, Derek asked if the officers had visited.

"Yes they came with their familiar talk about nothing."

"So you 'listened' to what they had to say?"

"Yes, we were listening. Pity they are not though."

"A bit much to expect from people blinded by a society of orders and compliance."

As they said hellos to everyone, Carmel, Tim, and Celia stood up to watch the fire spark into life. Upon seeing her father, Celia ran over to him and grabbed his hand as she pulled him over to the now blazing hearth.

"Why did you come over father?"

"Murray and I thought you and Esther might need some help getting home in this heavy snow dear."

"We will be okay now we are in this town dad."

"I think so too Celia."

"But we have to watch out. John knows and so does Asper and Carmel...and Chan - all of us."

Chapter 25

The Agent had chosen this very night as his time to escape. His own mania was undefined yet definite. Eric would be sleeping his allotted night time in a place without day or night, his own mania through his mechanical mind implants contributing to his dream state. Both men were intrinsically linked. They were convinced of similar rites of passage, and whilst the Agent's rites were shaped by megalomania, Eric himself was not so distant on his own path as a subject of experimentation combining human biological systems with nanotechnology.

The interface between human and machine exceeded the DNA telomeres management robotics designed to minimise oxidisation during cell reproduction. Ironically, the early studies done by Carmel as a former officer during her visit to Germany where she reported on the aspect of elemental biological systems, was the foundation research into this capacity. It enabled more humanistic systems over just programmed robotics responding only to specific programmed scenarios.

A lull in attention to him was never really a reality as the authority systems maintained a constant watch and monitoring of all personnel and prisoners. This was not an issue for George Smythe though - he had simply outsmarted Eric and so whilst he was sleeping, the Agent would escape and in his usual way, celebrate how this affected Eric and all others. The sheer prospect of a world at the mercy of him was provocative, and as unable to resist as he was nor was he willing to, this allurement of provocation excited him as he prepared for the right time.

He was almost in a childish sense, sniggering to himself now and then, and almost beside himself with anticipation. Normally he was bereft of such elemental feelings, and so his excitement emerged as part of his mania - it was driven by his mania, and it was reflective of his mania.

Unbeknown to Eric and also unanticipated, whether it be Eric's own oversight, an oversight by his mechanical mind implants, or a combination of both, the Agent had an extensive knowledge of computer systems dynamics. He had successfully hacked into the systems he had accessed via his link with Eric, he had determined a path of escape using those systems, and most remarkably, he had accessed a new type of flying craft the authorities had yet to reveal to the public.

The Agent had acquired significant knowledge after stealing the high velocity spaceship on Mars. His years of merciless flights and of configuring virus algorithms were catalysts leading him to this new type of monolithic systems flying craft. Using a false DNA profile he built during the long hours where he was mostly left to himself, his escape would be successfully complete precisely eight minutes and eight seconds after commencement.

George had calculated all variables in coming to this time, and for measure sent a virus to Eric's system for it to then be inserted into the main operating systems if all went according to plan. Eric would inquisitively open the file of data hidden within the last report he filed about John Matheson's location so he thought - thus the virus sequencing would then begin. It would start with a breakdown algorithm to access the monolith systems, and if successful, the virus would infect and destabilise any of its vortex amplification statistical reporting. Whilst not a virus to devastate Eric's work, it would prove to be a substantial nuisance interfering with progress for sufficient time to divert their attention.

Fundamental oversight was not something the authorities considered plausible, so sure they were of the thoroughness built into their systems. Eric had been instrumental in designing nearly all systems schematics, algorithms, and contingencies since the Agent began to force the authorities to take counteractive measures to his viruses. As sure as they were, simple fundamental oversight did not elude them during the time they sought George's help in their quest to find John Matheson.

Eric was both organically and mechanically confident all possible measures had been taken to ensure secure holding of the Agent. His mechanics did provide a sense of confidence through their workings as this facet of human behaviour was viewed to be advantageous for cognitive processing leading to further efficiency. Now, without flux stability from John, those mechanics were progressively undoing what they had constructed within Eric's persona. A mask was fading to reveal another mask beneath.

Eric's oversight was simply in allowing the Agent access to any part of the authority main systems. George was able to create a false DNA profile, he was able to hack all the access codes he required to escape, and he had been able to auto engage a new monolith flying craft for taking him beyond. Eric's data security measures in place proved to be ineffective against the maniacal volition of George Smythe. Eric had vastly underestimated him.

George slipped quietly out of the deep facility right then. The air was suddenly very stale to him. It smelled of nothing yet everything in a way he found repugnant. His mania was almost at breaking point as it realised its' release. Like bolts of electricity charging through him, his psyche took George all the way to the hanger where his new acquisition awaited. It was silent. His passage to the craft was swift as if like velvet upon a polished floor. Nothing opposed him. Even the air seemed at his back pushing him closer to release. George engaged the holographic controls to commence flight as soon as he was inside. All was perfect and the systems told of nothing happening to concern him. His mania was at the cusp as he always was really. It was time now to realise the truth and to enact its' virtue.

As he streaked away from the sombre night sky over New York City, he did not even burst into his usual maniacal laughter. Something had come over him. It was not a calmness or loss of mania, rather a growth of mania resonating with his directive. Whilst dominated by his states of mind, George had become far more cunning and capable of thoroughness than he had at any time during the years he had led the dark sect across the Earth.

When he engaged torus drive in the craft, it was as if he stood still for a second or so, before the craft rapidly accelerated to eight times the speed of sound. So advanced were its systems, George felt only a slight push from the forces bearing on him during such rapid ascent and velocity change.

When he decided to take a moment to consider his situation and decide on a destination, he had reached an altitude of one hundred thousand feet. There almost at the brink of space, the wondrous sight of the Earth below him bore no impact on his mood and mind. The view was not what one would have expected though, with only large cities here and there sending some of their central city lighting systems as beams upward through the sky towards him.

After a few minutes of wondering what to do, he decided to return to his original base of the time when arriving back from Mars in the stolen space ship years before. He engaged torus drive again, sending the craft in a spinning spiral as it turned on a heading taking him across the entire breadth of the former United States, then out across the Pacific Ocean to Australia.

Within two hours he could see the city of Canberra as a few dullish lights far below him. After stopping a moment to gain his bearings, he adjusted his heading taking him to the east of the city where he once had begun his reign as the Agent. All this time, the authorities had no knowledge of his destination, his heading, his speed, his altitude, or even if he had left New York City. George had ensured his theft of the craft would go un-noticed in the authority systems where the only way it would be detected was if an officer did a physical inspection and count of craft situated in the hangar.

When he saw the holographic display indicate he had reached the designated co-ordinates, George commenced rapid descent from the edge of the Earth to then land softly and un-noticed in the grassy field just outside the old abandoned farm warehouse. He pushed open the front doors to the building a minute later to find it was in a poor state inside, but relatively intact. Debris and broken machinery was everywhere all throughout the building. It was in the far corner where George went to see what it was like. Debris was also all over the floor here, but this was of no consequence to him – he had one thing he needed to find.

After scrabbling about clearing everything out of the way of where he thought he would find what he wanted, he stepped back in a moment of maniacal glee when he discovered the secret doorway in the floor was still secured with the same combination lock he had placed their prior to moving his operations base to Seattle years before.

George fumbled a little as he unlocked the door, so excited he was with the prospect this first part of his escape was going so well. He almost stumbled as he took the stairs to the chambers thirty feet below ground. With a hand held light, George hurried to inspect the chambers. First he found the energy cells he had stashed as if he had known then this time would come now, and so he engaged a few to light up the rooms.

There was nothing much to see aside from scattered remnants of his previous life, and a few scurrying rats. The rats did not bother him – to George they were not even worth acknowledging in presence. He had no need to search any further either, for he knew precisely where he would have to go. At the far end of the last room branching off the wide corridor running the entire length of the underground chambers, George found the beacon. He immediately activated the beacon and silently it sent a signal to all others who possessed sufficient technology to receive. It was a unique channel only those who sought the ways of dark sects would ever hear. Amongst the many groups they had shared this knowledge and subversive means to communication without being detected by the authorities then or now. In fact, they had remained so removed from society, their secretive ways had prevailed for centuries unbeknown to the population at large.

He cared nothing for this call. Care was beyond him. If anyone came, they would serve the greater purpose. It was beyond George now. He was really no longer serving any personal need. It was an elemental expression of mania and so it would do through him what was meant to be done.

Satisfied to this length, he decided to hide the flying craft and so he set about clearing enough space inside the building above the underground chambers. George knew the authorities had never discovered this former lair of his – it was evident through his experiences prior to moving to Seattle, as it was by its' relatively undamaged and uninterrupted condition now.

Within the two hours, eight of his former minions had made their way to the secretive location nestled amongst steep hills in a dead end valley. George did not greet them with any form of exultation. He merely acknowledged their presence defying their outward exhibitions of enthusiasm.

"Well...we are again. I am again. You are again in service and again to service you are to be bound. Enact this fortune as your own and you will be punished by the mere circumstances you arouse. This time we are not stopping for anything idle like any of your petulant behaviour in the past. I have vital data for our cause. Now get to work and re-build this place and our path to our self denial will be revealed."

George knew Eric would be very troubled by now. Not only had he failed to keep Matheson for his precious Monolith project, now the maniac himself so despised by all was free again. His deranged half smiled was aroused as he considered how this would immediately erupt into a cataclysm for Eric. His plan had worked flawlessly through hacking into systems and creating false profiles when he needed them. Beyond Eric, George was likely second only to John for knowledge of flux systems and so could always hold one last upper hand over Eric when the opportunity came. It would always come – George knew this and he had again played the game to exploit those moments of weakness within people.

His mind taunted itself further – the mania rising and swelling, erratic and testing. For an instant he was distracted by his erection and then immediately it sent him headstrong on a pathway almost carnal as he delved into the animal of his psyche to express the rage of unabridged wildness. Ideas raced around, each vying for a stranglehold urging him into action. He had no need to contain his mind. He had no perception of containment during these moments, and without sense of same where containment establishes boundaries founded in moral and empathic feeling, George overstepped these imaginary lines, bereft of existence beyond absence towards oblivion neither here nor there.

George Smythe former Agent Eight, victim in his mind to the condescending mannerisms of the superior officer bitch making him furious when she almost succeeded in exiling him to asteroid mining. George Smythe, the notorious daring agent who stole a spaceship for return to Earth to then take over as head of the dark sect. Then George Smythe, the Agent who had delivered so much terror and misery as he flew the Earth almost entirely to his own volition, choosing what and where he would strike through computer viruses sent to microscopic robotics inside people's bodies delivering horrors never imagined.

Once again he felt an iteration of self to be realised as a sudden attack – an affliction of burden. Like a fever, like a schizophrenic attack, or a sudden bout of epilepsy, George existed at this edge, at a fine line between composure and lack of control. Like all people who evolve through life experience, his position of disposition was yet to mature as its potential growth beckoned to him now. It was as if he was possessed and in a way he was, but not of the beast so many of the dark sect would secretly wish for themselves – George was simply possessed by himself, who he was, and who he was to become in punishment of self.

George was very much human without restraint for expressing the darkest traits found within human embodiment. He had feeling. It was mania, as was his volition. His will unfounded in reason contained all the symmetry required for chaos. This was his reason and his utter contempt held for almost all who were not exactly like him. He hated them anyway. It held him, it spoke to him, and it controlled him. George was merely the vessel for this entity, cast adrift on a sea of misery without heading yet all the while on a course to nowhere beyond space and material, beyond concept, and to an oblivion of irreverence.

He was simply the next incarnation of what was as old as humanity itself. This was his reason. Unconscionable in apparition as his manifestations beyond quantum particles and beyond his wildest imaginings, he was the trauma of human being, he was the utter reversal of all in place for the seat of the soul, and he was the action so many never dared approach.

In an instant he was immersed in ways to establish some algorithms he knew would be suitable for making his monolithic flying craft invisible to detection. Eric had provided him sufficient access for obtaining key specific resonance data for monolith operations during the time he was asked for calculations to stabilise the anomaly.

Without pausing to think, he set about putting the small quantum components together he had stolen during the course of his escape. Every docked monolith craft had a device for monitoring attached to the docking bar. George had simply removed the device during start up of the craft. It was his, and whilst not a full quantum processing device, it contained monolith components and algorithms he could easily adapt to suit his purpose now.

A small holographic field emitted from the fully operational device within a second after the Agent barked a command. He immediately then set to work building an algorithm to bypass its torus drive systems, so he could then removed the small ring for use in the vortex amplifier he would later build. After ten minutes of work, the field changed slightly as torus drive was diverted through pseudo parallel systems. Before the torus had even stopped its mild pink glow, the Agent had removed it from its holographic housing to hold it in his hand.

For a few more moments he stood just looking as his mind took him on a wild ride of possibility awaiting him for when he had successfully replicated previous efforts in building a vortex amplifier. He then put it in his pocket and returned to his immediate objective. When he was sure he had done all required to create a masking algorithm to conceal his monolith craft, he decided to take it for a test fight and to further understand its capabilities.

The algorithm was working as he rose steeply into the air oblivious to authority monitoring systems located in the nearby city of Canberra. Numerous times he took the craft to the brink of space, trying each time to push it a little further. But he was unable to break free of the atmosphere, and amongst screaming systems warnings, he spent a moment in anger bashing the clear front view screen, before lunging earthward at sickening speed until when only one hundred feet above ground, the craft came to a sudden stop.

Anti gravity inertia systems cancelling the effects of gravitational forces permitted this erratic style of flying motion. No wings were evident on the craft.

Aerodynamics adapted to conditions in real time using the programmable matter construct of the craft. Capable of changing shape in response to forces and atmospheric conditions, the craft was ideal for any situation during Earth bound flight. It was limited though, and could never be taken to space.

As he sat hovering a hundred feet in the air, George thought of this contingency. It troubled him for he knew more powerful technology than his was above him beyond reach, meaning the authorities would have this upper hand to counteract anything he did. He decided stealing beyond Earth technology was inevitable for his cause and this made him snigger a little as he set out on further flights of fancy, all the while conjuring plans to realise this theft.

Despite the considerable task it would be to steal a space capable craft, George knew where their flaws were, their inefficiencies, and of their ignorance. Whilst barely capable in many instances of applying logical lineal processes to thinking, George's mania had become his instrument to thoroughness. Years spent captive in body, locked away from the world by a mere array of holographic cell bars, had evolved his manic mind. It was an irresistible seduction to George and he took to it without consideration of where it may lead.

As suddenly as he did, the Agent changed tact by engaging pseudo torus drive – 'what a marvel even Matheson would admire,' he thought. His heading was directly back to his new home and to oversee progress by his minions.

As they were, these people had taken to immediately pick up from where they had left off a few years prior when the Agent had been captured. So embellished in their beliefs to an extent where they had all crossed a line never to return to life previous, they had each lost sight of themselves, including their heart as they delved deeper into vestiges of darkness and their own individual insanities. They merely obeyed the calling they thought was coming from the beast and yet this calling came from the negative aspects born from ego. This measure of circumstance was not abhorrent to them in any degree, nor was it a real sense of loss to them. They had simply lost touch with a true sense of being, instead relinquishing self actualisation to delusion.

Within a week, the Agent had been joined by almost twenty other people who had immediately contributed to re-building the former base where he had held Chan and the others captive years before. It was ramshackle in appearance then as it was now, yet effective in hiding what lay inside and beneath. Prior to the dark sect taking it over from the original owner, there had been caverns, rooms, and passageways constructed deep into the ground. The dark sect had therefore been naturally aspired to take such a place by killing the owner and his family, and then occupying the entire complex in force where numbers meant they were rarely threatened.

When he became satisfied with the state of repairs, he ordered them to leave him alone with his holographic array. George did not tell them he was about to build a new vortex amplifier. He simply gave orders for tending to surveillance and maintenance, ensuring they were at the ready to obey any of his mania based commands. He was right. So weak had they become in their own volition of authentic actualisation, they were easily moulded through his style of manic language and dominating sense of insanity. Each one aspired to be like him for some reason of self loathing then exhibited for all the experience both as an energetic low point and a psychological density. It was their way to express this degrading of light so minimal it focused only just above the threshold of darkness to then view into the complete darkness of oblivion. They obeyed as it was their condition of self for they restricted their consciousness to self and only saw their deities and methods of evil worship as anything conscious beyond the meat body self. Their meat, their reckoning...immersed in blood. Now again in service they wanted to deliver this blood working feverishly to invigorate its apparition sooner and sooner – their hunger like their messenger alone with his holographic bank, sought to deposit their depravity upon others as his will lacking.

Inside the room where he had spent so much time sending viruses delivering terror, punishment for existence, and denial of self sent to oblivion, George again took to the pleasures of such vice. First he began to convert some programmable matter into two horned torus. The marvel of this monolith technology was how before one's eyes, solid objects changed shape as the program reached beyond the atomic level to reconstitute matter.

Chapter 26

Carmel's house was a little removed from the scene in town where buildings were situated side by side and separated by a fence. The house next door to her had been in a rundown state since she had first moved to the town after leaving San Francisco. Despite a somewhat dilapidated appearance, the house was in good enough repair for John, Lorraine, Chris, and Gareth to live there leaving more room at Carmel's, and to also increase their overall footprint of properties between the entire group.

Derek, Murray, and Esther had considered doing this as well in order to bring all three residences closer together, but after a conversation at the front of this other house they decided it would be best they remain where Derek and Murray had done so much restoration work themselves. Asper had already moved in with them much to Celia's delight, who was the only one to speak outright against moving. She had told them their location would also provide them with a view into the other side of town for watching what the authorities might be doing.

Everyone was pitching in to help restore the old house when two officers drove by in a vehicle nobody had ever seen before. John knew it was monolith technology as they all stopped working and stared for a moment when the officers slowly drove along the road. The vehicle appeared to lack distinction between operating parts, instead where wheels would normally be attached, it was suspended above the ground using anti-gravity technology. It cast an ominous presence before the officers deliberately moved slowly away still noticing the unease amongst the onlookers.

A short time after they had passed, John stood at the front of the house admiring the progress of the work so far. From its ramshackle look, the house had now taken to appearing liveable in a very short period of time. As a mark of acknowledgement, they all gathered for the evening to have a meal and converse prior to the authorities arriving to install technology. It was a relaxed time they all knew was to be almost the last before again they would face adversity.

Next morning the authorities arrived at dawn to install access to energy, and for the provision of entertainment and quality of life with the installation of holographic hardware. The attending officers seemed to be less friendly than any others previously, content to do just their work with a focused determination for efficient success. When Asper, Celia, and Carmel noticed the look of consternation behind their eyes, they could all see each officer was slipping away from themselves, slipping away from their soul, and slipping further and further into compliance.

As if natural forces were aligning to draw them closer to each other, everyone decided it was best to stay together at the house for the night. As Chan had said to them softly whilst they built an open fire outdoors, it was imperative they focus together to remain attentive to what they could be called upon to action.

Celia had spent a lot of the evening going around the house playing in one room, or asking them all to come and talk in another.

"We are spreading our energy to this house," she said to them without anyone actually raising a question as to why she insisted they follow her. They all loved her for such ways. Even Gareth and Chris had warmed to Celia's behaviour – both men sensing the elemental freedom she embraced and projected. This was something new to them as they had very little experience with children in life.

"Hey Chris, aren't you glad you came here with your father? I am. Father and I think this is where we are meant to be. It is sad mother is not here, but I know she is smiling about us. She is happy we are happy."

"Um, yes I am happy about it Celia. I see there is more to life than working for the author..."

"They are silly. Such closed up minds. I will never understand why they do the things they do."

"Come to think of it, neither will I Celia. I think I was sleeping...like you say."

"Yes maybe. I don't really know, but I do know it was silly and causes pain to people. You know, I have a secret too. I bet they wish they had it."

Everyone laughed knowing Celia's secret was indeed something the authorities would wish they possessed. Yet it was not a secret for possession or control – it was in the energy of essence, of mystery, of living, and of authentic experience they experienced together as a building momentum to where they did not know.

"Can we dance here Asper? Who can play music?" Celia turned to Carmel who was such a lover of music and its effects on feelings.

"I cannot play an instrument and I don't have one..."

"Then sing. We have all heard your voice and we like it. Sing Carmel. We can dance to your songs."

Carmel cast a quick glance around the entire group seeking their agreement. She was not nervous as she had no reason to feel such a way around people she loved, and as soon as they had all confirmed agreement to Celia's request, she began a song.

It was a folk type song telling the story of a young couple who fought whatever they came up against to realise their true love.

Melodic and entrancing, her voice captivated them all for a few moments before the tempo of the song increased inspiring most of them to join in dancing with Celia and Asper. Lyle and Jake had taken to drumming a rhythm on wooden barrels so Carmel held this tempo for a time as they danced along.

John, Tim, and Jenna were the first to break away from the scene as they went to Carmel's house and into the secret room to work on technology. When they sat for a while, Chan, Raynie, Lyle, and Jake began discussing the focus of intentions both laterally and as an intentional projection through the Torus of Eternity Chan still kept in his pocket. Gareth and Chris went with Derek and Murray to gather some wood stock and other supplies they could find, leaving Esther and Lorraine talking about what they could do for growing food in the coming spring just a few weeks away.

Carmel continued her song, more hushed now, holding Celia and Asper with her words as they sat listening. She was seated on an old wine barrel and in some way it was bringing out the best in her voice. Now and then she tapped the barrel in an abstract beat to her song, and this made Celia smile broadly as she attempted to copy Carmel's actions. Her smile grew taking her naturally into laughter. As child-like her actions were, both Asper and Carmel joined her feeling drawing upon their own inner child – all of them aboard a carousel feeling elation. When Esther noticed Celia through the kitchen window as her and Lorraine plotted out a vegetable garden at the rear of the house, she felt yet more sense of how Celia's life was progressing further away from the ordeal of separation after her mother's death.

"She is going so well now. I knew she would come through, but she is really in an element," Esther said when Lorraine had also stopped to watch.

"It's wonderful she can become...or just be like she is. We all could take heed of what she projects."

"I find it a bit overwhelming at times Lorraine. Perhaps her freedom of spirit is a lesson for me in letting go of the concerns with taking over from her mother. Filling a mother's shoes can be a challenge. I like your perspective on it. It um..."

"Frees you up a bit? Allows you be you and not what an expectation of whom you should be?"

"So she is our reminder."

"And teacher. We all are to each other."

Celia noticed Esther and Lorraine were looking in through the window, so she sent them a broad smile and a wave. They waved and smiled back to her, then returned to song with Carmel and Asper. By now they had reached a focal point of all the songs Carmel had so far chosen to sing. She had deliberately led the other two along a course taking them to a melodious dreaming. Celia loved this as she took hold of Asper's hand giving it a tight squeeze.

"We share dreams you know," she said out of childish enthusiasm. Carmel acknowledged her with a quick smile through the words she sang, before continuing on with the song.

Lyle entered the house just then with Chan, Jake, and Raynie in tow. They had become enchanted and compelled with the singing during their conversation outside near the road and allowed fascination with the feeling Carmel, Asper, and Celia were generating.

Chan retrieved the torus from his pocket to show them what he already knew, and could physically feel. The ring was a familiar yet richer pink as it vibrated on palm of his hand. Celia was immediately drawn to it, and whilst she too had a torus and a dodecahedron, she had nothing as beautiful as the Torus Chan kept. She didn't want it. She would never want it. She knew as long as he had it, everyone she loved had the torus. This did not stop her from wanting to hold it though as she reached out to Chan with a simple look deep in feeling. He responded immediately by placing it on her hand which she then drew tightly around the ring. After a second or two, she released her grip for the others to see, and what they saw astounded them. In just those small moments, the torus had begun to radiate outward as opposed to just within as it had been since any of them had first seen the pink hue. They were all taken aback for a few moments as they just stared in wonder at the enchantment of the spectacle. Chan then looked into Celia's eyes to find her eyes were already fixed on his.

"See," she said to him.

"Yes I do Celia."

"Well those authorities would want this secret wouldn't they?"

"Definitely. What did you...?"

"You know Chan. All of us know. The voices told me this type of thing would happen, and they said I am free in spirit to show this to you."

"Did they say you have a special power Celia?"

"No silly. Nothing special at all. Everyone has this ability. They just forget. You see it don't you Chan?"

"We all see dear, but perhaps you have a head start on us," Esther said noticing Chan seemed to be lost for words for a moment.

"Um, we have never seen such a rapid change in activation. Perhaps there are things you can teach us Celia," he managed after a few seconds.

"It's okay Chan. I can teach you but I am not a very good teacher who makes lessons. You just need to watch and find out for yourselves."

"I think we can Celia."

"I know everyone can, even those silly officers if they tried."

"To remember?"

"Yes. And we need to be very careful with this torus now. I saw what it did in my dreams last night. Asper was there and she saw it too didn't you Asper."

"Yes I did dear."

"Well, watch out because it is beaming this light out now and it means other people will learn where it is. We need to guard it very well."

"I agree...we all do Celia."

"Thank you Carmel. You and Asper are amazing."

"What about us?" Raynie asked.

"Of course you are. Here Chan, put it away now. It is time."

"Time?"

"Yes listen."

Merely a few seconds later, all energy and holographic monolith systems came on line at the house. Everyone looked to Celia astounded at her precognition and how she may have known when this was to occur. She looked back at them in turn with a simple expression as if she had absolutely no idea on how she did. When she finished by settling on Chan for a few seconds, she turned and ran outside to play, issuing a call beckoning everyone to come and join her.

"Don't worry about hologram stuff. We know what it is like already," she said to their concerned faces as they ventured outside.

"Can we play around a bit here? Maybe I can help make the garden. It is like playing. Can I help please Esther?"

"Certainly Celia. Anyone can help."

"I'm going to see Jenna for a minute," Lyle said as all the others started off for the rear of the house to where Esther and Lorraine had plotted a garden.

As he neared Carmel's house, Lyle felt a sudden pang of urgency to see what they were up to in the secret room. With the need to remain stealthy about anything the authorities would deem as suspicious, Lyle quietly made his way to where the room was located. He then knocked his foot on the floor in the agreed code, before Jenna opened the cover panel concealing the inner door.

"Come in."

Lyle gave her a peck kiss on the cheek and took her hand as they sat down to watch what Tim and John were doing. Both men were immersed in a holographic display whilst they entered algorithms and finetuned hardware.

"John has found a way into some decent systems," Tim said a moment later. "As we know, the authorities and the few remaining corporations left have basically merged in recent decades. The public are being told there still are large opportunistic corporations as autonomous organisations to the authorities giving the illusion of the old economics competitiveness. Most people are unaware they are actually part of one and the same."

"A lot of former executives have become authority figures."

"Precisely Lyle. John has found a way in - a hack into one of these pseudo companies who are listed as supplying hardware to the authorities and who also serve to assist in the reconstruction of cities the Agent decimated. Fortunately for us this company has a few little holes John has found."

"Access to the hardware side?"

"Yes. This so called company has a direct connection into the monolithic systems for monitoring of performance for their hardware."

"Yeah...a big error on their part. One they would not even be aware of," John added as he briefly glanced away from the holographic display.

"Well, this portal or access we hacked just now should provide us some interesting specifics on how those systems function. John already has significant knowledge, but these operational parameters are vital if we are to stay a step ahead."

"Your quantum computer helped Tim?"

"Without it we would be far too slow to effect a decent covert intrusion into the monolithic technology."

They all fell silent as John then proceeded to enter algorithms at a rate so fast Lyle was mesmerised by his actions. Jenna had encountered this many times over the years developing protein string technology, but she too was impressed with how John was going. As he worked, the display constantly went through change as strings of data, three dimensional renditions of data processing, and readouts for systems monitoring appeared and disappeared.

A few minutes later, he suddenly exclaimed he had done it, and there before them in holographic space, was a control section for monolith robotics.

"They will not detect any of this. I have constructed an algorithm bypassing all their security checks."

"You think they would have more stringent security measures," Jenna commented looking a little bewildered as to how they could make such an oversight.

"They do have wide ranging layers of security, but they did not count on my knowledge being sufficient for making inroads bypassing their systems. I suppose Eric felt confident his systems were secure and I wouldn't be able to get my hands on this technology."

"What next then?"

"Good question. Your insights into protein strings can help our next stage of operations."

"I thought similarly. Application of the string dynamics was useful before with the work you did after arriving here, but you might need to guide me through this event."

"By all means. To start with, they are using amino acid pathways for conducting high speed data transition during the stage where programmable matter interacts with nucleotide sub atomic quantum separation."

"Programmable matter?"

"Yes. Tim and I discovered it this morning."

"It was quite a moment really, as I imagine it is for you and Lyle right now."

"Ah, you could say so Tim," Lyle responded.

"So you are going to tell me they have adapted the protein strings to enable even more processing through these acid pathways."

"Precisely Jenna. You can imagine the processing required at any scale of this monolith technology is going to be huge. I discovered so when they had me in New York. Eric fortunately enabled me to find out more than he would have anticipated. Going through their access points was easy once I could understand the coding they use for the monolithic programming."

"Are the strings in parallel with these acids, or are they staged hardware for transferring the amino calculations?"

"Both really. The strings amp up the power more than the acids can provide, and then as you would know, they render the processing."

"Render?" Lyle asked.

"Well yeah. Remember the cupboard you worked in on the Moon? Well, very similar to the holographic readouts you were monitoring then, but...this render is at the brink of flux mechanics, so the systems need to lay down the preconception pathways in preparation for activation through tachyon transition. They just don't have the last bit yet. The authorities are close though, but they won't get there due to instability during focus of inter-dimensional source through their torus. They just don't have the complete mathematical set, whereas I do, and so I generate this using the flux lens, which I have come to discover has the same mathematical properties as the Torus of Eternity Chan keeps."

"Have you thought of using the torus?"

"No way at this stage. The authority systems would detect it immediately due to its crystalline high vortex energy. We don't have enough power to mask high throughput."

"So how does their torus connect with these monolith data systems John?"

"I can tell you," Tim said. "By using these organic foundations, the atomic manufacture streaming from the star sent into the anomaly, can interact at a more fundamental molecular level and pass through dimensional superconductivity without any slow down affect caused by more complex materials. It focuses the sub-atomic through the wave pattern whilst simultaneously angling perpendicular to light waves from within a torus to energise at the golden section. This accesses dimensions according to the amount of pressure running through the vortex in the middle of the torus. When the pressure is high and more dimensions are accessed through using amplification, then without stability you can see how easy it could be to open unfathomable chasms in reality."

"Therein is definitely a protein strings adaptation."

"You're right Jenna. John and I have seen where your work has been adapted across a number of areas for this organic and dimensional transition, particularly with how beneficial it is for rendering other materials. We were both sure you would not like it."

"My intentions were for systems in the positive sense...you know, progressive and exploratory. These systems are regressive whilst containing these extraordinary advancements."

"We'll get around them though. Okay, just wait a moment while I key in some data to skate around inside their rink a bit – take a look around and get some bearings." John immersed himself into the holographic display once again, whilst the others watched the visual renditions of where he travelled within the authority systems. As he worked deeper into their database, he found a way to access the systems governing authority vehicles and flying craft. Several craft were listed according to their use and capacity. Whilst the authorities had full control over how material objects could be made manifest through programmable matter, it made efficient sense for them to retain specific matter clusters such as flying craft, ground based craft, and processing hardware amongst others.

As they all discussed the idea of stealing a flying craft, John could not resist his pilot urge, so he changed the display to access where he could establish a suitable data cover for the theft and prevent the authorities knowing unless they did a physical count.

Amidst the streams of algorithms, John began to notice a few odd entries. From his thorough knowledge of monolith systems only bettered by Eric Gunter, he could see a pattern emerging only he or Eric would be able to detect. He stopped then at a particular point as the origins of this odd pattern came to him.

John turned to face the others, "I am sure...um, see these algorithms? Well I am sure there is only one conclusion as to why these exist. These are almost identical to the programming I would use to cover us stealing from the authorities, but they contain one key indicator in how they perform in parallel with the monolith, or any other system. I have seen them previously...in viruses sent out by the Agent."

"He's has already beaten you to it?"

"In a way yes. This is definitely his work. I have seen his coding numerous times."

"So he is free. Why didn't you do this John?"

"The systems were not on line when I escaped Lyle."

"Ah, okay."

"This is significant news and a whole new dimension to everything. He will be after Carmel and I, you can count on it. And my guess is he will have access to monolith systems as well."

"So what do we do?"

"I am going to finish this work for now so when it comes a time to steal from the authorities, we will be able to cover any data traces. I suggest we have a talk then. Can you stay a bit longer Tim?"

"Sure mate."

Lyle and Jenna took it immediately upon themselves to inform the others of this latest news. Celia was not crying, but appeared to be very upset when Jenna spoke about John's discovery. She knew something bad was happening but she was determined to not be too childish and begin to cry.

"Now you must think very hard," she said being the first of anyone to speak after Jenna had finished.

Chan took to a thoughtful look as he listened to all Jenna and Lyle had told them. He decided it was time for further discussion of elemental properties in life so they would be best equipped to deal with the oncoming challenges, both psychologically and physically.

"Where the true test of all spirit and intention, whatever the kind or context of application, is placed under exertion, then this true test of one's fortitude will manifest the strongest reach for being actualised in each. We are to face darkness prevailing and so we must also realise our own last vestiges of darkness in each of us if we are to overcome what we are up against in truth."

Chan had hushed their murmured conversations as they knew the intent of his words as soon as they understood his tone. He spoke not of a solemn sense, rather in such a way their attention was captivated into listening and feeling his words. Since arriving into each other's lives, they had explored the prospect of this calling where their own darkness manifested from inauthentic egocentric self identification, would serve to support their endeavours. Now with the news of the Agent's escape, they all sensed the implications of the coming struggle.

"He is dominated by egocentric mania tormenting him into delusion. To overcome his and the other implications currently underway, we need to study more of the elemental geometries so we can grasp them well beyond concept."

"Well beyond concept?" Jenna asked looking at Chan a little quizzically. "You mean actually using them or controlling them through intentions and connection to elemental energies?"

"Yes Jenna. They are instrumental in retaining focus whilst they provide the capacity to manifest life in so many ways when our minds and hearts are synchronised."

"But then would all people have to do this study Chan?"

"No Raynie. Once we have gained sufficient knowledge we will be amplifying it using the torus. Consider a tipping point. When a magnet attracts an object, the object may be slowly drawn towards the magnet until it reaches a point where it is suddenly drawn quickly into the magnet. This is a measure for assisting the learning of others without them actually doing the work as we do. Anyway, it is most have forgotten this and so once we show them their memories, they will find this second nature."

Jake chimed in. "It is time for those with the capacity to act with fortitude and not merely talk."

"All of us have gathered for this purpose. It is why we are here, not as an organised group following any formal dictum – we are simply engaging and activating what exists in natural elemental course and so ourselves take us to ideas, places, and feelings of from within."

"Releasing our memories and activating ourselves to progress from an aligned authentic presence in life," Carmel said softly.

"So graceful Carmel. As I watch you speak, your mannerisms, your voice so angelic, your effortlessness...I am spellbound."

"Hey watch it Chan, or Tim might think you are getting too interested," Lorraine said, prompting them all to laugh.

Everyone knew exactly why Chan had said what he did. Carmel carried a grace so evident of the elements, where their recognition of this now would be the first learning of the workings for geometries intrinsically linked in application to their authentic self intentions in paradox actually from the concept of intention. A way without effort, yet all encompassing. It was to be their first interaction combining geometries of invention with geometries of intention.

Her presence, and her delivery of intentions were to give all of them strength – even those not present at this moment in the same location. Where they could all learn from each other, they could also recognise the energy of knowing place and confidence in self emanating from Carmel, from Celia, and increasingly from Asper.

Chapter 27

Eric's holographic device was the first to use photon neutrino beams for analysing objects and rendering a projected hologram. The application of this technology was a minor phase of the monolith systems, yet would become one of the most widespread in general use. Beams passed through any object either organic or non-organic, to map the exterior and interior coordinates of every atom, thus providing a comprehensive projection of unparalleled clarity, with a capacity to then display any component or particle down to the atomic level.

This was already proving very useful during the first morning of testing of the new device as he zoomed in to inspect the inner workings of the very device he was using. Previous holographic devices created images as virtual light refraction of airborne particles using a plotting algorithm, but now with the photon neutrino beams, the detail was comprehensively superior. Eric felt a small interest in pride as he watched all the device's functions work flawlessly.

'At least these do not suffer from instability,' he thought. Constructed of programmable matter, the holographic projectors were subject to malfunction originating from within the algorithm used for all monolith developments, but in the absence of torus processing, they were unaffected to the extent the systems around Eric were now beginning to demonstrate. Whilst he worked tirelessly to overcome these errors, Eric had not reached the point his superiors were demanding from him, and so the holographic success gave him a little respite from their pressure.

"Sir. I have fully tested the holographic units and advise they are ready for deployment."

"So the DNA updating profiler and communications bugging are working?"

"Yes sir. Any user of this device will unknowingly provide constant information about their DNA, and any information they convey to other people using this device."

"You must be sure Eric. The DNA is important, but the bugging aspect is of most interest. We do not want to miss anything deemed as insurrection."

"I am sure sir. I have tested it thoroughly. The image quality is outstanding also sir."

"Well at least you have one thing right Eric. You realise your status is now subject to review after the Agent's escape."

"I am aware sir. I am doing whatever I can for us to be able to find both him and Matheson sir."

"Then make sure we get at least one of them Eric. You are only working on this still because you are the best we have. Without your expertise, you would find yourself relegated to scientific officer status one and we both know it means you are a lackey to whoever needs you to be. No projects of your own Eric."

"I am aware of the onus for efficiency sir and I will continue to serve the authorities as best as I can to ensure we make all projected outcomes sir."

"Hmm, I cannot share your confidence yet Eric. Get me what we need for stable flux mechanics, and capture at least one of those fugitives and I may begin to grow in confidence."

"I understand sir. I have made my own progress on flux, but I am holding off reporting these findings until I am certain they will make a difference."

"Then continue. I want a report as soon as possible though. I too have superiors and they like waiting even less than I do."

"Acknowledged sir. Soon all people will be affected by trans-human technology at all moments, both awake and asleep."

"We can hope for such a day Eric. Our previous efforts stretched to cover only a quarter of the population, as feeble as they were. We need nothing but one hundred percent compliance on this Gunter. There will be no room for dissent and no room for avoiding this system. We have invested a considerable resource into this."

"I am aware of the extent to which the authorities have gone in the development of the technology sir. I also hope to report on progress within the anomaly soon as well."

"Then make it happen."

The next item on Eric's agenda for the day – one to become significant in the minds of nearly all people, was to deploy the next phase of monolithic robotics - the military police.

Each device stood twelve feet high on two legs in a hominid way with two extendable arms. Eric again felt a slight tinge of pride due to the failing of his own internal mechanics. With an ever so slight grin, he commanded deployment for the police robotics using a mechanical mind to systems direct connection. No longer would anything other than a thought be required for monolith operations. One second later, all police robots came on line, and within each mechanical consciousness autonomous nanotechnology mind mechanics were fully engaged for the first time.

Barely one minute later had they begun to make their presence felt on the streets. People were taken aback and surprised at first when confronted with the robot often standing just over twice their height as it scanned their DNA without their knowing. Eric saw these results appear within his holographic display in a time so close to real time on location.

"I want a full spectral analysis of my mechanics," he commanded to the team responsible for monitoring his and those others who possessed such implants. "I am detecting..."

"Yes?"

"Well, can't you see the issue? I have a lot of work to do and I cannot afford anything like trailing off mid sentence."

"I will get on it sir. Do you wish to stand down temporarily?"

"No. I will work through this, but get me some kind of explanation." Eric was becoming short, with a feeling of terseness he was unsure he ever remembered having at any time during his life. "I need it now rather than later."

"Affirmative sir."

Word of these formidable police machines soon quickly spread amongst the population at large, especially concerning the method used in the apprehension of people. The authorities no longer had use for large numbers of organic officers – either Police or Military. Most enlisted officers from both sectors were either being fitted out with internal mechanics, or simply had been dismissed from service and left to their own device for earning a living. As they no longer required active personnel on most fronts, so too did they abolish any sense of compassion, leaving many people who had dedicated their lives to achieving status with the forces, without any acknowledgement or assistance.

Those who could no longer afford their particular level of residence in the newly constructed high rise, and amongst the fringes at the edges of these centres, became homeless on a path to dereliction if they were unable to acquire new employment. With very few businesses outside of those run by the authorities, their chances of finding an income suddenly became greatly diminished to almost nil.

For those already on the street, this new menace was to be their nemesis. As if their circumstance was not already in such a poor state being stricken to poverty and mere survival in most instances, now this latest type of law enforcement would ensure their lives ended or became a path to nightmares.

People were being forced into choice – to become trans-human or face an effective slow death. In a way, neither choice would avoid death of self and of any remnant traces of human and individual spirit within a combined race. Humanity was to face its' most confronting reality as part of a vision of its evolution – an evolution beyond human in service to society's new machine technology system.

Many looked at this without a hint of reluctance as they envisioned a future of mechanics supporting their desires within a life free of illness and deprivation. Little did those who chose so willingly, understand the very path to deprivation they decided to take. For those who held an enquiring mind, soon enough if they failed to comply, the authorities would detect this without their knowledge, and they too would face suppression.

A few groups and the odd individual decided to refuse any interjection into their selves by the authorities – their numbers had grown in recent years after the plight of the Agent wrought havoc around them. They could see where the path of technology was taking humanity, and like those in the small town north of San Francisco, they were at their wits to defy issues of compliance and yet remain able to function in an increasingly controlled and managed world.

Across the planet in all nations and in places no longer regarded nationally and now governed as administrative zones, some people could see the discord coming as it was already apparent, and in their hearts connected to their minds energised in toroidal flow as is the way of energies throughout the universe, they began to search for personal answers they already possessed.

Now, with the latest incentives driven into minds and homes by the authority propaganda machine, the population learned they would no longer require the use of a vehicle due to the authorities providing safe and sanctioned travel routes for all of the people to enjoy. The streets were becoming empty of transport, they were becoming empty of character, and those rebuilt after the Agent had brought destruction to so many places, were simply being made as pedestrian and public transit thoroughfares.

Any hint of character within the cityscapes, along main routes through large towns, and amongst the old sectors still standing in many cities, was being lost to a history quickly receding. Style and charm were recognised as inefficient and to be of a dissenting mind by those in high office.

Endless supplies of holographic vision would come from the monolith, to project endless supplies of propaganda for what was to be an endless supply for consumption. People wanted objects and they wanted the latest technology with entertainment to marvel over. From these provisos would also come their enjoyment. Naturally the higher your status in your working credibility, the more access you were granted to both content and technology.

One particular transmission caught Eric's eye. He could see a dead person being collected from the street where she had been left by a Police robot. This was his first ever vision of the support robotic units he himself had designed and once again he was pleased, to his dismay. With a slight grunt and a shaking of his head, Eric tried to dispel these idioms of character by focusing his attention solely on the incident unfolding before his eyes.

Eric saw it place the body into an opened cavity, close the cavity door, run a two second calculation, and then shoot straight upwards at great speed. Torus drive was working as per designed specifications. Eric could see the refined motions, the precision, and the capacity to reach great speeds in mere seconds. As he watched from cameras installed on the robot, the ground receded at dizzying velocity before the robot abruptly halted and changed direction at precisely ninety degrees for a straight course to the human recycling centre.

"Eric. Wake up What is wrong with you?"

"Um, nothing sir."

"I have been monitoring you for the past ten minutes and I know inefficiencies when I see them. Your mind Eric...is in a degree of trouble is it not?"

"Yes sir it is."

"Just now I caught you dreaming. Not for a moment would I have thought a mind like yours could afford such a thing."

"It cannot afford...sir."

"I have some news for you Eric. I have a report here compiled by those responsible for monitoring your situation Eric, and it is not good."

"But how? I only asked them a short while ago."

"Surely you don't think they would have waited until you asked them do you Eric. We have had a close eye on you ever since you received your mind implants.

"I see. I know."

"Do you? How are those eyes of your working Eric?"

"Fine sir. They seem to be unaffected."

"Spectral analysis?"

"Functioning normally sir."

"Well, you are going to need it. After you engage the next phase of monolith technologies, I want you to go and look for Matheson. I am sick of this issue going nowhere, particularly now the Agent is gone as well."

"Look for Matheson myself sir? I do not understand. My work is here and..."

"And it will soon be over entirely unless you bring him to me, or bring the Agent to me. You need a break from this Eric and we want to see how these mechanics in your mind will respond to such a mission, given their propensity to fail now and then. Take what you need with you. Everything is at your disposal. Your mind is only indicative of a larger problem, and with all these errors creeping into yours, I am at pains about what to do. So...I am sending you out."

"But the work sir."

"The work will only proceed if we have Matheson or something to a lesser degree from Smythe."

"The Agent is nowhere nearly as knowledgeable as Matheson sir."

"Without either of them, we are exposed to both failure of these monolith devices, and to attack if they decided to infect our systems."

"I have worked on the assumption to some degree sir."

"And?"

"I have identified the algorithms used by the Agent. He has a particular style."

"One we want to eradicate."

"Um, yes."

"Look at these new capacity mechanics for application to the anomaly and make some progress Eric. Then I want to see you personally. We have a lot to discuss best done through a one on one meeting."

"May I ask why we need to meet?"

"Because Eric, I have not yet told my superiors of the Agent's escape. As far as they know, he is still locked away safely down there helping you. They have demanded I report soon though, so get to work on the anomaly. Otherwise, if they receive advice of Smythe's escape, then it will be both of our heads, especially yours, and I don't just mean a loss of status."

"Understood sir. I have made progress with multi-dimensional flux capacity sir. It is one step further towards the mechanics Matheson is so expert with."

"Then hurry up and get more of this. We can mask it as work done by Smythe can't we?"

"Yes sir. Easily sir."

"Is it stable?"

"Not yet sir, but I have almost been able to model stability. There are just a few key algorithms I am unaware of at this stage."

"Well get them Gunter and make it fast. I want this stage of development reached as soon as possible, no excuses. Then you go on a field trip for me."

"I will double my efforts."

"We'll be watching you...and your mind."

Eric returned to his display readouts as soon as his superior disappeared from holographic view. After two minutes of work, Eric became a little horrified by the data readout coming through from the anomaly – something those monitoring him instantly picked up. At first he thought instability within the vortex had rapidly increased as he examined hundreds of lines of data streaming from the monolith star. He quickly worked in response based on this assumption, but to no avail as his entries failed to counteract the effect of the instability.

Eric turned to his most intellectual thoughts on flux mechanics, searching within for answers to the apparent disarray growing before his robotic eyes, but none came. Whatever he tried, utterly failed. He could see the exponential growth of the issue causing what he thought was instability and he was unable to remedy the situation.

Fear then began to rise within as he thought of the meeting he had with his superior officer just moments before. Such inefficiencies would eventually lead to his downfall in status, meaning he would no longer be in charge of any science project, or he could lose his life if there was a catastrophic failure.

For a further fifteen minutes, Eric was bordering on angst until he was able to determine the cause. Signals were coming in from the spacecraft sent into the anomaly several years prior – something sure to please his superior. At once he was able to decipher the meaning of the audio data he had detected for some time now. It was a carrier wave for the formation of geometrical golden ratio calculations accessing inter-dimensional transmission – he had discovered evidence of other dimensions.

Only when he had deciphered a tiny fraction of its meaning, did Eric relax and then feel a tinge of excitement at the possibilities waiting to be discovered. As he delved into this new data, a holographic construct began to form in front of him. Eric even felt a slight pang of excitement as he realised the image was of a torus. As details emerged within the holographic image, pathways to other dimensions appeared as angulations perpendicular to light as it travels forward. Eric then entered a few commands to prompt further investigation of this contingency where he discovered access to stable pathways leading off between the sideways oscillation of light at an eight thousand cycles per second.

As the data matured, Eric could determine the elemental alignment of energies meeting at the angle of torsion between dimensions, aligned with the golden ratio. As each new dimension became apparent, so too did pathways to dimensions beyond at the same ratio angle. His efforts began to surpass his expectations as again and again he ran tests to ensure the data he was viewing was of flux in stability.

An aligned torus with energy flows accelerated from other dimensions in flux, then harnessed through a vortex pattern to emerge as collective energy in this dimension, was Eric's best result in years. Yet, this data was coming to him and as such was not of his creation.

Questions began to arise as to its origin. Was it from the computers aboard the space ship sent into the anomaly? Was it a reflection or echo of his own data? Could it be entirely alien to his knowledge of sentient life in this sector of the galaxy? He had no way to be certain.

Then as suddenly as it had arrived, the transmission ceased. Eric could not see anything, but he had a recording of what had just taken place. He would work on this new information as soon as his other duties were completed. Maybe he would not have to pursue the Agent or John Matheson after all.

Deployment of the next monolith technology phase proceeded immediately thereafter, as Eric engaged the holographic controls once again. Additional robotics were sent to towns all across nations where authority controls were dominant. In those places where deployment of hardware was effective, people were controlled already through their dependency on other centres for trade and goods as it had mostly always been, but Eric was determined now to go to the deepest levels where survival for many was the new dependency.

Chapter 28

Celia was almost beside herself with joy. Asper and her had recently woken up at precisely the same time from a dream they had been sharing. Since Asper had taken up residence with Celia and the adults in their house across town, she had shared dreams with Celia almost every night. Celia even insisted they sleep in the same room at the rear of the house overlooking the recently dug vegetable garden awaiting spring sowing.

"You know today will be the day Asper. We saw it in our dream just then."

"Yes I know dear. Funny though, seeing Carmel there as well."

"It is because she is growing very strong and we will need her."

"Hmm, maybe you are right dear, but I wonder what we will need to..."

"Oh you're not going to be silly and pretend you don't know."

"No. I was thinking about what Carmel will do."

"We will have to wait Asper. Her being here is only the first step. Now she is in our dreams too, we can be sure the next step is just around the corner."

"Well, I'm sure it is. Life seems to be changing regularly these days."

"It always did. Just you didn't look at it like you do now."

"Yes I know. It is exciting and scary too."

"It can be, but never mind. Anyway, I'm sure she will do a great thing today."

"Yes she will. Are you hungry?"

"Sure I am Asper. Let's go and have breakfast and then we can go over to Carmel's house. It has been three days since we last visited."

"Okay. I'll go and see what your father and the others are doing. You get ready."

The walk to Carmel's house for Asper and Celia was a leisurely stroll along grassy tracks covered in a thin layer of frost. Celia took to stopping now and then to observe frozen over puddles of water. As she prodded them with her fingers, bubbles of air would bobble back and forth under the thin sheet of ice. This captivated her so much she insisted they stop at every puddle they saw so she could play. Asper was of no mind or heart to object to Celia's requests, as she too was fascinated by the same visions, and like Celia, was loathe to actually place enough pressure on the ice for it to crack or break.

"Let the warmth of the sun melt it back to water," Celia said at one time as they both squatted beside each other over a puddle.

"Then the water progresses to a liquid state."

"Like it was before it had progressed into being ice. It is a wonderful cycle isn't it Asper?"

"Yes it is dear. The others like to observe these things too, and appreciate the simple beauty surrounding us."

"I know...and within us too. Don't forget."

"How could I ever forget?"

"Maybe you did once."

"Yes, I am sure I did once, but not now. Hey! Do you want to race to Carmel's house? It is just around the corner."

"Okay. Bye." Celia set off as fast as her legs would carry her, leaving Asper surprised at first, but then soon she caught up. Just as they approached Carmel's front gate, they were running hand in hand, laughing and challenging each other to take the lead. At the last second, Asper let go of Celia's hand so she would win the race and be the first through the gate.

"I expected you two this morning. Come inside. I want you to help me with what I have to do today." Carmel said before stopping and looking at both of them silently for a second as she remembered the dream she had shared earlier.

"The dream..."

"Yes we know," Celia responded. "We knew it was best to come over straight away and talk about it...and help you."

"Well, you can sure do both. Come in."

Carmel had laid all the pieces to her dismantled steam engine on the dining room table after she had shared breakfast with the others at the house. Each piece had been carefully cleaned and was now waiting to come back to life within the engine as a whole.

"Shall I fetch some drinks before we start?"

"Oh no. I'm Okay thanks."

"Asper?"

"I'm good too. Let's get started. I want to see this thing running."

"So you both knew I would be doing this today then," Carmel said as they worked together at the table.

"Oh yes. It is a symbol. It represents something you adults know about. I know too, but I would not call it the same name."

"Why not Celia?"

"Maybe I don't know the right words. But...I would say it is a symbol of how we are building things to overcome other bad things and this engine is part of it."

"Well, I think your words are just fine. You are right. I have a strong desire to rebuild the engine today. It is a bit like the dream we had about doing things we need to do so we can be strong."

"Yes the dream was right. The voices told me. I know you don't hear them like I do, but they are there. I am so glad Asper and I came over to help."

"Me too," Asper added.

"I am glad also. Once we finish this we can have lunch and then talk about our dreams some more."

"Chan and the others could come and listen. They will like what we say."

"I'm sure they will Celia. Carmel? Pass the piston assembly so I can attach the drive rod please."

"Here you go."

When they had finished, Carmel went to fetch some fuel and water as Asper and Celia stood admiring the reconstructed steam engine. It had taken the combined efforts of the three of them a little over two hours for the rebuild task and now Carmel was about to ignite the firebox. Celia was particularly excited as she had never seen any other steam engine besides Carmel's in her whole life. Asper had seen an old dusty engine once in a shed as a young girl, but it had long since ceased working back then, so now to see a steam engine in action, would be an entirely new experience for her as well.

Three whistles let off in quick succession brought John and Tim out of hiding from the secret room. John had not heard the sound of Carmel's engine since he had had been at the farm near Arequipa in Peru, before then being captured by Eric Gunter's apprehension robot off the southern coast of Chile. He had spent some years deprived of most sounds, smells, and sights other than the walls of his prison cell, and then later, the holographic quantum computer projections when Eric sought his help. Upon hearing its' familiar sound, he was reminded of how Carmel saw this as symbolic for progression, positiveness, and perseverance.

John then thought of Tobias. He had not seen his friend since their apprehension at sea where they were transported off the old fishing vessel. Tobias had remained a mystery the entire time, and it struck a chord of deep sadness in John. He missed his friend and he hoped some day they would be reunited.

When John and Tim had reached the lounge room, Carmel had sent steamy tendrils throughout, with some beginning to drift towards the kitchen. Tim had never seen his lover behaving now as she did letting off steam whistles. Carmel had spoken to him about the engine many times since she had arrived home to find him there. Now to see her in such a carefree and happy way, served for him to love her more deeply.

Her elegance was apparent as she danced within the steam where her movements cast eddy and wave patterns into the mist. She was angelic, so giving as was her nature, and most of all to Tim, she was mysterious and loved an invigorating life every moment.

"Here Tim darling. Come and dance," Carmel said as she grabbed Tim's hands.

Tim took the lead within a few moments, prompting a squeal of delight from Celia, who then seized Asper by one hand to lead her around and around the room. Every now and then, Celia grasped at the steam floating and whirling around her face, with both her free hand and her mouth. Before long, everyone was involved in a conga style line back and forth until the steam began to dissipate. As the last few wafts hung around them, Carmel sounded one more whistle before she disappeared into the kitchen to fetch them all some drinks. Tim was again reminded of how special she was to him, as he recalled their first time together in the very same room, when Carmel had done the very same thing. For a moment he felt as if he was back in time – all the others seemed to fade away around him then as he entered his memories.

All he considered and all he could feel was important, had come to him during his first meeting with Carmel. He did not really know then, but he had a notion of feeling it was to be this way since the very first time.

As they ate lunch an hour later, Chan and Carmel agreed discussion of geometric alignments and wave patterns would be best done after their meal. They kept their conversation to a minimum, often speaking in coded methods they all knew, even Celia. She delighted at the times when the adults took to such talk, feeding on the air of mystery and their almost childlike secrecy.

Tim and John told them of the work they were doing when they had all gone outside after lunch. Their achievements thus far were inspiring to them all – even Celia knew what they were talking about.

"We all know what it means to hold a weapon. How the body, mind, and heart are all challenged at once, but John and I think it is imperative we take a minimal stance of having at least a few pulse rifles for our safety."

"Inherent in your words are challenges beyond what you speak of," Chan replied. "Understand as we do, there is particular attraction at play when weapons are held...and for the very reason of doing this."

"I recall thinking a similar thing on our way to Dunhuang," Raynie added.

"I recall your speaking of this Raynie. It was during this time where activation of elemental intentions was paralleled with your course to discovering the Torus of Eternity."

"And so the activation continues..."

"I can help," Celia interjected.

"We know," all the adults replied simultaneously.

"Just saying." Celia almost looked hurt for a second or two, but was unable to hold her face in a sorrowful look for long before her natural exuberance returned.

"And we love you for it dear," Esther said to her rubbing her arm.

"Thank you Esther. I think mother would love it too."

"I'm sure she does and I think your father would agree."

"Of course he would. He is happier so much more in his heart. Since mother died, he has had lots of times where he has been sad, but I think he is much better now."

"I'm sure he is. He loves you very much."

"He does Esther. Do you think I would remind him of mother?"

"Very much. Every child has a special essence to their parents Celia dear."

"I'm glad. It would be awful to have parents who did not care and only thought about the silly things."

"Indeed. So whilst we are very lucky, we should retain our focus and our intentions on remaining happy..." Carmel added.

"And lucky Carmel. But...it isn't really luck is it. More like what we make happen in our lives."

"So very true Celia. So very true."

"Um John?"

"Yes Celia?"

"Can you take Tim with you now? I know you are discovering lots of things, especially about the anomaly. I think you and Tim will find out about the voices I hear soon. And look into the anomaly. There is something there."

"Indeed there is Celia..."

"Yes I know you know, but keep looking. It has to do with those two sounds you can hear coming out."

"Okay. Come on Tim. Let's get some more done. The sooner the better."

"Yeah mate," Tim gave Carmel a quick kiss and then followed John back inside the house.

"I always wonder with Celia. She says something to make you think there is more just when you thought you had it all."

"I agree John. Maybe we should look at the anomaly from some different angles."

"Run some test scenarios and flux simulations?"

"You have it there...just what I was thinking."

"The signal coming from the anomaly could be intelligent."

"I have thought the same."

"I want to look at the quantum computer you retrieved. I have an idea I can alter the cubit array and how atoms are held in superposition. If I am right, we can infuse an additional flux state within the tachyon establishment phase. If this is the case, then we can make a start on much faster processing well beyond a tiny fraction above light speed."

"Alignment of simultaneous geometric transference could accelerate atoms."

"Exactly! What a breakthrough if we make it. The monolith technology could assimilate the extra algorithmic extensions due to the multi dimensional flux capacity being much larger."

"Almost infinite."

"Well yeah, you could say almost. Ironically it is leading to infinite causation for manipulation and processing in a particular context..."

"Still limited by the speed apparent?"

"Yeah. Once we can take speed differential out of the equation, it becomes a true lateral application, rather than the lineal facets attached to establishing tachyon pathways we have at the moment. Acceleration well beyond light will come from losing the concept of both time and therefore lineal speed so we can draw from dimensions at angulations to this one."

"A bit to wrangle with in the mind."

"Yeah I know, but once we let go of preconceptions we can allow it to happen. At this level, quantum mechanics going into flux can depend a lot on the observer's intentions without them even knowing they are having an effect."

"Um...but we will have to retain an elemental dimension by which to measure our success."

"True. In theory we cannot go so fast as to time travel. It is alignment with energies giving rise to manifestation, be it data or hardware. I'm sure Chan could help us explain it a little better."

"I'm sure he could."

Carmel, Raynie, Jake, Lyle, Jenna, Esther, and Lorraine had followed Chan to the recently dug vegetable garden patch outside the house adjacent to Carmel's. Gareth and Chris had joined Derek and Murray at their house, having left just after dawn to scout for building materials again. John was pleased to see Chris mixing well with the group and appearing to really have left his authority life behind him.

The others all looked to Chan who appeared poised to say something to get the conversation underway, "Our goal is to reach an understanding sufficient for us to retain strength of intention through adversity. We know and feel it as part of the activation process we have been living for some years now."

"I have my torus and my dodecahedron. Will they help us?"

"Yes they will Celia," Carmel replied. "Chan is very interested in what you have to say about those two, aren't you Chan."

"Yes I am. Aspects of angulations in both objects are to be our focus to get this started today. Remember when I discussed the angle of torsion in human DNA called the dihedral angle, being aligned with the golden ratio? This appreciation of creativity when observing this ratio in art...or music, and other things, correlates with elemental forces of both creativity and of intention as they proceed along the energetic geometries hidden from our eyes."

"Should we attempt to relax ourselves and even assume a type of meditation state?" Raynie asked.

"This is apparent in all our moments, but if you like, assuming a state similar to meditation may help your focus." Chan looked at Raynie quizzically, testing her to see if she understood his message about focus. She did and so her question tapered off in momentum.

"Clarity is required in each given moment. There is no such concept as relaxation from this clarity. Our alignments seek similar for actualising outcomes based on authentic intent."

"This is a bit new for me Chan. Perhaps I need to study further to understand?" Esther asked.

"Not so Esther. Study is fine because wisdom always grows. Just follow what we say and understanding will soon come to you. Be aware this is not a doctrine we are discussing. It is simple elemental geometry human beings are a part of and so what comes is already there."

"You'll be okay Esther. I know a lot of this stuff and I am just a child."

"Yes, but you are unique to us dear."

"Unique, huh...?" Celia was a bit mystified at this. She thought herself normal without any idea of being special.

"Regardless, our focus is for alignment beyond anything we have consciously experienced. Subconscious experience includes these alignments for transition into the conscious mind. Invariably, this includes also the heart as the central focal alignment geometry as it is a constant connection, yet within this comes many variations. "

Raynie proposed a question to interrupt Chan for a moment to ensure her thinking was in the right direction. "Are we going to explore how to project our intentions whilst aligned, um...to give them more power?"

"You could say so Raynie. It could be described as more power, but it is simply more aligned and so without disruption to the intentional focus. It is not knowledge. Rather you will find it is your nature. Once we realise this as part of life...particularly when many people experience this recollection, then combined energy amplifies for progression. It is the natural law of how the universe works and so we too as part are bound to this. When this is clear energy, then results are more powerful because they set up the next progression without the debris of actions cast into creation attached to doubt and from an inauthentic perspective whatever this may be. It necessarily may not be deceit towards another, yet often is deceit of self and resignation. A sense of giving in."

"Lyle and I studied how momentum continues to build exponentially within torus after we came back to Earth from the moon."

"Indeed Jenna, hence seeing and feeling the crystalline facets of the torus as an object capable of amplifying energy as it is within the natural construct of this reality. Torus are found in many different forms as we know, from Earth cycles to entire galaxies...quantum level. It is universal energy."

"I like my torus and this," Celia said holding out the dodecahedron. "Keep it safe dear," Esther remarked, suddenly feeling weary of the authorities being about. Celia put the object back in her pocket making sure they were safe and deep down.

Jake decided he would take a walk around the house just to make sure there were no officers lurking – either coming to interrupt them with more demands, or hidden away spying. He and the others knew of the risks they posed to being investigated. Such a large group of people who for all intended purposes were not appearing to be so ready and willing to take up a life of status, were sure to attract attention.

Lyle jumped up immediately after Jake indicated he would check the property, joining him as they casually strolled around the perimeter. They noticed a few new buds were beginning to appear on the deciduous fruit trees – a sign of spring not being far away. Winter still had some grip for the sun was bright but it offered little warmth.

Jake had become especially fond of growing food whilst they had lived at the steam farm near Arequipa. He had become particularly fascinated with fruit trees and the seasonal offerings they gave. Since he had taken up this interest, he had planted two small orchards on the farm with Ricardo – a man from whom he had learned significant information for the care and maintenance of fruit trees.

When they reached the front of the house, there was no sign of anyone from the authorities, so they decided to continue around to the other side. At the last, Lyle cast a glance back before they went around the front corner of the house, and he caught a glimpse of something metallic coming along the road. He grabbed Jake's arm spinning him around to see what he had just seen. For a few seconds neither of them could figure out what it was walking towards them.

Such a sight was entirely new, until after a few more seconds, they realised it was a robot of authority making.

Instantly, Jake ran back around the house out of sight from the front, and kept going until he reached Carmel's. He gave the coded knock on the door of the secret room to advise those inside trouble was coming, and then ran back to join Lyle and the others talking at the back of John's house.

"We should all just look casual. Here. Grab these tools and do some work on the garden. Lyle and I will muck about here cleaning up a little."

"Good idea Jake. I know we are very much able to focus our intentions, but we are yet to encounter this type of robot, so it is best we act as you say."

"Okay then Carmel. Why don't you take Chan over to your house? It appears as though we have run out of tools."

"After this, we must continue our discussion," Chan said before he and Carmel departed.

Esther, Asper, Lorraine, and Celia were hard at work in the garden when the robot demanded both Jake and Lyle present themselves at the front gate. They both wore DNA profiling devices John had built along including creating records of their identities in the main authority systems. Each device would mask their true DNA using a stable flux field the robot could not penetrate. It stood waiting for them to come to the front, and without the men's knowledge, it had already run a full scan.

"You reported in at San Francisco. You advised the authorities of your destination to a rural setting where you would seek work. You are not employed. Explain."

"Um, I haven't found anything I could apply my skills to yet officer."

"Me neither."

"There are no excuses for inefficiencies. Whatever your skills are, you at least have one, and it is you are able to work. You are required to report to the authority office in this town to be assigned employment. Are you listening?"

"Yes officer."

"I have detected others at this location. Bring them to me for scanning."

"Yes officer," Jake said after the robot had pointed one telescopic arm at him.

Lyle remained on the spot as he thought it best to not upset this officer in any way. As it stood waiting, the police officer robot remained silent, aside from a low hum coming from deep within. Lyle assumed this would be its torus drive linking into the monolith energies. The robot was impressive, yet entirely menacing. Its head featured dual cameras for eyes glowing a faint red around the rim of each. There was no mouth other than shaped facial angles vaguely representing a chin. Weapons were not visible on its smooth rounded body, but he was sure it would contain lethal devices somewhere.

As the others approached, including John and Tim who eyed the robot very carefully looking for any information they could use, they were all DNA scanned. When they stood in front of the officer, it spoke to them in its monotone voice, advising they were to be assigned employment, except for Celia who was to attend a local educational facility. Immediately thereafter, it left the location to continue its first scan run of the town and its surrounds.

Dismay flickered across all their faces as they stood for a short time at the front of John's house. They had decided to call it his house so they could make a reference point for any time they thought they would need.

"I just hope Gareth and Chris were not scanned. At least they will not have to report for work if they are not in the system."

"Maybe father and Murray missed it too. I wish I had. I don't want to go to school."

"Let's hope so Celia. I don't want you to go to school either. Maybe we can work around it somehow."

"It poses a bit of a problem. I can regularly change our identities and avoid work, but if it does a face scan, our files are linked. You can tell if it does a face scan by a flash in your eyes. I noticed the robot's eyes were the same scanners I saw when I was still in New York."

"So we have to live with these false identities then?"

"I'm afraid so Raynie. But...look on the bright side. At least we are not going to be seen for who we really are by the authorities."

"I suppose so John. It would be risky to change and..."

"Attract attention. This will work as a cover. It is just the reporting for work issue I find difficult."

"Yeah, I had no idea they would force us," Tim said looking a little sadder for longer than the others.

"We can still nail them mate. With stable flux and our recent discoveries from the anomaly, we have a huge upper hand."

"Thanks John, it helps."

"Well, I suggest we get back to talking while the day is still good. Tim and I will join you now though. I'm sure we need to work on geometries to make this amplification greater."

"You speak wisely John. It is inherently a requirement for you and us in all manifestations, to align," Chan said.

"Yet it poses a sense of finality contrasting with facets of alignment being progressive," Jenna added. "My work on protein strings encompassed progressive alignment according to the changing state of the strings when data is applied."

"I noticed those results when Jenna and I worked the crystals back at Kennedy Space. The holographic readout showing the fluctuating carpet affect stands out."

"It is a cosmic carpet Lyle."

"Really Celia."

"Yes Jenna. What is woven into the carpet is what we feel and how we make life happy."

"John and I have shut down for now. We both think our progress will be aided by listening in on your discussion. As you said Jenna, it is a progressive response to the base alignment field. Otherwise the instability causes decay, eventually rendering everything useless. Flux can apply where it is the transition to a fraction beyond light, but from there it is still a bit hazy. This is why we need to listen in."

"And contribute," Chan replied to Tim reminding him and John.

"Of course. If we can crack this code and apply flux, we will be happy."

"I know what you are talking about. The voices told me this would happen and it would be wonderful."

"I seem to hear them in the dreams too Celia."

"We do Asper. I bet Carmel will agree."

Carmel was about to respond, when Jake interrupted her. The police robot was making a return journey along the road and would soon pass by. Nobody felt much like giving it any attention, nor was it required by the autonomous robot, so they slowly migrated over to Carmel's house, caring not to even look in its' direction. Automatic yet responsive, the robot had already made its presence felt through this harassment. They knew it would become regular, so they decided there and then not to suffer by allowing it to impinge upon their lives. It was ugly anyway, and whilst they never really assessed or judged ugliness, the robot was ugly to them as it would always. Whilst it had telescopic arms, there was no requirement for legs as it used anti gravity to hover over the ground.

"Perhaps we should talk this evening after we have all eaten. It may be wise to invite Derek and Murray so we can all discuss today's events along with the alignment information," Jake suggested.

They decided working on John's house was a good distraction for the afternoon where they could reserve focus later on when the time was right. Late in the afternoon, Esther, Celia, and Asper went back to their house to fetch Derek and Murray.

When they arrived back as the sun was setting over the hills to the west, nobody had yet seen Gareth or Chris. Whilst not actually worried about the two men, each of them secretly hoped they were alright. Then half an hour after dark, Gareth and Chris returned laden with supplies and building materials. Everyone was eager to ask them if they had encountered the police robot.

Celia spoke for them, "Did the ugly robot find you?"

"What ugly robot Celia?"

"The police thing. I don't like it at all."

"Nor do the rest of us," Lorraine added.

"We didn't see anything, though we kept out of sight most of the day."

"We are going to have to keep you out of sight Chris...and Gareth," John said looking carefully at each one of them in turn as he spoke. "I have already discussed what we might need with Tim."

"Why dad? What did it do?"

"It informed us we are to show up for compulsory work because we registered in the system after we arrived in San Francisco."

"We registered as well."

"Yeah, both you and Chris did Gareth. It was our only way to be able to get through authority checks."

"So if we keep out of sight, it won't recognise us?"

"Yes. Tim and I are going to build some little warning devices to detect if the robot is approaching. One for each of us."

"What about me, do I get one too?"

"I'm sure John has thought of you Celia dear, but..."

"What father?"

"He might not..."

"I'll make her one Derek."

Chilling winter winds from an approaching storm, descended into the valley as if on time to reflect the coming storm they could all sense brewing. Everyone had pitched in an effort to build a fire now burning brightly for them to keep warm as they stayed outside to discuss elements of geometry as agreed upon earlier in the day.

Chan began, "First of all, it is important for us to recall gestures or mudras, particularly those seen in the cave near Dunhuang. Especially those seen only under ultraviolet light. They present a key to understanding of conception just beyond the light spectrum a human being can see. This is where we are to focus in concept to stretch our conscious selves beyond what we consider as normal. These abilities are resident within us."

Raynie, Jake, Jenna, and Lyle were the only other people present to have actually seen the mudras in the cave at the fringes of the Gobi Desert of western China. They had shown images of the pictograms to John, Asper, and Lorraine, shortly after returning, but to all of them except Chan, the specific images were hazy in memory. It had been a long time since they had journeyed across the world seeking information for activating the Torus of Eternity.

"Asper has told me about those mudras and I have seen pictures," Celia said as the others sat in silence trying to recall details of the images featuring hand gestures and formations representing life pattern formations.

"Gestures were indicative of the way into seeking the truths apparent arising from within like a voice of self calling. Within this pure state of elemental self, one connects with the life force lines of symmetry integrating in progression with all other life forces. Where the term life is used, the indication is not only of living as it is the entire living organism of the universe and beyond," Chan said in his usual calm manner. "Consider the lines of force energy within a torus, your heart, your brain..."

"A neural synapse," Jenna interjected seeing Chan was looking for the term.

"Yes yes. If you imagine a neural synapse where just one neuron firing, sets off a chain reaction creating an outcome large enough to cause your body to move, or to generate a pattern of action leading to much larger events. In each moment of choice concerning the synapse we want to fire, we energise templates of manifestation. These come from the elemental organic energies and are available to us at all times."

"Templates are a unique geometrical signature I have used in developing protein strings for energy and data transmission," Jenna again interjected.

"When we energise a unique geometrical code, we energise an entire reality from this geometry," John added. "This aspect is fundamental to establishing tachyon pathways for flux mechanics."

"In realms beyond space and time we can manipulate and alter all manifestations by working with the source codes of the manifestations," Chan spoke seeing the progression building. "So if you imagine a geometry representing an action or presence in place or in feeling...all things, and compress the vision into a single multidimensional geometry or light code, you can utilise geometric light code to create and energise and therefore manifest as reality here in this physical plane...and beyond. It often happens without thought to us as second nature."

Carmel felt it was the time she spoke and added to Chan's words, "In each moment, we are shown different templates. We are shown geometries reflecting themselves as experiences, interactions, feelings, thoughts, and others. We are given the opportunity to choose which geometry we want to energise. This is also available to us at angulations for access to the many dimensions."

"Yes Carmel, I share this feeling for it is important to hold awareness of the codes, geometries, experiences, and templates in alignment with our elemental selves of who we really are."

John appeared as though he had just reached a point of reference, "I am thinking...to program certain geometries resonating with our higher self, we are looking at frequencies already there but not accessed due to the state of awareness preventing them to come into our physical reality and crystallise."

"Surprising coming from you John, but in essence you are correct and this is how to approach further development of your flux technology. They are not frequencies of divine beings or idols. The frequencies lay within the essence of organic elements...they are the manner of construct and of shaping our reality far beyond the mere building of objects with raw materials. The connected conscious applies respect to the actualised moment in order to fulfil the potential at the time."

"So I need some type of alchemy for the transition of these geometries when I manipulate them for use with tools or machines?"

"The authorities are already trying this with their directive and programmable mater. It is for us to find the frontier they seek. As we learn more on this, I share the same path, for this is information I am sensing as the torus realizes potential. Atomic acceleration within it transitions matter. Think not of me as anything more than the one who is providing this information for it is self evidently coming into being. Think again of the mudra cave and recall the feeling engendered there. It was of contentment, of alertness, and of human spirit uplifting. These are the ways of the authentic self, hence the connection. As an elemental self with a sense of positive ego sense of place as society demands, one is simply oneself...nothing else. As fundamentally it is always this way. There is no complication to this but it must be authentic and not conjured from thoughts and definitions learned through egocentricity. An openness allowing consciousness to deliver. Most of all, fear is almost lost. I say almost for there is a slight retention of this element coming from the survival instinct, but...the fear of all else dissipates as it is simply allowed to do so because the mind has allowed the flow of the self and not restricted this to create obstacles and the resulting negative outcomes."

"Even then Chan, fear can go away because you know what you are doing and where you should be. It is why I like the dreams I have with Asper, and a little bit with Carmel. We go to those places."

"And I know why you like to hold your torus and your dodecahedron..."

"Because of the geometries being pure Chan."

"Yes Celia."

"Alchemy is an in interesting prospect," Lyle said. He had been pondering the use of the word since John had spoken. "I have studied the ways certain cultures used alchemy in practice."

"So have I," Jake added. "Raynie and I looked at this just before we met you and Jenna in San Francisco. She was showing me quantum mechanics information and we both thought some type of alchemy could be required to transform atoms. The atomic responses at this level often result according to the observer's intentions."

"Precisely. This alchemy you speak of is in truth, a way to access this geometric control and alignment. But it is not so the alchemy of the past though similar in intention. It is what the authorities seek."

"They are creating programmable matter," John stated.

"Yes and this is the response to interpretations of their elemental selves clouded by negative ego. They manifest machines to do this in awareness of themselves, but their intentional use for the results created by the machines, is the negative ego having a blocking dominance over their elementally flowing self. To look beyond the field and sense the energetic responses giving rise to the information to create matter is the frontier I think we are approaching."

"We will do it without machines then?" Chris asked.

"A difficult question to answer. It is likely a combination but still I am only assuming for I cannot now otherwise it could be occurring as I speak."

"Well, I used to do alchemy as a chef," Gareth added. "Here, everyone take a glass, I think we should share this bit of whiskey stash I have. And for Celia, some grape juice from another little stash I have."

Everyone paused for a moment as they each had a drink. Esther, Derek, and Murray had been silent the entire time so far, content with listening in so they could build their own individual understandings of what was being discussed. Before long, Chan felt it imperative to continue as everyone agreed the momentum was more than just knowledge but also a feeling and communication energy undeniable and relevant.

"Alchemy of geometries is a little like quantum entanglement. Where one acts or is present in one place, a corresponding twin correlates with its distant sibling, despite physical distance. This alchemy is similar where it applies a catalyst agent to correlate with progression not yet apparent. The progression only becomes apparent due to the foundation laid down in real time like John laying tachyon pathways. So...with alignment, this potential is realised and then amplified due to the inherent nature of the organic elemental pathways established always being exponentially progressive in any form. From this realisation, we can access more potential exponentially, like...um."

"Say how technologies grow exponentially Chan?" John offered.

"Yes, a similar analogy. Going on then to manifesting matter is not so much as a lineal process we observe with construction. It is more of alignment occurring prior to our presence in the place or moment and the provision of manifestations based on our intentions leading us."

"And what of the other information we have learned since activation of the torus began?" Raynie asked.

"It all ties in. Our investigations into the properties of waveforms, the appeal of creativity aligning with the golden ratio found also in our DNA, and the affect of sound and the constitution of water molecules, of which we are so much made up of, all relates to the understanding of this method used to activate geometries. Then...it is no method for its is natural and without the burden of the mind interfering instead of complimenting, then the idea of method is irrelevant."

"So we need to understand these fully to then take the next step and become more empowered?"

"You could say. Our journey of understanding is always growing...as wisdom does all life. As part of this wisdom or alignment and synchronisation with pure information untainted by negative egocentric identity seeming to often seek problems, we must feel and therefore base our intentions on this fine tuning, otherwise we are striking out in lineal journeys as you say towards a better way and this does not exist. Our intentions become clouded when this material mind aspect affects us where egocentric thinking leads to actions reflecting such thoughts. The results of our actions are self evident but many are deep within requiring the self inquiry in pursuit of truth...the flow...nature for consciousness instead of fighting against."

"Surely if we were just told about this then Dad could have developed flux mechanics more by now," Chris said trying to grasp a fast understanding of what Chan was saying.

"Not so Chris. Understanding comes from experience, to then realize it is not dependent upon experience. Often theory serves well to build understanding, but application through self is always a requirement for experience and thus to gain more knowledge. There is no finite point to knowledge and this is definitely the case with the alchemy of geometric alignment as it is an exponentially growing facet of reality. It never ends."

"So there is never a perfect point then?"

"Correct this time. Alchemy is this context is the art of liberating parts of the cosmos from temporal existence and achieving perfection for a particular instance, but this perfection is not a finishing point. In a sense it is a transmutation of reality and nothing of a secret society or cult or any type of collective establishment. This is fundamental to life and to the atom. There have been instances of this in the past, and for their endeavours, most of those people were cast as heretics. This type of alchemy is simply becoming master of oneself in alignment with geometrical forces and wave forms as part of natural existence. This is not heresy or anything related for it is to simply allow truth and self respect through truth."

"So in context, it comes down to how I look at flux mechanics and how I intend to achieve results based on my connection as an organic life force with the geometrical forces at play?"

"I assume you are already doing this, but to take it further may require direct connection of self with the technology being used. This is for you to determine. Through trans-human technology they are reflecting a growing awareness within themselves as all humans recall their inbuilt memories of their relationship. It is just they are not refined in their intentions coming from the negative ego rather than from the heart in a balanced way to facilitate organic connections."

"Interaction of self is a definite requirement. I have felt this in the dreams I have shared with Asper and Celia."

"I know Carmel. When I started dreaming and Asper appeared, we were able to change things because of how we felt and how we were a part of everything around us."

"And you are so clever at doing this Celia," Chan said looking at here faithfully. "Soon enough, we will all experience this direct relationship, and John will be able to create technology he had only ever dreamed of previously."

"And Eric Gunter. I am sure he has similar dreams."

"He does, but they are clouded so he will not reach this type of awareness unless he changes. Also, there is more to learn if you remember Tim mentioning ultraviolet light – study this as well,"

"We are all within a relationship with the geometries and are remembering this," Carmel added.

"And this will empower our intentions into realisation through this method Carmel. We are just beginning this activation or reactivation. See how the torus reflects this back to us," Chan spoke as he took the torus out of his pocket to show them all its even deeper pink hue. Geometric patterns of flickering gold were obvious across its surface and around its construct.

"I admit I am having trouble understanding or seeing this Chan," Esther said as Derek, Murray, Gareth, and Chris nodded in agreement

"We all do Esther. It is our openness unhindered by expectation aside from our intentions we are to recall. This memory unlocks how to understand what we are potentially capable of doing and how to live. Imagine you are awakening from sleep and your awareness becomes sharper and sharper as you wake. This is a similar way to understanding how we are to work with geometry and when we awaken sufficiently to enable this to come from within, we will then know how it is done...and feel how it is done. It may well be through using technology John and Tim are building, but...there is always to be the organic resonating connection and this learning will surprise us in the least I think."

Chapter 29

Despite high efficiency ratings for all new projects the authorities were undertaking, there remained small gaps, anomalous events, and oversights through lack of forward vision. These were already affecting outcomes in their supposedly flawless execution of the new machine world to be constructed, and whilst they learned quickly of these issues, their response was burdened with instability both in mind and in technology.

Eric could sense the breakdown of his internal mechanics long before the official order to report came. He knew some type of servicing surgery was required – he just hoped in his remaining self, of it being less than brutal. Surgery was a marvel of technology, yet through such marvel, it had begun to reach places never before touched by such instruments. Whilst painless, one could sense the very core of themselves being intruded upon, tainted, and altered.

Live readouts were studied as Eric commenced this acceleration phase of the project. They showed his flaws, the potential outcomes based on their learning capacity for human behaviour, and the slowing of his responses. Eric set the last command into action within the holographic display, before reporting immediately for surgery.

Everything Eric envisioned in respect to a sense of ordeal was realised during surgery. He could sense declination of his soul in a way where his organic pathways were being genetically manipulated more and more through such deep penetration of the almost impossibly small nanotech robots. His mind became the workings of a machine, where swarms of the tiny bots went to work reconstructing organic connections to the implant technology. It was a warm buzz, almost sensual and intoxicating, yet it was penetrating so far into him, he felt tinges of horror as wave after wave of technology swamped his deepest thoughts.

Feeling remnant of his emotional self as he did, Eric was coupled to a machine almost unfathomably incoherent to his natural essence. Like a grinding wave of distortion, the surgery cut into him both physically and spiritually, reconfiguring his persona, his projection, and his purpose.

Aside from this trauma soon to be forgotten, Eric was otherwise unaffected by the surgical intrusion. Now as he sat on the edge of the bed rubbing his temples, he was again confronted by himself. He could hear the questions being asked, he felt discomfort at being removed from his pure organic composition given to him at birth, and then he shuffled as he attempted to create a comfortable condition for his seated physical body. All this took place whilst trying to smother the deepest sense of regret he could feel. Eric had been here before when he had his eyes done followed by the implants and he had regretted it both times then...until he had forgotten.

'It is like a drug now,' he thought as he analysed this growing cycle of regret. Drug users of any time were so often bound to incessant cycle of behaviour – Eric had seen this research during autonomous monolith development.

As he continued processing these thoughts, he gradually lost sense of precisely what he was thinking about, and like the addict, he began to forget his regret as the trauma of surgery rapidly faded away. Within an hour, he was back at his work station determined to perform at his peak and investigate the idea of multidimensional flux mechanics he had recently discovered.

Matheson had the information for flux beyond the ability Eric possessed, but he was not privy to all of the information now coming from the anomaly vortex. Eric knew John had not given him all he knew. Additionally, John Matheson's strength of mind was at a new level surpassing anything Eric had encountered during his life and his research. He had beaten mind implants. He had beaten his systems and escaped from beneath New York City, and he had no doubt already put himself on a path to working with flux. This would be adversarial for Eric – John could pose a significant threat to him and his superiors.

'Ruthless in pursuit of efficiency,' came time and time again in thought to Eric as he continued his work. The surgery had worked, and he was improved beyond his condition prior to the technology breakdown. Eric felt a clear determination emerging as he realised the monolithic directives he was to carry out in order to establish and maintain peak efficiency as an officer.

He ordered four squadrons of four jets each to scour the countryside along the co-ordinates provided by the Agent – each with corresponding ground based teams searching the field for any trace of John Matheson.

The Agent had provided some vague information and Eric knew the most valuable information was not included. Eric also gave all personnel involved a new device based on the most recent developments coming from the monolith in the anomaly. The created star was bending the continuum in a manner where multi-dimensional flux equations were becoming apparent to Eric.

New aircraft were a vast improvement on previous HyperJet technology where the authorities now made every aircraft military capable. Whilst confined to similar atmospheric speeds, most craft were out of atmosphere capable accelerating rapidly to atmospheric escape velocity whilst the occupants rode in a dampened force field skirting the upper reaches of the atmosphere to breach the sixty two mile high Karman Line and officially launch in space. With atmosphere re-entry engine technologies and near zero gravity navigation systems, the populations who could afford or who were of sufficient status to take this new HyperJet travel, would soon be embracing the thrills of being off world.

Each craft could be weapons enabled with plasma bullets, laser pulse canons, and wide or narrow dispersal human and technology suppressant weapons including sonic bombs and limited electromagnetic pulse artillery clusters. Central drive systems included a torus in situation to accelerate the atomic matter drive.

Far from atomic drives of the past, these burnt no fuel, nor did they create any pollution – they used an excited field of matter resonating at the verge of this dimension. It was incidental energy, created on demand for reprocessing or recasting atomically. At its centre, the torus was indeed a fine instrument if only a facsimile of one very distant in detail from Eric.

Mathematically it processed geometric pathways within its crystalline structure capable of accelerating processing for a result almost the instant data was entered. As it amplified fusion and thus changing matter, geometries blended drawing energy from dimensions slightly different in frequency, and then forcing them through its centre with a pulse as the combined energy amplified.

For Eric, his next action was to engage full facial scanning for all monolith technologies. If John Matheson showed his face to any device, Eric would be able to pinpoint his location in an instant. Each robot was enabled to make its own decision for proceeding with a facial scan if any failures occurred within the DNA scan. Now they would conduct and transmit a scan of everyone's face every time, for the sake of Eric's need to find John.

Readouts coming from the monolith acceleration phase immediately drew Eric's attention to the next task. In his understanding of the anomaly thus far, Eric had determined the event horizon for venturing into multi-dimensional flux capacity. Beyond this point, the ability to establish energy channels into dimensional shift attributed to frequency variations from non-constant events, was an opening to shifting matter beyond the speed of light.

Within the vast holographic array in which Eric was immersed, he could see the parables for establishing organic nodes within pre-photon pathways. Laid in geometric formation, these nodes were the alignment principles for objects and life in physical manifest, and in balance with organic elemental intentions. Within each he could see the prelude to dimensional angulations - a view into taking life beyond the speed of light, and all he had to do was design a machine to take him.

These thoughts then prompted Eric to analyse more of the data recently received via the harmonic transmission coming from the anomaly. On this occasion, he could determine a differential not observed previously. Within minutes, it was obvious to Eric - the accelerated phase of monolith production had revealed something he was sure could lead to stability. A quick sequence of algorithms to process the new data was an almost instantaneous unthinking response by Eric. His surgery was proving to having worked well, as he processed and actioned data faster and more efficiently than he ever had.

Ideas of conquering space beyond the mere local neighbourhood of the Earth and Moon systems and also Mars were erupting within the mechanical aspects of Eric's mind. His organic self soon realised these same notions and basic projections for steering his research to reach his new goal of inter-dimensional travel.

He could see one has to bend the concept of lineal dimension to travel laterally as flux between dimensions transcending light speed. Within these equations, he determined flux can bend the dimension locally on a small scale, thus bringing mapped tachyon light receptors in contact earlier than through lineal passage. Eric could see this as a dimensional precursor set up for manifestation in this dimension with data geometries in waiting when the action is made to send or reconfigure an object.

Working further, Eric determined the alignment parameters would originate as an intention immediately in manifest as opposed to then being made manifest at the speed of light a fraction in time later.

Would Matheson have this level of understanding as yet? And what of the Agent? He was surely working devilishly hard to ensure he remained at the forefront of developments in order to make his mistakes of the past disappear into irrelevance. With constantly operating flux in this context, anything would be capable of being in readiness to instantly convey the entire data or result within multi-dimensional fields.

Chapter 30

Inevitably, the Agent was destined to regain a stronghold – such is the way for the persistent megalomaniac who would continue affecting people and places even after their death. A newly constructed vortex amplifier was his type of endearing apparition for his ongoing self actualisation towards destruction. Where self is a notion of individuality, within the Agent this idea of self was only in pure servitude to his mania now. Equipped with the torus removed from the stolen flying craft, the amplifier was remnant of his previous machine, yet this time with added capacity derived from monolithic technologies.

This time he was not restricted to sending out viruses, nor could it have had the same effect as its predecessor. Eric Gunter had ensured monolith technologies could not be affected by any type of virus other than what they were inherently plagued by – instability. Provisions in the atomic accelerator ensured programmable matter could immediately take over any virus affected system, thus rendering the virus immediately obsolete. Whilst they contained some flaws, any type of shut down due to virus was simply eradicated through the nature of the advanced exponentially progressing algorithms. Heuristic in nature, the algorithms were capable of learning and adapting to any anomalous event and thus, were able to constitute autonomy for several types of monolith machines.

The Agent now had access to this information and he was beset with exercising this in the most extricating way to life as possible. He knew the ineffectiveness of any virus he could send out and this was not an issue for him. Devastation could be caused in ways relating to the atomic acceleration and matter construct easily surpassing those history based notions. Progressing then to overrun key components, he was confident the learning algorithms would soon find ways into more vital systems.

Once access was obtained where he could undermine the very core systems, he would affect untold mannerisms of distortion and melee. Where he once trod, he was to trounce in degrees menacing in darkness unregulated and unchecked. Degradation encompassing all beyond physical venturing to the realms of psychological depravity, his nemesis of self purged any sense of humanity in respect to grace. His fulfilment was apparent as it is for any living soul, yet he was not of this ilk, nor was he of mind to consider anything more important than finding Matheson.

George knew Carmel would be close by – he had encountered them and had captured the bitch he despised. Both of them meant nothing yet everything to him. Twisted in expression, never bound with grief, unmentionable in any positive context, he was filled with ire so much so, it would clench him and torment his remnant heart. Regardless, he would extract what he needed from them on his course of discord, until utter annihilation beyond measure serviced his ongoing mania...albeit temporarily and in whatever senseless to reason context it assumed.

"Information for Matheson," he said in a low voice. The holographic array surrounding was impressive enough, though sparse due to his lack of available technology. Dark holographic shades played with data readouts, appearing like minions in shadow, tending to his processing needs.

Monolith programmable matter was proceeding well with atomic acceleration drawing on fluctuation states between resonant physical and geometrical dimensions. George knew of its potential and Matheson was vital to him because he was the only one who could help realise his maniacal destiny. Gunter was also an object he was determined to extract a sinister type of revenge upon when he had him and his systems under his control, his direction, and at his disposal.

Not a single explosion would be required and this brought a moment of solace to the Agent. He dearly loved the thrill of setting off weapons and seeing people flee below his spaceship to begin along their journey towards oblivion through his viruses. Both sanctified his pure nature of endless menacing, feared by all and thus respected by all in a type of glory to nothingness.

George spoke seldom at most times. Now and then he would bark an order to those who considered themselves worthy to be his minions. 'What an absurd expectation being a minion to a maniac,' he thought.

In an instant his mania told him to ignore most of the data floating around him and focus on various potential locations with the best possibility to begin the trace of John. Torus processing provided outcomes in an instant after he requested it via telepathy control. Monolith technologies had unveiled this technology – aged in concept, yet only now being fully realised. Characteristic brain wave identification signals were a blueprint for identification between operators, and for connection to produce the planned command result in the quantum computer. Within an hour, George mapped out a covert course of action to search from Seattle towards the south after he paid a visit to his least favourite farm.

Summer sun was finally giving away to twilight in the orange red skies above the Agent's base. Heat still rippled in the air, curling leaves on vegetation and draining moisture as life was strained and sapped of energy. Then amongst the last lingering rays of sun casting pink, purple, and red hues into the tops of fierce clouds approaching from the south, George had taken to flying, free from almost all detection by the authorities. Pseudo torus drive was working according to expectations including overcoming the immediate elements of instability.

He realised a recollection of freedom and in an instant it brought forth a crescendo into mania. He turned the craft engaging full power. Far to the east he headed – out across the South Pacific Ocean at great speed eighty thousand feet in the sky and chasing the night towards Peru.

Dawn was some hours away when Steve was awoken by what he thought was flying craft thrusters. He was right. The Agent had landed in a type of flying craft entirely alien to him. By the time he had assessed the situation and decided to gather the others living at the farm, aside from Kerry-Anne and their son, the others had emerged after waking.

"All I want is Matheson, Carmel, and the torus. I can see with your steam engines, you are still lingering amongst the aged."

"They are not here and neither is the torus. You can destroy us if you like but it won't change the fact," Steve replied.

"Any reason not to destroy this place of impartiality to me is a feeble reason. But...I am forced to take this pathetic excuse. Never the less, there will come a time when I will not have to be so sickly."

"What's stopping you? Afraid we have an even better laser weapon now?"

"Don't stir him up Steve. He gets mad."

"Nothing is stopping me. I simply have no need to destroy you at present. I will look around though. Oh...and don't mind me, but I have quite a great deal better technology than you know."

The Agent ran a series of scans looking for John, Carmel, and the torus, but found nothing.

"I'll be watching, you know it." With those last words, he immediately left the scene without any indication he was about to do so.

Upward at astonishing speed defying anything a human body could withstand outside of a dampening field, he rose to eighty thousand feet with the long west coast of South America stretching in a curl away behind him. On a heading for Seattle, he then set the speed to hypersonic six.

Dawn was halfway across North America by the time George had arrived at a location near Seattle. He set the craft down in a small clearing amongst some trees not far from the now abandoned HyperJet factory on the city's outskirts. George was running the gauntlet of being visually detected. His technology sufficed only to keep him covered from electronic detection - it would not render the craft invisible. This was the one drawback of his current status.

'Those minion types were sure to be lingering around looking for something to do,' he thought as he scanned the vicinity around his landing position.

He need not have waited long for someone to come to his position and present themselves. A disjointed group holding a forest ceremony in worship of some pagan idol had seen the approach and landing of his craft only two miles away. They had sent three to investigate, where at first they remained hidden spying on George until one of them recognised his bland face.

"We welcome thy return. We are in servitude to..."

"Enough of your rubbish words so pretentious and insignificant. If you work for me, the benefits will come to you. If not, then I may annihilate you now...or I may not. Make a decision."

"We choose. We choose. How can we help you?"

They were pathetic in his eyes, bowing to his every breath as already they showed weakness.

"Find yourselves some holographic devices so I can communicate. Then I will provide information you will need."

"How will we contact you once we have a device?"

"Be here precisely three days from this time. I will return. You had better be successful as failure will not be tolerated.

"We will not fail you."

"Of course you will...eventually. Be here or I will come looking. Are there any others like you south from here?"

"We only know of a few people to the north of San Francisco."

"Where exactly?"

"We don't know. Try the old Redwood Highway. Out along those lonely disused roads would be a good place to look."

The Agent bade no farewell. Without further word he ascended again, eager not to be flying around anywhere as daylight came. He would have to find somewhere to stay for a day, but this did not bother him as he could detect any authority presence nearby with his on-board scanners. Twenty minutes later, he landed at the rear of an old roadside cafe appearing as though it had only been abandoned in recent years. Inside, he smashed aside a few photographs of an old couple on the counter so he could position his portable scanner on the surface. Obviously, the owners had left in a hurry not even bothering to take the photographs now smashed in pieces on the floor.

He felt a restlessness and impatience leading to an escalation of his maniacal urges as he waited merely passing the daylight hours. By day's end he felt flustered, full of angst, and riddled with psychological pain. When dusk finally came, somewhat quelling his state, George looked skyward during the walk to his flying craft from the cafe. He noticed several moving lights amongst the stars he was certain were the next phase of Eric's monolith technologies.

As soon as he was seated inside the craft, he took to the sky, this time maintaining a low altitude. If the advice he had received was anything close to accurate, he should be able to scan for heat signatures coming from fires. It was a long shot and George took it on. He was concerned only with finding people on the ground to assist in his search, otherwise, he would leave them alone to minimise rumour and maintain a low profile.

It took the entire night and the entire next day at the cafe before he made any further progress. Almost at the break of dawn on the second night, he found a group who had not been a part of his previous following, and who did not have any idea who they were dealing with. It lamented him to have to resort to these measures, as his mania demanded more to find itself than to be involved with such compromises. He relinquished under the guise he was looking for dissidents to join in a life not bound by the authorities.

This group were themselves interested in such a life and were also part of a growing number of groups who had become distant to the proviso the authorities offered during the time of the Agent. They were willing to help and already possessed a holographic projector. George gave them the information he wanted them to use in helping find John Matheson and Carmel. No mention of the torus was made as he told them these two people would be of great assistance to their overall cause. He spoke an element of truth in this, yet it was nothing near the impression his new followers gleaned from him.

When George had simply had enough, he returned to his home base, tired with waiting and not prepared to risk knowledge of his whereabouts any further. His future strikes against those whom he sought and against the authorities, would require diligent stealth tactics until the time he had gathered sufficient capacity to take the authorities on out in the open.

Back at base, he began to plan how he would strike at the authority systems. His impatience would not suffice to allow him just to sit around killing time while he waited for news of John and Carmel. In earnest, he went about researching algorithms for creating tangible naturally appearing errors striking at the very heart of programmable matter manufacture.

The first wave of intrusion sent out in his next wave of intrusion into society to affect the purity of atomic resonance building. This meant the resonant frequency of the atoms used in manufacture of systems was slightly askew even from its original slightly unstable state. Like a cancerous cell, it began with one insurmountably small component, and from there it would grow until officers like Eric were called in to repair the damage.

Chapter 31

Life in the small town was being affected by more restrictions now. The authorities had deployed the latest in 'personal attribution' so Eric named this next phase. He had initiated this new round of restriction through incursion into personal liberties of self after being satisfied with the output of monolith manufacturing.

No longer were people allowed to roam freely where they pleased as a heightened authority presence lay down people movement restrictions. Broadcast via the holographic news service, citizens were advised they would require permission to travel at all times. Aside from work purposes, people were basically restricted to meandering about where they lived as permission to travel anywhere beyond town was difficult to obtain. Sentry robots now accompanied the police in positions spaced at twenty mile intervals everywhere – they were surrounded, all were surrounded.

No real sounds filled the air aside from the gentle calling of distant birds trying to hurry up spring. Everyone was quiet. Nobody spoke much, if any. Homes and buildings everywhere were subdued, and somewhat cast into a gloom reminiscent of the days of the Agent. It was not quite the same gloom, but gloom nevertheless.

People were struck with a sudden relinquishing of themselves as if they had unwillingly given away part of their very being to someone whom they did not know, and by no means had given permission for them to take. Sure enough, they had dulled senses anyway, but this was different. Many people likened it to a feeling of futility and for no reason. They began to wonder if by pursuing status, they had overlooked themselves during the act. Their minds did begin to wander, but the authorities were prepared for such an eventuality.

As soon as those many began to wonder why they had let it all come this far, they began to lose this very cognition. Eric Gunter had unleashed the first wave of torus based psycho technology – beamed directly into the very core of people.

Automatic sensors were applying this wave to subdue minds where systems were adapting in real time to procure these emotions and feelings. Outputs Eric was viewing revealed three dimensional holographic images of people simply staring for a moment, or breaking down in despair, only to rise again with a similar stare seconds later after the wave form had passed through their brain.

He felt a sense of pride he was not meant to feel. All sound around him seemed to slip into low tones as he paused a moment to feel this new feeling. It welled up taking Eric further away from his work.

'Oh,' he said to himself as if he almost broke his composure and showed emotion. Then a moment of pure pleasure erupted within.

It was ecstasy for someone so dedicated to work. He was lost to it for a moment before all the busy sounds of the other officers at their stations came rushing back to him in a bombardment. Eric was not meant to feel this way – nobody was. It was a blend of artificial intelligence and human intelligence, combining to process and respond to emotion. It was a failing.

Despite his earlier sense of triumph, Eric began to come around as he realised the serious flaw in his own psycho technology. He had linked into the system as it had dispersed the wave throughout the populace in almost every place, every valley...but not all. As a result, his senses now began a descent into oblivion as they cancelled out each other. Eric was heading towards nowhere and he had to make it stop. Other officers around him continued to bombard him with their noises, as too did the internal transit vehicles meant to run silent, now sounding as if there were in a serious state of disrepair as they transported other officers about.

As he switched off his connection to the torus inter dimensional amplification and therefore his connection to inter dimensional energy, Eric came to one graphic realisation. He had stumbled upon the core of the viruses the Agent had used to overthrow the authorities in so many places. A sense of oblivion was the common thread amongst those who had been afflicted with his viruses in their implanted nanotechnology, and for a few moments, Eric had felt this loss of purpose. It was ultimately to him the most life draining force imaginable. It was beyond death – it was nothing.

Eric had siphoned energy inter-dimensional in scope. This siphon had opened up in an instant when he had engaged the third phase of monolithic operations. The artificial star was sent literally into overdrive, processing at an exponential rate as Eric tested the parameters of the algorithms John Matheson had provided not knowing they were fraught with errors John had subtly included so as to avoid immediate detection.

John had known Eric would reach a monolith technology stage where he would extend systems beyond their physical constraints. This was the first phase to flux technology. But...John had given him a pseudo flux assimilator algorithm which simply meant he was only ever going to be able to sample tiny filaments of faster than light manifestation with the slightest hints only of the dimensional gateways. It was a mock up or construct based on interceding algorithms being laid upon energy transit tachyons established by the monolith star.

Almost eleven hours later, Eric had concluded all necessary review of psycho data, provided reports to his superiors who had authorised him to proceed to the next phase, and now was well into analysing data in order to track down the Agent. As he walked the corridor to his personal quarters, Eric dreamt of the splendour awaiting him when he returned with both the Agent and Matheson – yet another indication of his mechanical failures.

They were more visions over dreams. He was a logical person who never really assimilated the idea his mind could be so creative as to have imaginative dreams, so he called them visions. His personal ideas were constructed of Earth as a machine planet with so much more than what the authorities had planned. This would be a planet to rival the best utopian dreams of any person throughout the ages. It would be mechanical in the best vision of heightened perfection his mind could hold.

Secretly he wanted it to be a showcase to alien life. Eric had thought about other civilisation many times, working towards a conclusion where if life existed on only a tiny fraction of planets within the vast expanse of known space, these numbers could still add up to millions. Eric could see himself at the pinnacle position to showcase humanity to any alien – a dream he had held since childhood.

He was grasping the true implications for flux in multi-dimensional access. It thrilled what was left of his real self, it enticed his enquiring mind to explore deeper, and it unleashed his own inner darkness inevitably leading to confrontation. His mind took him to the search ahead to find John, the Agent, and those with the Torus of Eternity.

In a position opposite to Eric in location across the breadth of a vast continent and in a position oppositional in intent, John and Tim were working endlessly to come up with a counter punch to monolithic technologies.

"Now we have established what those harmonic waves from the anomaly mean, we can be sure Gunter has some idea of how to construct stable flux mechanics. You can bet this latest wave of deception affecting feelings is his first look into psycho monolithic systems."

"Will it be a tough one to counteract John?"

"Not really. We have enough gear to build force field devices for preventing those types of transmissions entering our personal field."

"Using the geometry definitions for energy vortexes at the meridian golden ratio angles?"

"You have it. Let's build them now. I'll do the software whilst you put the hardware together."

An hour later, they had built force field transmitter devices for everyone they knew, with a few spares in case any were lost.

"What about the harmonic signal? Do you think it is alien in origin?"

"I cannot say for sure as we can only speculate. Once you go deep into and beyond flux, you can basically transmit across light years in mere moments. I think we can take some time to explore the option considering we have just about all we need for defending ourselves at this time."

"Aside from the weapons we mentioned previously."

"I have thought about design for those and I think we are best taking it up as our next task. We don't have anything else to work on aside from understanding the anomaly."

"Any chance we might score jobs to help us?"

"Hopefully we can avoid compulsory employment, but if provided with half a chance to look into their systems, I will take it. Anyway, let's make some guns."

"A little hardware defence never goes astray."

"Just remember what Chan said and why we have it. Psychology is important to us all if we are to remain inconspicuous and focused."

Later in the evening, everyone had gathered at Carmel's house to have dinner together.

"There is something about to happen Chan. I can feel it."

"I can feel it too Celia. We are best to remember ourselves and the geometries if we are to find the pure energies we require to see light within us prevail over darkness."

"I agree and so do the voices. They told me they are from far away and yet also within, and our planet has been disturbing the balance...um, they called it equilibrib..."

"Equilibrium?"

"Yes. Humans have been affecting this part of the galaxy in bad ways for too long. It is the time to wake from our sleeping and take inia..."

"Initiative?"

"Yes Chan. This is the focus on us and not anything even like the torus."

"She's right," Asper added. "Ask Carmel too."

Everyone looked at Carmel to see her respond in the affirmative.

"Are you sure these voices are coming from somewhere else and within Carmel?"

"Positive Esther. I have analysed them over and over and have thought they might be an echo from our own planet, but there is a peculiar feeling one feels when asking oneself as to the truth. It is this feeling..."

"The one we share when we dream walking through the flowers and bees. We can talk to each other without talking. We do it all the time anyway."

Chan chose this moment to speak as he was satisfied his contemplations to this point were worth mentioning, "Our intentions are amongst the stars and they are born from the stars. All energy is within and infinite in connection. Like the wisdom of connection told by many ancient peoples of this land and others, we are in the place where spirit of life is the essence of soul expression. This is present for all life regardless and as we let go of the bind from conditioning, we feel the nostalgic connection to alignment of geometries beyond perceptions within light."

Chapter 32

People in towns and cities everywhere began to feel the wrath of the new imposition being forced on them by the authorities. Many had no qualms in simply obeying officers when told, yet many others could feel there was a resonance to the authority methods unsettling to their nature and prompting questions in their minds and hearts. They could tell something was amiss with these new offerings – it was their soul conscience speaking to them. Despite their latest wave of suppressing energy, something was awakening in people the authorities had no idea was present. Resistance was building against them of a type they had not considered at any stage or time in memory.

As a guise to enhance compliance amongst the many, the authorities began offering a new range of products many were eager to uptake after so long without anything new. The latest in Geiga wear was now available. Devices were replaced with miniature versions of the torus now distributed widely. Rather than carry a holographic medium, people were offered rings packed with technology for all their communication and holographic requirements. One could simply use their unique telepathic connection established through DNA scan to display holographic material at the highest resolution. Soon they would become conversation pieces, excite people with their future possibilities, and deliver a comprehensive service linked to authority systems.

Vehicles at large operated using anti gravity technology, but people were restricted in both ownership and use. No longer was it permissible to simply own a vehicle – the authorities required strict criteria for anyone to even apply for ownership. All other vehicle travel was in accordance to newly passed legislation as law where public transport was seen as the proviso for nearly all public travel requirements. The transit tubes elevated twenty metres above ground and for years left to become dirtied with the passing of time and with the passing of virus affected people, had been given an upgrade with restrictions in place for use by public transport and authorised vehicles only.

As they embraced this new life shown as significantly improved since the reign of the Agent, little did anyone know how the Agent was about to make inroads into their lives so soon after they had thought his reign of terror was finished.

Most did not even bother to think of the past in any way, relieved as they were to finally have some semblance of normal life back again. They could see the monolith craft flying overhead and were tantalised by the prospect of being lucky enough to travel in one.

His mania felt a sense of love for the potential to once again have space flight capacity as part of his hellish dream of dominance. Though the original torus was his objective, his off Earth ability was a must to accompany his manic driven volition.

He began this on the very day the public were permitted some freedoms where they could again consume products and add value to their lives, as told by the authorities via hologram in all homes, on the streets, and in passageways inside buildings. Any minions he had managed to summon were now gathered in the disused HyperJet factory outside of Seattle. Enthralled with his breakthrough in devising a method to scan for the Torus of Eternity, he was eager in his own way to be on his way. He left his minions under instruction to make good this base for his return. The Agent wanted ill winds to blow again and soon he would fan their course with the torus atop his machine.

Using his superior knowledge for creating algorithms, the Agent was able to mimic monolith systems and prevent any detection. As his relatively brief flight south from Seattle neared the outskirts of San Francisco, he initiated scanning for the actual torus. It was an obvious means to begin for the Agent, as the resonance properties of the ring still held by Chan were easily detected if he was able to calibrate the instrument correctly.

At first he found nothing. This came as no surprise considering the ambiguous nature of his search, and as such it did not deter him considering his unwillingness to embrace uncertainty. He operated on such levels anyway – never building his macabre ideas upon anything other than his maniacal desire to extol his lack of virtues.

The readouts gave a radius of one hundred miles and there within the holographic display, the signal finally emerged after he tuned the algorithms to focus on key components of its construct, mostly diamond. Immediately the idea of the small town north of the city came to him and without hesitation he took to a course directly leading him there. His gamble was already paying off.

"They will never outsmart me," he said aloud as the craft rapidly accelerated. "This time they die." He had taken to expressing himself to himself often now, clear there was nobody he could trust for anything meaningful if in fact meaning existed.

The landscape passed by rapidly below him as he approached the speed of sound. He refrained from accelerating to trans-sonic for the sake of alerting anyone to his presence by way of sonic booms. Ten miles from town, he slowed as he rose to a high altitude so he could take further readings without being seen from the ground. The last distance would have to be covered on foot. He did not possess the weapons required to simply overwhelm them and so he decided at first on creating a diversion.

His sensor readings indicated the small town was populated, though judging by its' size, the Agent estimated it was only a quarter of its capacity. This did not affect his plan as he knew the first house he checked was likely the place he would find them. The bitch lived here and he would send it all to cinder along with her and those pathetic others.

An hour later he watched them about the small house appearing to be homely and happy. He despised this and he despised them. The years spent underground deprived of his senseless mode of glory for holding the Earth as his dominion - she was to blame and Matheson. He then set his craft down an hour before dawn where all was quiet and frosty.

A light was in the window of the house next door so he decided to sneak up and see who might be visible. Matheson was there before his eyes – the Agent could barely believe it. He wanted to kill him now but it would only alert others to his presence. His most important objective was the torus for without it his new machine would not be effective. Carmel must be close by. Her house was the other one and judging by its tidy condition, she was home.

He thought of leaving Matheson to himself, deciding once he had the torus and was on his killing spree, he would devote a particular pleasure in seeing his demise.

John was working on construction of a magnetron device he could use with the newly acquired torus from Tim. The Agent knew enough technical engineering to recognise the similarities it shared with his vortex amplifier. Within the intense magnetic fields, access to universal source energy could be derived and thus affect manifestation of matter. He could see a future of atomic manifestation without limit.

According to George Smythe, former Agent Eight, creation had all been in error. Mistakes and ill conceived notions only served to illustrate the very need for it to be sent to nothing. He was a mistake of a system birthing billions of errors – all of them in defiance of sense.

He saw Carmel Madeline appear looking distressed. He heard her call to the others at the two houses, including the old mystic. They gathered in a group, a small child amongst them. She struck him as peculiar in a way she seemed to hold as much energy as he did, yet he could tell she was benevolent as opposed to his undoing. Tears were streaming down her face, as all gathered around her with comforting gestures. This almost made him sick. How could humanity in all its imperfection, even begin to think such emotion was real?

When they all went in to Carmel's house, he decided to return to his ship. Nothing more would come to him now. He needed a plan to find who had the torus and where it was. George heard one woman cry out, 'Oh Celia, you are so brave,' before crossing the road and disappearing into the forest.

"Father would only want me to be this way Asper. I know I will cry, but it is not the right time now. He would want me to be strong."

"So this robot just appeared and then told Ester, Derek, and Murray to accompany it without delay?"

"Celia and I were returning to the house from the forest at the rear. We could hear it all. It told them they had been deemed unemployable and were to proceed to a holding camp for processing."

"I think we should take Celia for a little walk don't you Asper?"

"I think so Carmel. Time for us all to go for a walk." Asper indicated to Raynie, Jenna, and Lorraine to join her and Carmel. Celia showed strength, but she would need the nurturing energy they could provide while the men decided what they must do next.

"I have some developments on the magnetron drive. It will make our weapons, scanning, and data capabilities a lot better. With the new algorithms, I can hack central systems without any bother."

"We need to hunker down dad. Gareth and I were thinking there is going to be a sweeping authority weapons command coming through here at any time. Look at what happened to poor Celia's father and the others. There is no use just trying to remain out of sight. We need to strike an offensive."

"What ideas do you have Chris?"

"Well take this torus thing. We have the means to create our own weapon. All along we have been looking at this poorly...concentrating on trying to remain aloof. Why don't we assert ourselves a little? After all, we have the upper hand and the authorities are so desperate to get their hands on your flux mechanics, they'll not ruin their one chance to have it."

"I could work with Jenna and make some adaptations to her original ideas with protein strings," Lyle suggested.

"Good idea Lyle. We're going to need you to conduct research as we develop. You know, one thing leads to another," John spoke as he considered the validity of Chris' words.

"Take these times to pursue this clarity. I can see the alignment taking place. These are your times to be called and to be mindful of our sky's vortex. It is paramount this be considered in all your work," Chan advised looking serious but not overly so.

"Any reason Chan?"

"None other than what I have said. It will become apparent to you when it is right for it to do so."

"The authorities will have scaled this place by now John. Chris and I thought we should do a little bit or reconnaissance and compile some data on what we have around here. We'll map out the installations around town, any technology placements and any readings we take from scanning."

"Keep a low profile though Gareth."

"They won't see us. None of us want to end up in some processing camp."

"After I modify our identification sequences to show we are already employed, I am going to see if I can find Esther, Derek, and Murray in the system. Maybe we could get a location and consider a retrieval mission."

"Let's just hope they don't become buried deep like Tobias."

"There is still hope for him Gareth."

Chapter 33

Calamity was lingering near the surface. Across nations, zones, and precincts, technology was undoing. Time was apparent for the intervention to take place now regardless of flux stability. Eric had to take the chance and engage the satellite, robot, and flying craft network to encompass the Earth in a net of monolithic influence on the physical, emotional, and light bearing fields of experience. The technology was taking control to the deepest level without enough conscious recognition in the many who were already feeling its affects.

He knew not all would succumb to the sway of nanotechnology mechanics entering their soul. Some were beyond the transmission frequencies of the technology as they resonated atomically at a rate preventing such intrusion within their cells. Yet many would be affected and to them it was to become a platform to launch the evolution of artificial intelligence humanoids in service to the master machine. No longer was it suitable for society to rely upon the unreliable. No longer were many able to withstand the unreliability of even an enhanced body – they were to be an augmented self enhanced through the blend of technology and cells with humans biologically powering their internal devices.

Immediately results were apparent as consumers took to biologically powered internal tattoos rendering patterns and images within the skin using a self controlled bio-luminescence. Others took fantasy to new heights indulging in sexual mechanical enhancement with nanotech skin designed to be ten times more sensitive than the usual nerve related human sexual arousal experience. Geiga suit parties, hyper reality addicts, orgies of self indulgence almost macabre – elements were unleashed as desire gave way to a sensation as part of the bio mechanical experience. Similar to any addiction, they came back for more and those many who sought this expression held nothing back as the authorities offered more and more to tantalise them.

For those north of San Francisco, it was a time they focused on tracking down their stolen friends – amongst them Celia's father. The robot would have removed them to an internment camp without doubt and in reality they were likely lost to the system for now. Celia had a look of resignation of this already being the case. She looked sullen mostly yet at times she felt certain Esther, Derek, and Murray had the strength to persevere and come home safe whilst her friends like John made enough devices to help.

John had constructed enough devices for them all to now remain free from detection by the authorities thus eliminating the prospect of compulsory work and school for Celia. Chris had been right and so John had taken the offensive approach to create a small device for each of them taking care of all their identification and records needs. Both he and Tim had worked all night.

"I can see why we found the crystals near the Leibnitz Mountains on the moon. Lyle and I always had a hint of the connection with Leibnitz himself researching mathematics and metaphysics."

"It seemed too synchronised to overlook Jenna. The principles of mathematics and of the esoteric he researched are coming to light as we decipher more alignment modalities within the toroidal matrix."

"I think John and Tim will find the gateway we have theorised to access inter-dimensional space."

"Do you think it will align with the flux technology?"

"Without a doubt," Chan said interrupting. "I could not help but overhear your discussion on the latest information about the torus. We will quickly find ourselves swept along its path sooner than we realise now such awareness has entered. It is imperative to know how to steer the path ahead."

"It is our place to remain hushed and out of sight. John has enabled us to see through this pathway and beyond our measure of application for the material sense. We have trained to this time as have the others to theirs. As all parties meet in all places, the strongest call will be for authentic presence in whatever the context to be realised."

Chan held the torus closely to his body with a slightly open hand to reveal a mere glimpse – enough to see its glow. He spoke softly, "Our understanding of how faceted crystals, life, emotion, construct, even dimensions, helps us align with knowing these elemental presences are where abundance originates without shaping by negative control mechanisms. Authentic presence determines the integrity….this is aligned with the quest they have for stable flux technology John will not give them. Aligning this consideration for the dynamic human spirit and essence in connection is so much like the technology – beyond this self, beyond this light, beyond…"

"Aligned with other metals and crystals, the torus can amplify the universal properties of each, especially gold. Lyle and I have just worked this out from some calculations we put together."

"I was thinking there must be something for this peculiar sparkle," Chan replied to Jenna as he revealed the torus a little more to show it had a few sparkling flecks of gold now revolving around its inner ring.

"Within this is all our calling as we realise the nostalgic signature to these pure elements and thus realise ourselves as an expression of such purity for they are intrinsic to our very being."

"The authorities are only mimicking this alignment as they do using my protein strings."

"Yes they are Jenna. As we know, there is an effort to see this as a control mechanism where it can never truly be."

A short time later when a patrol robot floated by past the front gate, they were relieved to see it failed to even notice them as its' automatic sensors detected no unusual activity or illegal presence in the house. Carmel had them feeling comfortable and with Asper and Celia they were establishing a presence together of calm and of mindful application without thought.

"People are beginning to be lighthouses Carmel. Asper and I were just talking about how the energy of people here and in other places is being sent out."

"Projected?"

"Yes, projected."

"How do you know Celia?" Carmel asked as she also looked to Asper.

"It is like the dreams Asper and I shared before you came back Carmel. The ones we had since you were included are different in some ways aren't they Asper."

"Yes they are Celia. It is more of a communication feeling coming from some other place for how people enter into a moment and project their intentions."

"A connection from some other place. I sense there is a reason there why Celia has so much to say about how John and Tim are getting along finding the energies coming from the vortex."

"Yes, and now they know sound is a wave carrier there will be more coming from the other dimensions so they can discover what it is we need," Celia said looking determined. "Soon with the lighthouse people, there will be a transmission way for the energy to spread. It will be like it is going through wires but through people and invisible too."

"Our dreams showed us this coming from ourselves and connecting with others. Celia and I thought it was just like what you say about connecting with people immediately around but in the wider sense without anything blocking their way."

"We have talked about this and…why haven't you told me before Celia?" Carmel asked almost as if she had sensed she had been missing something all along.

"It is because now is the right time otherwise the focus would not have been enough."

"She is correct," Chan said as he emerged from the hallway into the lounge room with Raynie, Jake, and Lyle behind him. "Her intuition comes not from her mind but from her heart and it is a guide towards the information we seek as are the objects she likes and the objects and alignments we all know. All this information coming together is finding its place and soon we will see but not for now."

Celia could tell something was about to happen and she studied each of the adult's faces carefully to see how they were dealing with the situation. Her

248

losses in recent times were somehow urging her determination rise beyond and to see through this time in a manner seemingly unbefitting for one so young. Her wisdom was in her allowance as she was certain the prevailing energies would lead her father, Esther, and Derek back to them in time. This self assurance was giving her the strength to overcome emotions though sometimes she almost let them go to just be an eleven year old child needing adult comfort. She was fortunate both Asper and Carmel gave to her now – their natural presence being the very support she did need.

In the evening they had gathered at Carmel's for dinner together. She had lightened the mood by starting her small steam engine and allowing the steam to build before she set off a few whistles to release some pressure and set forth steam billowing about the room. John and Tim had given them the sanctum of being free from listening devices installed by the authorities. Using sensor algorithms, they had detected installations in both houses and were now able to mask their actions using scramble signals emitted from their personal device. Chan was relived as it allowed them to talk naturally and allow ideas and feelings to flow rather than being under threat of constant fear of surveillance.

"My work with Eric Gunter gave us more than he would have ever assumed. I have knowledge into the depths of their systems sufficient for us to advance beyond their monolithic technology and begin to see what is going on inside the vortex."

"Along with mine and Lyle's help."

"Of course Jenna. Tomorrow we are going to launch a transmission of our own into it and see what happens."

"Requiring us to be of place in authenticity for the discoveries can only occur if this is so," Chan said looking at each of them as his eyes conveyed the seriousness of the times. This would be their calling for all they had strived for, endured, and imagined, along with dreamed would come to find a place and so they would be the aligned instrument of its delivery.

"Together we will find the quantum singularity zero point energy using the energy of the universe to find our way as our guide," Raynie added. She felt assured her and Jake had prepared along with Jenna and Lyle. With Carmel also present, she was certain their combined energies would allow them authentic resonance and energetic apparition for the discoveries they made.

Tim and John looked at each other with Raynie's mention of the singularity. It was their most imminent purpose as they sought this point and the gateway to apply stable flux mechanics beyond light speed and beyond dimension. The singularity inspired an idea of further calculations they could perform to determine the nature of the transmissions coming from within the anomaly. With focus on the layered sound waves along with the projections of transition to breach light speed, John set to work along a line of thinking with a view to finally establishing the source of these energies. Tim knew John was looking for the spaceship sent into the vortex, and so he too set his directions to establishing what they both wanted to confirm.

"There it is," John said tapping Tim's shoulder to gain his attention. "The spaceship is caught between matter and flux outside of time."

"What about the pilot?"

"Maybe the systems keep him in stasis inside this dimensional paradox. "

"We can bring it out can't we?"

"Sure, but we will need you to determine the data pathway to reach the craft and engage its' systems to reverse it out of the vortex."

"I'll get on it."

"Do you realise though?"

"What John?"

"The craft cannot be responsible for the transmissions."

"Meaning…it is alien?"

"It could be alien. Maybe not. We have to determine a few more factors but for now alien speculation is imaginative enough."

"Well mathematically the stats add up to there being at least some other life in the galaxy."

"And maybe Eric Gunter found it."

Two and half hours later, John called Chan and the others together to discuss what lay ahead.

"Where will it land John? And what about the authorities?" Jake asked.

"I won't bring it any further than out of the vortex. I'll let the authorities deal with it from there."

"So the signals come from another world maybe. Interesting…"

"I thought you would be interested Chan."

"Well, I would say we all are," Lorraine added.

"John and I think the craft in position is the only thing keeping their monolith technologies stable. The element of fluctuation at the dihedral point within the vortex retains the sufficient torsion to keep them in situation."

"So when you bring it out they will come apart?" Lyle asked.

"You could say so Lyle."

"Meaning we will require our best attention free of the material mind and resident on the variations of dimension we are exposed to subtly through our sub-conscious. All we have learned will be required for this overcoming will unearth the darkest of elements so bereft of light they will strive as if they are battling for the survival of their very existence," Chan said noticing Jenna looking a little distant.

"And the aliens then. I guess they would have some systems far surpassing anything I have developed," Jenna said seemingly more focused on the material technology at the moment.

"This too is evident of our intentions and the elements we strive to retain in connection and not allow the material mind make us forget our true authentic presence. I remember images in stone when we visited the glyphs in Peru. At the time then, we discussed the notion of concept for life outside the Earth. Still, it remains as speculation though feasible in the context of this event. Within presence the motivation to transcend the very distances we see lineally could be accommodated laterally. So you can see your work in developing protein strings was a part of the journey towards what you may be considering now as alien technology."

"I suppose once technology went organic then the evolutionary step would be reflected in the use of mind and intent to access what John would say are tachyon pathways just beyond light speed."

For a second or two there was complete silence and stillness until everyone began to look at John. He had suddenly fixed his eyes on Carmel with a look communicating to all the others. Even Celia nodded in appreciation of where she observed the adults around her progressing to in understanding. Both Asper and Camel had already shared this and Chan too, but now to see all the others embrace what had only been present as feelings inside dreams, made her smile the broadest she had ever smiled.

John now knew where he and Tim along with Jenna were to look. Breaching light speed as a physical manifest was now a step closer as his mind reeled with ideas. In opposition of the times when his diligence of thought was sufficient to keep authority mind probe devices at bay, he was now in chaos – a chaos leading to an order and within this order would again be chaos, only controlled with intent elementally.

The place beyond light was in part reached through the mind and its capacity to create. With an ethereal sense as reflected in the glowing pink Torus of Eternity Chan held, transition to dimensionality beyond the present could encapsulate not only the mind and the heart in essence, but the entire body as well. Access to these other dimensions was their next focus and so without delay, he and Tim set out to conquer this next aspect of their plight together by returning to the secret room once again.

John sent the first transmission knowing Eric Gunter would be able to detect it but would not be able to trace its origin. He would then know John was actively trying to undermine him and must of by this time now realised John had always refused to provide him the stability with flux technology he had so ardently sought.

As the craft began to emerge from its state of flux into the present dimension, Tim was able to confirm there was a pilot on board and from all signs coming from a chemical spectrum analysis, the pilot was still alive though somewhat only partially as the readouts showed he was likely the most mechanised human being in human history. This man was almost half machine with barely any system unaffected by nanotechnology mechanics. He was both a marvel and a monster.

John stopped a moment to examine the readouts Tim was achieving, "Fine tune the bio-signature alignment, we might be able to integrate with the ship's systems as it emerges fully into this dimension."

"Get an identity?"

"Yeah. I never saw or knew of anything like him during my stint with Eric Gunter."

As the ship emerged fully into the present dimension, they were able to key into its systems immediately. Tim wrangled the data until he found the lead to the identity system for the pilot.

"Here we go, ship pilot Tobias Engelmann…"

They were stunned. John immediately thought of Asper not more than fifty feet away outside the house with Celia and Lorraine - her beloved was now emerging out of stasis as the world's most mechanised man.

"Tim, fire up the other processor. We need to control this ship and bring it in. It doesn't matter any longer about where."

"Gunter will find us. He will know it is you."

"Then we need to make a plan and not allow them to know where the ship lands."

"Not near here though. It means a trek."

"I know. I'll go along with Jake and Lyle."

"I'll tell them."

"Keep it a secret. Only us four to know. It avoids any of the others having to tell lies if asked."

Within the hour John had been able to mask the ship's location and directed it for landing eight miles away in a clearing the Agent had recently spent time in. When it was time to leave, the others asked about what they were doing only to be met with hushed glances. Celia had an idea. She knew the spaceship was coming back to Earth anyway – it was inevitable to her.

Dusk was approaching as they left. After half walking and half running, by the time the three men had reached the clearing, the ship stood there ghostly in the half moon's dull gleam still hissing with vapours after a heated re-entry into the atmosphere. All lights were shut down as John brought the ship in on minimal power. Now it stood there exposed and powerless brought back from the void with Tobias visible in the pilot seat.

The craft was angular representing military ships of the early twenty first century. When Tobias had been retrieved, John set the craft to auto destruct wanting nothing to do with a ship designed around his mechanised friend.

John may as well of relaxed a little at this time for Eric Gunter was far too busy working to retain his own personal alignment. Since the craft had emerged, monolithic technologies had descended into turmoil for John had been entirely correct. As Eric faced the largest calamity of his career to date, the devices he so worked to bring about his vision of a mechanised world, began to malfunction, turn on each other, and attack people at random.

From his newly established base, the Agent watched this erupt. It evoked a special kind of mania to see this chaos begin. He knew now his eternal calling was being made and so he would launch himself regardless of whether he had the torus or not.

Chapter 34

Everything was coming undone for Eric. As the instability of the monolithic technologies increased, so too did the instabilities build within his own self – the nanotech inside him erupted surging and evoking emotion, imprecision, and inefficiency. The barking of his superior regularly over the Broadcomm did nothing to alleviate the situation. Eric could see John's work in almost every algorithm now rendered so magnificently in three dimensions about his head. The more dynamic the rendition, the more dynamic the failure and as he watched, monolithic robots began to fall from the sky, take to illogical actions, and begin to shut down.

He could see the artificial star was collapsing in on itself soon to become a human generated super nova. As Eric continued frantically working through systems, he at last found something for preventing a system wide complete failure. He could launch attack robotics and weapons systems situated outside the main monolithic network data management system. He had always retained this element to back up the directives and now it would prove its worth.

"Sir, I have a plan to launch weapons systems so we can assert authority prior to complete monolithic shutdown."

"Then do it Gunter. Now!"

Eric initiated the launch sequence to send authority forces into the field everywhere. With a link to other nations and governed areas around the globe, he successfully deployed similar systems in most national capital cities and other strategic places. The entire force almost matched the monolithic hardware now being seen as functionless junk by people everywhere, and so Eric was confident in some confused mechanical way of at least asserting control until he could develop a remedy and re-instate monolith devices.

He refused to see any type of failure as an option and in doing so set about trying to determine the algorithms John had used in case he could discover some element of stability. But John had covered his access well and the more Eric tried, the further deliberate implants John had placed took Eric away from his goal. In frustration he then tried to source the location of the spacecraft until he thought of the Agent. Eric smiled a moment thinking the Agent would be stricken by the failure event taking place for monolith devices not knowing the Agent had replaced the torus drive in situation and so the craft was quarantined from the effects of the instability.

Eric's judgement based on this assessment prevented him from immediately seeing the reality of his adversaries. He was being outsmarted by those who all along had this potential. It was then he decided deep within of the elimination. He would destroy either of them when he had the chance. Both were responsible yet one would need to remain alive if he had any chance of rescuing his failure.

To Eric there was no surrender, no looking back, and no option other than to pursue action now at all costs. Intent as he was, for a moment he failed to see the destruction taking place.

As the star exploded, it gave off an inter-dimensional shockwave resonating through the entire vortex to any path beyond. Within seconds it launched outward as it torn itself to fragments – some quantum size, others as large as a human hand. In tandem, the vortex itself began to shudder sending energy waves back through the system entirely destroying most of the monolithic hardware deployed around the planet. When it completed its amplification, the vortex remained stationary appearing almost stable. Eric then realised the reason. Another force, another conscience, and another mind were directing this event. He learned then he could have been responsible for opening a gateway affecting other civilizations. Immediately he advised his supervisor who informed Eric to stop everything and focus on the vortex.

"It may not last long sir and the weapons systems…"

"Never mind the weapons Eric. You don't think we would leave such control only to you. The war is now our business. I want you to get some real answers fast. The Agent, Matheson, these aliens if they exist. I want to report Eric and I want it in the affirmative."

"Yes sir. I will attend." Eric was then left silent as his superior disappeared from three dimensional holographic view. His mind though confused at times as the mechanics continued to intensify their loss of logic, was capable enough as he set out to establish anything he could.

The Agent was his first prerogative as he returned again to finding him based on any residual signature left by the stolen craft. One facet of monolith drive was the faint residue of fluctuating atomic material remaining present for some days after use or shutdown. Within a minute he had traced recent activity in the far west. He had previously sent officers out searching for Matheson in this area so he at once doubled the force numbers with focus on a particular region still two hundred miles across.

After completing the order Eric thought of how he not seen such an obvious plot where the Agent mastered a few algorithms to conceal the theft of the monolith craft. Feeling disturbed, Eric knew this indicated the strength of conflict his mechanics were presenting. Some sense of personal efficacy arose reminding him of how much work he had been doing and how his human self could make such an oversight.

Eric knew anything from the extra terrestrial presence now evident would come from Matheson most likely where it was certain he would be involved. He continued to weigh up his options. He knew the Agent would be up to something and he would see the failures everywhere adding to his maniacal motivations to then unleash something. He decided then of there being nothing to be gained from his presence any longer on the Earth. The Agent must be gone and Matheson could end up the same way. Either coerce or force him to release stable flux mechanics information would be the only options. Eric knew he could exercise means to an ends if it came to threats against those Matheson held dear, and this idea was one now of appeal rather than efficiency. He was finding himself feeling desperate and Eric had almost forgotten this long past notion for many years until now.

John had become the instigator of his greatest downfall much more so than anything the Agent George Smythe had ever done, even at the height of using his torus amplifier to send authority systems and nanotechnology assisted people into virus driven chaos.

He returned to the holographic array around him, settling his eyes on the statistics of weapons systems deployments. Using the remaining thought control mechanisms in his own mind, Eric then changed the display to show the actual deployment of hardware taking place in San Francisco. It had just occurred to him how it might assist with capturing the Agent and Matheson.

The Agent was aware of the war now waged by Eric. It was a natural response with the loss of almost the entire monolith technologies everywhere. It was now the catalyst for yet more deliberate insensitivity to the real human condition where George rendered mania in all its personal forms. His lopsided grin resembling anything but happiness, his now slightly bent stance resembling the warped nature of his mind, and the look of oblivion in his eyes – cold not steely, just absent and merciless without any remorse.

Such behaviour took hold at will and part of him enjoyed it. Lacking any sense of self preservation for a moment, he indulged in electrifying with sufficient charge to give himself a jolt. One mistake and the amperage would be wrong and dead George would be. The electricity excited him. George knew his death would arrive at any time. Any sense of reign and power over people was a barrier to his ultimate fate. He wanted it and felt the excitement at being close to his destiny. Comforted by the idea of oblivion – a place where all relevance is lost, is devoid of feeling, and obviously is absolutely removed from the warmth of creation, he felt a moment of arousal before turning his attention back to the display.

As he watched authority machines, George was pleased to see weapons directing fire at seemingly innocent people who appeared to be beckoning mercy in most instances. How wonderful to see their existence terminated and he only hoped they indeed found no solace on their way to oblivion.

He could see many people being taken down by machines reigning in from overhead, appearing around street corners in numbers, wrangling people into sections to gather them and then kill, and most brutal was the random nature of these attacks. Artificial intelligence had gone mad, its' instability in reflection of the minds responsible for its creation. Amongst this melee so wonderful, an opportunity for George presented to attack them at will.

His new machine was comparable, the technology was present, his skills had been honed during his time incarcerated by the bastard Eric Gunter whom he had a particular urge to place high on his to be killed list along with the others. In fact, he decided Eric was no lower than third after Matheson and the bitch Carmel who as Superior Officer One had driven him insane with her condescendence because of errors he had made. There would be no such errors this time though. George wanted her to suffer the most, particularly as she had been there in Peru and helped prevent his retrieval of the Torus of Eternity.

He hated the torus. He hated them and Chan too. He hated the whole idea of even bothering with some type of sect anymore. They had gathered to him numbering almost one hundred but to George they were useless. Nothing they could do would satisfy his self as his fate unfolded now in holographic vision. He was taken anyway with the pathway ahead he could feel was his destiny to wherever he would end. No conscious plans of using the minions came to him and when they came to him, he told them merely to keep things secure and he will show them later what it is all about.

As the war heightened so too did the intensity of both George Smythe and Eric Gunter. Both men were beset now with closing in for the kill. Events had quickly escalated where the urge to dominate for each in their own ways, determined their thoughts, their actions, and their individual mania.

Despite the conclusion coming to Eric as his mechanics time and time again were absorbed with making up for failures rather than providing the optimisation to him as a person according to design, he pushed on still eager to please his superiors. Eric could see the hopelessness growing as holographic monitors revealed an increasingly disturbed population prone to erratic actions, death, and loss of dignity as their own mechanics failed. People behaved in absurd manners barely making sense where others took to physical depravity entirely humiliating themselves as if devoid of all human decorum. They were losing a mind almost already lost, spiralling downward into an abyss where the fake lives of their times were in-fact a precursor to their significance at any level – a sense of oblivion rivalling the disassociations sent forth by the Agent.

The monolithic shutdown was system wide, planet wide, and for many, people wide. No longer was an efficient society being enacted – rather a breakdown at all levels was slowly permeating through all and soon it would be calamity for a planet often affected by calamity through history. Eric knew John had beaten him also, for the stability of the vortex along with the collapse of the star, had rendered this defeat Eric had tried to deny all along.

Contrary to the objectives as sought out through their play of dominance, Eric could see the dynamic energies at play and thus he could see a place to where humanity would quickly arrive if the stranglehold over consciousness they held was lost. Within minutes he had set operations on automated deployment leaving the remainder to his superiors as they waged the actual war of assertion. He then left his station immediately for a transport vehicle – one of the remaining few in operation he had managed to isolate from monolith systems. Within seconds of Eric engaging the controls it had lifted off to ascend rapidly to seventy thousand feet.

George knew Eric was coming. He could sense the urgency as he watched the destruction. Cities were being taken again, though many people resisted causing the newly deployed weapons robots to work overtime killing, maiming, and rounding up groups. George felt a little pleasure at seeing this suffering as he sensed his own and now he would add it to Eric's and bring humanity to its undoing.

Working as fast as he could, he had created a few viruses he was about to send out, but before doing so, his mania allowed him to feel its presence sending him into erratic jerky movements as he almost danced within the holographic array. When it had subsided, he entered the last few holographic controls to actualise his latest vortex amplifier and then sent such devastation through the air, people had barely enough time to realise the virus had even been contracted.

George had exquisitely designed these few viruses to creep in and attack the DNA with an insidious sub atomic unravelling leaving molecules and cells to suddenly lose cohesion and send people into meltdown. Similar to times in the recent past, people began to experience the horrors of disembodiment in the physical sense as they lost themselves to his sickness.

Chapter 35

Chan was directing them at this time as they focused on the ethereal energies associated with physical manifestation and how they interact with other dimensions. It had come to their realisation as a group where the authentic elemental presence and awareness upon the geometries of energy at play on all levels were vital to understanding the capacity to go beyond light. John was sure Chan had the right idea now as Chan's words prompted him to investigate the alignment of flux for opening gateways to other dimensions present at all times, just unseen.

"Within the gateway lies the question of truth John. At this presence one is required to answer with an authenticity we have not really contemplated."

"How come you have not advised this previously Chan?"

"It is only now for it to be the right time and it is only in this moment do I feel the authentic presence to make it apparent. One always must consider the feeling of intuition and the right timing according to the gut feeling."

"So it is your gut telling us now?" Tim chimed in.

"Yes Tim. It is consciousness all pervasive. You really do know this already. Go with this as John does and soon we will find the answers we seek. But we must not delay or become distracted."

"The others doing their energy focus through intention as it comes to them, are there to assist?"

"Yes, so focus and stop asking questions otherwise they will become fatigued."

"Sorry Chan."

John and Tim worked as best they could with Chan guiding them after short stints in a meditation like state. He was communicating with the others and aligning with them to experience the geometries beyond the lines of sight to the dimensions coalescing in a sense to support the actualisation of their own dimension. Access to this universal energy tuned into frequencies of atomic and other manifest vibration outside the normal confines of constructed reality to a conscious place yet sub-conscious. It served to uplift their knowledge in addition to exponentially expanding going beyond for inter-connection with people in other places – Celia's lighthouse people. The evolution of psyche taking place was not only drawing upon the energies of the whole group with their technology, but upon the energetic awakening of others who in connection were to attune energy of potential arising from authentic presence. Within, the elemental geometries would reveal the gateways John sought for humanity to transcend light speed.

He had suspected this would eventually be the case to achieve fully stable flux technology. To appreciate the capacity of speed beyond light, one could not just observe from a modality of the third dimensional mind. Concept beyond the limitations of scope presented through knowledge and science requires the conceptualisation in the present moment or as Chan put it, ever so slightly in the past for the intention of spirit sets the path for light to follow. At this thought, John whispered to Tim where to take the next algorithm. He was certain the intention would lead to the knowledge.

Eric would find such a concept difficult as too would the Agent, yet John knew in both of their capacities as both scientist and cult leading maniac, they would be aware of the properties required to traverse the dimension. The anomaly and the breakdown of the monolithic technologies had provided all the answers both men had required in order where to next direct their search. Both though were of no mind, no heart, and of no spirit to enable realisation of the alignment in a true sense, for their ways were dark and devious be it annihilation or authority control of a machine planet devoid of emotion without any real reason for living.

The Torus of Eternity was now glowing so brightly in Chan's pocket it easily filled the small secret room with a pink and gold glow. He dared not take it out in case it was too bright and became a distraction to the energy all three were working to establish.

Chan suddenly sent a though image to the other two. For a moment he watched them intently to see if any trace of the energy projection could be detected. Then a moment later, his eyes diverted as his conscious recognised his success. John was creating holographic crystalline structures as Tim leaned in adding facets to make the structures resonate and appear to blur at the edges. As this occurred, faint perpendicular lines appeared within the image – they had constructed their first insight into a dimensional gateway. Bearing off into infinity at right angles to the crystals, these gateways at first flickered and then remained solid seemingly to grow with intensity during each algorithm correction and instruction made. Both men were now fixated with their objective and Chan knew they had reached the focal point where soon enough their concept would bring about the required state of being to enable a true gateway rather than just a simulation.

"The field where soul energy resonates is close John," Chan whispered when the two had broken their work to watch the growth of the simulated dimensional gateway. "Your focus has enabled the actualisation Celia, Asper, and Carmel, have found in the dream state. This place free of mind is the void yet it contains everything connected. As images appear they are of elements authentic and so bare notice for they heed you and invite you to experience. Everything you are free of from mind construct ego, is the link to this so let it become as the torus does in flow."

"They spoke of voices, well Celia did."

"Those are the voices of others yet they are you and I. They are the voices of all yet of none and so they are to be cherished for what they give as this insight is rare amongst us and is to be considered barely ever known."

"Some through history may have when you think about it."

"There are always those who are connected – our time now is merely the next iteration, but at this time important steps must be taken."

"Otherwise we are lost?"

"Almost. We would dwindle and then have to spend so much on mere survival outside of the strict confines the authorities want. This distracts us and would set us back."

"Could this just be more of the same?"

"It is yet it is not. Our recollection of self dissolves our reckoning with more of the same. It is an evolving place from which no turning back can be."

"See how the crystal is showing a gold colour John," Tim interjected after noticing a sudden change to the projection.

John studied the projection for a moment before announcing the hue was appearing from an angle perpendicular to the sideways oscillation of light waves. He turned to Chan who immediately knew what was happening.

"This is the universal metal John where all comes to align through dimensions such are its' properties. It is the golden dawn, the golden star, the golden section, and the golden age. Recollection of this within our memories is now being unblocked hence it appears to us now. "

"So the energies finding the dihedral point of torsion in the golden ratio of DNA opens the capacity of body to align would you say?"

"It is why our studies and experiences have brought us to this place. We require this knowledge gained authentically to elementally actualise the gateways of dimension existing even in our DNA…"

"Now look," Tim again interjected. He was pointing to the sectors at each gateway where toroidal fields formed the interaction capacitor between each. Energy from the other dimensions was flowing through the torus to appear in the next dimension.

"See the flux Tim. The moment it passes the threshold within the torus, it appears to lose cohesion and then accelerate through to appear again in this diamond shaped region within the inner toroidal horizon."

"I would never have imaged seeing this happen in my life time."

"But you have Tim. Both you and John and the others have. So too have I and perhaps many people who are helping us to find this medium of exchange."

"Making it a physical reality might be a lot different though."

"Only in how you approach it John. Think nothing more of it being more complex than your simulation. The principle is the same and if the intention is established, then the outcome will be determined."

"But what if it is determined in a way other than how we want it?"

"No such question can arise Tim. We are approaching a dimensional gateway and in order to be able to pass through, our intention must be of the gateway otherwise it simply will not present itself."

All three men continued on for the next few hours until it became apparent they had made all the progress and inroads possible at this time.

"As the energies are present, we can expect him," Carmel said as she cleared the table for dinner.

"It is an attractor like moths to a light. We are of the place to confront him otherwise he would not be coming," Tim replied.

"I have been trying to tell them about it for ages. Asper and I first saw it."

"Yes Celia and it is your vision in particular where we should pay attention."

"Why Chan?"

"You have the essence to guide us without the difficulties we have experienced."

"But my parents…" for a moment Celia looked sad before she thought of Asper. This brought a lull in the conversation generally.

Since John and Tim had Tobias back from the now disintegrated space craft, Asper had spent most of the time taking care of him in a room set aside in John's house.

Nobody spoke much of the condition Tobias was in – all was self evident as he exhibited as a man half machine at the brink of mechanical turmoil. His systems were failing and it was taking all Asper could do to keep him alive.

Tobias held no memory of how he came to be there. He held no memory of the past couple of years, and he held no memory of Asper or any of the others. Tobias was beyond them to a point where even Chan was grim in response to the outlook ahead.

So it had become a hushed reunion and a resignation to where Tobias was heading. Now all they could do was to allow Asper her final moments in caring for the man she loved.

Raynie was the first to bring them out of silence, "Tell us how we can find ourselves if we manage to travel faster than light Chan."

"A good point Raynie. I am reminded of the effect a Fibonacci spiral has…"

"Not a fib or nasty then Chan?"

"No Jake. Surely such an old joke is past its time. I was saying the spiral effect is the carrier as we effortlessly allow it to find the balance of alignment always resulting in an ever progressing sense of such motion. Through this we may pass and so it would be of such in experience."

"I am not sure on my being wound and unwound in such a way." Lyle commented feeling his stomach as if already being in some type of sympathy pain.

"Not as such Lyle. Allow Jenna if you will. She looks a little concerned at your discomfort."

Jenna gave Lyle a good shove sending him over from his seated position on the floor.

"Feeling straightened out by the looks of it now Lyle?"

"Can we help Tobias at all John?" Lorraine asked. Her best friend had been through a tough time in recent years and now she was confronted with her love being a dying mechanical man.

"We can only see what eventuates. His mechanics are just too extensive. We don't have the facilities to remove them," John replied.

"Surely you can stabilise…"

"We tried Lorraine. Tim and I exhausted all we know."

"What about now with this new information?"

"Our intentions are to guide us is all I can offer. We might find something…"

"The energy is becoming erratic within us. I suggest we quieten and solve any dilemma of focus. We are finding inner emotions rising to challenge and we must find our authenticity within each in order we do not succumb to distractions."

Chan was right. The entire group were disjointed. Chris and Gareth basically found themselves out of place and decided to go for a walk. Celia was in the bathroom washing her hands as Raynie, Jake, Jenna, and Lyle sat quietly.

Collectively they all shared a bond Chan knew had the potential for great healing in the future. They had all come together and brought the torus into reality as the catalyst for immediate events and international events over these past years. The emergence of the energy surrounding the awareness represented by the torus had brought forth an unsettling to some within society as they had revealed more of the dynamic potential to be recollected through authentic elemental presence in the true organic sense free of mind constructed by negative ego. They had realised this too for others as the invisible pathways geometrically inter-connecting all became subtly activated stimulating memories where life was more than they were at present.

There was loss of self to find true sense of self. Therein the golden ratio facilitated the flow represented and also facilitated by a torus – the Torus of Eternity glowing so bright now Chan had to conceal it within a metal box he had found.

"Don't forget," Celia said as she returned. "We all must remember the little thing inside out head, um, the Pine gland…"

"Pineal."

"Yes, pineal gland is like our extra eye. It has the memories of how to connect better with everyone rather than just thinking it. You could say it is like another sense we have."

Her eyes met Chan's for a half second surprising Chan with how deep and determined they were.

"I was just thinking to allow anything to come into your mind as an image opening your insights."

"I will Celia. It could give us precognition."

"Yes, pre…cognition. We need to see what is coming."

"I think we are already."

"I know, but more."

"It is amazing how she goes on after what has happened," Jenna said when Celia had left to inspect the garden.

"She might be suppressing something…"

"I think she is somewhat as you say Raynie, but she also has a very clear vision of her purpose at this time and so it may allow her in time to then grieve her losses."

"Derek, Murray and Esther might come back," Jake offered.

John had seen Celia go outside as he was about to enter the secret room. He wondered at how she articulated such vision through her simply yet assertive words. When it came to him it was as if she simply prompted him into altering his perspective. Celia's fascination with both the torus and the dodecahedron had now stimulated a new aspect to consider the moment he was securely inside the room.

Working within the holographic array, John entered new algorithms he deduced after studying the data from the gold hue within the dimensional gateway simulation with Tim earlier. He was currently spending some time with Carmel, so John thought it best they be alone and he be alone to focus on the ideas now coming.

Magnetic resonances emerged through the toroidal simulation to then be aligned with properties coming from theoretical perpendicular constructs of other dimensions. As soon as he engaged the gateway sequence again, the evidence became clear. There was stability within the vortex projected along the dodecahedral planes.

Application of universal gold properties combined with the sound resonances he had recoded coming from the anomaly in space, enabled him to establish a focal atomic pathway to deliver stable flux via a tachyon upsurge amplified through the torus. At each angle the torsion was aligned and within the experiment John could also see a method for delivering stability to presently unstable vortex phenomenon. Chan was right. The resonance of gold had proven to be universal in application and was one ingredient of atomic sequencing required to transcend the boundaries of third dimensional physics.

As a further thought, John decided to send a pulse to mimic a physical transition upon the dodecahedral plane. He could see the dodecahedron containing three golden proportion intersecting rectangles, each made from the Fibonacci number spiral, the fundamental compression ratio of the fabric of space and time in this dimension. A second later he was delighted. The pulse emerged into a simulated dimension intact. He pushed it along giving it instructions to travel the dimension and then emerge back into this one at a destination. Within a moment it responded delivering the most surprising result.

Travel through the perpendicular dimension enabled the pulse to arrive at a time just above light speed. Accessing the perpendicular dimension enabled the lineal pathway from one point to another, to be laterally expressed as a much lesser distance. To his self amazement, he had discovered theoretical faster than light travel. It was this lateral application crossing dimensions where gateways opened avenues of travel disproportionate to this dimension. One facet then came into play as he realised the sound waves gave definition to the gateways. He had studied cymatics at length over time and was now reminded of the multi faceted expressions of dimension Chan had discussed. Light, matter, electricity, sound – all were relevant to this breakthrough as was the human intent, organic and elemental without the irregularities of resonance caused by negative ego characteristics.

After a few seconds to realise this, he aligned the equations with the torsion angle in DNA purely out of interest. As a further moment of utter surprise, John then observed a meridian network of what appeared to be helix within and through the DNA totalling twelve in all. This was a bonus as it confirmed the inter-dimensional capacity of human DNA. Then what became apparent was the indication of a thirteenth helix being revealed as this insight into dimensions was made.

He immediately left the room to go and find the others, but refrained from saying a word when he noticed an authority machine outside the house. Everyone else was already tense and standing still to avoid any unwanted attention. After what seemed an eternity, the robot finally moved on allowing everyone to breathe easier…for a time.

Chapter 36

Eric could see the spacecraft in the clearing twenty three miles away as an image on his holographic scanner scope. Matheson would be nearby – his own intuition free of any mechanics made it obvious. Eric had placed Tobias aboard the craft after extensive mechanical implants knowing John would not be able to resist if he ever discovered who had been pilot sent into the vortex.

John would surely be within two days travel. Eric knew he was good at escape and at moving undetected covering long distances in short time, but this was the time. Eric knew it and he was sure Matheson was aware of him closing in. As for the Agent, Eric expected him at any time and so had prepared for this eventuality.

Unknown to anyone even his superiors, Eric had developed a small quantum computer. His internal mechanics had directed his organic self this way as a means of preservation given the analytical probabilities of failures now evident in monolith systems. This computer was Eric's personal device and it contained the power to encode in various states...matter, wave, plasma, and audio whilst harnessing the electricity in each. Eric knew fundamental principles at play here and those potentially of flux John had provided. Such power with reach into the electric rhythms along geometric construct was required for any excursion beyond this dimension. With this knowledge there also was the certainty the Agent knew of the same. He had sent amplified vortices prolifically across distances creating unfathomable dimensions to oblivion.

He must find Matheson first. Even as his superiors sent commands to him, Eric's focus remained on zeroing in and re-capturing John before the Agent could stir things up. Neither his superiors nor the Agent could appreciate the potential for control ahead with the possession of stable flux technology. He was at the cusp, as were they – it was a bearing towards a town north of San Francisco where Eric decided to begin.

On his way he responded to the demands for his attention coming via the Broadcomm. His superior had begun to question Eric's integrity sounding a warning to him of the impending crisis should he disobey an order. Both men knew what was really happening though. The breakdown of internal mechanics was not allowing Eric to restore to who he was prior, instead, they were breaking down his character as they began dissolution towards oblivion. In effect he was in the early stages of a virus similar to those George had recently transmitted and was now affecting people at large as they too began to dissolve.

Upon arrival Eric commenced his scan. As he engaged the quantum device, the thought of finally tracking down Matheson and any cohorts turned to a moment of glee for him. Eric could sense the final stroke he could master appeasing his superiors with delivery of the only person who could render a realisation of the potential dominance monolith technologies could have. No other solution was now viable – humanity could only be controlled at the whim of Eric and others through manipulative technology where the element of choice was no longer considered. Everything had become far too inefficient with the advent of the monolith star and the imminent failure. They had taken the technology too far too soon and now the price was the ultimate for such ignorance unless Eric could devise a plan to ensure Matheson would help him.

Eric sensed one deception immediately as he gently landed hidden by a copse of trees on the outskirts of town. The Agent could have given him this area as a location to begin looking for John but had declined, instead hoping to secure something for himself before Eric could have arrived. It had failed as Eric was first on the scene this day and so without delay he set out to find any trace of flux technology.

So far his scanner had detected nothing as John and Tim had shielded the secret room from detection by any known or potential device coming from recent developments. He was frustrated as he was certain of the infallibility for his quantum scanner yet it was delivering nothing.

Two hours had passed and still Eric was without a lead. All he could do was to keep searching, but now he watched people more keenly looking for a sign from anyone who might lead him to John.

Nearby, the Agent could not resist. He could see Eric waiting looking lost and it was a perfect opportunity to confront him over his recent incarceration and deprivation of liberties. George also knew if he was to achieve his objective over Matheson, then the assistance Eric could provide until he no longer needed him, came as a logical consideration amongst the chaos of his brewing mania.

The moment he reached sufficient elevation to avoid any detection, George ushered in the next phase of his rapidly developing plans by thought issuing instructions for his monolith craft to proceed. As a gesture of will in celebration of the outcomes about to unfold, George sent forth two more viruses – he had rigged a connection to his amplifier for dispersal at his leisure and this time it would attack the synaptic sugar conversions inside the minds of many sending them to hysterical bouts of psychopathic behaviour.

He had now mastered these algorithms drawing out the darkest facets of personality within and so the people then lacking the mind control to suppress their inner beast were now prone to erratic spontaneous killing and maiming before emerging from this state to be confronted with the horrors of their own doing. George felt inspired by this level of conscious discomfort knowing those affected were bound to end in misery.

Unfounded and so entrenched – George's destiny was all too apparent now. Once again he would unleash calamity through mannerisms previously unseen as the moment of his emphatic pinnacle of oblivion approached.

Eric could see there was a craft on approach. No knowledge had come to him as to an authority vehicle being despatched to track him, so he engaged defence weapons in case they were required. A moment later, scanning systems confirmed what he was thinking – the craft was the one taken by the Agent. There was no predicting the behaviour of George Smythe so Eric accounted for all types from calm and conniving, to manic and chaotic. Certainty was on his side in the least where he could destroy the other craft now only a few miles away and be finally and fully done with the Agent once and for all.

Smooth as silk, George landed the craft silently beside Eric. There was barely room to step around between them such was his intent to immediately show his dominance. Eric aided by his internal processing where the nuances of human behaviour were processed with nanotech enhancements, deliberately allowed George to believe he had the upper hand.

"Our collective efforts have rendered an almost identical situation my former captor. Naturally I have every reason to despise you and even more to enact revenge or some other form of violence…hmm, it does sound tempting yet I consider it futile for the present time. Your assistance and mine could bring an advantage to us both."

"You don't sound convincing to me George. I can sense the snideness in your voice."

"I see using my name appeals to you. Then let it appeal to me also for this moment is one of deliverance and such idleness as becoming irate at something so trivial would not serve our objectives."

"What is it George?"

"Tell me Eric, how is it you have become so similar to me?"

"By what measure do you say George? I am nothing like you…a maniac."

"Oh but yes, for the maniac in you may be different yet it is present all the same."

"Be of whatever mind you choose. Our objectives are Matheson and the torus they have."

"The Torus of Eternity. Do you fancy eternity Eric?"

"We all do George."

"Apparently those fortunate enough to have the torus do not agree with our sentiment."

"It will be their undoing."

"Do you really believe so Eric?"

"More than anything I can believe otherwise. Their ideas of some energy beyond the present are absurd."

"Surely you have seen the data from the anomaly. The scientist in you must question at least some Eric."

"Some, but there is always a scientific explanation, or a geometric definition – again science."

"Yet there is the unknown we know surely is there. It is over these past years where both of us have to come to pass of this knowledge as has Matheson and his cohorts…Chan."

"Yet more science to be discovered and defined. There is nothing mystical other than what it is you think you can do for me George."

"I can offer a mystery Eric but it is not worthy of you so I will only consider our combined efforts to take Matheson so we can take each what we require, and then we depart."

"Do you think I am so foolish as to believe such an obvious lie George?"

"Surely Eric, I have built a degree of trustworthiness unsurpassed…"

"Yes, trusted to erupt in to mania or to send dismay and horror to the people."

"You practice the same Eric. Your methods are not so different to mine. Why, even the system coming to pass is a remnant of the greed from the twentieth century - an old world of manipulation and control. Nothing you are doing is really new Eric."

"Interesting you think so George for I see you oh so similarly. The snide, the conniving, the deceit and manic moods. All of it is just repeating what has passed before."

"There is nothing like me in the past Eric. Sure those methods of motives may be matching, but there is so much more waiting in oblivion - a place no person has been capable of delivery previously."

"How do you know George? There have been many tyrants."

"We know beyond light now Eric. We know there is more. We know there is now more to lose than ever before. Mere loss of life is just part of it."

"Your perceptions are limited George."

"We will see Eric."

"Shall we negotiate an agreement?"

"It is not a notion of negotiation George. Simply present your data and then we investigate further."

"How can I be sure you are not hiding something?"

"You cannot, as I cannot."

Both men progressively remarkably worked together for over an hour running with ideas and testing data until they had reached an agreement on how to approach John.

As the grey dawn light rendered a colourless landscape, George was reminded of the cold grey light he had installed in buildings and instilled in the psychology of many, and how it lacked the colour of life. This inspired him enough to take to the air before the agreed time causing Eric to hasten and give chase.

"They are coming soon," Celia told the entire group as they gathered for breakfast. "They are near and will find us."

"We know the time will come dear. We all must be in focus to address whatever happens."

"I know Carmel. It is more important for you and the others because your adult minds have been persuaded in the past enough times to make it like a second nature popping up."

"She is right. As I have recently conveyed, all we have practised and been made aware of is coming to pass and so shall be ultimately tested for its' purpose for the very time," Chan added.

"There is more Chan," Celia told him determinedly.

Chan looked surprised for a moment before calming asking what more there was.

"It is a telepathy thing. You know when minds connect. This is the next place for all of us and why Carmel came back so we can do it when the time comes."

Carmel's voice was soft yet re-assuring, "It comes from the dreams Chan. Sharing with Celia and Asper has opened my heart to sense the torus nature of extended mind fields – our true heart intentions are projected through its electrical field. We have this to connect."

"Interesting Carmel. I know of this yet why has it not been brought to my attention here?

"We needed to know ourselves before putting the energy of its concept to you. The concept of it is already here between us."

"See Chan. Carmel is telling you about what I said, how you must focus."

"It aligns with our work beyond light – the inter-dimensional aspect of connection through accessibility present to the authentic nostalgic state. Unhindered we can travel faster than…well, not yet but I am sure Tim and Jenna will help me come up with something."

"John knows in his way Chan. We must have this intuition with each other before they arrive."

"I am sure we have the approach for this Carmel."

Eric had tabled the telemetry and set course alongside George. There was not a fleeting moment in time where George would consider following Eric – such a notion was the domain of useless minions of which he was nothing.

The town had nothing to offer other than the pathetic sight of new residents trying to live in a normal sense. George fired a volley of laser shot into them as he flew alongside Eric who neither approved nor disapproved. Eric was beset with far larger concerns than the fate of a few murdered townsfolk, yet he was annoyed enough to speak.

"Did you have to? How is it you manage to find yourself causing such turmoil yet have no control over such childish outbursts?"

"Condescendence is unbecoming of you Eric. Where you see child is merely your frail attempt at definition. I consider your antagonising as insignificant."

"A typical Agent response. I feel you would have served well in Earth's past when those ridiculous peoples allowed lying politicians to basically screw them over."

"I sense a hint of something in your tone there Eric. Are your mechanics functioning well? And how is it the authorities are any different now?"

"They are functioning well enough. As for the difference, it is vast. The authorities now are much more aligned with the best outcomes for all rather than just for a wealthy few. Anyway, never mind yourself with my state of being George. Our task is simple. We must maintain focus as time is of the essence."

"Indeed time is of the essence for soon it will disappear for all."

"Your logic is unbecoming George. Such simple assertions of mania have no foundation in science."

"Yet my successes to date have been exquisite."

"A label of your own making George."

"Surely you must acknowledge my mastery using the amplifier. It was my work helping your pathetic officers do theirs all along."

"You might see it as such. I can assure you, we have our own developments still kept from you George."

"Something more than the monolith?"

"A method we have achieved. Complete failure is never an option."

"Oh but it will be Eric, just wait and see."

Once again, Eric felt the presence of George's final blow coming closer. He was certain the moment Matheson and the others were approached, the Agent would do what he could to take all. Eric could not allow this to occur in any way and was now in the last stages of developing his own method for disposing of the Agent.

Their flight was an exchange of daring where they taunted each other in a mania destined to become frenzy. Pressure as amplified through a torus, extracts pathways to dimensions and as both men felt this pressure now as the final act for dominance, there soon was to come an episode where logic was absent and frenzy took hold.

Eric could see there was no longer anything the Agent could do for him. Without warning he fired three times hitting the Agent's craft before suddenly shooting two thousand feet vertically within a few seconds. The instant he had reached safe distance, Eric engaged the destruction sequence.

George knew what was happening. He could not have done anything to prevent this measure. Eric had built a fail mode independently into every monolith device. George followed him instantly matching his speed. There was no time for anything else and in those very few moments, George reckoned a sense of personal efficacy of calm resolution knowing his place had arrived. In those fleeting seconds he saw himself as a boy growing into a young man free of the burdens his experiences in life had placed upon him in his youth. No sense of bitterness from the rejection came to him – George saw it all and knew it was his reactions to events where his life had begun a downward spiral. His hatred, his lack of remorse, and his sense of futility had all been a construct his mind had cleverly manipulated him into believing. And so as it strengthened over the years, it had become a mania where all memories of the innocence and light of the unconditioned purity he was given at birth, had been forgotten until now.

Eric could see him approaching as the safe distance readout numbers rapidly declined. They gave Eric an audio reading of the display - five, three hundred feet, four… thr…two hundred feet, two, one…one hundred feet…. The counting ceased. A small detonation within George's craft immediately disengaged gravitational dampening and stopped its ascent sending him headlong into the viewing window.

In a brief moment George met his oblivion yet it was in agony as he realised he was never going to reach such a utopia. He sensed meaning, he sensed what life meant, and he sensed himself free of mania in those fractions of seconds. His last remnants of life were as he had given such moments to others. George realised he had been smashed against the front window of the craft with his body to be left like those who had lost integrity and form through his viruses, before finally dying. His craft then fell away as did his body, descending until moments later it erupted into a fireball on the ground. George was gone. He was dead. There would be no more Agent and in fulfilment of his quest, an end inglorious.

Within minutes Eric was located at the house a mile from town. He did not threaten those inside, rather he calmly arrived to commence negotiations. He wanted John and the others alive as their knowledge could mean a lot to his superiors, so his first tactic was to go alone and avoid any backup forces.

"You will be pleased to know I have just killed our greatest adversary George Smythe. He died a most inglorious death so unbecoming to his mania. I have a video recording to prove this too," Eric announced via the broadcast speaker from his seat inside the craft. "Be assured I speak the truth and am glad to be doing so as his nemesis."

"We don't want anything from you Eric. Why can't you just leave us alone?" John shouted through the partially open front door. Everyone was gathered together waiting silently in the room behind him.

Eric's choice of the word nemesis struck John for a moment as he realised how far Eric's mind was deteriorating with each moment.

"You know there is really no choice John," Eric chose to remain in his craft and issue demands. "You alone have the best knowledge to take humanity to places never imagined. We cannot allow you to keep it to yourself John. And now there could be charges against you for the unstable flux you intentionally gave me."

"You don't honestly think I would have given you the correct algorithms Eric."

"Surely no John, yet we held a degree of faith in you I see was ill placed."

"Why the faith Eric? Such a notion is far from the mechanics of your mind."

"Not as far as you may think John. Let me say we are aware of the dynamics of geometry and what the role humanity has in realising this as an apparition for potential access beyond light and dimension. It would be the new birth of the human race if you were to share this with us John."

"Only as your version of the human race Eric and we know how tainted it can be."

"We are free of the Agent. The time of adversaries is over. Our collective energy could instil a new order for humanity, a prosperous way of life, and luxuries beyond imagination."

"All produced as a means to keep people distracted as you and your superiors shut down what it really is to be human. You intend to blend humanity more and more with machines making people so dependent on products to survive and taking away so much of their natural selves."

"It is natural for humanity to progress this way John."

"In some ways yes but not at the mercy of minds like yours and the authorities. Deceit is your game and the so called betterment of humanity comes at a high price. I and we here and no doubt some others, would prefer you keep all your progress to yourselves. We like ourselves Eric. We don't need outsourcing to you."

"There is no real choice John. Humanity has always required a guide, a leader to take them where they require to go and so this will be the obvious role now for us. You and your friends can join sampling all the finest as we go."

"I nor the others here are tempted by your luxuries Eric. I have just told you how we feel."

"How you feel plays no part John. You must decide to come otherwise being forced to comply will be not to your benefit, and I can force you."

"You can try Eric."

John's tone of voice was so confident, Eric was stopped for a moment as he considered the potential secret John may hold.

"Why make it difficult John? You and your friends can all live well if you comply."

"We already live well Eric. Your version of living well is quite opposite to ours."

"A response I have anticipated John. It is late and I am tired. You can have until the morning to think this over." Eric left the scene so suddenly those present who were yet to witness the dynamics of monolith technologies, were astounded at the precision and speed. Jenna was even taken aback some. She had worked on the very first systems now evident physically and had imagined seeing such operations as Eric's sudden ascent.

"See him really Carmel and Chan," Celia said being the first to break a temporary silence. "Mister Eric is no better than the Agent was. He killed him. It is his measure."

"Your words are wise young Celia. It is as if you are much older."

"Chan, I am you see. This time I am here to confront you and help people think."

Asper looked to Celia. She had shared dreams and within there was the idea of their lives having been shared previously across time and dimension. Carmel whispered something to Chan. She did not speak – it was a thought. He heard her, as did Celia, and within a few seconds Celia was smiling broadly as she encountered notions of telepathy with them.

Celia took Asper's hand and led her outside, "See the stars Asper. We are already almost there."

Asper felt Celia's presence but her mind was still distracted by Tobias' plight. She missed this first instance approaching telepathy but Celia did not mind. Dealing with Tobias was exhausting for Asper both physically and emotionally in her heart.

"We can always dream Asper. You know I love you."

"Yes, I love you too Celia. Our dreams are special, they…"

"I know they help. As we listen we grow and things will become better."

"Let us hope Celia."

Chapter 37

Energy in many faceted manifestations can be hewn like diamonds are cut yet smooth and rounded – the torus reflected energetic facets of manifestation showing details half felt and half seen. Somewhere deep beyond what they could detail yet they could still see, were geometric properties now responding to their conscious state. As if electrically and magnetically charged, there appeared filaments of plasma like energy emitting from angles originating at the golden section within the flickering images. As they focused yet let go to allow the self, tendrils of this plasma were attracted to them in a manner similar to the behaviours for the polarity of magnetism.

Chan had considered it was time to expose the torus as they sought the fine alignment to form the pathways of geometric infusion where they could begin to expand the potential telepathic experiences. He knew it was not so much as a mind speaking words to another mind. Rather it was the impressions from each other exchanged within the invigorated medium of energetic presence they felt.

"In authentic presence, the torus will act as our amplifier similar to the way the Agent once used it. Our focus as a group is now to remedy our own misgivings for aligning our true human dynamic potential to access dimensional gateways laid before us but invisible to the eye. We can go there no other way…"

"Sorry Chan," Celia interrupted. "We can simply be present. Our misgivings…are they our doubts? Anyway, we can easily align with the reality as we see it."

"Of course Celia. Perhaps my word was not clear enough. We are to allow our true selves the presence here in these times. All other events of the mind, our experiences, and doubts are of the past yet they teach us the presence here now and our alignment elementally."

"I'm working on it," Gareth added."

"Same for me," Chris said before turning to his father. "Dad, can Gareth and I take a break from this. We feel there is something else we need to do."

"Um, Chan what do…?"

"Where they see fit to be at this time is their place. We are all together regardless of what we are doing as our efforts combine."

"Not ready for the mind meld stuff then son."

"It is not really about being ready, but more of a feeling. Gareth and I have talked about it some."

"I want to work on a few things with Tim before he comes back anyway. I guess he and I will not be far behind you."

"Then let them go John and we now are to focus for I feel Jenna will want to join you so we need to do some preparation for our entire understanding."

The group remained guarded. Embracing the moments as levels of conscious slipped away allowed them to retain a level of alertness based in feeling as if they could almost physically touch and senses its' presence.

"We find our nostalgic signature in our DNA where meridians invigorate additional dimension helix at the dihedral angle mirrored in number by the dodecahedron. Twelve is the universal gateway to the birth of a new helix the thirteenth. From this golden point we realise universal properties including gold itself as a metal of transcendence and alchemical to conscious awareness progression based on the natural laws of the universe as it exists. Exciting these other DNA will provide us with the ever present opening to access those gateways aligned perpendicular and fashioned through dihedral forces where torsion of physicality renders a state of flux enabling the body to pass through."

"It is the same place we dream isn't it Celia?"

"It is Carmel. Asper and I have been there enough to know where we are don't we Asper."

"Yes Celia, I can feel it now and somehow I can feel Tobias is there."

"His presence is always with us Asper despite his body."

"His heart Chan?"

"Calls to you."

Asper felt a tear well up in her eye. Celia noticed and put a hand out as comfort.

When silence once again took hold it was time for John, Tim, and Jenna to leave for the secret room and commence work. They had already communicated their ideas – their next endeavour would be to construct a device to channel the torus energy for opening the dimensional gateways. In combination with their newly discovered conscious, the algorithms would work in conjunction with the dynamic forces created and controlled through authentic connection to the geometries subtly permeating realities.

Raynie along with Carmel, Asper, Lorraine, Jake, Lyle, Chan, and Celia, remained in a close group. As the hours grew old and the first grey light of dawn began to show, they worked through focus and projection to the others not present.

Gareth and Chris had arranged some barricades making it a little more difficult to access the house but Eric would easily overcome any obstacle. He was determined to make this the final time and a successful time, so he surprised them as he had planned to by returning before the sun had risen.

The readouts showed him the intensity of the energies present and central to all was the readout showing the Torus of Eternity. Eric knew this time it was to be the moment he would surpass all expected of him and deliver to his superiors the most sought after people and object. Soon enough, the vision of Earth he shared with those superiors, would come into being despite most monolith directive technologies now in an utter state of chaos.

Matheson and the torus would take him beyond light and beyond dimension. With the mind powers obvious amongst the group Eric could suffice to say he would be the catalyst for humanities furore deep into artificial intelligence and the eventual mechanisation of the entire human condition.

Eric saw the barricades and although part of him wanted to assert authority there and then by vaporising them, he refrained, preferring to make a dignified approach in the hope he would receive a similar response. This time he set his craft down gently just beyond the front gate before casually approaching the house on foot. Eric had no fear – his internal mechanics still managed to keep it at bay for now and he saw no reason to be afraid of anyone given they were not the types prone to violence.

Celia was the first to greet Eric as she hurried to intercept him before the adults could make a stand, "Why do you persist with these silly control things Mister Eric? Surely you know all your failures are showing how much you miss."

"My failures are mere learning along the way young girl. Minds articulate in the provision of focus can achieve objectives knowing any setbacks are mere incidental to success."

"You sound very sure of yourself yet I know there is still enough of you inside to have some doubt. All people have this element otherwise they would not need to be here. It is the way they are taught to trust themselves…"

"Trust is long gone from these parts and is something your friends here are going to need to place in me if they wish to survive. There can be no room for the inefficient dissent you and others like you present."

"But you can never stop us. We will be there as long as people exist…"

"They will become their next evolution as machines little girl."

"There is no way such a dark thing can prevail Mister Eric if you consider the strength of light as it represents the strength of life and love of will. There are others too. They will make sure of this."

"Who are these others you speak of? Other people?"

"No Mister Eric. They are like beyond our place and mind as we see it here. They speak to us and from us knowing our spirit to live connected."

"Who are they?"

"I do not know but I listen. Why would the voices be there if they were not for listening?"

"And why do you think such a thing is important?"

"It is because it shows your behaviour as a mistake to the true nature of elemental humans and how they express themselves."

"How do you know these things? Who has been telling you…? And mistake. What an absurd idea from a little girl. You are yet to realise the ways of adults."

"Nobody tells me silly. It is a way of knowing many adults have learned to forget and now at this time, it is being asked to act. I know this enough to see it is good and not like the horrible things you bring."

"How do you mean act?"

"Act on the efforts you make and the ones my friends make…and my dad…"

"You miss your father. I can see your sadness."

"It is very sad but I know he is strong just like my mother. I am strong too and so are my friends."

"We will have to see now they have arrived outside. They do look worried for you little girl."

"My name is Celia and you should know already. You are rude Mister Eric."

"Leave her alone Eric. You came to speak to us…to me."

"Indeed I did John. How are you now we no longer have our insidious adversary the Agent to contend with?"

"As expected and expecting you to exert all you can Eric. It is a cliché. Your will is so easily readable."

"Oh so you may think John, but you have no idea of the capacity of my…"

"Failing mechanics. I know entirely why you are here Eric. It is no different to when you took Tobias and I years ago. Do you want to see him? He is here. You can see in him where you yourself are heading. Oh, and don't forget there is the compassion element you so easily overlook, so please when you see his love Asper weeping as he lies there dying, perhaps your mechanics might help you."

"They eradicate all such wastages John."

"Well then I imagine you will eventually be their target when they realise how your wasted self is such a burden to efficiency."

"Never such a place shall be attained John. You know I will merge prior to any such failure."

"Don't count on losing yourself Eric. I can see a lot of pain in you. Your eyes show nothing, but your sub-conscious is alight."

"You know nothing of my sub-conscious and soon if you are given to reason, you will be able to witness me enact such travesty through using the real torus of Eternity, any resistance to the way ahead I and my superiors are to deliver for the good of society, will be meaningless."

"Never such a notion shall arise within any of us Eric, nor any others who are surely aware of just how far we have come from the submissive pathways the authorities want to drive humanity along where the spirit of living is gridlocked in a psychological melee corroding the very authentic nature of people. Why, even Celia here who was so bold as to intercept you at the gate. She shows the strength of character determined to be more than any pathetic rendition you may offer."

"Ah but you are so few, and the many are so many and are so willing. They have suffered John and now they can be emancipated…"

"What an extravagance coming from the very person so willing to be in charge of technology to bring about precisely the opposite."

"I can have forces here at any time John but I thought if you saw reason then you might like to come quietly and in so much less pain."

"Pain is never the issue Eric. Any idea you have for me and the others here only entails a form of slavery and submission you choose to practice for the interests of control. In know why you do it being as cowardly as you are."

"Cowardly is hardly appropriate John as it is I who has endeavoured to work hard and deliver humanity to a better world with uncertainty almost eradicated."

"More rhetoric from the ignorant."

"So what will it be John? I know you speak for everyone here. You can tell me what you know peacefully…including these voices the girl speaks of."

"You already know my answer Eric. I know nothing about where voices come from but even you cannot eliminate the idea of other sentient minds somewhere…maybe watching you Eric. I guess we will be seeing you later."

"Oh by no means John. Later is not the issue for it will be much sooner than you realise. I am sincerely offering you a place to use your mind and whatever else you think it takes to enable true flux beyond light speed…"

"I already have decided there is nothing I or any other person here would do in respect to help you in any way."

"Then I am going to have to force you John. There is much advantage for humanity to have this under control. We cannot have rogue elements like you upsetting the efficiency of our authority."

"Then do what you can Eric for we may surprise you yet."

"I am counting on it John."

Eric departed calmly leaving John watching him. Almost everyone else was gathered in the lounge room of Carmel's house behind him except for Celia who had stood by John's side the entire time. As Eric disappeared from view, she gave John's hand a tight squeeze, "You told him just what he really wanted to hear John. It is just his silly mind thinking he does not."

"Yes I know Celia. It is strange how so many people go around in two worlds."

"They can be very silly when they could just be happy."

"He's dead. He's dead. Oh dear." Asper had arrived in the next moment to announce the fate of Tobias.

In the past few minutes before Eric left them, Tobias had suddenly awoken a little to himself as his last act of will before death. He had smiled at her and mouthed her name in silence. His eyes showed a hint of their familiar twinkle to her despite their mechanics – it was in his face around his eyes from where he spoke to her. His last few seconds pledged his love…their love. It was as if he had come to gift her one last time and as he did, she had smiled for the first time with him in many years. It was this as their last experience where he willed her to take only this with her forward – to remember him at the last in presence for her, in love with her, and alive only for her. With a slight wheeze his face then lost its smile as it renounced into a pale nothingness signalling the time had arrived. In the last he had been himself and had died knowing love and for all she could have ever given him.

Celia ran to her wrapping her arms around Asper. As tears welled for all in the room, Celia remained steadfast despite her own. She knew the sensitivity of such a thing having lost her mother and with her father missing – it was this learning she now gave for Asper and the others and in the essence of this time, she gave them strength and the determination to be in truth their authentic self. It was nothing she spoke. It was her will, her energy, her projection. Even Chris and Gareth knew what was happening, and as for Chan, he was looking to see the evidence of interaction on all their faces. As his eyes met Carmel's, they both recognised an element of relationship from deep within their ancient DNA now recalled. It was an activation in a moment where Celia had assisted.

In the next few seconds, Chan and Carmel took this and gave it to the others.

They focused their cognition and telepathic potential to harness and focus and then in those few seconds afterwards, the others felt a sense of exultation. It was so evident of self and so evident of intent it was impossible not to feel. Unseen yet surely felt, this exponential wave of human consciousness evolution came as a breath of fresh air.

This breath, this wind, this wave – energy of form yet not of form, was set to render form and amongst those who could feel its presence was Eric as he analysed the energy signals at Carmel's house. He knew they were up to something threatening so he called for enforcement technology to attend the scene. He decided a dozen monolith robots designed to herd people effectively without causing harm would be sufficient.

Inside, Chan lead them all to a place where they could focus on…nothing. Everyone was asked to help and as they came to reckoning within of their position to elevate the potential of energy following each wave.

When they had returned together to the immediacy of the room, John, Tim, and Jenna broke off from the group first after securing the Torus of Eternity from Chan. It was time for the object to be placed in situation and bring about the next elemental stage of its' progression.

The alignment came elementally as the dodecahedron geometries were applied to the torus in an interplay forming a diamond at the amplification focal location of the dimensional gateway. With calculations and algorithms being constructed in real time as response mechanisms to the energies aligning, the evidence of the gateway became more apparent. At the perpendicular meridian to the light wave oscillation, a tiny prick of jagged light appeared for an instant. It was not a holographic projection – rather a point within the space in front of them where the energies had been focused to direct flux. Immediately Tim and John set the instruments to focus on the point whilst Jenna regulated the amplification signal to expose more aperture in the gateway.

With each oscillation came a greater opening until they had established a portal some two inches across. It was a strange sight looking into another dimension. Almost beyond description, it encompassed feeling, intuition, and poignant elemental authentic presence to allow the geometric pathways to align sufficiently. Within seconds information came to them as images, as thoughts, and as direct communication to their minds. There was a presence aware of their intrusion into this dimension and as such were attempting to communicate.

Outside in the lounge room, Celia, Chan, and Carmel suddenly took a gasp of breath – the portal had opened the eternal link now to become part of the wider human psyche. Instantly they communicated as best they could hoping the others would receive the intuitions coming from this first endeavour into another dimension. Chan felt the potential to be realised now the gateway was established so he took Carmel aside for them to discuss them further.

Celia saw Chan's and Carmel's departure as an opportunity to give Asper some comfort. Asper knew Tobias was in a better place and her heart felt the enrichment of his last moments. She knew she had to be strong, but she also knew the others would extend their empathy for her. Celia was evidence of this as she came up with a slight smile trying to encourage the same from Asper. She realised her energy and returned the favour, setting them both off in an effort of consolation where Asper was grateful for her connection at this time.

In contrast to the urgency of the situation with Eric's pending return accompanied by force, all remained calm for they knew precisely what had to be done. Carmel was instrumental in maintaining an ease about the place, choosing this time to fire up her engine and when the steam had built sufficiently, she let off a volley of whistles. Celia was taken with this as her fascination in Carmel's ways at how she could so easily elevate herself beyond the material mind, never ceased to make her smile and feel a growing confidence.

It was about fifteen minutes later when the group felt the surge within extending beyond themselves and beyond sight. There was no denial in feeling – it was a result of the flux gateway now becoming wider and wider within the secret room. John and Tim had now constructed a portal measuring twelve inches in diameter and still expanding.

"We'll stop at thirty six inches Tim. It should be wide enough. Jenna, make sure we set the coordinates. There is no room for us to go wandering off just anywhere."

"It is such a risk John."

"We don't really have a choice do we Jenna."

"I suppose the alternatives are more or less what we have been through in the past and I think we are all fed up."

"Better to make this choice than to submit," Tim added.

"I agree…"

Jenna was suddenly cut off with the sound of a soft knock on the door. They knew it meant Eric was back.

"I will heed no words from you old man. Where is Matheson."

"I speak for us all." Chan remained calm and persistent. "Nobody is going to give you anything Eric. Your efforts are wasted yes. It is your choice to see darkness in a manner so similar to the Agent."

"I am nothing like the maniac George Smythe, former of this planet."

"Are you so sure? Look at you. Look at what you bring for the sake of what you call efficiency. You are blinded by your own blindness. There is nothing for you to see other than what those mechanical eyes allow Eric. You are wasted. So inefficient."

"How absurd coming from an old man who leads people on chases to nothing. You have done nothing with the torus old man. It is I who can realise its true potential."

"Therein you fail to understand Eric. You covert the torus, yet it is not for such things. Your mistake is the evidence."

"Just give me Matheson or I will come inside and get him."

"He is unavailable at present Mister Eric. He has to be calm now as you try this otherwise he will lose his wisdoms to you."

"What is it you speak of? I have no time for your riddles little girl. Get Matheson now. You have two minutes."

Chapter 38

The opening was growing as they watched in anticipation. As each moment passed laterally as a matter of concept and not of time, they peered in looking further and further seeking answers. It was to be the first encounter as the catalyst of connection for placement within for the dimensions of realities and of creation. From so far they were about to encounter something so near – a concept now realised naturally to them as much as to any others who were the instigators of this gateway.

As they watched, John made the opening accelerate in size by amalgamating some algorithms to speed up the effect of the torus. Jenna and Tim were both busy with their heads down calculating algorithms to maintain stability of the entire energetic event. The torus was glowing so brightly, the entire room was bathed in its hue – now also extending beyond into the portal in front of them. As a final measure, John instigated the sound wave generator they had discovered from the emissions out of the anomaly. It was a requirement for stability and to render a smooth edge to the now jagged portal smelling of burning electricity. As the two notes sounded in accompaniment, the hole rounded itself to a perfect circle now thirty six inches in diameter.

When they saw this, it invigorated a sense of excitement and confirmed the intentions of those opening this portal. They now held an eagerness as anticipation became reality, yet they retained a sense of composure for this was to be the very first instance and the correct feelings and intentions had to be conveyed.

Chan and Carmel went immediately into deep meditative like states. Celia was excited as she held Asper's hand. Both of them then took to feeling this new energy as a matter of nature and like the others, projected it outward for all present. When all were harmonious in their field of energy together – even Chris and Gareth were able to sense this and project their own interpretations despite their relative recent exposure to the subtle aligning geometries. They had gathered now as a number, a group, and as an energetic sense of humanity reaching beyond the body and the mind as it sees the world.

"All life force mirrors us," Chan said quietly. "In this time we are to recollect this true sense further than our previous experiences. This is the universal competence allowing us to explore as it is naturally. This place is ours and is for all. Mostly it is our responsibility to enable transmission of the energies to uplift others. There is no sense of personality – it is a synchronicity and we are authentic in place."

Celia smiled knowing the feelings were all soon to be shared and the wonder of her dreams with Asper and Carmel were to become the wonder for the hearts restored in many.

As Eric organised his force of robotics outside, for those still in the secret room, the time had arrived for the revelation – they all were to travel, to test, and to be the first taking risk for the sake of future vision.

"I do not want to use these tactics. Bring the torus out now and make yourselves available and then this day shall continue to be in your best interests."

"Such a notion can never be in my best interests Eric. You are beginning to sound a little like the Agent. Your language, your assuredness based really on nothing…"

"Nothing! No such reality exists old man. You know such a thing already. Energy is transformed, there is no end."

They could see this negotiation was going nowhere and would never reach anything favourable. Eric wanted only one thing so one track his mechanised mind had now become. Obsession was in fact a distraction he sought to eradicate with his nanotech mechanics shaping an efficient mind, yet here it was demonstrated in full view. He could not see it so focused he had become. It was now or never and he would accept nothing less than a full apprehension of this entire group in any way deemed necessary. Their lives although easily extinguished, were of importance to him if he was to extract information from John.

Tim and Jenna were ready to usher the others into the secret room. The element of risk was high – the portal through dimensions was un-tested. A human had never walked such a pathway in any of their knowledge, but something deep inside John resonated the authentic nature and elemental geometric calculations required to open the passageway. He was confident they would be able to travel the dimensions if in true alignment with their elemental self. Any aspect of negative ego could trip a travesty where transgression within the portal could be a nightmare of conflicting realities potentially sending one either insane or to the abyss of oblivion.

"I can wait a minute or two longer. Afterwards, expect the full force of my accompaniment."

"Okay Jenna, take Chan first as he holds the torus." John had returned the item to Chan after using it to open the portal. He knew it would require a human touch at the last to activate the object to its' potential. Chan had advised him it was itself an amplifier of proportions beyond the scope of algorithms and forces. It was a lesson he had consistently alluded to since their first encounter with the idea of the torus.

Less than a minute passed before Eric began to act. He knew they would not give in to him and so he engaged the preliminary scanners on the robotics. The entire line of machines standing fifteen feet tall suddenly came into action with a slight whirring sound before each one used an array of sensors at its head position to scan the entire scene.

It was time. Jenna indicated to Chan. He discreetly made his way towards the secret room door just out of view from Eric and the robotics at his side.

The air about smelled electric as if lightning had struck somewhere close. Constant transmission between the robotics and the portal still hidden in the secret room, were causing the atmosphere to slowly burn off in a way where electrons were being sheered at their angle of torsion relative to their nucleonic orbit.

As Chan held the torus for all to see, geometric forms and patterns glowed the brightest pink with gold in a never ending cascade without beginning or end flowing about the entire object. Elemental alignment was now heightened as forms broke off indicating its presence at the point between dimensions.

As Chan showed them, Eric sent the first command to prevent any escape from the house. At seeing the discomfort arise in the eyes of Raynie and Jake who were holding each other at this time, Eric sensed an opportunity to give one last chance for them to come peacefully.

"Your last moments, will they choose my offer of freedom or will you choose oblivion?"

"John was right. You do sound like the Agent."

"Jake is it? Well Jake, I am no agent but I did dispose of him thoroughly. You could be happy to see his demise."

"Only to be replaced by you as you lose your mind. John has told us how your mechanics must be going by now. The proof is here. Your behaviour Eric is the issue, not us."

"Oh is my behaviour the issue? Well, I would consider my behaviour as appropriate considering the fact I am assigned with the role to ensure the mechanised future of humanity goes unchallenged."

"Like a heartless corporation, a dictator, a…"

"Any of those will do. Where I and my superiors are taking us is beyond the material concept as applied to controlling the masses. Our ways are far more intrusive and subtle. People will recognise the benefits as they strive to find meaning through status and consumption. There can be no other way Jake. Humanity requires leadership."

"Some do when they fail to…no, I won't debate with you. It only serves to give you merit Eric."

"Certainly something I deserve."

"Ah, see. Again John was right. You are seeing deservedness. Surely your mechanics are not working efficiently."

"They are working. Where is Matheson? I am through with this. I want him here now or the command to retrieve him will be sent."

"He's not coming Eric and your robots will not work."

"Oh they will. I know it was you here who interrupted the glory of monolithic technology. This time I have prepared and as such there is no way you can invade the systems for these robots."

"Who spoke of such a thing? You will fail Eric."

"I will not fail Jake."

"Oh yes you will."

"I will not. Get Matheson now."

"No."

"You must, otherwise you will not endure through being forced. I cannot take you all with me and there really is no need."

"You can do nothing Eric."

"I can do what I please. Matheson only has the final stable flux algorithm. I still have all the rest.

"It will not help you without stability Eric. We all know."

"You know nothing."

"We know more than you."

"How can you know more than the leading scientist?"

"We know John Eric."

"Where is he?"

"Inside but he is not coming to see you. What would be the point? It's too late for you Eric."

"Too late. It is never."

"It is now. We really do become tired of you Eric."

Raynie was silent at Jake's side giving his hand a squeeze now and then as he boldly defied Eric.

"Then you are destined to become ever more tired of me." Eric instructed the robots to move in and disable the people in and just outside the house. Without reliance on doorways or windows, each robot took a direct line with an intention to smash through whatever was in its way on course to the targeted occupants.

At the moment they all simultaneously reached a wall, door, or window, Chan took the first step into the three foot wide dimensional gateway. In the first instant of time he breached the horizon between dimensions, the monolithic robots were affected. They suddenly become erratic in their operations seeming to fumble and stumble before they mostly went silent. A few careered off taking random directions on pathways of destruction until they destroyed themselves. The house next door bore the brunt of one robot as it walked straight through the walls and in a few moments of changing directions within the house, it emerged from what was now a ruin.

The pulse surged outward in the instant Chan entered, eclipsing all laid to and before humanity in a simultaneous lateral appraisal of self. These energies revealed the coded DNA sequencing attached to the dynamic principles of angulations and the access of photons to calculate the elemental self in place with the entirety of universal connectivity across dimensions. No longer was the paradigm of doubt or lack of alignment to be the construct of so much thought. Allowance of awareness through experience clarifies such density where burden brings weighted mind and heavy heart.

Jenna had left the room to fetch the others. As soon as they saw her face, they all started towards the portal. Raynie and Jake were at the last, leaving Eric bewildered as he stood there watching the demise of his robotics.

He knew it was something they had all done beyond anything he could manage using technology alone. When he turned to see them all heading inside, he felt a surge of anger unlike anything he had ever experienced. At this time with energies emitting from the nearby portal he didn't know existed, the mechanics of his mind took to turmoil as they were unable to cope with the data load being thrown at them. His anger then became a mania when he realised how much be had just lost and how much potentially was at stake right now.

From his belt, he first grabbed at his electric ray pistol before steadying his hand and carefully taking it out of the holster. Time was almost standing still for him as he watched Raynie and Jake run in through the door as if they were in slow motion. As he levelled the gun, he knew he was wrong – Eric never wanted to be a killer. Despite his conscience, he took aim and then pulled the trigger.

A bolt of blue ten inches in length shot out heading for them as they were about to round the doorway and disappear inside. It struck sending a charge all over Jake causing him to writhe about and scream. Where in a moment he was active, the very next he was subdued to only slight movements, before in the next moment he lay completely still.

Raynie screamed and Eric felt the same as he had when he killed the Agent George Smythe. Lyle was nearby. He grabbed Jake's arms and dragged him along the floor.

Eric saw this rescue and so proceeded on foot inside. When he saw Lyle and Raynie disappear through a small door with Jake's body, he knew then they would affect an escape if he didn't act. He ran to the door and kicked it open only to see the portal through which all had passed, now being closed with an instrument John had made for this very purpose. Eric then fired his ray pistol again to no avail. Instead of destroying the technology around him, Eric slumped into a chair resigning to defeat. The very power he sought through technology had just been exhibited to him where his first experience was of its insurmountable potential rendering all else obsolete.

"He won't be able to affect us as this portal in consciousness is like a phasing of reality. What seems like moments to us is merely a fraction of a second to him."

Raynie wanted to scream again but she could not. Jake looked dead in a place they all felt estranged in somehow out of mind, time, and place. There was a lack of definition yet there was definition. She did not know why she couldn't scream about Jake. It was confusing. They all had lost a great sense of self yet gained the same in a way they had never conceived. It was as if the sudden inroad into a wider scope of connectivity through mind and heart had taken to concept for which they had no previous knowledge.

Entering a different dimension outside the boundaries they had all become used to was a place where the endless was present, the most intricate was observable, and where millions of geometric pathways constructing their immediate reality, were visible and active as if powered by some electricity.

A moment later, they felt their genetic code changing. It was as if they were being re-written or some blockage was being cleared. At the DNA level they were integrating the active connection to the elemental geometric forces. They were observing the construction medium through which differing frequency oscillations of consciousness create manifestations of reality and of thought. These intentions come before the passage of light as it is set on its pathway to follow. Chan had told them this long ago where spirit sets the path for light to follow.

They could all associate with a presence, not in the physical sense yet seemingly there beside them. It talked to them. Instantly Celia, Asper, and Carmel recognised their dreams – they were speaking to those who had spoken and had revealed the facet of conscious self through the anomaly in the sky.

Carmel's house was the point where this portal had rekindled memories of alignment offering the authentic presence for progress – an evolutionary step natural and unhindered by the material mind. In a moment, humanity began to re-align its memory and sense of nostalgia for true self over the oppressed legions of the authorities. Once established, most of humanity as a species evolved in an instant beyond the confines of their material minds occupied with futility so often causing their problems.

Eric nor his superiors could deny what they too felt at this time. Their motivations subsided as they were taken beyond the limitations of their own ways and exposed to the wonders none of them had taken time to imagine ever. Derision and degradation were their forte until this moment where for the first time many experienced the light aspect of life rather than focusing on darkened methods of control either for personal situations or as an operative.

They had always been useless anyway. Attempting to stave off a natural elemental progression of the human experience for the sake of control maintained by the few over the many was an idea of such lacking it always required enforcement to keep a weak hold over the many. Those who had challenged its worth through the centuries were now vindicated. There would be attempts to maintain control as those who missed this event or were unable to fully let control go, but in most they were only short distractions to the universal acceptance of life of here and more than just planet Earth.

When John and the others stepped from the dimensional gateway, they emerged into the same house – the portal had not been to a physical place, rather it had touched the sub-stratum of all pervasive consciousness. An energetic sense undeniably greeted each of them. It was a home coming and even Celia felt the same as all the adults. John had enabled stable flux mechanics to open a gateway between dimensions for humans to grasp what they already truly were and understand all pervasive consciousness. Nothing Eric or the authorities could do, would affect this present moment realization for them all. They were free and without thought had set so many others free simultaneously.

Time out of dimension was due only to experience beyond the lineal passage as they understood. What had seemed like minutes was actually less than a second beyond the speed of light where consciousness precludes all other in reality and matter is a derivative of consciousness.

It had been six years since the crackdown had begun. Now it was the last year. Further than time permits, unhindered by material boundaries, and lifted to the recollection of authentic dynamic presence, society was to be more than the lineal years and so those years were to fade from conscious. The flow, the energy and imagination, restored and reflected in the torus, for as it is with the cosmos, authentic energy flows through the geometry of a torus majestic in geometrical splendour as the bridge to understand the phenomenal plane as part of all pervasive consciousness. The truth once revealed was set on course for progression. Eric nor anyone of similar ilk from the authorities or any sect with its senseless minions bound to traits of ego, could pose opposition this as the resonant frequency of humanity was being restored and exponentially set to grow and progress. Yet as is reality, nothing was set in stone and forever unchanging for the universe and dimensions were bound to elemental characteristic of consciousness affecting matter within the intricate nature of geometry underpinning the values of construct permeating dimensions through the golden section of both material and of intention as the act of cosmic law.

Humanity was no longer alone, was not bound through time, and no longer was serviced through years. The last year was passed, it was of past, and presence was now the beginning of an authentic alignment not just for some, but for many and this was a tide of light golden and unstoppable as humanity took a deep breath and was finally set loose from the binds of power control mechanism for at least the foreseeable future. It would be an easiness releasing the human instrument as a body and energy to be genuinely present and build society accordingly. There was no prevention for this elemental progress for one may as well try stopping the orbit of the planet Earth itself given the energetic and dynamic momentum humanity was to experience.

Fear was gone, the anomaly was gone. People could look to the clear blue sky rather than the drudgery of times past. A heavenly breath was what many described their new feelings, their new outlook, and the embrace of so much more than any status could have ever offered. The passage of time took no relevance to them as invigorated senses were not burden with such density. It began to slip from the conscious towards a future already apparent where the moment is the presence and so requires no intent for authentic intent is lived. It has been about loss of status, loss of materialism, loss of the projections through control, loss of dependency, and mostly, the loss of egocentric self identity. They are eternal as a fragment of eternity...the universe...all pervasive without second or ending.

Through resistance to authentic presence constructed in the minds of many, feverishly manifested within maniacs, and dominant in those who sought domination and then enforced through technology, toxicity arose to reflect the abrasive nature of society. Consistent dramas, seeing lacking through accepting struggle, and hungry with an eternally insatiable hunger, and worst of all, the propensity to destroy each other directly or through coercion and submission, were to become the frequencies of old – a stale paradigm now well past its time where even the ignorance of those who set about trying to re-institute power in the old dense ways, were seeing their ignorance begin to wane. To remove the ego in its dominance was to embrace spirit setting the path for light to follow – a simply allowance of the authentic self in the moment, free from construct yet immersed so intricately within its grace.

Chapter 39

Raynie O'Day sat by herself in the library of the old house she had returned to where she had first began her journey of discovering the Torus of Eternity. The house was liveable but in an obvious state of disrepair after numerous desperate occupants and their neglect. Close friends had all become a little scattered now after the uprising events for humanity. Jake was not coming tonight – the night when they met in this very house seemed distant, yet close. She had shared some of her life with someone she adored, her love for his sense of humour, his longing for mystery, and his spirited genuine self amongst others, were dearest in her heart. She had been blessed with his presence in her life, and he with hers. They were inseparable across all dimensions, souls travelling experience together.

The winds swept the house as they often did, except they were not of winter descending upon the landscape – they were hot and dry, cast from deep in the heart of a continent often brazen with dust. There was no dust within Raynie though as she sat reading alone. She was the only person for miles around.

The two lights at each end of the house, one in the kitchen and one in the library were the only beacons of life shining into the moonless night. Her essence was touched with magnificence and she felt love beyond measure.

Many people across the Earth now shared this elemental connection and a realisation of self removed from the bind so many had lived with in recent years stretching to decades and even centuries. She could feel her connection with the others she loved, especially Celia and Carmel. She searched for Asper, but her signal seemed weak and indeterminate. They all shared this connection, as did many others, and it had been the one evolution of human consciousness they could never synthesise with machines.

Technology had already proven to be an easy medium once aligned intentional understanding was activated. The Torus of Eternity was the instrument by which all attributed this elevation of awareness – though not as an object of affection, rather of reflection. Humanity had come to understand the quantum and beyond mechanics of dimensional existence, and were now venturing further than they could have foreseen.

Raynie felt all this as a matter of contentment. She often felt this way all her life and celebrate the spirit she was naturally. Where life would now take her was a mystery and she could not resist. Within all she admired the beauty, like the time she saw Lyle staring at Jenna in the HyperJet over Korea where the ethereal beams of sunlight entering the cabin appeared to endear him with love for her. She had also seen the beginning to the Himalayan roof of the world, and admired the mountainous landscape of stark contrasting beauty at the fringe of the desert where she had stood.

Moonlight shining in the clear water springs during the time she began to feel more love for Jake than ever, stirred her inner most deeply. She could feel a tear well in her eye - it had been so beautiful on the night in the magical light of the springs and gardens. Jake had shined with such a mischievous twinkle in his eye, she felt compelled and drawn toward him.

With a sigh, she put the book down and walked the long hallway to make herself a cup of tea. The old radio was still there from years before, but it had long since been broken by people who had visited the house prior to her return. It lay in a few pieces on the floor by the fireplace. Old things still fascinated her, so she picked up the pieces and placed them on the table, thinking she might be able to fix them later.

She went back to her chair in the library shortly after, where she sat and stared out the window as she sipped the steaming tea. The day was hot, the drink was hot, and the land was hot. Midsummer could also bring spectacular thunderstorms where great anvil shaped clouds would build up ascending high before cracking with thunder as the atmosphere smelled of charged particles - something she loved. One looked to be brewing on the far southern horizon, and she thought it would at least bring some humidity back into the air.

Many long hours after the sun had relinquished to dusk, Raynie still sat in the library, reading and then dreaming, dreaming and then reading. Accepting her place now in this time was inevitable for her – somehow it was an inner calling like the one Carmel had experienced for returning to her house north of San Francisco. One had to feel this calling and give it their best attempt at realisation, and Raynie considered she had done this. She was only forty one, so it was not by any means the end of her life. This was the time for change and she had taken it on with others, emerging with wisdom, love, and free from the bind life seemed to hold for so many.

Acrux the southern star of the Southern Cross, shone brightly overhead like a beacon as she passed through the old door leading directly out to the garden. The old oak tree whistled in the wind, its leaves shouting amongst themselves. Above her, the band of the Milky Way stretched across the clear sky, ablaze with thousands of potential world harbouring stars. Now with faster than light travel capability, humanity would soon visit some of these stars. In time, they were bound to meet at the proper moment and begin to share their wealth of cosmic experience.

A place in the cosmos was here and at one in all places, like Chan had told them when they viewed the petro glyph in Peru. Indeed it was, and so onward endeavouring to go beyond the frontier, was the progress ahead for humanity. The dark ways of the Agent and the constraints from the authorities were both gone. George Smythe was no longer of the Earth or this dimension, and the remnant authority officers were on a similar path to nowhere.

Raynie stood there for a time recalling moments and learning. She remembered seeing her light body being caressed by wonderful geometric snowflakes. It was how she felt then and now and in each and every moment since she had first begun to awaken properly when Jake had come to this very house and they commenced their journey together in love. Such was their progression to conscious awareness to be in a meditation like mind in every moment, yet alert and active, their growth together had taken hers and many other's breath away.

Light and love had awakened humanity from darkness with potential realised for progression organically connected to geometric alignment of intentions born from nature and not coercion. Darkness it seemed, had been suppressed, though the revolving of the Earth still brought upon the night and it would again try to arise from those few destined to be its' vessel. For most the way ahead was of this brightness and the field of intention they could create together, but as wisdom is realised, growth is ongoing through life beyond into dimensions of influence and experience. Science was now to merge with the organic spirit – the soul being the most complex energetic organic essence they had come to know.

At dawn the next day Raynie awoke as she often did, to greet the rising great eastern sun bringing light into her world. The weather had calmed to a soft still morning, dashed with splashes of colour on the clouds to the east. Birdsong greeted her coming from a few small wrens flittering about the vegetable garden catching bugs. One was calling to another as if to say the food is over here, and sure enough, a moment later, Raynie saw its mate appear and join in on the feed. These simple natural acts inspired her to feel her personal sense of connection as she admired their grace and their purity. She saw how they progressed to each moment looking for sustenance, glad they had survived the horrors of recent years. She thought humans were no different and it had come to pass where they had chosen to remember their true selves and relinquishing false ideals.

Movement coming from the front of the house suddenly caught her eye. She had not seen the transport vehicle arrived, nor had she seen the occupant exit the vehicle. He was waving to her calling out her name, "Raynie!. Hey, come outside. Raynie?"

"Yes. Who are you?"

As the man walked over closer, Raynie began to recognise him.

"Raynie, it's Mike. Mike Edgars..."

"Mike so glad to see you! Come and give me a hug. I really need one."

"Raynie. Wow...last time we saw each other was on the way to Ryan's place near Lake Tahoe years ago."

"Time sure does travel fast. It only seems like yesterday."

"It was in a way," Mike said as he gave Raynie a long firm hug.

"Well, what brings you here? I'm sure you must have a reason other than to just see me."

"Yeah, Chan told me you would be here, so I came as soon as I could. He said to pass on a personal greeting through me."

"Then I accept. So what is it you have to tell me?"

"I have some interesting information I have recently learned about connecting with soul energy and I wanted to talk about it with you. From what Chan said, you would be best to discuss this with at the moment, so here I am."

"It's a long way to come for a talk."

"Is it? How about some tea and a chat. I have been travelling a bit and do like the look of this relaxed country home."

"By all means. Come into the kitchen and I'll put the pot on to boil. This could be fun you know."

"First, have you heard any news? It travels fast among those who want to know."

"Jake was hurt very badly. They say it could be some months before they have an outlook for his future."

"But he does have one doesn't he?"

"I think so. Yes, I love him, of course he does."

"You look troubled though."

"Well, he might not be the Jake we all used to know."

"He is still Jake though. Remember we are consciousness witnessing this body and mind."

"Yes we are. Thanks Mike."

"Anyway, I thought you might like this information on a group in San Francisco gave to me. We could be talking all day and well into the night, if you are okay."

"Then I had better fetch more wood for the stove fire. Of course I am okay," Raynie replied giving Mike a jab in the ribs showing she was glad to have his company on this night.

"What about just using free energy?"

"I like the romance of the fire and there is a lot of wood needing to be cleared from this land. It has become a fire hazard. Come on. Come and help me. I do love sitting and chatting. Mystery is exciting."

"Invigorating even."

"Of course. Out here through this door to the wood pile. I remember coming here with Jake back in eighty eight. Gee so much has happened since then."

"It is nigh impossible to predict what out futures are, or even if they exist. Now we are beyond time as a constraint in our identity, I guess such thinking out of the present is not really going to be the way."

"So true Mike. Jake and I were thinking similar those years back. It was during a snow storm...somehow an indicator to what was coming."

"Hmm, yet it had been coming many years, but not to such a resolution as it is now."

"I'm glad. I bet a lot of people are. To lose so much about the egocentric identity and free yourself from all those burdens and fears of the mind. How was it such bliss and invigoration existed for so long yet was so ignored by society?"

"You answered your own question. The egocentricity."

When they returned laden with enough wood for the rest of the day and the night, a young dark brown Burmese cat about three years of age darted in through the partially open kitchen door.

"Oh puss you have come back."

"He seems to like you."

"He arrived from nowhere and has been hanging around about five days now."

"Maybe in his wisdom he wants you to keep him. Perhaps the universe has sent him to be with you. Well, it seems so anyway. He's here isn't he?"

"I did think he wanted to stay. It is not like any of the houses near here have cats. You know, I think I will keep him. You are such a smooch aren't you puss."

'Meow'

"There, he agrees with you."

THE LAST YEAR

And so concludes the Torus Saga for now...as progression never ceases.

THE LAST YEAR

www.ingramcontent.com/pod-product-compliance
Lightning Source LLC
Chambersburg PA
CBHW021424200626
46814CB00015B/370